ROSE OF TRALEE

The year is 1925, and in Liverpool Jack Ryder, a tramdriver, and his wife Lily are bringing up their only child, Rose, to be as decent and hardworking as themselves. But Lily's sister Daisy and her daughter Mona live very differently. Daisy is a lazy slut, and Mona no better than she ought to be, and Jack discourages any friendship between Rose and her cousin. Over in Dublin, Eileen O'Neill has to bring up her children alone, since her husband Sean is working in England. Colm is a good son to her and takes care of his little sister Caitlin in addition to working hard at any job he can get. However, when Colm is sacked, Sean insists that his son goes with him to England because work is starting on the Mersey tunnel and labourers are needed. When tragedy strikes Rose's family, they are forced to take in boarders, including Mona. And it is to the Ryder's boarding house in St Domingo Vale that Colm and his father come when they arrive in Liverpool . . .

ROSE OF TRALEE

Katie Flynn

THE
WINDSOR
SELECTION

CHIVERS PRESS
BATH

First published 1998
by
William Heinemann
This Large Print edition published by
Chivers Press
by arrangement with
Random House UK Ltd
1999

ISBN 0 7540 1347 2

British Library Cataloguing in Publication Data available

Printed and bound in Great Britain by
REDWOOD BOOKS, Trowbridge, Wiltshire

For Vicki Turner, who patiently read reference books to me and cooked me wonderful meals whilst I wrote this book—thanks!

I am most grateful for the generous help given me by Jack Gahan and his colleagues in the Merseyside Tramway Preservation Society—Jack has done his best to stop me from making and really bad mistakes about the trams in the twenties and thirties, but because of a rush to get this book ready for the printers, he has not been able to check the MS—so any mistakes are mine, but the good research is his!

As usual, I've used many facts given me by the wonderful people who helped the Everton Library production of VILLAGE WITH A VIEW, and I'm particularly grateful to Mrs J. Spruce, whose delightful reminiscence of Everton in the thirties—and in particular her memories of her tram-driver father—inspired me to write this book.

I do apologise if I've left anyone out, but since the start of M.E., my memory has been totally unreliable.

CHAPTER ONE

1925 Dublin

It was August, and a hot and sunny day for once. Colm O'Neill, sitting on the canal bank holding in one hand a long willow wand from which dangled a length of line, with his eyes half closed against the noontide glare, was indulging in a beautiful daydream, which was rapidly becoming the next best thing to sleep. In his mind's eye he was seeing the straightness of his line suddenly jerked out, the rod itself bending from its natural shape into a perfect curve as the huge salmon that had taken his bait fought to get free. The salmon was a dream one, so it was, pinkish, with a great, ruby-red eye and a mouth which gaped wide as a railway tunnel. In his dream Colm played the giant up and down the bank, scattering the other kids who were fishing alongside of him, whilst bigger boys envied and smaller ones oohed and aahed.

The salmon, when he had got it ashore, would be for his mammy, of course. And wouldn't the mammy be pleased with him? His dream skipped a mile or so and there he was in their room, holding out the giant fish, whilst his mammy, with tears in her eyes, thanked him for providing her with enough food to last a week.

And then, all of a sudden, Colm was back on the canal bank and the giant salmon had somehow managed to get the line around his foot. It was heaving and pulling with painful force ... Colm opened his eyes and got half way to his feet, all

1

ready to hit the salmon over the head with anything handy . . . and came back to earth with a bump. His line hung slack, nothing was nibbling his bait, but his leg was still being half torn off him so it was, and even as he stared at the calm, unrippling water, he realised what was happening. Caitlin was on the move and the rope with which he had tethered her was heaving urgently at his ankle as she reached the end of it.

With a sigh, Colm bent down and untied the rope, shouting: 'Caitlin, ye devil's spawn! What on the good earth d'you t'ink you're doin'? Haven't I telled you, times wit'out number, not to stray when we're by water? You'll be drownded, so you will, and who'll get the blame? Answer me that, you eejit!'

Caitlin took no notice but continued to heave at her rope, so Colm, well used to this, jerked and watched with some satisfaction as his young wan sat down on her bottom with a bump. Hastily propping his rod on a stone, he set off in pursuit, reaching her in a couple of strides and swinging her off her feet into his arms. She giggled and wriggled but made no protest and Colm, carrying her grimly back to his rod, reflected that divil though she was, she could have been worse. She was only five and the sit-down had been a hard one, but not a sound of protest had come from his little sister. She often yelled with temper or cried with rage, but apart from that she was of a sunny disposition—Mammy often said they saw more smiles than frowns from Caitlin and, though his friends always groaned when he appeared with his young wan in charge, they had to admit that even at her tender age she was game for most things.

Colm sat her down on the grass and took his place next to her.

Beside him, his friend Seamus rolled over onto his stomach and peered down into the depths of the canal, then sat up once more and addressed the child on the end of her rope. 'Did you run off, you bad gorl?' he enquired cheerfully. 'What a good t'ing it is that you've a big brother to look after you! Have you forgotten already bein' near on drownded in this very canal when you was a little mitchin' babby? And you've frighted all the fishes away, so you have—we might as well go home right away, wit' such a turble young wan to turn our hairs grey before time an' scare the fishes away.'

'She didn't go far, not wit' the rope round her middle,' Colm assured his friend. 'Phew, don't you go remindin' her of that other time, you great eejit, or she'll likely fancy another dip.'

'I dare say she don't need much remindin',' Seamus said lazily. 'I bet your ould wan gave you the rough side of her tongue that day.'

'She would have, if she'd knowed,' Colm acknowledged. 'Isn't that why I rope the kid whenever I'm near water? I'm just t'ankin' the Lord above that she didn't go straight down the bank just now, but only along it.' He turned to the child, sitting on the grass and picking daisies as though she had never done anything more adventurous in her life. 'Didn't I tell ye not to stray, now? Whyfor did you go off?'

Caitlin looked vaguely around her as though searching for the explanation, then turned a pair of large, dark-brown eyes reproachfully up at her brother. 'You'd goned asleep, an' I wanted the yellow duckies,' she said in her small, clear voice.

3

She pointed a chubby finger further along the bank. 'See 'em, Colm?'

There were no ducks further along the bank, yellow or otherwise. Colm heaved a sigh and picked up his rod, pulling it carefully clear of the water and missing the reedy margin more by luck than judgement. 'You aren't supposed to go anywhere wit'out me, Cait,' he reminded the child, though without much hope. 'You promised Mammy, so you did. What'ud she say if I telled her you'd been strayin' off after yellow ducks ... or anyt'ing else, come to that?'

'You won't tell,' Caitlin said tranquilly. 'I never tells an' you never tells, Colly. When will you catch the fish?' she added hopefully.

'Soon,' Colm said. Truth to tell, he was beginning to get bored and was sure he would never catch anything worth taking home, anyway. Because it was a nice afternoon the bank was crowded with young fishermen, all using an amazing assortment of tackle. Bits of string, half a clothes pole, bent pins, a length of orange rope ... and the bait was almost as varied. Colm had some precious pieces of bacon rind, Seamus was using earthworms, someone farther along was putting his faith in bread pellets ... spoiled for choice the bloomin' fish should be, Colm thought crossly, but no one had had a bite so far as he knew. The denizens of the deep seemed indifferent to the fine feast being wafted before their goggly eyes.

'It's too hot and there's too many chisellers, all wit' the same t'ing in mind,' Seamus said lazily. 'Did you see that feller ground-baitin' wit half a loaf? He's spoiled the sport for the rest of us, feedin' the buggers like that.'

4

Colm gave his friend a warning look; Caitlin loved new words. But since she was still gathering daisies and murmuring to herself as she cast them into the lap of her dirty cotton frock, there seemed little danger there. 'You're right about the fish,' he said. 'I'll give it another ten minutes, so I will, then I'm off. The ould wan wants some spuds washed an' over the fire by when she gets home. Wit' the littl'un along it'll take us half an hour to walk from here; might as well start sooner than later.'

Since neither boy possessed a watch the ten minutes passed by guess, but during that time no one caught a fish and it was with only the pretence of reluctance that Seamus, too, pulled his line out of the water and wrapped it around his hazel wand, whilst Colm quite happily made his own preparations for the walk home. The canal had proved a disappointment so they might as well leave now as later.

If it hadn't been for Caitlin he and Seamus would probably have gone further afield—maybe down to the Liffey, where the fishing was better, or even to the big pond out at the Brickfields. But the ould wan was terrified of the child drowning and had made Colm swear that he would take her to nowhere dangerous. The fact that his mammy would consider the Grand Canal dangerous was a mere woman's whim, he and Seamus had decided. The water wasn't deep ... well, not very deep ... and because of the tow-path there was no need to get too close to the edge. Some kids fished from the tow-path, of course, but he and Seamus were happy enough to sit on the long grass, well back from the water, and fish as best they could from there.

5

When the two of them were ready Colm wound in Caitlin's rope and lifted her to her feet. 'We're goin' home now, alanna,' he said cheerfully. 'If you get tired, I'll carry you. But you can walk for a whiles.'

Caitlin still had the daisies in her skirt but she trotted along beside him, the rope dipping between them. Colm did not intend to let her off it until they were in their own home since, with the best will in the world, he could not keep watching her every minute of the walk. Past experience told him that she would stop by every other grating to push a daisy or two through, or trace a picture in the dust with a grubby forefinger, or dart into the road in pursuit of a mangy dog, or a pigeon, rootling between the paving stones. On the rope, at least she would stay within a foot or two of him, so that he could curb her worst excesses.

As he had told Seamus, he had never forgotten the day he and his pals had gone to fish for crabs alongside the Liffey. They had begged or borrowed lengths of line from older brothers or fathers, and had baited them with scraps of long-dead and stinking fish, found down on the quays. He'd had Caitlin with him, of course, because his ould wan was working as a cleaner in one of the smart houses in Ely Place and could not look after the child, but Caitlin had been a baby then, not even a year old. He had brought her along in a wooden fish box to which he had fixed small wheels, and had satisfied himself that she was sound asleep before sitting down on the quayside and dropping his line hopefully into the gentle brown water.

She hadn't made a sound on waking, either. She had climbed out of the fish box and crawled to the

6

edge of the quay ... and before he had had the remotest idea what was happening he had seen a flash of white and there she was, bobbing in the water below, too startled even to shout as it closed over her head.

Colm had been eight then, not thirteen as he was now, and hadn't been as strong a swimmer as he was now, either. He had screamed, though, and Seamus had echoed the scream, and then he had hurled himself off the quayside and into the water, which was a dozen feet below, for the tide had been out.

'You might have killed your young wan be landin' on her head, boy,' the man who had rescued the pair of them told him as he hauled them to safety aboard his boat. 'Never jump into water feet first until your swimmin' is a deal better than it is now. But you won't do it again and you're safe, the pair of ye. Now tell me, how did she come to fall in?'

Colm had explained, tearfully, what had happened, and their rescuer had seen them both ashore and had bidden Colm to take the young wan home right now and put her into a warm bed. 'She'll be none the worse be tomorrow's morn,' he had declared cheerfully.

He had been right, too. And Colm's ould wan had never realised that her precious baby had landed in Anna Liffey; Colm managed to make it appear that she had got wet by somehow slipping into the fountain at St Stephen's Green whilst watching himself and other chisellers sailing boats made from matchboxes—and he had done it without telling any downright lies, either. But even so, it had taught him a lesson. A little sister was precious, so she was, and though he had felt ill-done-by, at first, when his mother had made him take the baby with him whilst she was working, he soon began to look on it as an honour rather than a penance. Other boys his age had sisters, it was true, and sisters automatically looked after younger brothers and sisters. But he and Caitlin were the only kids in their family, so they had to look out for each other; it stood to reason. So whilst his mother did her housework or marketing, or worked at her cleaning in the big houses around Ely Place and Merrion Square, he took his sister with him and put up with the sneers of other chisellers who were not so burdened.

That had been at first. Now it was generally accepted that going somewhere with Colm often meant taking Caitlin too and Seamus, who was the youngest member of a very large family, actually seemed to enjoy the child's company which, since he and Colm got along just great, was as well.

So now, making their way through the dreamy, dusty summer streets, the two boys talked over their plans for the morrow.

'We can't go swimmin', 'cos me mammy's workin', so we'll be takin' Caitlin wit' us. But the mammy'll give us some pennies . . . an' she'll give us bread an' cheese an' mebbe an apple so's we can spend the day in Phoenix Park. We might hear the lions . . . if we only had some money we could show Caitlin the animals in the zoo!'

'We could fish in the pond,' Seamus said, grinning. 'There's some big 'uns in there!' He glanced down at Caitlin, trotting between the two of them, one hand grasping the hem of her brother's shirt though the rope was still knotted

8

firmly round her waist. 'Tired, alanna?' he asked. 'Will I be after carryin' you for a bit?'

Caitlin looked consideringly up at Seamus, then shook her curly head. Colm guessed that she, too, had napped now and then in the hot sunshine on the canal bank, with the bulk of Polikoff's clothing factory looming up behind them, and now had no objection to stretching her legs a little.

'S'awright, Shay,' he said, therefore. 'She'll be good an' tired be the time we get home, then she'll gobble her tay an' straight to bed wit' her. Less trouble for the mammy an' me.'

The three children continued to walk together until their ways parted at the junction of Kevin and Cuffe Streets, where Seamus turned left towards his home just off the Coombe and the O'Neill children turned right, towards Cloddagh Court which ran behind Grafton Street, quite near Switzer's. The O'Neills had not lived there long. Until five months ago, they had been almost next door to Seamus's large family on the Coombe, but Colm's mammy had been determined to get nearer her work and, as soon as she could afford it, she had rented the rooms in Cloddagh Court.

'It's handy for Merrion Street and next time Switzer's want a char, it's goin' to be meself, so it is,' she told her son as she washed the dishes and he wiped them and put them away. 'Can you imagine workin' there, me laddo? Eh, an' they pay better'n the big private houses I've heared tell.'

So now when Seamus turned left towards the Coombe, the O'Neills turned right and made for Grafton Street. Even late on a sunny summer's afternoon it would be crowded, but no one took any notice of a small grubby boy and grubbier girl,

9

making their way past the smart shops and imposing buildings.

Presently they turned left and found themselves suddenly transported. Gone were the wide pavements, smart people, brilliant shop windows. Here the narrow streets were dirty and crowded with noisy, ragged children kicking a ball, rolling marbles, playing tag, skipping rope. Colm and Caitlin made their way between them, exchanging greetings and insults.

'Where's ye been? Oh, you t'ink you're a Mickie dazzler, goin' off out wit' the kid in tow 'stead o' playin here wit' your pals . . .'

'Whyfor's she on de rope? You skeered someone'll kidnap her, an' send yiz a ransom note an' a lock o' hair?'

'Don't I wish they would?' Colm replied untruthfully. He would be doing Caitlin no favours by admitting he enjoyed the company of a five-year-old—and a girl at that. 'Still an' all, she's not bad as young wans go.'

Caitlin, never slow to learn insults, simply said 'Shut your bloody gob!' to anyone who addressed her, which startled even the rudest of the surrounding kids and would have mortified her mother, had she heard.

Even Colm, who knew well how to swear when adults were out of the way, was taken aback and reproved his sister as soon as they entered the quieter area where they lived. 'Cait, you mustn't say that,' he said earnestly. 'You'll be in big trouble, so you will, an' you'll mek our mammy cry first an' beat your little bum next.'

'You say it,' Caitlin stated. She was kicking a nice piece of red tile ahead of her, head down, eyes on

10

the ground, concentrating. 'You said it to the chiseller who told you to t'row in your line somewheres else. You said he was a greedy bugger.'

'Ye-es, but I'm ... I'm older'n you and I'm a feller. Fellers can say t'ings which gorls can't,' Colm said after the slightest of hesitations. 'Swearin's bad ... have you ever heard Mammy say bad words?'

'No-oo. But I'm a kid, she's a mammy,' Caitlin said complacently. 'It's different for kids. You telled me so.'

They reached their door and Colm pulled his sister to a halt with a tug on the rope, then bent to untie it from her small waist. 'You'll be a mammy one day,' he said cunningly. 'Just like our mammy. But only if you don't say bad t'ings. You hear me?'

Caitlin manoeuvred her piece of red tile up to the bottom of the two scrubbed steps which led to their rooms and, after a moment's frowning thought, nodded. 'Awright. I won't say bad t'ings no more. Well, not when our mammy's listenin',' she added hastily. 'But them boys was *rude*, Colm!'

'You can be turble rude back wit'out swearin',' Colm said, lifting her over the steps and settling her on his hip as they approached the door. 'Mammy's out ... d'you want to pull the key up?'

The key was kept on a piece of string attached to the letter-box. You put your hand very carefully through the slit, found the piece of string and hauled the key through. It was odd, Colm thought as he stood his small sister down and watched her fumbling through the slit, that everyone he knew employed this device yet thieves did not take advantage of it. Mammy was always on about thieves, yet so far as he knew no one in the vast,

11

sprawling area that was the Liberties had ever been robbed by someone hauling up their key.

'Got it, Colly,' Caitlin said breathlessly. 'Me open?'

''Course,' Colm said at once and lifted her to keyhole height. 'Remember, turn gently and it'll open sweetly. Turn jerky an' it won't open at all.'

The child clung grimly to the key for a moment with both hands, breath held, eyes almost shut, then she squeaked triumphantly, 'It's worked, Colm! You do the handle!'

Colm turned the handle, the door opened and the two of them entered.

The room was both their main living-room and kitchen, for the parlour next door was kept for special occasions only, so that this room was crowded with all the impedimenta of family living. There was an open fire, unlit on this warm day, the mantelpiece over it a refuge, at the moment, for all the ornaments and breakables which had once been scattered about the room, for well Mammy knew that if any of the china figurines or pretty crockery was within reach of Caitlin's small, busy fingers it was unlikely to last an hour out, so she had put her treasures out of reach as soon as the child began to toddle. 'As I did when yourself was at that age,' she had reminded Colm. 'Caitlin's no better an' no worse than any other child—she likes to touch. And look how careful of me nice t'ings you are, now you're a big feller! There's no one I'd trust sooner than you, Colm, an' that's gospel trut', so it is, and one day Caitlin will grow more careful, just like me boy has.'

Apart from the mantelpiece, all the other surfaces held more utilitarian objects, save for the

12

stoup of holy water by the door and the pictures, mostly representations of the Virgin, which crowded the walls. The large scrubbed wooden table had a box of cheap cutlery at one end and four tin plates and mugs at the other. In the centre was a tottering pile of dry linen, awaiting the iron, while under the table lurked a large basket full of what looked like folded—and ironed—sheets, pillowslips and tablecloths. There was a rug by the fire, made of pieces of brightly coloured rag, the back of it sacking, the edges neatened with a border of raffia, and on the topmost sheet was an apple and a sheet of paper.

Caitlin dived for the apple with a squeak of joy but Colm grabbed her before she could snatch it up. 'There's a note from Mammy on the paper, Cait,' he said rather breathlessly. 'Let me read it forst, then we'll have halves, eh?'

'Sure,' Caitlin said cheerfully. She stood back, staring up at him as he perused the lines. 'What's it say, Colm?'

'It says to scrub the spuds an' then to tek the basket of linen round to the back door of the Merrill place in St Stephen's Green Street South and knock the door. The housekeeper'll give us one an' ninepence for the washin'.' He stopped reading and heaved a sigh. 'There! Mammy's not supposed to do that old crow's washin', she's got enough on her plate, so she has, but at least she'll be paid for it this time.'

'What's one an' ninepence?' Caitlin said as her brother went over to the washstand and poured water from a bucket which lurked beneath it into the round blue basin that stood on the top. 'Is it money, Colm?'

'That's it,' Colm said. He crossed the room to where a box full of potatoes stood against the wall, neatly hidden from view by a clean but ragged piece of cloth. 'How hungry are ye, Caitlin? One spud or two?'

'T'ree,' Caitlin said promptly. Ever since her third birthday she had understood three and had used it whenever she could do so. 'Can I pick 'em out, Colm?'

'No, 'cos they're covered wit' earth, so they are, an' you'll get your little pawses all filt'y,' Colm told her. 'Besides, they're huge ole spuds, alanna. I doubt you'll ate two of 'em, let alone t'ree.' He saw his small sister's lower lip begin to wobble ominously and said hastily: 'You can fetch me the piece o' salt, though, from the cupboard. Or will it be too heavy for you? 'Tis on the bottom shelf, in a brown paper.'

Whilst Caitlin stood on tiptoe to open the cupboard door Colm hastily chose three enormous potatoes and stuck them in the water, forgetting to knock the worst of the earth off them first so that the water quickly began to resemble a swamp. Sighing, he did as good a cleaning job on them as he could under the circumstances, then put them into the large blackened pan which stood between the buckets beneath the washstand. One bucket was for slops, the other for fresh water, and he saw with dismay that by the time he'd covered the potatoes with water he would have to go down to the ground floor to replenish the bucket, as well as taking the other one to empty the mixture of water and mud which his carelessness had brought about. It was a nuisance, because he had planned to put the potatoes to one side of the fire, then take the

14

empty bucket in one hand and carry the basket of clean linen in the other, but now he would have to make a double journey.

'Here's the salt, Colm,' a small voice said breathlessly at about pocket level. Colm grinned at his little sister and took the big chunk of salt, the size—and weight—of a housebrick, from her. He stood it on the dry piece of the washstand and chipped a piece about the size of a walnut off it with the old kitchen knife which Mammy kept especially for the purpose, then handed the salt back to Caitlin, who received it in both arms and staggered proudly back to the cupboard with her burden. 'Is there anythin' else I can fetch for you, Colm?' she asked, slamming the salt down on the lowest shelf with an audible crash. 'Are you goin' to light the fire? I'll bring the matches if you like.'

Colm knew very well that Mammy always kept the matches on the topmost shelf, and knew, too, that Caitlin could never reach them in a million years. 'It's all right, alanna,' he said, however. 'We'll not be after lightin' the fire until we've delivered the linen.' He bent and picked up the bucket of water, pouring it over the potatoes, then stood the bucket down again and tossed in the salt. 'And anyway, you know you aren't allowed to touch matches, they're ...' he turned as he spoke and what he saw made his eyes bulge. Caitlin was calmly struggling from shelf to shelf like a goat up a mountainside, heading straight for the topmost one. 'Why, you wicked little ...'

He leaped towards her on the words, just in time to see her clutch at what she clearly thought was a shelf edge ... and topple backwards, holding his mammy's wooden chopping board in her hands for

15

one brief second before releasing it to clutch at the air as she crashed floorwards. A number of objects came off the shelves with her, landing on or around the child, and Colm, his heart beating so loudly that it almost deafened him, pushed everything wildly aside and looked down into her white face. 'Caitlin! Are you all right?' he gasped. 'What devil possessed you to go climbin' like a mountain goat on Mammy's cupboard shelves? Oh, if you've been an' gone an' kilt yourself then it's my fault, for not rememberin' as how you're always game for anyt'ing, any'ting at all!'

He pulled Caitlin into a sitting position and realised that a good deal of her pallor was due to the bag of flour, which had tipped most of its contents over her as she fell, and indeed, a second later she sneezed several times, very loudly, before pulling herself out of his arms and getting waveringly to her feet. 'I went crash-bang-wallop,' she said breezily. 'The shelf breaked in me hands, so it did. Will—will Mammy be cross?'

'She will so,' Colm said thoughtlessly, then saw Caitlin's mouth begin to turn down at the corners and repented of his cruelty. 'Ah, it's all right, alanna, for I'll not breathe a word to the mammy; you were doin' your best to help,' he said reassuringly. 'Now just you sit in the chair be the fireside whiles I clear this mess away, then we'll go off to deliver the washin' an' no one the wiser.'

He shovelled the flour back into its sack, hoping that the next time his mother came to need some she would not notice what a deal of dust had somehow got mixed with the topmost couple of inches, then began to tidy the other things. What a blessing she'd not actually broken anything, he thought, returning things to their proper places and giving a quick look back over his shoulder to see what the spalpeen was doing now. With Caitlin you could never be sure. But she was kneeling on the floor and dusting flour off the lower shelf with an old rag, clearly intent on making amends for her accident. As it was, Mammy would not scold for a mishap—and besides, with luck she need never find out.

'All done,' Colm said presently, returning to the washstand to heave the slop bucket up in one hand and the empty one with the other. 'Come on, Caitlin, we'll deal wit' the water first.'

Caitlin got to her feet and as she stood up Colm noticed the state of her for the first time. Oh Mary, Mother of Jesus, the kid was covered in flour; it mingled with the dirt of a day's play and gave her a terrifying appearance! Sighing, he stood his buckets down and reached for the floor brush, then led Caitlin back into the pantry cupboard. He might as well brush her down where all the worst mess had been, then brush all the mess between the boards.

Twenty minutes later he and Caitlin set off at last, Caitlin looking suspiciously pale still, though Colm comforted himself with the thought that she looked pale because he was not used to seeing her so clean. He had brushed her hair, retied the piece of orange string which kept it out of her eyes, washed her face, hands and all the leg you could see under her skirt, then got rid of the evidence to the best of his ability. So now he took her hand, picked up the buckets and set off down the stairs.

The tap was inside the house, towards the back—a huge luxury in a city where a great many houses had no piped water indoors at all—and the

17

slops were emptied down a rainwater grid. Colm performed both his tasks with Caitlin trotting beside him, then headed for the stairs once more, the buckets full. They would need the water later for making the tea, washing up the crocks and for their own ablutions at bedtime. Mammy liked to have her buckets full and provided he gave the slop bucket a good swill she would not object to it being filled instead of the big blue-and-white enamel one with the fitting lid, which he did not feel capable of carrying down as well as the other two.

Carefully, Colm carried out his tasks, then trudged up the stairs again, deposited the full buckets and picked up the basket of linen. 'One more trip, Cait,' he said happily. 'Then we'll come home an' light the fire an' get the spuds on before Mammy gets home.'

'An' . . . an' you won't tell the mammy about her cupboard, will you, Colm?' Caitlin said in her most wheedling and soulful tone. ' 'Cos I does hate it when the mammy's cross, so I does.'

Colm laughed and rumpled her dark curls. 'I'll not say a word,' he promised cheerfully. 'And now let's put our best foot forward so's we're home the sooner.'

*　　　*　　　*

All the way to St Stephen's Green Street South Colm thought about his mother and how hard she worked to keep the family. He admitted, grudgingly, that he supposed his father worked hard too—but he was so far away. Diggin' ditches in England, Colm thought sourly. Drinkin' ale, fightin', havin' a fine old time. He sent money

18

home, Colm knew that, but it wasn't the same. Mammy slaved at her cleanin' jobs, so she did, and brought home washin' and cooked them good meals, took them out for days, gave him money for the penny rush at the picture house on Saturday mornings and for a tram ride from time to time, or a new second-hand pair of trousers from the market, so's he was as smart as his pals. And in his turn, Colm did his best for the mammy. He did girls' work around the house, he looked after his little sister, he ran messages and when he earned money, he handed it to his mammy without a second thought. She loved him and he loved her, he reasoned, and since she was good to him, he must be good, in his turn, to her. But for some reason best known to herself she still got very excited when their daddy came home, which was usually only once or twice a year. And after she'd put out the best food for their daddy she changed into her smartest clothes and the pair of 'em went off out together, and there had been times when his daddy came home the worse for drink, singin' an' shoutin' an' fallin' about. Doing the things, in fact, which his mammy thought dreadful in other women's husbands but apparently accepted in her own—'Because,' she explained, 'your daddy's far from home so much. When he's back wit' us sure an' hasn't he the reason for gettin' a bit over-excited?'

But Colm didn't excuse him, not in his heart. Sean O'Neill was over six foot tall and strong with it, and sometimes Colm thought that his daddy didn't understand why he did so much around the house for his mammy, why he took Caitlin with him whenever he went out. Sean thought he had fathered a milksop and sometimes he showed it in a sneering sort of way, which made Colm long to rush at him and batter him. Only Sean was hugely strong—if any battering were done, it would be done by his father, Colm realised regretfully.

Not that Sean had shown the slightest sign of attacking his son. It was just the look in his eye sometimes, particularly when Mammy got up to clear away the tea-things or the dinner-plates and Colm jumped up too, and wiped whilst she washed, or poured the tea from the tin teapot into the cream-and-blue pottery cups which the mammy had saved up to buy from the market stall in Francis Street. Then Sean would lean back in his chair and whistle a tune, or pick Caitlin up and put her on his knee and tell her stories of life in England. Colm tried not to listen, but sometimes he couldn't help it, and it was from these stories that he'd got the impression that his father had a high old time when he crossed the water.

And his mammy was so wonderful! She was no taller than Colm himself, and thin as the long pole which lifted their washing line up high in the courtyard at the back of the house, yet she was strong enough to scrub all the floors in the Merrill house and the O'Grady house and the Thompson house, then bring a mound of washing home and iron it with the flat-irons which he or she heated by the fire until they reached a sufficient temperature to press without burning. And she almost never got cross, no matter what went wrong. Colm knew that other fellers had mammies who roared with rage, used a stick on their kids, wept and bellowed when something happened to vex them, but his mammy said the best thing was to 'count to ten', and she did just that. When the milk burned, when the spuds went to mush, when Caitlin dropped her cup and it smashed into a thousand pieces, when Colm played late and forgot a message, it was always the same. Mammy would sigh, smile, count to ten and then say lovingly that sure an' wasn't it just the sort of t'ing which had happened to her once, long ago? 'No one's to blame,' she would say comfortably. 'We'll put it down to experience, so we shall.'

Sean O'Neill wasn't home long enough to get aggravated with his son and daughter, Colm told himself, but once or twice his daddy had slapped him across the legs and wagged a reproving finger at Caitlin, which just showed, Colm thought, that given a bit more time his daddy would be like most of the daddies he knew—he'd beat his kids and his wife, and make their lives a misery, given the time to do it in.

But Mammy couldn't—or wouldn't—see it. When they'd been out for the afternoon, perhaps, and had a fish and chip supper, she would squeeze onto the same chair as Sean's and he would put an arm round her and pull her close. And Colm would have to go to bed in the next room while they were like that—he hated doing it, hated leaving them, but he didn't have a choice. Mammy would smile and say, 'Bedtime, Colm me boy' and he would be on his feet and half way out of the door before he'd thought of one little excuse.

Colm slept in a cupboard of a room next to the living kitchen. It was a snug, windowless little place, with his bed, a chair, a holy picture and a row of hooks to hang his clothes on. He loved having his own little space, except when his daddy was home. Then he envied Caitlin, who had a cot next to

21

mammy's big bed, and could keep an eye on their parents all night if she wanted. Only she would be sound asleep really, Colm knew that, and come to think of it, judging by the way his mammy snuggled up to his daddy in the fireside chair, perhaps he did not much want to share their room, either. You'd have thought they were like the young lovers who hid in the doorways on Grafton Street to carry on when respectable people had gone to bed and not two old people, long married.

'Are we nearly there, Colm?' Caitlin said, bringing Colm back to earth once more. 'Will we go in, eh? Will the lady gi's a piece of soda bread or some liquorice sticks?'

You had to admit that for a young 'un, Caitlin had a way with her, Colm told himself as they rounded the corner into St Stephen's Green. Only twice could he remember being given anything by the important people his mammy worked for and each time it had been because of Caitlin's undoubted charm. But it didn't do to get hopeful; better to expect nothing and be pleased if you got something, he thought, and answered accordingly, 'I don't know, alanna, but when we got the bread and the liquorice we went into the house to fetch Mammy out, didn't we? This time we're only deliverin', which isn't the same.'

'You get a halfpenny or an apple or somethin' good for goin' messages,' Caitlin pointed out. 'That's why you do it; you told me so last time. Isn't that why you're after goin' round to Mrs Gillis to see if she wants messages runnin'?'

'It's because she's old and can't go for herself . . . but you're right, I'd not be so prompt if she didn't give me somethin' for me trouble,' Colm admitted.

'I'd still go, though, even wit'out the pennies. Mrs Gillis is nice.'

'Yes, I love her, so I do,' Caitlin said cheerfully. 'Is that the house?'

'You've got a memory like a bloody elephant,' Colm said, then clapped a hand to his mouth. He was forgetting his own vow not to say anything in front of Caitlin that one did not want repeated. 'Sorry, Cait, that was a bad word. You didn't hear it; right?'

'Sure I didn't. Which house is it, Colly? If it's a house wit' kids in they might be makin' treacle toffee!'

The incident of the treacle toffee had happened a year previously, but like most nice events it had clearly stayed in Caitlin's memory. Possibly she had not included it in the recollections of things given at big houses because the giver had been a child, but although Colm had not forgotten it, he knew they were not revisiting that house today. 'The toffee was give by the kids of the woman on Lower Bagot,' he said regretfully. 'I dunno if they's kids here. Come on, it's this house, but we go round the back, same's Mammy does.'

There was a narrow passageway down the side of the house and they turned into this, crossed the courtyard where the dustbins were kept and knocked loudly on the back door, which was half open because, Colm assumed, of the heat of the day. Through it they could see a very large and splendid room with red tiles on the floor and a big wooden table almost the length of the whole room. There was a huge oven, an open fire, shelves and shelves filled with exciting-looking kitchen equipment—Colm knew it was kitchen equipment

23

because Mammy had told him so—and a very large fat woman hovering over the long table, which was laid with a great many dishes and pans and trays of food. The woman had her hair wrapped in a white cloth and a white apron covered her person . . . and her face was scarlet from the heat and from bending, so that two trickles of sweat ran down her cheeks and joined into a little stream under the fat pile of her chins. She heard their knock and glanced up, then straightened and shouted to someone out of sight: 'Door, Biddy! Delivery, be the looks of it.'

There was a rustling sound and a girl not a lot older than Colm appeared in the doorway. She, too, wore a white apron, but it was speckled and stained with dirt, and the hair which straggled out from under her white cap was greasy and unkempt. She had a thin face, reddened now by the heat, and she held a bowl in the curve of her arm and a big wooden spoon in her hand, but she smiled pleasantly enough at the two children hovering on the doorstep. 'Yes?' she asked, half turning away from them to stand the bowl down on the edge of the table.

'Laundry, Miss,' Colm said promptly. 'Me Mammy's Mrs O'Neill, she said to bring it over for her.'

'Oh . . .' The girl turned and said to the fat woman, 'It's the washin', cook. You know, the staff tablecloths an' sheets that O'Neill took a couple o' days gone.'

'Right. Tek it in, then,' the cook said abstractedly. She sighed. 'Sure and isn't it just my luck that everyone's comin' to the door an' me wit' a dinner party for two dozen to get ready?'

'Thanks,' the girl said to Colm, holding out a hand.

But Colm had delivered too many parcels to great houses to allow her so much as to touch it until he'd had his mammy's money. 'There's money to be paid, Miss,' he said politely, therefore. 'Me mammy said there was money owin' and I was to fetch it.'

'Bloomin' blood out of a stone some of 'em would ask for,' the cook said in a goaded voice. 'We'll pay your mammy tomorrer, sonny, or the day after that. Tek it in, Bid, and get on wit' beatin' that batter.'

Biddy looked hunted and Colm hung onto his parcel harder than ever. He knew the quality, so he did! They would mean to pay, his mother had explained many times, but you could fall between two stools, with the mistress thinking the maid had paid and the maid assuming that the mistress had done so. Accordingly he stood his ground. One and ninepence was nothing to these people, but it was a great deal to the O'Neills, and a poor sort of son he'd be if he meekly handed his mammy's work over without first getting his money!

'There's one and ninepence owed,' he said in a singsong voice, hoping that the cook and this Biddy would think him a bit stupid ... anything, rather than leave here and be the one to blame because his mammy hadn't been paid again. She herself had more than once not stood out for money owing and Colm always chided her when she told him about it. After all, he was the man of the house whilst his father was away and it was up to him to see that at least Mammy was paid for all the hard work she did. So he looked hopefully up at Biddy and

25

repeated, 'One and ninepence owed please, Miss,' in a slightly stronger voice. His mother had taught him to address the older ladies, like the cook, as 'ma'am', and younger ones, like the maidservant, as 'miss'.

'Cook says ...' Biddy began in a slightly apologetic voice, but Colm abruptly decided that he could have none of it.

He knew very well that his father, whatever his other faults, would not have handed over the parcel and walked meekly away. If I'm standin' in for him, then I've got to act like him, so I have, Colm reminded himself and spoke firmly across the other's voice. 'Then I'd best take me parcel back home again,' he said. 'Me an' the littl 'un brung it along when Mammy said, but if there's no money until tomorrer ...'

There was a flurry inside the kitchen and cook, who had been on the opposite side of the table, suddenly appeared at the door side, her face redder than ever, oddly stifled sounds coming from her mouth whilst her eyes almost popped. Colm realised she must be very angry and quailed inside, opening his mouth to add some more conciliatory remark, but before he could do so she was upon them, vast as a mountain, hands held out towards them. Startled, he took a step back but she ploughed onward, seeming not to notice as the maid hastily squeezed herself out of the way, and suddenly he saw that she wasn't angry but was actually laughing, that the stifled sounds were mirth and not fury. 'Well, well, young feller, your mammy's taught you well, so she has,' she said, mopping at her hot red face with the back of a huge hand. 'I like a boy wit' spirit ... One and

26

ninepence, you said?'

She was fishing around in the pocket of her apron as she spoke and produced a large and shabby purse, then looked at Colm again with enquiring eyes.

Colm nodded. 'That's it, ma'am. One and ninepence.'

'Right. I'll pay ye now and the housekeeper shall pay me back after I've done this dinner. You're O'Neill's boy?'

'That's right,' Colm said, not quite liking to say that Mrs O'Neill would sound better. Besides, he knew that servants in the great houses were very often called by their surnames alone. 'Thanks, ma'am.'

Cook fumbled briefly in the purse, then produced a two-shilling piece and handed it to him, taking the parcel, which he immediately held out.

'I don't have any change, missus,' Colm said, flustered. 'But me mammy will bring it tomorrer, so she will.'

'Oh, and it's all right for me to wait for me money, is it?' the cook said, but with good humour. ' 'Tis only the likes of yourself which must have money what's owed immediate-like?'

Colm hung his head but Caitlin was not to be so easily put down. 'Sure an' me big brother 'ud give you the money in a trice if he had it, missus,' she assured the woman earnestly. 'But we've done no messages today—we've been fishin' in the canal down behind Polikoff's.'

Cook laughed again and sighed, too. 'Sure an' didn't me brother and meself fish down there when we was kids?' she demanded. 'Lovely an' cool the water was to dangle your feet in . . . wish I were still

27

nine or ten, an' fishing on a hot afternoon.' She sighed, then added unexpectedly, 'As for the thrupence, you can keep it for makin' me laugh. It takes somethin' to mek me laugh on a day like this 'un.'

'Janey, thanks, missus,' Colm gasped. Three pence! He and Caitlin could go to the penny rush at the Tivoli and still have money over for sweets. Or if his mammy would give an eye to Caitlin he could go to the swimming pond on Tara Street—he could give the other penny to the little girl to spend. Since girls were not allowed in the first-class pond he could not have taken her anyway and as she could not swim she could scarcely expect to take part in that particular outing.

'That's all right, young feller,' the cook said. 'Here . . . we've a dinner party in an hour so I was just goin' to get the staff a snack . . . will bread an' jam suit you?'

Too astonished to answer, Colm and Caitlin stood side by side, Colm with the two-shilling piece safely stowed in his pocket, and waited whilst the cook cut and spread, and then handed them each a thick slice of bread and jam. 'There you are,' she said. 'That'll see you home. Now young feller, I've had a thought. You've got a head on your shoulders, that's plain to see, and won't be shuffled out of the money your mammy is owed by any means. But what if it wasn't your mammy, eh? What if you was asked to collect money owin' for someone else?'

Colm didn't quite understand the question, because he could not imagine having to collect money owing for a stranger, and he was about to say so when he thought of the people who came round the Liberties to collect money owing. Tally men. People who needed good clothes for some purpose could buy them a bit at a time and if they were short one week they were supposed to pay double the next. Then there were the shops which delivered their goods and sent in a bill every so often. They must send someone to collect, he supposed vaguely. Was that what the cook meant? 'D'you mean the 'surance men, an' the tally men, ma'am?' he asked politely. 'I don't think I'd like to be one o' them!'

Cook laughed. 'No indeed. But what I'd got in mind, young feller, was deliveries. It's me brother, see? He's got a butcher's shop in York Street an' he needs a young feller to deliver on a Saturday—his boy's just left. If you go round there an' tell him Mrs Emms sent you an' give him a note which I'll write, there's a good chance he'll tek you on, so there is.'

'And would I have to collect money?' Colm asked rather nervously. He could not imagine asking for money from all the cooks in the big houses to whom he would be delivering—it was one thing standing out for what was owed to his mammy, but to try to get money from total strangers was a different matter. 'I don't know as I'd like that, ma'am. It 'ud mean carryin' money round wit' me, an' I'm only thirteen, bigger lads could set on me easy. An' suppose I couldn't get the money owed an' your brother thought I'd put it in me pocket?'

Cook, who had gone to the table and was scribbling a note as she had promised, shook her head, folded the paper and came back to the doorway. 'No, it isn't done like that, young feller.

When you take an order, there's a bill in wit' it. Then during the week the feller who delivers collects the money owed. All you have to do is hand over the bill, see? No messin' around wit' change, no fear of gettin' things wrong. But it seems you're a trustable young feller an' me brother needs someone he can trust. Well? D'you want this note?' She waved it at him. 'It's only Saturdays but you'll mebbe get as much as t'ree bob if it's a long day.'

'T'ree bob!' Colm said. His mind made itself up for him at the very thought of such riches. 'Thanks, ma'am . . . I'll go round there just as soon as we've tek the money back to our mammy.'

'Good. Mind, I'm not promisin' anything, because me brother might ha' got someone else in the meantime. But you're polite, tidy and well-spoken and because of me recommendation you've a good chance o' the job.'

'Right. Many thanks, ma'am,' Colm said eagerly and turned away from the door. What an opportunity! Like most lads, he'd done his share of earning small sums of money by breaking up empty boxes from the quays and fruit markets, and selling the wood as kindling, or selling newspapers, or running messages, but delivering was a proper job, the sort that paid real money. And I'm only thirteen, he reminded himself as he and Caitlin hurried back along the way they had come. Mammy will be so pleased if I get the job.

He voiced the thought aloud to Caitlin, who said: 'Mammy does her washing on a Saturday, Colly, so she can look after me an' you won't have to drag me round, devil a bit you will.'

'That's true,' Colm said, forgetting to tell her

30

that 'devil' was a naughty word not suitable for a young lady such as herself. 'Shall we go round to York Street on our way home, alanna? Will you be very good and quiet whiles I talk to the feller?'

'Quiet as a mouse,' Caitlin said at once. 'Oh, won't Mammy be pleased when you tell her you've got the job, Colly!'

*   *   *

She was. 'Wait until I tell your daddy,' she kept saying when he told her he had the job, her eyes shining. 'He wants you to go to England wit' him when you're a man growed, but if you're good, an' do as you're told, you'll mebbe have a job in butchery for the rest of your life. Then you won't have to leave Dublin.'

Being a butcher didn't appeal particularly to Colm, but he did not say so. Indeed, he was so shocked to hear that his father planned to carry him off over the water to dig railway lines and such that he decided, over the matter of his future, to keep his own counsel. After all, he was only thirteen; there was time enough to think about it.

What was more, he liked Mr Savage, the butcher, and Mr Savage seemed to like him. At any rate he had not quibbled over giving him the job and had added that he would pay half a crown a day, with extra for overtime. 'It's good money for a lad of thirteen,' he observed. 'You can ride a bike? It's quicker'n footin' it.'

'Sure it is,' Colm agreed, for like most boys of his age, though he had never owned a bicycle he had had 'goes' on other people's. 'But the bike, Mr Savage . . . will I be hirin' one from ole Whalen on

31

North King Street? Only I don't have one of me own.'

Mr Savage laughed. 'I keep a delivery bike wit' me name on it,' he said cheerfully. ' 'Tis a big 'un, but you'll manage, I don't doubt.'

So on the Saturday following Colm started his new job and by the end of the day he had done well, big bike and all. The basket on the front made it a cumbersome vehicle, but when it was full and too heavy for him to ride he pushed and as it emptied he began to cycle, at first very slowly, and gradually faster and faster. He took care, furthermore. He made sure that the right parcel and the correct accompanying bill in its brown envelope were handed in to each house, and whenever he went back for more orders he slid between the customers waiting to be served with a murmured apology. He wanted to keep this job. To his delight and surprise he was frequently given something at the kitchen door when he delivered a parcel.

'You're a little feller for that gurt big bicycle,' a cook said, 'and it's a good way you've cycled wit' me leg o' mutton. Here's a cut o' bread an' jam to keep you goin' as you cycle back to Savage's.'

At first, when this happened, he pushed the food into his mouth as he wheeled the bike back onto the roadway, but later he learned to give enthusiastic thanks and put it in his pocket. No need to ask his mammy for a carry-out when the rich were so generous.

When he mentioned this to Herby, who had been the delivery boy until Mr Savage had promoted him to working in the shop, Herby said he shouldn't take it for granted that such

32

generosity would continue.

' 'Tis because you're only a chiseller,' he explained. 'When you're older they're not so free wit' their grub. Still an' all, make the most of it. Time enough to bring your own food when the hand-outs stop.'

So it was no wonder that Colm headed home that night warmed by the exercise, the thrill of having a whole half-crown in his pocket and his full belly. And when he got home, the thrill of handing his mother his wages, like any other man of the house, and of being sat down at the table before a big plate of mutton stew, whilst Caitlin, long abed, called out to him to come in and tell her if he'd had a nice day, now, could not be bettered.

What was more, as soon as he'd finished the stew, for he was ravenously hungry, he produced a present for his mammy. Mr Savage had let him buy at a specially low price a nice piece of pork which would do them fine for Sunday dinner and when the mammy saw it she had been as delighted with it as with anything else he had given her. 'Sure an' haven't I the best son in the whole world?' she had said, her eyes shining and the joint pressed to her bosom. 'Not only did ye hand me your wages wit'out taking a penny piece for yourself, Colm O'Neill, but you managed to buy me such a lovely present! How did you do it, son? Don't say Mr Savage paid you over the odds?'

'He said I could have another sixpence, or the piece of meat,' Colm told her. 'He's a dacint feller, so he is. Will we have it for our dinner tomorrer?'

'We'll have it for supper,' his mother decided. 'If it's fine tomorrer I'm takin' you an' Caitlin down to Killiney Strand. We'll catch the train an' take our food wit' us ... now you're a workin' man you deserve a treat now an' then. Will you write a letter to your daddy tellin' him all about it?'

But this Colm did not intend to do. Sometimes he added a couple of lines to the ones his mammy wrote, but even that much he did grudgingly. 'You're better at letters than me, Mammy,' he said at once. 'You'll make a good story of it, much better than I could. Besides, it's nice for you to have somethin' different to write about ... I'll put a couple o' lines on the end of the page.'

'I thought you might enjoy tellin' your daddy about the new job an' the day out be the sea,' his mother said a little reproachfully. 'Still, letter writin' was always a labour to me when I was a young wan, so I dare say it's the same for you. Now you'd best go an' tell Caitlin how ye got on before she bursts a lung wit' shoutin'.'

Colm obeyed, but he had barely begun to tell his sister of the huge bicycle, the basket laden with parcels of meat and the kindness of the staff in the big houses, when he saw that she was asleep. And so he was able to go thankfully off to his own bed, where he followed her example very quickly, worn out by his day and by anticipation of the morrow.

*   *   *

After her children were in bed, Eileen made herself a cup of tea, smeared margarine on a cut of soda bread and sat down by the open window to relax for a moment or two before she, too, went to her bed. I've a good son, she told herself again, leaning out a little so she could see into the dark and deserted street below. And a good husband, for all

34

he's so far away. But why in the name of God don't they love one another, my two good men? Sean tried, but he expected too much, was too critical of the lad, and Colm, sensing this, responded by showing a sort of jealous contempt for his father which not only hurt Sean, but Eileen, too.

If only Sean didn't make it so plain that he thought Colm a bit of a molly—and for why? Because the young feller helped around the place and took his sister out with him, sooner than stay at home all day. And whilst she continued to work she hoped that Colm would go on taking Caitlin around with him, otherwise she would have to spend money on a child minder, and they could do without that, so they could. If she'd had more children, if Colm had been a girl instead of a boy . . . but she loved her bright, intelligent son and most certainly did not envy her sisters their large families. She and Sean were well off by most standards, and that was because they only had the two childer and they both worked.

Sean, over in England, was well paid in comparison with wages in Ireland. He sent what he could home and when you remembered that he had to pay his lodgings and buy all his own food, clothing and the baccy for his pipe . . . well, he was on good money, that you had to admit. Many of the men in the surrounding tenements brought back less than a pound a week to raise their families on, so the wives worked, and the older children, and even so, life for them was a constant struggle.

Eileen, who worked in the big houses, had never quite understood the economics of the rich, nor why they had so much and gave so little. As she scrubbed huge tiled floors, whited steps, washed

35

paintwork, she saw out of the corner of her eye the waste, the greed, the selfishness of their lives. The children of the rich had for pocket-money what she was paid to work as hard as she could for eight hours, but a poor crippled beggar would get more from herself than from her employers' children. The lady of the house would quibble over what she paid her servants, then throw out the dress she'd worn only twice, because 'Everyone's seen it and you won't want folk saying your wife has only the one decent dress'.

Another bob or two on me money wouldn't hurt any of 'em, but they'd never dream of payin' over the odds, Eileen told herself, more in wonder than in pain. And Sean had said that in England she'd be paid better, too ... not that she had any intention of going over the water. Not she! Ireland was ruled by the Irish now, since they had kicked out the British back in 'twenty-two, and the civil war was over, so there was no need to flee from the fighting. No, Ireland was Sean's home as well as hers and her children would be brought up here, so they would, as she and Sean had been.

The soft air coming through the window smelled of dust, and chimney smoke, and the salty odour of the river, but even so, on its breath Eileen could smell the Irish countryside. Wouldn't it be grand, now, to live in the country? There was a little village not far from Dublin, Finglas, where there would be space to grow, fresh air, grass and great trees ...

But that was just a dream and well she knew it. She and Sean would work hard, and her good son would do the same, but their chances of moving out of the Dublin slums to live in a village were remote indeed. Besides, she had no idea whether she would like it, because she had been born and bred in Dublin and knew only the life here, understood nothing of village life. True, she had gone out with the other women of the neighbourhood when the spuds were ready and picked them for the rich farmers, and her kids had sat in the grass at the edge of the field and played games with the village kids. But that wasn't like living there.

Still. Everyone needed some sort of dream-future and Finglas was hers. And one day Sean would give up the navvying, because he'd not have the strength to go on with it, and they would settle down together to live happily somewhere—why not in Finglas? It would be wonderful to have a rose-covered cottage with tall trees around it and a bit of a garden where they could grow spuds and cabbages, and she would sit on a chair in the sunshine and make lace, or embroider collars and cuffs, and sell the results of her industry to the rich Dublin ladies who had money to burn, and they would live happily ever after.

But that time would not come for many a long year, and right now she had better get herself out of this chair and into her bed. Tomorrow she was going to take her kids to Killiney, where the stony beach ran down into a shallow sea, whilst the tall mountains at the back brooded over all. She would need to get her sleep, for they were a lively couple, Colm and Caitlin, and would not expect her to sit on the shingle and doze, they would want her to enjoy herself, too.

Eileen got up off her chair, pulled the window almost closed and carried her empty cup over to the washstand. Then she checked the buckets

37

beneath it. The slop bucket was empty, the water-carriers full. The fire was out long since, but it wouldn't take a moment in the morning to stir some life into it with fresh kindling, then she could mash the tea and send Colm out for bread and milk. Earlier in the day she had made two tea bracks and a dozen potato cakes, and with a bag of the little rosy-cheeked apples that were being sold in the markets at present, a bottle of cold tea to drink and a few of her home-made toffees, they would have a feast fit for a king, so they would.

Yawning hugely, Eileen went through to the room she shared with Caitlin. The child was slumbering soundly in the truckle bed and Eileen undressed down to vest and bloomers as quietly as any mouse, untied her rain-straight, light-brown hair from its bun and brushed it until it crackled. Then she climbed stealthily into the big bed and let her head relax onto the pillow.

In less than a minute, she slept.

CHAPTER TWO

1925 Liverpool

It was a mild night for September, so the window in Rosie Ryder's small bedroom was half open, letting in both the soft night air and the glow from the gas-lamp outside in the street.

Rosie had been in bed a good hour or more, but she couldn't sleep. It was too hot and besides, she had a piece of poetry to learn for school and it refused to stay learned unless she kept going over and over it in her head. Past experience had taught her that a poem repeated just before sleep somehow stuck, she did not know why, so she hadn't bothered to learn it earlier but had gone out and played in the road with her friend Peggy, first quietly enough with their skipping ropes, then far more rowdily with the rest of the kids in a game of relievio, with the yard at the back of the public house on the corner—Ricky Elliott was the landlord's son—as the gaol.

It was a noisy game, popular with kids but not with grown-ups because of the noise. For not only were there screams of 'Comin', ready or not!' from the hunting team, but the hiders would shriek when they were caught, warn others at the top of their voice that the enemy were in the vicinity, and when packed into the gaol they would shout 'Relievio!' until a member of their own team, uncaught, came to rescue them.

There weren't a lot of hiding places unknown to both sides, of course, because it was an unwritten rule that you didn't hide on private property. That was why it was best played at dusk, so that hiding was easier and seeking harder, for the most exciting part of the game was sneaking past the seekers to let your pals out of gaol and this, also, was easiest in the dusk.

The boys usually organised relievio, so you had to be tough to join in. Boys didn't appreciate girls who cried when they were caught or objected to being barged aside by a male shoulder, they liked the ones who didn't complain, and took the rough and tumble as fair game. Rosie's hair was tied back for school in two long plaits and many a time young Alfie Morris, who lived next door to the Ryders, had caught Rosie by grabbing a pigtail, or even by doing a sort of rugby tackle, which brought them down at speed and caused a few startled phrases to erupt from them both. But Rosie, an only child, knew better than to complain. Alice Fitzgibbon, who lived near the end of the street, was an only child and considered a right little ninny by the boys. She never played rough games, and liked to sit on her mother's front step and knit blanket squares or play cat's cradle with the younger kids, and of course the boys despised her and told her so. She didn't mind, though. She would just give them a slant-eyed look, as though to say 'Just you wait!', and continue with whatever game she was playing.

'She'll be more popular than the lot of ye one of these days,' Rosie's mother was wont to say darkly. 'A feller won't fall in love wit' a girl he's chased up the road and brought with wit' a crack in the dust. No, when the fellers are searchin' for sweethearts it's the little Alices of this world they turn to, you mark my words, Rose Ryder.'

'I don't care, I don't want sweethearts,' Rosie said airily. 'I like playin' wi' the fellers, Mam.'

And now, of course, she was suffering because if she'd done her homework for Monday earlier she could have let herself go to sleep. Instead, the words of the wretched poem went round and round in her head ... she even found it hard to concentrate on listening for the sound of her father's bicycle as he creaked homewards.

Jack Ryder was a tram driver and when the weather was fine he cycled from the tram depot on Smith Street to his home on Cornwall Street. Since his bicycle was an elderly machine, Rosie knew the creak of it by heart and usually heard it first as he turned into the street. If he was on an early shift she would drop everything and run to meet him, casting herself into his arms with a cry of 'Oh Daddy, it's good to see you—there's pig's liver an' onions for your tea, an' Mam's gorran apple pie an' all!'

But when he got home late, all she could do was to call down the stairs the instant she heard the back door open, 'Daddy, I'm in bed, will you come up an hear me pome that I've learned for school? When you've had your tea, I mean, norright away.'

But he always came up right away, because he knew she'd not settle until he did. So if she missed the bicycle's creaking progress, she might also miss the opening and shutting of the back door, or worse, she might fall asleep before he got in. But she wouldn't, of course. She wouldn't miss saying good-night to her daddy for anything, not even if she had to prop her eyelids open with matches, the way Daddy used to tease her.

She said the poem over once more, then pushed it firmly out of her mind and allowed herself to think about the game of relievio and her close encounter with Moggy Highes, who had seen her crouching behind Mrs Fitzgibbon's backyard, half hidden, she hoped, by the dustbins, and had reached for her just as she sprang forth and roared off down the jigger, with Moggy so close she could feel his hot breath on her neck. But she'd got away all right, hadn't she? Girls were often faster runners than boys, and she had sped along the jigger and turned right into Cornwall Street, which meant a long run past her home before making a quick dive into the backyard of the Queen's Arms to free the prisoners cooped up there with a joyous

41

shriek, then pounding off once more along Netherfield Road this time.

She was in the middle of reliving the glorious moment when she had glanced back and seen Moggy clutching his side and obviously about to give up on such fast prey, when she heard the back door shut. Immediately she shot up in bed and prepared her lungs for a good yell. 'Daddy! I'm in bed, I've been learnin' me pome, when you've et can you come up an' hear me say it? Daddy, can you come up when you've et?'

Rosie paused for breath. She had shouted at the top of her voice, he always heard, but . . . ah!

Footsteps crossed the kitchen and trod along the narrow hall. Rosie, who had bounded out of bed to shout, now jumped hastily back in. Her father would not come up if she was out of bed, he had made that quite plain. So now she pulled the sheet up under her chin and bounced up and down on the mattress. 'We played relievio, this evenin', Daddy, an' our team won, mine an' Alfie's. Alfie picked me first, Daddy, afore all the fellers, 'cos I can run so fast, an' Moggy come after me—I was hidin' behind the Fitzy dustbins—only I ran so quick he couldn't even sprinkle salt on me tail!'

Her father's head appeared round the door; he was smiling. 'All right, lass, all right . . . is it a long poem? Only your mammy wants me down again, pronto. She's cookin' me a pork chop, wi' apples an' sultanas, an' there's mashed potatoes an' fried onions too, so I don't want that little lot gettin' cold, for I'm hungry as a lion an' me carry-out was et hours an' hours ago.'

'Yes, I had pork an' mash for me tea earlier—it were grand. An' the pome's norra long one.' Rosie

42

fished the exercise book containing it from under the bed and held it out. 'Page seventeen, Daddy.'

'Gorrit,' Jack Ryder said after a moment. He looked up at her expectantly. 'Fire away, chuck.'

Rosie recited the poem falteringly and her father nodded, then put the book down on her counterpane. 'Well done, queen. And how's my Rose of Tralee, then? Did you have a good day in school?'

'It were awright,' Rosie admitted. Her daddy always called her his Rose of Tralee because he said she was just like the girl in the song. 'Did you have a good day on the tram, Daddy?'

'Grand, thanks, Rosie. Well, if that's all I'll give you a kiss an' gerron me way to me supper, 'cos there's no time to serenade ye tonight. Now get to sleep, there's a good gal.' He leaned over the bed and kissed the tip of her nose, then brushed the wisps of hair off her forehead and bent lower, to tuck her in. 'You'll not be wantin' me coat over you tonight,' he observed. 'It's warm still—too warm, you might say.'

In winter, Rosie liked to have her father's tram driver's coat as an extra cover, for not only was it thick and warm, it smelled of him and was like being held in his arms all night, safe from all harm. But now, with the day's warmth still lingering, she smiled and shook her head. 'No, I don't need your coat, Daddy,' she said round the thumb which she had just stuck into her mouth. 'But won't you sing me one little bit of me song? It'll send me straight off to dreamland, sure as sure.'

'Awright, just one verse,' Jack Ryder said, sitting down on the bed again and filling his lungs with air.

'She was lovely and fair as the rose of the summer,
Yet 'twas not her beauty alone that won me,
Oh no! 'Twas the truth in her eye ever dawning,
That made me love Mary, the Rose of Tralee.'

'Thanks, Daddy, though I still think you ought to ha' called me Mary,' Rose said as she always did, as her father's voice sank artistically low and the song died away. 'I love your singin', honest to God I do. Will you always sing to me at bedtime?'

'As long as you want me to,' her father said from the doorway. 'Mary's a nice name, sure enough, but we liked the name Rose, it suited you. Now goodnight, my very own Rose of Tralee; sleep well.'

'You sleep well too,' Rosie mumbled, but once he had gone she lay awake for a little longer, listening to the familiar sounds of her parents in the rooms below: quiet talking, the scrape of a chair, the rustle as her mother pulled the kitchen curtains across. Then, when her mother had washed up and put away the dishes, she imagined them down there in the kitchen, carrying out their usual before-bed tasks. Her mam, who was fair-haired and pretty, with a round, rosy face and quick, neat movements, would be bustling about the room doing all the things she did every night. Turning off the cooking stove, making sure that Socks, next door's tabby cat, who sometimes came indoors when her owners were out, had not got shut in by mistake, checking the washing to be sure that anything needed for the morning had been ironed and was ready. And Daddy would be relaxing after his day's work, sitting back in his easy chair with the *Echo* spread out on his knee, sometimes reading a piece out to his Lily,

44

sometimes chuckling, tutting, exclaiming over a headline.

And presently, Rosie knew, her parents would come up to bed and would pop in, 'just to make sure', and she would pretend to be asleep, eyes closed, ignoring her mother's fussing round the room, straightening the sheet, picking a book off the floor with a gentle murmur of dismay; books must be treated with respect, she would have said if she had known Rosie was awake.

And tomorrow was Saturday, so there would be no school and she would have a whole lovely day to play in. Oh, she would do her chores first; even an only child in a moderately comfortable house had work to do. Rosie would make her bed and tidy her room, then go down to see if her mother had any messages for her to run. There was usually a bit of shopping to be done locally, then, if it was a fine day they might go out somewhere—to the big shops in the city centre, or to Stanley Park, or even out on the overhead railway to Seaforth, perhaps, if her mother was in a good mood. Lily Ryder was a thrifty housewife and always had a store of money in the old pewter teapot on the mantel. She said it was for emergencies, but she often used it for little treats ... Lying snug in bed, Rosie hugged herself at the thought of all those little extras. It might be ices at the park, or some new hair ribbons, or a trip into the country and cream tea at a farmhouse. Of course, there were other good ways of spending a Saturday, she knew that. Sometimes she and Peggy went to the cinema, to the special children's shows, but enjoyable though that was, it wasn't as good as going out with Mam.

Once more, before she slept, Rosie repeated the

poem. It came easily now, one word following another as though she had known it all her life. Satisfied, Rosie slept.

*   *   *

Lily Ryder had heard the shouts from her place by the cooker, and sighed and smiled, knowing very well that it was no use telling Jack to have his meal, then go up and see the child. For one thing, Rose would have fallen asleep and for another Jack would not have enjoyed his meal knowing that, upstairs, his daughter waited.

Lily and Jack had married when she had been twenty and he twenty-seven, and she had fallen for Rose at once. They had wanted a child, Jack especially, but neither had ever bewailed the fact that since Rose's birth there had never been a sign of any more children. The war had intervened, and in any case it was clearly easier to stay solvent when you had one child than if you had ten, Jack often said. They wanted the best for their girl, and the best would not have been possible had they produced a string of other children.

But there was no doubt about it, Rose was spoiled. She was a real tomboy, preferring boys as companions to girls, enjoying boys' games and pastimes, and though Lily sighed over her daughter's torn clothing and frequent scraped knees and ruined boots, she knew that Jack was delighted with his boyish girl.

'We've gorra lad, for all we've only gorra girl, Lily me love,' her husband would say bracingly sometimes, when Lily looked wistfully at a sturdy little boy, playing up at the park or on the sands.

46

'Not everyone can say that, you know.'

'Oh, you think Rosie's perfect,' Lily was apt to reply. 'What'll you do when she grows up a bit, an' wants pretty frocks an' silk stockin's an' such?'

'That's diff'rent; I like a young lady to be a young lady,' Jack had assured his wife with a grin. 'I don't recall expectin' you to play cricket or to come swimmin' in the Scaldy when we met up first.'

Lily laughed. 'You'd have had to want,' she had informed him. 'I weren't a tomboy even when I were a kid. Me mam brought me up proper strict, no street cricket or Kick the Can for little Lily Roberts! Come to think of it, Jack love, you'd not ha' wanted to marry me if I'd not been a bit of a homemaker by then. So I really think we should insist that Rose learns more than how to tidy her room an' make her bed neatly. She'll be the only girl in the neighbourhood who can't peel a spud or cook a meal at this rate.'

'She'll learn in good time,' Jack had said comfortably. 'She'll change as she grows older an' begins to see fellers in a different light. And then she'll want to learn how to mek an apple pie an' to sew a straight seam, as well as all the other things, like how to curl her hair, an' look cool an' pretty even in a heatwave.'

Lily had snorted sceptically, but in her heart she believed that he was probably right and besides, she had no wish to alienate their daughter's affections by insisting that she did household tasks which she hated and which were not really necessary, since Lily herself did not work.

So now, standing by the cooker ready to serve up his dinner as soon as he appeared downstairs again, she let her mind go back, nostalgically, to those

47

magical courting days, when she had worked behind the counter in a small drapery shop in Scotland Road and had first seen Jack Ryder strolling along the street, gazing into the windows as he passed them.

She had been just sixteen, then, for their courtship had taken all of four years. Lily, youngest of eleven children, had had a dependent mother on her hands at the time and though old Mrs Roberts had died a couple of years after Lily and Jack had met, Jack did not want his wife to work once they were married, which meant that they must have enough savings so that Lily's wage would not be missed.

But of course she had known nothing of the shared future that was to be theirs as she stood on the top step of the wobbly old step-ladder, cleaning the shop's big, slightly bowed window. All she was aware of was that there was a handsome young man coming along the pavement ... and she was up a ladder, with her skirts kilted round her calves, and her legs on view in very old, darned woollen stockings.

She had been half-way down the ladder when the heel of her shoe caught in a piece of uneven wood and she took a nose-dive for the pavement.

Jack had bounded forward and caught her. 'Bloody 'ell,' the young man had said breathlessly, with Lily Roberts in his arms, feeling the most almighty fool as she clutched at the strongly muscled shoulders. 'Strange things 'appen on the Scottie, that I do know, but since when did they tek on women window-cleaners? I know I'm a lovely feller, but it ain't every day that a beautiful young girl dives nose first into me arms!'

He stood Lily down on the pavement as he spoke but did not let go of her and Lily, blushing and laughing, had bidden him 'Let me go!' without, it must be admitted, meaning a word of it. She could see her aunt glaring at her through the glass, however, and because she knew it would annoy that lady to see her in such a compromising position she had not pulled away. The chore of window-cleaning, which was hers whenever the shop was quiet, was a bone of contention between herself and Aunt Em anyway. Other shop girls did not clean the windows, the shop owners employed a proper window-cleaner, but Aunt Em was mean and moaned all the time about the amount of money she paid her niece.

So now Lily gazed up at her rescuer, taking in his appearance. She liked the brightness of the blue eyes in his tanned face, the cowlick of brown hair which overhung his brow, and the humour and gentleness in the line of his mouth. 'It's me aunt's shop; I work there as a counter-hand,' she informed him. 'She meks me clean the windows, though—too perishin' mean to employ a feller and that's the truth.'

He smiled lazily down at her. 'And you go on workin' here, when she uses you as slave labour?' he said mockingly. 'Where's your pride, queen? You want to tell 'er where she gets off ... Me cousin Alice works on Great Homer Street an' she was tellin' me that there's a job goin' there in a drapery. She wanted to apply 'cos the money's good, but she's in ironmongery an' they want someone wi' drapery experience. Why don't you have a go, eh?'

In one moment of knowing Jack, it seemed, he

49

intended to change her life. 'I will,' she said without giving the matter any further consideration. 'What's the name of the place?'

He told her, and suggested that she go into the shop now and tell her aunt that she'd met an old friend and wanted to go along with him and have a word with his mother, or invent some other excuse for leaving off work right away. 'I can tek you along to Great Homer Street meself, to the very door,' he promised. 'Then, when you've got the job, we can get ourselves a bite of tea. We might go to the picture house, an' all—d'you like the flickers?'

Lily realised that this was all going a good deal too fast, but she wanted to leave her aunt's shop and try for the other job. She knew herself to be undervalued and underpaid, too, and had been keeping a look-out for a better opening for some time. She loved the cinema, what was more, and already felt instinctively that she would be safe with this pleasant, tanned young man whose arms had held her so safely and who smelled of fresh air and sunshine. But first, there was one question he must answer, if she was to go off with him right now. 'I love the flickers, but I don't know your name an' you don't know mine,' she pointed out. 'What's more, I don't know what you do with yourself— what's your job, that you can stroll along the Scottie as if you'd all the time in the world?'

'Me? Eh, sorry, queen, I never thought.' He sketched a bow. 'Jack Ryder at your service, an' I'm a seaman on the SS *Maria-Louise*, when I'm not livin' in Netherfield Road. And you?'

Her father had been a sailor and he had been drowned. She had told her mother she would never go out with a sailor so she should have backed off at that point and invented an excuse not to continue the acquaintance. Instead, she told him that she was Lily Roberts, that she was the youngest of eleven children and lived with her widowed mother in Eastbourne Street. And after that she went into her aunt's shop and said she'd met a friend and wanted the rest of the afternoon off.

Aunt Em was mean. She said, tartly, that if her niece took the rest of the afternoon off her pay-packet would be short on Saturday night. Equally tartly, Lily told her that since it would be her last one, it didn't really make all that difference. And walked out, whilst her aunt was still expostulating, and took Jack's arm and walked away with him up the road in the direction of Great Homer Street.

She had never regretted that moment, never looked back. Jack, informed of her feelings about marrying a sailor, had applied to be taken on at the tram depot, and within three months was driving the big trams all around the city though when the war came he had joined the Navy, ending up decorated for valour. It had been a worrying time, but they had got through it somehow and the small Rose had flourished despite shortages and adored her father more, perhaps, because he was not always on hand.

And now here they were, married a dozen years and as happy, Lily often thought, as anyone could be. She might pretend that she wanted a dainty little girl interested in dresses and playing with dolls, but she would not have changed Rose for all the tea in China and she knew that Jack felt the same.

Lily was still standing by the cooker, reliving the

51

past, when she heard the clatter of Jack's shoes on the stairs and hastily produced the warmed plate from the bottom of the oven and placed tenderly upon it the pork chops and the onions, fried brown, the thick gravy and the mashed potatoes which were to be tonight's dinner.

The plate was being stood down on the kitchen table as Jack entered. 'Me favourite!' he declared, taking a seat and pulling the food towards him. 'Have you eaten, Lil?'

When he was going to be late she usually ate with Rose and tonight was no exception. 'Aye, me an Rose had ours earlier, when she came home from school. But I've not had me puddin', so we'll share that. It's a nice treacle duff; I got the suet from the butcher's on Netherfield Road when I bought the pork chops. Our gal settled down, has she?'

'Aye. I gave her a bit of a tune an' she stuck her thumb in her mouth . . . she'll be asleep well before we go up, luv.'

'Good,' Lily said, sitting down opposite him and getting her knitting out of the pocket of her wrap around overall. 'I thought I might tek her out tomorrer when she's finished her chores. If the weather's as fine as it's been today, that is. 'Cos it'll be winter soon enough, wi' no chance of goin' to the park or the seaside,' she finished.

'That's it. You go off an' have fun,' Jack said at once. 'We might go somewhere Sunday, after church, but the chances are it'll rain. Why not go to Seaforth? Rosie loves the sea.'

'No, we'll leave that for when we're all together,' Lily said comfortably. 'We'll likely tek a tram to Sefton Park; our Rose loves the aviary, an' we can tek a boat on the lake an' have our tea there.'

'Sounds good,' Jack said. He scraped his plate clean, then sat back with a sigh of contentment. 'That were good, our Lil! Bring on the puddin'!'

Lily got up and fetched the duff, steaming hot still, from its nook at the back of the oven. 'Here we are,' she said, cutting off two slices, one large for Jack and a smaller one for herself. 'Want extra syrup?'

'I'll be so fat I won't be able to squeeze into me tram,' Jack protested as his wife put the tin of golden syrup on the table before him. 'No, luv, this is plenty sweet enough for me.'

When the meal was finished off with a cup of tea, the two of them tackled the washing up and clearing away together, then, hand in hand, went contentedly up to bed. As they undressed, Lily remembered something. 'If we're goin' Sefton Park way, I s'pose I oughter call on me sister Daisy. She might like to come wi' us, you never know.'

Daisy was the sister nearest in age to Lily and the two of them had remained friends, though Lily saw very little of the rest of her family. But Daisy, like Lily, had married young and borne only one child, though she had not been as lucky as Lily; her husband Bill had gone off with a younger woman some years earlier and Daisy had been left to struggle on as best she could. She had never remarried and Lily was in the habit of meeting her sister a couple of times a week for a chat and a cuppa. It would have been nice had their children been friends, but the age gap was too great, for Daisy's Mona was sixteen and had been in work for two years. She worked in a grocery shop on Heyworth Street and seemed to spend very little time at home. Sometimes it crossed Lily's mind that Mona dressed awful smart for a shop assistant and occasionally it occurred to her that she had seen Mona out with several different young men, but she didn't say so, not even to Jack. The girl was her niece and was probably at the age when she was testing her wings, so to speak. She would settle down one day and because Daisy did not care much for the house there was little incentive for young Mona to spend her time at home. Daisy seemed fond enough of her daughter, but the two of them never went out together as far as Lily knew. Indeed, that was why she continued to visit Daisy so often; someone had to try to get her out of herself.

'What, to the park? We-ell I suppose she might,' Jack said doubtfully. Lily knew that he thought Daisy was a real moaner, always complaining, but that was not her sister's fault. Life had treated her harshly and now Daisy had to work five mornings a week, cleaning in the insurance offices on Exchange Flags. 'Still, even if she doesn't want to come out wi' you I dare say she'd be pleased enough to see the pair of you. I expect you've got some bakin' for her?'

'A couple o' cakes an' a meat pie,' Lily mumbled. She often took food round to Daisy's little house and her sister was always touchingly grateful, but Lily knew that Jack thought Daisy ought to bestir herself a bit more. 'She does bake sometimes, Jack, luv, but it's a bit hard when you've no oven of your own. It means she has to take the cake mix round to Watts to get it cooked, an' then she has to collect it again. And wi' just the two of 'em ... well, it's easier to buy in.'

'I didn't say a word,' Jack said, climbing into bed. 'You know I don't grudge Daisy the food or your work, it's just that I think it would do her good to bake now an' then. Still an' all, you're right about gettin' it baked. We've gorra decent oven, so we do have it easy, I suppose.'

'We do,' Lily said eagerly. 'Daisy can afford to buy wi' the two of 'em earnin' an' Mona must make a regular wage at that grocer's. But our Dais do love me home-made stuff.'

'Yes, right, I'm not arguin',' Jack said again. 'I can't—I ain't never baked a cake in me life! Now gerrinto bed, woman, an gi's a cuddle.'

'You're awful, Jack,' Lily said, getting in and snuggling into his arms. 'Anyone 'ud think we'd been married twelve days, 'stead o' twelve years! I'm sure our Daisy weren't never so undignified.'

'No ... but look what happened to your Daisy chuck! No, don't pull away, I weren't being nasty but you asked for that, didn't you? Now you can jest settle down an' tell me about your day and when you've done I'll tell you about mine. Ready?'

'Ready,' agreed Lily. They always spent the last twenty minutes before sleep in swapping experiences. 'Well, our Rose went off to school wi' Peggy ...'

*   *   *

Next morning, Rose got up, washed, dressed and made her bed. She didn't make it neatly or tidily— no hospital corners here, no smoothing down of the sheets—but at least she made it and tidied her room, too, in a manner of speaking. Then she hurried downstairs. Her mother was already in the

55

kitchen, having got up to see her father off, and was diligently stirring porridge.

Rose yawned and went over to the stove. 'Mornin', Mam! What's for breakfuss?'

'Porridge, as if you didn't know, and toast and tea. Or I could do you an egg, I dare say. How hungry are you?'

'Eggs-hungry,' Rose said promptly. 'Will you have one too, Mam? A boily-egg?'

'I might at that,' her mother said. 'I've a few messages for you, then I thought we'd have ourselves an early meal an' go out this afternoon.'

'Out? Where?' Rose said, pricking up her ears. 'I do love an outin', Mam.'

'To Sefton Park . . . only I thought we'd pop in to Aunt Daisy's first, see if she'd like to come wi' us.'

'Oh Mam, not Aunt Daisy's,' Rose said, dismayed. 'You know what she's like, she'll keep us there for hours, grumblin' and moanin' about everything, an' she won't come wi' us into the park—which is a good thing, if you ask me.'

'She's me sister, an' she's gorra good deal to grumble about,' Lily said, taking a couple of eggs from the bowl in the pantry and putting them into a pan. 'Why don't you butter some bread, chuck, whiles I cook these eggs?'

'Awright, Mam. But I'd much rather go straight to the park—you know what Aunt Daisy's like, it'll be dark afore we get there if she has her way.'

'I'll mek you a promise, young lady. We'll not stay longer than thirty minutes . . . that's only a little old half-hour . . . because I'll say we're meetin' a pal o' yours in Seffy. How's that?'

'Well, if we're goin' to say that, how about us takin' a pal really, so you won't be tellin' no lies?'

Rose said hopefully. 'Peggy might want to come . . . or Alfie, or Moggy. They all love Seffy like I does.'

'Get your breakfast et an' your messages done, an' we'll talk about it,' Lily said prudently, taking refuge in delaying tactics. She wanted her daughter to herself, she didn't want to cart half the neighbourhood along to the park. 'Is that bread an' butter ready, chuck? Right, here's your egg, then. Now get eatin'!'

*   *   *

By the time Rose and her mother arrived at Aunt Daisy's small house in Prince Edwin Lane they were both cross: Lily Ryder because she'd been jockeyed into bringing Ricky Elliott, who was a year older than her Rose and a good deal more street-wise. At twelve, Ricky knew all about the seamier side of life and Lily was anxious that he should not pollute the ears of her darling daughter with tales of Saturday night drunkeness in his parents' pub, or stories of his older brother's exploits with the 'young ladies' who walked the pavement alongside Lime Street station. Ted, Ricky's eldest brother, was a notorious womaniser.

And Ricky, when told to take himself off to Sefton Park and to wait for them by the aviary, had not been best pleased. 'Why can't I come round to Rosie's aunt's 'ouse?' he demanded querulously. 'I ain't gorrany money for ices nor nothin' whiles I wait for yez.'

Rose saw her mother give Ricky a slant-eyed look and knew that the older woman was thinking 'What a common boy!' and that didn't please Rose, either. She and Ricky weren't best friends, like she

57

and Alfie, but they were good mates and you didn't like your mam thinking your mates were common just because they said 'yez' instead of 'you'.

'If he came to Aunt Daisy's as well, Mam, you could say you'd promised his mam to take him to Seffy and we's both wanted a go on the boating lake,' she said craftily. 'Besides, if there's two of us we can play in the yard, whiles you an' Auntie have a chat.'

Lily Ryder could see the sense in it and she did feel, a trifle guiltily, that if young Ricky got into trouble of some sort whilst alone in Sefton Park then his mam would blame her and put it about that 'that stuck-up Mrs Ryder weren't to be trusted', so she grudgingly agreed to Ricky accompanying them, then had the satisfaction of seeing the youngsters disappear into the mucky little yard where Daisy kept the dustbins, apparently much preferring it to the inside of Daisy's small house. At least that way Ricky was less likely to take back a bad report to his mam.

'Bring 'em in, they can 'ave bread an' conny-onny, or some cake,' Daisy said, her eyes fixed greedily on her sister's basket. She was banking on that basket containing a cake, Lily knew, but it wasn't poor Daisy's fault that she wasn't domesticated. She'd never taken to housework or homemaking and, when you thought about it, why should she? Her man had gone off before they'd been married a twelve-month, she'd borne her child alone and lived alone ever since. And why should she clean her own house when she spent her mornings scrubbing other people's floors? Lily knew very well what Jack would say—that Daisy was a slut and that was why her man had left—but she didn't let it influence her feelings for her sister. Daisy had had ill luck whilst she, Lily, had been fortunate in everything she did and Daisy was fond of reminding her of the fact. Nor could Lily deny that she had the best husband in the world and the best daughter, too.

Now, however, she had to think fast so as not to hurt Daisy's feelings. 'Oh, lerrem play out,' she said, squeezing past Daisy's bulk and entering her untidy kitchen. 'You know what kids are, Dais, they'd rather be outside than in a palace. And as I said, I promised 'em a go on the boatin' lake, so I can't stay long.'

'You never stay long,' Daisy grumbled, but Lily ignored the remark and began emptying the basket onto the table. 'Anyways, I'll pull the kettle over the flame.'

'Aye, a cuppa never went amiss,' Lily agreed. 'Gorrany milk, queen?'

'Only conny-onny,' Daisy said through a mouthful of the rich sponge-cake which her sister had brought. 'The milkman never calls 'ere.'

'Never mind, I've not got time for drinkin' tea right now,' Lily said. She did not take sugar in her tea and disliked condensed milk. 'You know how it is, Dais; if we don't gerra move on there'll be a queue a mile long for the boats an' I can't let the kids down.'

'But you can let your flesh an' blood down,' Daisy grumbled. 'I'm that lonely on a weekend, Lil. Why can't the kids go to the park by theirselves, eh? You an' me, we could sit down wi' our tea an' have a jangle whiles they play. Why not, eh?'

'Because I promised, like I said; and besides, Rose *is* me flesh an' blood,' Lily said equably. 'But

59

why don't you come wi' us, eh? We could have that jangle you wanted, and we'll have a cuppa over there an' a bun or something. Come along, our Dais. You'd enjoy an outing. And it would do you good to wash up an' put on some shoes an' a coat an' come along wi' us.'

She waited for Daisy to object to her last remark, for her sister was barefoot and dirty, with food stains down the front of her grey dress and runnels of dirt across her arms. But Daisy just sniffed. 'No, me feet get quite tired enough walkin' to work an' back each mornin', I'm not givin' meself more grief, walkin' when I don't 'ave to. No, no, you go off an' enjoy yourselfs, don't worry about me, I'm used to bein' alone.'

'All right, then, I'll just stay for a cuppa,' Lily said. 'Now what've you been up to all week, queen? An' how's our Mona?'

'Oh, I been doin' the usual—workin', an' waitin' on Mona hand an' foot,' Daisy said wearily. 'That reminds me, chuck. Mona wondered if you'd let your Rosie come over 'ere tomorrer, for Sunday dinner. She thought the pair of 'em might go off together in the afternoon. Well, it wouldn't be just the pair of 'em, because Mona's gorra lovely young feller, a real gent. Mona's tek a rare shine to him and she told him she'd like to settle down, see, and 'ave a nice little place of her own, kids one day, perhaps a car, even. And there's no gettin' away from it, Dennis—that's 'is name, Dennis Brannigan—is 'ead over 'eels in love with me daughter. Well, I mean, when Mona suggested bringin' Rosie along there weren't no 'esitation, he agreed right off, said 'e'd mug the pair of 'em to a day in New Brighton, Seaforth, anywhere Mona 'ud

60

like to mention. Your Rosie 'ud love that; kids love a day at the sea.'

'That's ever so kind of Mona,' Lily said at once. 'But Sundays our Jack teks us somewhere, after we've been to church, that is. It'll be the seaside this week, that I do know, for we've discussed it and I couldn't disappoint him, queen. But thanks for the offer, it were a lovely thought.'

'Why don't you ask Rosie if she'd rather spend the day with 'er cousin? After all, she can see 'er dad any day of the week,' Daisy was saying persuasively, and Lily was wondering how to refuse without causing offence when Rose burst into the kitchen. Lily turned to her daughter with considerable relief. 'Manners,' she said chidingly. 'What's up?'

'There's kittens next door,' Rose said longingly. 'The lady looked over the wall an' said we could go an' tek a look. Have we got time, Mam?'

'Ten minutes, then we'll be off,' Lily said, glad not to have to admit that she had weakly agreed to have a cup of tea with her sister. 'Shall I give you a shout?'

'Oh Rosie, luv, your cousin Mona asked me to see if you'd go out wi' her tomorrer,' Aunt Daisy said, breaking into the conversation with heightened colour in her cheeks. She plainly considered that she had been snubbed by Lily and was thus taking matters into her own hands. 'She thought you might like a trip to New Brighton wi' her an' her feller.'

'No thanks, Aunt, Sundays is me dad's day off,' Rose said with a promptitude which endeared her doubly to her embarrassed mother. 'You don't need to shout us, Mam. The lady's bringin' the box into the backyard, we'll see you in the jigger as you leave Aunt Daisy's.'

'An' we'll come away wi' you as soon's we've seen the kittens,' Ricky said, hovering in the doorway behind Rose. 'We want to have a good go on the boats. Come on, queen, there's six of em to see, you know!'

'Why it makes a difference how many there are I can't even begin to guess,' Lily said as the two children scampered out of the yard and round to the next-door house. 'Let's mash the tea, Dais, an' you can tell me what you've been up to this past week or two. And don't be upset because of tomorrer, only Rosie loves to be wi' her dad an' five years is a big age difference, really. When they were younger I know they used to play together, your Mona an' our Rosie, but Mona's a young woman now and Rosie's just a kid still. My goodness, this tea's hot!'

*   *   *

'So that's your Aunt Daisy,' Ricky said thoughtfully as the two of them crouched beside the cardboard box full of patchwork-coloured kittens. 'She ain't much like your mam, chuck.'

'She's ten year older,' Rose explained. 'An' her old feller left her years back. Her gal's growed up, an' all.'

'Your mam took your aunt cakes an' that,' Ricky said after a moment. 'Don't she have much gelt, queen?'

'Yes, she's gorra job an' so's her daughter what lives wi' her, me cousin Mona. But me aunt don't bake,' Rose said briefly. No lover of Aunt Daisy

62

herself, she did not much fancy having to explain her to Ricky, particularly as she did not really understand Aunt Daisy herself, so she strove to change the subject. 'If you could have one of 'em, which would you choose?' She pointed to the kittens.

'Dunno. Kittens is grand, but they grows into cats awful quick,' Ricky observed. 'An' we've gorra cat—two, in fact. Ain't you gorra cat, Rosie?'

'No. Next door have got one called Socks—I like Socks all right, I wish she was ours. Though I'd like a dog, really. But a kitten would be next best,' Rose said. 'But these ones are too little to leave their mam, ain't they?'

'Yeah. The lady said another couple o' weeks,' Ricky reminded her. 'I like the one what's gorra black patch over his eye. An' the one that's nearly all white ain't bad. But I tell you, Rosie, cats ain't no fun. Try an' mek em play an' they either stick their bleedin' claws into you or stalks off wi' their noses in the air, honest to God they do. But a dog, now . . . if I could have a choice I'd go for a dog every time.'

'Oh, well, perhaps you're right,' Rose said, standing up. She knew, really, that she was unlikely to get a dog or a cat just yet. She had assured her parents that if she had a dog she would take him walking after school each day, but her parents did not seem to believe that she would and, in her heart of hearts, Rose thought they might be right. She did so love playing out, and though a dog would be great fun, it might not think that games of Kick the Can and Relievio were as good as a nice, long walk. And Mam said that she didn't intend to squander her precious housekeeping money on

63

feeding a dog and if they had one Rose would have to use her pocket money to buy dog's meat and biscuits. Rose had a number of uses already for her Saturday pennies and thought she might love the dog less if it meant no more Saturday flicks or bags of sweeties. 'We'd best go back to me aunt's, Ricky, or Mam will get going on another cuppa an' we'll never shift her.'

'Right you is,' Ricky said, standing up as well. He called out: 'Thanks, missus, they're grand kittens,' and got an answering shout from the back kitchen before setting off for the jigger and Aunt Daisy's house once more. 'Your aunt's not wearin' no shoes!'

He sounded shocked, as well he might, Rose thought crossly. She had heard her father calling Aunt a slut and saying he couldn't make out why Lily didn't have a word with her about her appearance, but Rose understood only too well. A sister who was older than you by ten years must be nearly like your mother, and you wouldn't tell your mother to wash and put her shoes on, would you?

'Me ... me aunt's a bit careless, like,' she said apologetically now. 'Mam says when a woman loses her husband she sometimes gets a bit that way.' She knew it was a mistake as soon as the words were out of her mouth because in a neighbourhood like theirs, everyone knew everyone else's business, and several women living in their area had lost husbands one way and another and they hadn't turned 'careless like'. And Ricky was on it like a ton of bricks—he would be. Rose was beginning to regret asking him to come to the park—but she never would have done so had she realised that a visit to Aunt Daisy was part of the trip.

'Mrs Johnson's a widder—you do mean that your aunt's a widder, don't you, Rosie?—an' she wears shoes ... she's smart, is Mrs Johnson. Doesn't your aunt work? You said she wasn't short of a bob or two.'

'She ain't. Oh *dear*, Ricky, why must you ask so many bleedin' questions?' Rose said, deciding that honesty was the best policy. 'Me da says me aunt's a lazy slut, but she's me mam's sister, so I can't say what ... ay-up, here comes me mam, better leave it.'

'Right,' said Ricky and began to talk enthusiastically about the kittens.

'Nice, were they?' Mam said as they made their way towards the park. 'I wouldn't mind a cat—less trouble than a dog.'

'Ricky says they're no fun once they's growed, though,' Rose pointed out, skipping along beside her mother. 'What'll we do first, Mam, when we get to the park? Go on the boats or have us sarnies?'

'Have our sarnies, you mean,' her mother said, then bit her lip. She tried not to correct Rose's speech before other children, since she knew it was important to sound like them and not to be pointed out, jeeringly, as 'the posh one', or 'the kid what purron airs'. Besides, she was well aware that Rose would not speak carelessly in her own home. 'Which 'ud you rather, queen?'

'Boats,' both children replied in chorus and Ricky added, 'We gets to eat sarnies every day, mostly, Miz Ryder, but I ain't never been on the boats in Seffy.'

'Right, then boats first it is,' Mrs Ryder said. 'I'm fair parched an' longin' for a nice cup o' tea, but I agree, we'll go on the boats first—or rather you two

65

will. I shall sit on a seat an' watch.'

'I thought you had tea wi' Aunt Daisy,' Rose said. 'You telled her to put the kettle over the flame.'

'Aye, but she doesn't have milk, only conny-onny, so I had it black an' it don't quench me thirst the same,' her mother explained. 'Look—there's the park gates! First one there gets a penny!'

*   *   *

Jack Ryder was driving his tram past Lime Street station when he saw Mona. She would, he reflected wryly, have been difficult to miss. She was wearing a bright scarlet coat, a small green hat and very high-heeled shoes, and her skirt was so short that he could see her knees. She was standing at the tram stop and as his vehicle approached she raised her eyes and saw him. For a moment she looked startled, then she gave him a practised smile and a small wave and, as he stopped, moved casually away, as though she had not been waiting for a tram at all.

But she had, Jack knew that. She was with a middle-aged gent in a bowler hat and a dark overcoat. A businessman of some sort, Jack presumed. Years older than herself, of course ... oh Gawd, why had he noticed her? He was pretty sure, after a number of such encounters with Mona, always accompanied by a different feller, that his niece was no better than she should be, but while he could shut his eyes to it he would. He couldn't understand why she did it, either. Street-walking was dangerous, as well as against the law, and Mona had a job which brought in regular, if

66

not good, money each week.

Daisy had spoiled her when she was a kid, Jack remembered that all too well. Fancy clothes, lots of trips out, pictures whenever she wanted to go. Sometimes he wondered how Daisy had managed that ... if Mona's present behaviour was 'like mother, like daughter', whether Daisy had gone with sailors to make a bit extra after her husband had left her, but naturally, he could not voice the thought aloud. Lily, he knew, would be outraged and terribly upset with him, and even if he proved himself right she would be dreadfully hurt.

But it was why he didn't like her taking the kid round there. Children weren't stupid and his Rose was as bright as a button. If she twigged what Mona was up to ... well, suppose she thought that since her mam took her round to Daisy's place and let her chatter to Mona such behaviour was acceptable? She was his heart's darling, was Rosie, he wouldn't have her getting the wrong idea, not even if, in the end, it meant that he had to put his foot down over Daisy, tell Lily what he believed and make her see that, for their daughter's sake, they would have to steer clear of both Daisy and Mona.

The trouble was, Jack liked a quiet life and he liked the people he loved to be comfortable. Lily behaved towards Daisy as though she were the elder, he sometimes thought. She was forever going round there with food she had baked, she spent time with her sister even when she was busy herself, she gave her presents. Sometimes it was a pretty blouse which she would have toiled over for nights and nights, at others a pair of thick woollen stockings for winter wear, or some embroidered pillowcases, or a thick, soft towel to take to the bath-house. Not that Daisy ever visited the bath-house so far as Jack knew; she always looked unwashed to him.

An elderly woman tottered across the tram's path and Jack, who had not been going fast anyway, moved the handle to cut the power and slow them down, then gradually built up speed once more as the road cleared. Daisy Mullins had been a thorn in his flesh ever since he and Lily had first met, and her disapproval of him—and his of her—had not become less with the years. But he had no right—or reason—to grumble, because he rarely saw Daisy now. She had grown lazier and lazier with the years, and for a long time now it had been too much trouble for her to come to Cornwall Street, and because of his work—and his feelings—Jack never went round to Prince Edwin Lane, either.

Yet it still made him uneasy when Lily took their daughter to visit the Mullinses, which was absurd, really. Rose didn't even like her aunt and the age difference was too great for her to have had much to do with Mona.

'Rotunda!' Jack was jerked out of his thoughts by his conductor's shout combined with the ringing of the bell and he turned the wheel which applied the brake, at the same time reducing the power, and drew to a halt by the queue which waited to embark.

It was a pleasant afternoon and Jack looked kindly at the throng outside the theatre. Some must have been to the matinée performance, others had been shopping, others still simply enjoying a stroll in the sunshine with the fresh breeze from the Mersey bringing the river and sea smells to their nostrils. Lily and Rose, he reflected, would be at Sefton Park by now, perhaps even on the boating lake. He imagined that Rose would be trying to row whilst Lily lay back in the boat and laughed at her daughter's efforts. Not with the greatest effort of the imagination could he put Daisy into the scene and this cheered him. He told himself that she wasn't a bad woman, just idle and feckless, and that probably Mona wasn't a bad girl, either. She just liked male company and because she was a pretty girl and spent all her money on pretty clothes, she got male company. But the feller she'd been with when he'd seen her earlier wasn't a young blade, he was a stolid, middle-aged, middle-class office worker, by the look of him. He had looked . . . married, Jack decided uneasily. And he had been holding Mona's arm . . . as though . . . as though . . . well, as though he had just bought her and was anxious to hang on to his bargain.

I'll have a word with Lily this evening when I get home, Jack decided abruptly. There's something very odd going on and I don't like it. If Mona is going with men for money—even in his own mind he would not use the words which would utterly condemn his niece—then it's time Daisy had a word with her daughter. And since he had to assume that Daisy did not know what her child was up to it was time that Lily asked a few questions and told her older sister a thing or two.

Having made up his mind to act, Jack was able to concentrate on his job once more and was happy to do so. At the next stop he pulled out the heavy metal pocket-watch, which helped him to keep pace with his schedule, and consulted it. When they reached Hopwood Street he would have a pull at

69

his bottle of tea, because the heat would get at him, else. He glanced back over his shoulder and old Georgie Allen, his conductor, made a gesture as of one drinking. Jack grinned back and nodded; if he was hot sitting out here in the open, with the breeze of his going helping to cool him down, then poor Georgie, wedged in the middle of a large crowd of sweaty passengers, trying to collect their fares and hand them the correct tickets, must be parboiled. And since they were five minutes early they could have a break at Hopwood Street and share his cold tea.

'Hopwood!' shouted Georgie, fighting his way to the back of the vehicle and tugging on the leather strap to ring the bell. 'Come along, folks, there's no room for them outside to gerron till you're off, y'know, so move along the car please!'

Once the descending passengers were out of the way and the new ones aboard, Georgie came round and hopped up onto Jack's running board. The two men had been working together for long enough to know the ropes when a short stop was indicated and Georgie had brought both their tea-bottles with him as well as a couple of cheese and pickle barms which they had brought with them.

'Cor, wack, I wouldn't mind bein' a driver in this weather,' Georgie said, mopping his brow with a large red spotted handkerchief. 'It's 'ellish 'ot inside, I'm tellin' yez.'

'Oh, you conductors are never satisfied,' Jack said with a chuckle. 'You din't like it when we 'ad open trams, you said it were cold, now you don't like the nice glass winders! Think back to January, ole feller; I don't recall you envyin' me then.'

'I can't think o' nothin' but the bleedin' 'eat. It's

70

like bein' a loaf in one o' Sample's ovens,' Georgie groaned. 'Still an' all, it's better out 'ere. An' the wust o' the sunshine'll be over soon. Where's your tiddler, then? Gone to the seaside, I dessay?'

'No, they gone boatin' at Sefton Park,' Jack told his mate. 'Gi's a swig from the bottle, ole feller!'

'Boatin'!' Georgie sighed, handing the bottle over and wiping his mouth on his sleeve. 'I wouldn't mind that either, Jack. But be the time this shift ends all I'll want will be me bed. Oh well, at least I'll be cooler there.'

'And tomorrer you can tek your Nellie down to New Brighton on the train,' Jack reminded him. 'Or into the park, if you've a mind.'

'Ha! Nellie's mam an' dad's comin' for their dinners to our place,' Georgie said gloomily. 'Allus the way, ain't it? When it rains we's free as birds, but the moment the sun shines the old folk decide to mek our day an' come visitin'. You don't know 'ow lucky you are, ole man, that your Lil's the youngest an' ain't got no parents livin'.'

'She's gorra sister,' Jack said gloomily. He glanced at Georgie. He and the older man had worked together now for ten years and trusted one another absolutely. 'I've gorra problem there, if the truth were known.'

'Oh aye?' Georgie said, interested. 'What's wrong wi' her sister, then?'

'Well, I ain't sure, but ...' And Jack proceeded to tell Georgie his fears.

Georgie listened seriously, then whistled. 'An' you don't want your Rose mixin' wi' a gal what's no better'n she should be?' he asked at length. 'Nor you don't want your Lil gettin' any thicker wi' her older sister. But do Lil know what's goin' on, Jack?

71

She don't strike me as the sort o' woman to put up wi' behaviour like that.'

'I don't think she knows, an' I don't much fancy tellin' her, 'cos I can't prove a bleedin' thing,' Jack admitted. 'But I seen Mona wi' another bloke earlier, Georgie. Not a young feller, an old one. I'll have to tell Lil, I can see that.'

'You should,' Georgie said at once. 'She'll likely thank you once she's over the shock of it. And you'll feel better in yourself once it's out in the open. No good bottlin' things up, Jack. That's not your style. You tell Lil. You'll feel better for it.'

'You sound like a quack recommendin' a cure,' Jack said with a grin, then leaned over and smote Georgie's shoulder. 'Thanks, wack, I know you're right an' I'll do it this very evenin'. An' now we'd best get goin' or we'll lose the five minutes we've gained.'

*   *   *

'Ricky, if you splash me once more I'll bleedin' *drown* you,' Rose said threateningly, as Ricky dug in the oars and sent water cascading into her lap. 'This is me best dress an' you'll shrink it till it's only big enough for a doll. Let me row, will you?'

'Women can't row, nor gals,' Ricky said breathlessly, clinging grimly to his oars and digging them deeper into the water. ' 'Sides, I were featherin', like they do in that there boat race they holds in London. You're *meant* to skim the water, so's a feather o' foam comes up. I jest digged a bit too deep, that's all.'

'Let me have a go,' Rose repeated. 'My mam paid for the boat, so I should have a go. Come on,

72

swap over, will ye?'

'Your mam paid so's I could gi' you a nice ride,' Ricky insisted, rather red in the face and very wet himself but clinging grimly to his male rights. 'Besides, if you muck about an' try to change places very likely we'll both git soaked . . . an' gals can't swim.'

'I can,' Rose said. 'On me front an' on me back. So there. Oh, come on, Ricky, or the feller'll be bawlin' "Come in number twenty", an' it'll be too late for me to 'ave a go.'

'We-ell, we'd best go in to the side then, if we're goin' to swap,' Ricky said, abruptly caving in. 'It's time I had a good laugh, any road, an' you tryin' to row is bound to be a laugh. What's more, I could do wi' me tea, couldn't you? It's hungry work, rowin' a big lump like you all round the boatin' lake.'

'You cheeky bugger,' gasped Rose, rising wrathfully from her seat and completely forgetting that they were in a boat. 'I'll gi' you a thick ear for that, Ricky Elliott. I can't think why I asked me mam if you could come along wi' us, because you're rude an' horrible.'

'Well, awright, you aren't a big lump on *land*, I give you that,' Ricky said, shipping his oars and accidentally hitting Rose on the ankle with one of them. 'But you feel a big lump in the boat . . . oh, oh, don't, Rosie! Why d'you have to git such a cob on, an' keep *hittin'* all the time? That's typical of a girl. Look, you'll regret it if you turn the bleedin' boat over, I'll mek sure o' that!'

As soon as the boat got near enough to the bank Rose had risen to her feet and clumped her companion hard across the head with the flat of her hand. Since he was still seated and encumbered by the oars, she was able to get in several more telling blows before Ricky pulled himself together and swung an oar threateningly at her legs. It found its mark and Rosie shrieked and snatched at it. She was tugging hard when Ricky very unsportingly let go. With nothing to pull against Rose tipped immediately backwards and plunged, oar and all, into the water.

'Oh Gawd, I knew it 'ud happen,' Ricky said and knelt in the bows to pull her out. The boat, which was round and tippery, promptly upended and both children found themselves struggling in the warm and shallow water.

'Look what you done, Ricky, me best dress is ruined!' Rose shrieked, regaining the surface and staggering to her feet. 'It's all mud under there ... Ricky, I said I were goin' to drown you an' I meant it. Hold still for a second ...'

She grabbed at him and the two of them grappled furiously with each other for a moment, then Ricky pulled her to the bank and sat her down on it. 'Your mam's watchin', Rosie,' he said warningly. ' 'Sides, if anyone gets drownded it'll be you, 'cos I'm a year older an' a good bit stronger, so stop bein' such a marred kid an' get back into the boat an' you can show me what you can do.'

Rose, dripping, climbed back into the boat, sat down and picked up the oars. 'But Mam's not lookin' at us,' she informed him. 'If she'd seen the boat tip she'd ha' shruck out; she's probably sittin' over there wi' her eyes shut, havin' a bit of a snooze. Come on then, gerrin!'

'Well ... awright, awright, fair's fair,' Ricky said, climbing back into the boat and lowering himself gingerly down in the thwarts, with an anxious eye on the oarswoman sitting grimly on the centre seat. 'You have a go now, then ... an' we'll see what we'll see.'

Rose began to row and was making a reasonable job of it when she suddenly began to giggle. The giggle turned into a laugh and Rose leaned on her oars for a moment, then sighed deeply and began to row once more. 'When Mam sees us she's goin' to go mad,' she said conversationally. 'You're older'n me, so you'll cop it worse, I dare say. What'll we tell her?'

'That we were changing places so that you could row an' the boat tipped up. It's as near the truth as meks no difference,' Ricky said after a moment. 'My, you do look like a drowned rat, gal! That frock'll never be the same again, that I do know.'

'It'll wash,' Rose said, suddenly cheerful. She looked up from her own mud-streaked skirt to examine her companion's equally muddy and dishevelled state. 'You ain't no oil paintin' yourself, I tell you. What'll your mam say, then?'

'Norra lot, so long as I'm dried out afore she sees me,' Ricky said indifferently. 'I puts all me clobber down for washin' on a Sat'day night, it'll just get washed, that's all.'

'Then we might as well row back to Mam, an' get outside o' that tea she promised us,' Rose said. She began to row faster. 'I'm rare hungry now—I could eat all them sarnies to meself, never mind sharin'.'

'I know. It's the rowin'. I'm so hungry me belly thinks me throat's cut,' Ricky said amiably. 'You're doin' well, queen. I don't know as I could row much faster meself.'

And on these amicable terms the two returned

75

to Mrs Ryder and the sandwiches.

*   *   *

I wonder why that Mona wanted our Rosie along tomorrow, Lily asked herself as she unwrapped the sandwiches and helped herself to an iced bun. She meant to buy the children ices and a drink at the café later, when she got herself a nice hot cup of tea, but the sandwiches and little buns would keep the wolf from the door until then. And who is this young feller Daisy was so keen to tell me about? I've seen Mona with half a dozen different fellers, and truth to tell not all of them could be described as young by a long chalk. And what young woman wants a kid cousin along on a date? It's got me in a rare puzzle, because Mona's always had her own way and I don't imagine she *wants* a kid like our Rosie along. Unless she's really interested in this man, and ... and hopes she'll seem more respectable, like, if she turns up with her cousin.

The next question, however, was one she preferred not to ask herself, but she knew she must if Daisy was going to continue to pester her to let Rose go around now and then with Mona. If Mona needed a young cousin to make her seem like any other respectable young woman then what was she hiding? Was it true what she, Lily, was beginning to suspect? That Mona was a member of the oldest profession in the world in her spare time?

The thought was a horrid one, but it would have to be faced. I can't ask Daisy outright, Lily told herself, because that would be the final straw. She was already aware that the only way she retained Daisy's affection was by the constant stream of small gifts and Daisy was the only member of her large family with whom she was still in touch. She had been so much younger than the others that they had scarcely seemed like brothers and sisters; only Daisy had still lived at home by the time Lily was old enough to go to school and Daisy had been carelessly kind to her then. Now, of course, it was different. Daisy was greedy and lazy, she knew that, and her sister sensed Jack's disapproval and consequently made no secret of the fact that she was not particularly fond of him. But she wanted Lily to go round to her house and she would have liked to have been invited to Cornwall Street, too. And the reason she wanted a closer relationship, if the truth were known, was in order to show folk that she and Mona were a normal, respectable mother and daughter whose relatives exchanged visits frequently. Lily had realised some time ago that many neighbours and friends must have begun to wonder just why Mona wore such showy clothes and spent her evenings wandering around the city. They must have jangled amongst themselves and come to the obvious conclusion. And now, from what she could gather, Mona had met a really decent young man and she wanted him to see her not as a flighty piece no better than she should be, but as a respectable young woman who took her little cousin along on a date and had to be home at a reasonably early hour.

So really, I ought to go along with it and encourage Mona to take Rose to meet this feller, Lily thought uneasily, staring unseeingly across the bright, reflecting water of the huge lake. She's me niece, after all, and I ought to want the best for her. And the best is a respectable marriage to a decent

77

feller, so why am I hesitating?

The truth was, she knew that she did not have much faith in Mona's apparent eagerness to get married. The girl was too young for settling down and if she had been spending as much as she appeared to have done on herself, she'd not take kindly to the restrictions of being a wife. The thought of sticking to one man instead of being the darling of a dozen might not appeal once the novelty wore off, either. So by and large, it seemed sensible to keep Rosie well clear of whatever imbroglio her sister and niece were cooking up.

Having made up her mind to this effect, Lily brought herself back to the present and stood up to stare across the lake. The children were out of sight, but the lake was large and hunger would bring them back to her soon enough. The man who hired out the boats was rowing off into the middle distance, shouting through his loud-hailer, and though Lily could not hear what number he was shouting and had in any case forgotten which boat the children had chosen, she guessed that they would be coming ashore any time now.

Accordingly, she walked down to the water's edge to wait, deciding that she really ought to confide in Jack about Mona. It wasn't as if he ever saw her sister, or her niece so far as she could tell, and he would agree, she knew, that Rose and Mona were best apart. The trouble was that she didn't want to set him against Daisy and the knowledge that Daisy was prepared to use Rose for her own ends would not exactly endear her sister to Jack.

She was still mulling over the problem when the boat came into view with Rose at the oars now, vigorously rowing. Lily watched them right up to the bank and exclaimed, 'My Gawd, whatever have you two been doin'? You're both drenched—and mud up to the eyebrows, what's more! Come on, what's happened?'

'The boat tipped up,' Rose said in a small voice. 'I wanted to row and Ricky said we shouldn't swap over, but we went right in close to the bank and stood up, and . . .'

'Well, it's a warm day, thank the Lord,' Lily said resignedly. 'Come on out of it an' we'll eat our food. I dare say by the time we finish you'll be dry, if not clean!'

'You are kind, Mam,' Rose said gratefully, clambering out of the boat and actually wringing water out of her gingham skirt. 'And it's quite nice to be wet an' cool on a hot day, ain't it, Ricky?'

'It ain't bad,' Ricky acknowledged. 'Tell you what, Mrs Ryder, why don't me an' Rosie have a race to the ice-cream kiosk an' back? We'll dry off sooner if we run.'

'Well, run wi' a sandwich, then,' Lily said. 'Then run back an' tek another. When you've dried off I'll give you both a brush-down—not that I think it'll do much good, but at least I can try.'

*　　　*　　　*

'I like your mam,' Ricky panted as they reached the ice-cream kiosk for the third time and turned to race back again. 'There's a lorra women would have nagged somethin' rotten at the sight of us. An' them butties is good—what's in 'em?'

'Cheese an' Mam's home-made chutney,' Rose said proudly. 'Come on, I reckon one more run an' we'll be dry enough to stop runnin' an' start on the cake!'

79

CHAPTER THREE

December 1927 Dublin

There was a blizzard blowing as Colm rounded the corner of Abbey Street and crossed the quay, heading for the Halfpenny Bridge. The wind was fairly howling and Colm realised that it was snow which was stinging his face now, not just rain. Just my bleedin' luck, isn't it, he thought to himself, that the longest delivery ride of the lot has to take place on a freezing December day when the weather decides to be the worst of the year so far. And just my luck that Mr Savage is too busy to take it himself, as he would normally have done, and the woman who wanted the biggest turkey in the shop and the enormous ham needed them, she said, for a pre-Christmas party and had to have them now, not in a day or so.

Unfortunately for Colm, the customer lived out at Clontarf, an area which Mr Savage usually covered himself on his way home in his pony cart, but with Herby off with the flu and everyone pushing in to give their Christmas orders, Colm's employer had no choice but to send his boy. And Colm, who had not yet managed to get himself a full-time job, was pleased enough to be employed all over the pre-Christmas period, even if it did mean some extremely long bicycle rides.

But tonight he was worn out and cold, despite the thick serge coat which the mammy had bought him, and the woollen scarf and gloves which she had knitted. It was a long way from Savage's shop in York Street to St Lawrence Road, and not only were Colm's legs aching, but his scarf and cap wouldn't stay in place once the blizzard really got going, so his face was like a block of ice and his ears had long ago ceased to be able to feel anything at all. But they will when the warmth comes to them, Colm reminded himself grimly. He already had chilblains on his hands and feet, and could only shudder at the thought of them on his ears as well.

As he approached the Halfpenny Bridge the wind gave an extra loud shriek and spattered what felt like small stones, but was probably hail, into Colm's face. He could feel it rattling on his cap and hear it clattering on the metal bicycle basket—empty now, thank the good Lord, Colm thought reverently, remembering the weight of the huge turkey and how difficult it had made steering earlier.

He had dismounted his bicycle to cross Bachelor's Quay and because of the fierceness of the wind, did not attempt to remount, though the Halfpenny Bridge was empty of people for once, and no one would have stopped him. But the wind, howling up the Liffey, was simply too strong; Colm and his bicycle might well have been blown over, and it was bad enough to be frozen with cold without adding a nasty tumble and numerous bruises to your woes. So Colm sank his head between his shoulders, half-closed his eyes against the stinging sleet and trudged on, enduring. Half-way over, a pleasant thought occurred to him. His daddy was supposed to be coming home today, but surely he would not have been able to make the crossing in such weather? A glance down into the waters of the Liffey showed that it was as high as he

81

had ever known it and that waves were crashing right over the quay in places. No weather for a sea voyage, Colm told himself with guilty satisfaction. There was even a chance that his father would be stuck in England for the whole of the Christmas holiday ... it would be a real treat for him and Caitlin if they were to have the mammy all to themselves, and no father to boss them around and tell them what they might and might not do.

But it was no good thinking about it just yet, for no doubt Mr Savage would have further deliveries for him when he reached the shop once more. So Colm fought his way over the bridge, which was surely the most exposed part of his journey since the foot-bridge curved up to cross well above the river, then hurried along Wellington Quay and dived down Capel Street with a moan of relief, for the buildings of either side of the road protected him, to an extent, from the bitter wind.

He crossed Dame Street, where the snow lashed at him again for a moment, and then he was in Great George Street and on the home stretch. He stopped for a moment to tug his dripping cap further down over his eyes and to remount the bicycle, then he wobbled at the best pace he could manage in the direction of York Street and Savage's shop.

*   *   *

'Well and aren't you a sight now, young O'Neill?' Mr Savage sounded more contrite than amused, though Colm guessed that he looked a real orphan of the storm indeed. 'Did you get to St Lawrence Road wit'out dumpin' that bloody gurt turkey on

82

the carriageway now? I hope the cook gave you a Christmas box for cyclin' all that way.'

'She axed me in for a warm be the stove, so she did,' Colm said through his thick scarf. 'An' she give me a slice o' gur cake to line me stomach, but not a penny-piece had the old girl left for me, just the right money. An' isn't it a grand house now, wit' a motor car standin' in the drive an' the place all lit up wit' electricity an' holly wreaths an' glitterin' paper chains in every window. An' I never tipped the bike over once, though I had hard work to keep upright once the storm really got goin'. But we got there wit'out a stain on either meself or the turkey.'

'Well done, lad,' Mr Savage said. 'I'll put an extry bob in your pay-packet, for I'd not ask a dog to go out in that ...' he nodded towards the doorway where the snow whirled faster than ever' ... in the normal way of t'ings. But it was an emergency, so it was, an' you came up trumps, young feller.'

'Thanks, Mr Savage,' Colm said gratefully. 'Is there anythin' else to go tonight? Only I'm wet to the skin.'

'No, not tonight, though I've had orders for tomorrer,' Mr Savage said. 'We've done well, I've near on sold out o' capons an' geese, but everyone who bought this evenin' either wanted 'em delivered on the twenty-third of the month or they took 'em themselves.'

'How's my goose money goin', Mr Savage?' Colm asked, taking off his dripping scarf and trying to wring it out through the doorway. Ice crackled against his fingers and he shook it so that a tinkling shower fell onto the step. 'Janey, d'you see that, Mr Savage? Me scarf's got icicles on it!'

'Aye, I see. Come through into the back an' have

a warm before you go home,' Mr Savage invited. He kept a small paraffin stove in the back and though he liked to keep the door between the back room and shop shut, so that the warmth did not invade the shop itself and thus turn the meat, he usually allowed the lads to warm themselves whilst they ate their carry-out.

'No point, Mr S., 'cos I've got to go out again into the storm. I might as well go straight away an' be home the sooner,' Colm said through chattering teeth. ' 'Sides, me clothes is so wet I'd only steam the place up. No, if you've no more deliveries for me tonight I'll mek me way home, so I will.'

'Right. I'll gi' you the extry bob here an' now, an' a packet o' mutton chops for your mammy,' Mr Savage said, producing a brown paper parcel from under the counter and sorting out a shilling from the money in the till. 'Can you be here at seven o'clock tomorrer mornin'? I've a feelin' Herby won't be back yet awhile, so if you could serve in the shop until it's time to start deliveries you'll be doin' me a service.'

'Sure, Mr Savage,' Colm said, but all he was thinking about was getting home and warming up. He took his shilling and his parcel, shoved both in the pocket of his overcoat and set off for the door where his bicycle still leaned. 'S-seven in the m-mornin', then.'

With chattering teeth, now, he mounted the bicycle and turned left into Aungier Street and then right into Kevin Street, which led to the Coombe. The snow was still falling and the wind howled, but at least he would be within doors quite soon and able to get dry and warm, and to relax. Let tomorrow morning take care of itself, Colm

84

thought as he pedalled. After a night's sleep I'll probably feel up to anything, so I will!

*   *   *

Caitlin was sitting on the bit of a rug by the Murphys' fire, reading to Paddy, the youngest Murphy, out of her school reading book, when her mammy knocked on the door. She knew it was her mammy because there were three quick little knocks and then two slower, harder ones, and the mammy never came in but went straight on to their own place, so she could have the lights on and the fire started before her daughter arrived back. So Caitlin jumped to her feet at once and called across to Mrs Murphy, who was scrubbing the spuds for supper, 'T'anks, Mrs Murphy, I'll be off, then. See ye tomorrer.'

The door opened a crack and Caitlin's mother's face appeared round the edge of it. 'I'm poppin' to the shop to buy a screw o' tay,' she shouted. 'You wait for me downstairs, Cait, there's a good gorl.'

'Awright, Mammy, I won't be after hangin' about tonight,' Caitlin shouted across the room, running to fetch her outdoor things from where they were hung on the hook on the back of the door. 'You go an' get your tay. Are you goin' to Donovan's?'

'Sure I am. But don't come after me, alanna, it's wild out there.'

Mrs O'Neill withdrew her head and the door closed behind her.

Mrs Murphy half turned towards Caitlin, her hands still in the bowl. 'Oh, are ye off awready, Caitlin? Ye wouldn't like to hang on for a few moments, so? Only I just sent Dervla on a message

85

an' little Paddy's only quiet when youse is readin' to him.'

'You could read to me, Mammy,' Paddy suggested. 'Or tell me a story ... tell me the one Cait telled me yesterday, about the big ould boggarty giant what catched the chisellers 'cos he wanted 'em for his supper, only brave wee Paddy knew what big ould boggarty giants like mostest, so ...'

'You've telled it yourself, so you have,' Michael Murphy remarked. He and Billy were sitting up to the table, biting their pencils and occasionally scribbling a line or two. Michael was ten and Billy twelve, which meant that they had schoolwork to do most nights. Michael, who was a good friend of Caitlin's despite the fact that she was a much-despised girl, turned and grinned at her. 'You stayin', Cait? If you are so, I'll walk you home later, 'cos it's mortal dark out there an' the wind's a bleedin' hurricane be the sound of it.'

'I can't, Michael, not tonight, you heard what me mammy said, an' besides, me daddy's comin' home for Christmas tonight,' Caitlin said importantly, pushing her arms into her coat and tugging it around her. She buttoned it and turned her coat collar up to give her some protection against the rain which she could hear lashing against the window. 'He was catchin' the ferry from Liverpool an' should ha' been down on the quays this afternoon, but he said he wouldn't go straight home, not wit' the mammy an' Colm both out workin', so he was goin' round to see Gran first. But I 'spect he'll be home by now,' she added.

'Can I walk Caitlin home, Mammy?' Paddy squeaked, dancing up and down on the linoleum at

86

his mother's side. 'Aw g'wan, Mammy, say I can walk her home!'

'Paddy, you're five years old, much too little to walk anyone anywhere,' Michael said, winking at Caitlin as she donned her woolly gloves and crammed her red tam-o'-shanter well down over her eyes. 'Besides, you know Caitlin, she never walks if she can run, an' her mammy's waitin' on her, an' if her ould feller's really home . . .'

He left the sentence unfinished. Caitlin, pulling a face at him, remembered how she had told everyone over and over how wonderful it would be to see her daddy at Christmas and had wondered aloud what he might bring back for them from across the water. She enjoyed playing with dolls and prams and similar things, but she had one particular dolly she adored, Long Meg she was called, and a nice pram made out of some old wheels and a stout orange box. No other doll could be as dear to her and a real dolly pram, she knew, would only make her different and arouse bitter envy in the breasts of other little girls. However, she and Colm had long wanted a sledge, a proper one, with runners which curved up at the front and a streamlined shape. Tin trays were all very well, but if you had a real sledge you could get some stupendous rides, so you could. She had confided in Colm that she wondered whether Daddy would bring them such a sledge but Colm, who was fifteen and had a real, six-day-a-week job, only codded her about it.

'I know, like the Snow Queen's,' Colm had said. 'So you're too grand for a tray or a common old orange box. Do you fancy bein' pulled be white reindeer an' puttin' a spell on some poor little chiseller, then?'

'I'll put a bleedin' spell on you if you say one more word, Colm O'Neill,' Caitlin had said wrathfully. 'What's wrong wit' wantin' a real sledge, 'stead of a miserable orange box, eh?'

'Nothin', nothin' at all,' Colm had said soothingly. 'But the ould feller won't be bringin' sledges all the way across the Irish sea, alanna. It'll be a story book for you if you're lucky an' a bit o' money for me. So don't go raisin' your hopes, 'cos they'll only be dashed down.'

'Well, I don't care. Whatever me daddy brings me is bound to be good,' Caitlin said loyally. She was always torn when she discussed their father with Colm, because she was uneasily aware that the two did not much like one another and she found this terribly hard to understand. Wasn't Colm the best brother in the world, now, and wasn't Sean O'Neill the best father two kids could possibly have? So why couldn't they like one another? She had asked her mother and had got only the sort of vague reply that was as difficult to understand as the problem itself.

'They're both men, alanna,' her mother had said. 'And men don't always get along. But they'll learn to appreciate each other one of these days, no doubt.'

But right now Caitlin was going home to see her daddy and had no time to mull over difficult questions. So she wrapped her scarf around her neck, pulled it up to cover her mouth, said cheerio to the assorted Murphys in a muffled voice and opened their door onto the landing.

Before she was married, Eileen had lived next door to young Bridget O'Mara and they had been

88

inseparable. Even after their marriages they had been good friends, though Bridget Murphy had rapidly become the mother of a large family whilst Eileen and Sean O'Neill had only the two children. Then James Murphy died, and the family suddenly found themselves in dire straits. The eldest boy was fifteen and in work, and the eldest girl was in service with a rich family who lived just outside the city, but apart from what little the older children could provide, the five younger children were completely dependent on their mother. Mr Murphy had never saved a penny, so Mrs Murphy had moved out of her rooms in the Coombe and across to Marrowbone Lane where she'd rented a couple of rooms over a small shop. During the day Mrs Murphy worked in the shop, but as soon as school came out she returned to her upper rooms to prepare a meal and look after her fatherless children, so when Mrs O'Neill wanted someone to give an eye to Caitlin until she got home from work, her friend Bridget Murphy was the obvious choice.

Caitlin, for her part, liked the arrangement. In summer she played out anyway and doing so in Marrowbone Lane was just as much fun as in the Coombe, and in winter she liked being in Mrs Murphy's big kitchen, handing out cuts of soda bread like a mammy would have done and telling the little ones stories. She liked having Paddy and Kieran to boss about and amuse, too. They were the little brothers she had never had and appreciated her vivid imagination in a way which no one else did.

'Cait tells the best stories in the world, so she does,' the little boys would assure their playmates.

'G'wan, get her to tell you a story ... she knows a *million*, honest to God she does.'

But right now she was leaving the Murphys and returning to the Coombe, and she was anxious to go because of her daddy. Surely this time Colm will see how nice it is to have a daddy as well as a mammy, she mused, clattering down the stairs and pausing at the bottom to shriek a last farewell to the Murphy kids, clustered in the open doorway looking wistfully down at her. How Michael would love it if *his* father were to come home tonight for Christmas, how his face would light up! The Murphy boys had adored their father, fond of the drink or no, and missed him dreadfully. Even the tiny ones remembered him, or thought they did.

'He played a leg an' a wing wit' us, in the park,' Paddy said wistfully. 'He brung back good t'ings to eat, an' gave us pennies for peggy's leg an' humbugs.'

Caitlin knew that this was probably true, for Mr Murphy had been a docker, one of the ones who was regularly in work, furthermore. He had had money and had spent it on his kids, his wife . . . and the drink. And his sons had loved him.

Our daddy doesn't come in the worse for drink, an' he sends nearly all his money home to us, Caitlin mused, so why on earth can't Colm see how lucky we are an' love the daddy like I do? She waited a moment, mindful of her mother's instructions, then opened the front door of the tenement block. Immediately, all thoughts of fathers left her head, for outside snow was dashing past the entrance, going horizontally, and the wind which had sounded loud enough in the rooms above was deafening. It howled and screamed like

90

an injured animal and Caitlin paused for a moment, wondering how long her mother would be, then remembered that Donovan's was only ten or fifteen yards down the street and pulled her scarf up over her mouth again. No point in hanging about here, when she could reach the shop in less than a minute, and it would save time, too. She and Mammy could set off at once for the Coombe, for she had no doubt where her mother's loyalties lay. Mammy would be as desperate to see Daddy as she was herself, and every moment away from their rooms was a moment missed with him. She plunged into the storm.

She had not gone more than a couple of yards, however, bent double against the shrieking elements, when a figure loomed up ahead of her. A white figure, completely covered in snow. But Caitlin would know the mammy under any circumstances and grabbed at her mother's arm.

'Caitlin! Didn't I tell you to wait for me in the hallway, then? I got me screw o' tay an' a piece o' gur cake an' a loaf so's we can mek toast round the fire ... catch a good holt of me, alanna, an' we'll mebbe arrive home in one piece.'

'I'm holtin' as hard as I can,' screamed Caitlin above the storm. 'Have yez been home yet, Mammy? Is—is Daddy back? Oh, I'm excited, so I am! I'll *die* if he's not waitin' for us, wit' a *grosh* o'stories an' tales to tell!'

'I don't know if he's back, I've not been home yet,' her mother said, shouting the words into the teeth of the wind. 'But we'll know soon enough, alanna. Oh janey, but the wind's fair cuttin' me in half.'

Somehow, the two of them fought their way

91

down Marrowbone Lane, turned right into Pimlico and into the Coombe. Here, they ran for it, slipping and sliding on the icy cobbles but gaining their hallway at last, to stand staring at one another at the foot of the stairs, unable to believe how much snow had piled upon them during the ten-minute rush.

'You brush me down, Cait, an' I'll brush you,' Eileen O'Neill said breathlessly, beginning to dust the snow off her daughter's coat, tam-o'-shanter and scarf. 'I'm beginnin' to wonder how our Colm's gettin' on, but I dare say Mr Savage will send him home early. No point tryin' to deliver in weather like this.'

'Let's go on up,' Caitlin begged as soon as they had rid themselves of most of the snow. 'Oh, if Daddy's waitin' I want to be up there! Will he have lit the fire, do you s'pose, Mammy? I do feel like a sit by the fire before we have our suppers.'

'Right. Up wit' you,' her mother said briskly, pushing her towards the stairs. 'No use hangin' round here, we'd best see what's what.'

Caitlin ran up the stairs as fast as she could but her mother was on her heels. Even old folk get excited at Christmas, Caitlin reflected. Mammy never runs up the stairs in the ordinary way. But for all that, she was just ahead as they reached their door and she beat a hasty tattoo on it, knowing that their father, if he was not busy lighting the fire, would rush to open it for them.

But the door remained firmly shut, so she pulled up the key on its string, fitted it into the lock and turned it, then threw the door open. 'Daddy, we're home!' she sang out, thumping her sack of books down onto the floor of the kitchen and seeing, all

92

in a moment, that she was talking to herself. The room was dark, the fire unlit. She turned a disappointed face to her mother. 'He's not back, Mammy,' she said. 'Not yet, anyway. Do you s'pose he's at Grandma's house?'

Her mother sighed and entered the room, then closed the door behind her and went over to the lamp. She lit it carefully, stood it on the table and lit a taper with the last of the match and carried it over to the fire. She held it against the paper and sticks until it had caught, then turned back to Caitlin. Her face was sad. 'He'll not be at Gran's, not now,' she said. 'Oh, alanna, if they've had this storm across the water the ferry won't sail. He'll be stuck in Liverpool until tomorrow ... oh, and the day after that's Christmas Day! Surely he'll not be done out of his Christmas holiday?'

The storm didn't start here until an hour or so ago,' Caitlin said. 'Mebbe the ferry's sailed but it's late, Mammy. Look, the fire's comin' on nicely, we'll be able to take our coats off soon an' hang them on the clothes pole up by the ceiling, where the heat'll dry 'em. And storms don't last for days, Mammy, it'll be over by mornin'. Daddy will come in time for Christmas, sure he will!'

Eileen sighed and began to fetch vegetables from the cupboard and a piece of meat from the wirefronted safe. 'Sure he will,' she said wearily. 'Sure your daddy will be back in time for the holiday. But I'll be happier when I've got him under me roof. I don't like to t'ink of him tossin' on the Irish sea in weather like this.'

'He'll be fine, Mammy,' Caitlin said, struggling out of her coat, hat and gloves. 'It's warmin' up nicely now, by the time Colm gets home it'll be lovely an' snug in here. Now, what can I do to help wit' the supper?'

*   *   *

Colm came slowly up the stairs, carrying his heavy bicycle. His arms felt as if they were about to come out of their sockets, what with wrestling against the weather and now humping the bike up the stairs, but it was too risky to leave it down in the hall no matter how foul the weather. There was a cupboard on their landing with a lock and every night the bicycle was put inside it, to wait safely there until morning.

Colm reached the landing, opened the cupboard door and wheeled the bicycle inside, then closed the door, locked it and pocketed the key. It wasn't easy to turn the key in the lock with frozen fingers but he managed it, then pulled off his iced gloves and went over to the door. Outside, he hesitated for a moment. He felt like a stranger, standing there, knowing that his father would be inside, that his mother's greeting, though loving, would be absent-minded, his little sister's attention half-hearted, because the women—*his* women—would have eyes for no one but his father for a while at any rate.

Still, it had to be faced; the mammy didn't see his father clearly but through rose-coloured spectacles. And he'd got the parcel of mutton chops, which might be a means of gaining his mother's attention for a moment. Mammy would be glad of the nice fresh chops no matter how wrapped up in his daddy she might have become. So Colm took a deep breath and tapped on the door, because it would almost certainly be locked. It led directly into the kitchen and no one wanted a total stranger suddenly in their midst because he or she had mistaken the landing.

There was a pause, then he heard the patter of approaching feet, the key grated in the lock and the door opened inwards, showing his sister's small face, surrounded by its halo of light-brown curls. Caitlin smiled at him, but it wasn't her usual cheerful beam. 'Come in, Colm. Sure an' you must be froze,' she said, catching his sleeve and towing him into the kitchen. 'Get that wet coat off your back before you die of the pneumonia! Ooh, what's in the parcel?'

'Meat,' Colm said briefly. He came fully into the room and began to take off his wet outer garments, hanging them on the clothes pole which, he saw, already held Caitlin's things and his mother's, too. 'Where's Daddy?'

Caitlin did not answer but his mother, working at the stove, half turned towards him. 'Not back,' she said in a flat, weary voice. 'He should've come in on the ferry hours ago, but he's not arrived.'

'Oh, janey,' Colm said feebly. 'But there's tomorrer, Mammy. He'll come tomorrer, sure he will.'

'Depends on the weather, I dare say,' his mother replied, turning back to her work. 'If the storm goes on, the good Lord alone knows whether he'll get home this side o' the new year.'

'Storms don't last, they move on, so they do,' Colm said quickly. 'You mark my words, Mammy, he'll be back in time for Christmas, no matter what.'

His mother nodded and began to talk about her

95

day, and they all marvelled over the bitterness of the weather and the suddenness of the storm. Colm described the horrors of his ride out to Clontarf with the heavy great turkey wobbling this way and that in his bicycle basket and the worse ride back, with the storm in his face. Caitlin chattered about the Murphys and the story she had told young Paddy. She tried to make her mother laugh, but it was hard work to so much as raise a smile and Colm, doing the same, praising the delicious Irish stew which his father should have shared, felt as miserable as anyone. This will ruin our Christmas, he told himself when at last he went off to his little bedroom. It's strange, because I thought a Christmas without the daddy would be grand, but I do believe I was wrong. It'll be teejus dull wit'out him, so it will.

And when, presently, he climbed into bed and began to say his prayers he added an extra one, though self-consciously, as though God himself would raise an eyebrow at young Colm O'Neill's sudden change of heart. 'Please God, let me daddy be safe, not drownded at sea, an' let him come home to us for Christmas,' Colm prayed. And slept better for it.

*   *   *

The following day was Christmas Eve and Colm set off for work earlier than usual. His mother had obtained the longed-for job with Switzer's Department Store and was off very early each morning, and since she had expected that Sean would be home, had made no arrangements for Caitlin. However, she dared not miss her work at the store, where each morning she scrubbed every inch of the stairs and the marvellous rubberised cream-and-brown flooring, so she woke Caitlin very early, bade her dress herself and saw her round to Marrowbone Lane before starting work herself.

'I'll finish at nine, as usual, and I'm not goin' in to the private houses today, so I'll call for you then,' she told her daughter, as the three of them hurried down the stairs. And then I t'ink we'll just go down to the quays, see what happened to last night's ferry.'

'Thanks be the weather's better,' Colm said. 'I thought we were after havin' a white Christmas last night but there's little enough snow left, be the looks.'

Indeed, there was not. Hail and snow had been blown into odd corners but the streets were icy and not snow-covered, and though icicles hung from a good many eaves the wind had dropped and the sky overhead, though dark still, was clear.

They walked together, Colm pushing his bicycle, until they reached the roadway where Colm turned left for York Street and Caitlin and her mother right for Marrowbone Lane. Colm gave his mother a kiss, rumpled his sister's hair and then said, on impulse: 'I'll go along to the quays right now I t'ink, Mammy. If there's any news I'll come to Switzer's before I go on to York Street, but if there isn't, you'll learn more later.'

'You're a good boy, so you are,' Eileen O'Neill said thankfully. 'I scarce slept a wink last night for worryin'. All I want now is to know your daddy's safe, even if he can't get home for the holiday.'

So Colm went straight down to the quays, glad that the gas-lamps were still flickering smokily, and asked everyone he met if they knew what had happened to the previous day's ferry.

'Sure an' it never would have sailed,' said a middle-aged man with the badge of the port authority on his jacket. 'Was your daddy meant to be aboard, young feller?'

'Yes, he was. Me mammy got in a turble state,' Colm admitted. 'Will the ferries be sailin' today, then, mister?'

'Sure to. We've heard no word of trouble other than that she didn't sail because o' the weather,' the man assured him. 'Don't worry, she'll sail today.'

So Colm, much relieved, left a message with one of the cleaners at Switzer's to tell his mammy that the ferry hadn't sailed the previous day but would certainly do so today and hurried along to York Street.

*   *   *

Sean O'Neill had lodgings in Toxteth, in a little street called Lavrock Bank right opposite the Corporation Yard. Mrs Caldicott, his landlady, was a small woman in her late sixties with an earthy sense of humour and a good deal of placid common sense. She had three lodgers, all Irishmen working on the Corporation dustcarts, and treated each of them like a son. She was, furthermore, a good plain cook, her terms were reasonable and she encouraged the men to spend the evenings with her in the kitchen, yarning round the fire. As she said, she much preferred it to having lodgers who went out of an evening and came home late, and probably the worse for drink.

So Sean knew he had landed on his feet when he found the lodgings in Lavrock Bank, and had no intention of leaving so cosy a billet. Indeed, when Mrs Caldicott told her lodgers that her younger sister was coming to share the house with her and give a hand, he felt no apprehension. Any sister of Mrs Caldicott's, Sean had thought, would be a pleasant sort of woman.

He was wrong. Mrs Maisy Evans was a skinny, shrill-voiced harridan who hectored the lodgers as she had probably hectored her own husband before he fled. When Mrs Caldicott went off to Crosby to visit her daughter, and left her sister in charge, Maisy skimped on their carry-outs and gave them such a meagre evening meal that the men went to bed hungry. It didn't matter on the odd occasion, Sean told himself, but he knew one thing: if Mrs Caldicott ever retired then he would be finding himself new lodgings within a couple of days. He would not stay in the house under Maisy Evans's rule.

But on the morning of 23 December Sean was not worrying about his landlady, for he was about to go home for the holiday. He had gone into the country the previous Sunday with one of the other men and come back with a great bunch of holly and mistletoe for his landlady, together with a box of chocolates, which he had bought from a fine shop on Church Street. Now, he gave her a jubilant hug and wished her a merry Christmas, and swung out of the front door, his bulging bag in one hand. He could not wait to get aboard the ferry and make his way up to the bows to watch Ireland appearing out of the mist and drawing gradually nearer.

He had reached the dock from which the Irish

99

ferries sailed and immediately caught up with half the population of Dublin, or so it seemed, for wasn't everyone going home for the holiday now, and hadn't they all got their tickets for this particular ferry, so that they would have a day at home to visit the pubs and their old pals before the obligatory family gatherings of Christmas Eve and the day itself?

But the ferry from Ireland had been late arriving and consequently would be late departing, and in the meantime the weather had got worse and worse. The passengers were actually boarding when the storm hit. Hail, snow, a raging wind, you name it, they had suffered from it. And been ignominiously bundled off the small craft so that it might ride out the storm in the shelter of the dock, whilst the passengers did the best they could to find somewhere for the night.

Sean went back to his lodgings, as miserable as he had ever been, and told Mrs Caldicott what had happened. She was very sorry, but made him a scrap meal of bread, jam and cocoa, and told him to go to bed and pray for a change in the weather. 'Though they'll sail tomorrer, chuck—sure to,' she said comfortably, handing him a dog-end of candle. 'My, the wind sounds as if all the devils from 'ell was out there, a-screamin' an' a-screechin' round the chimbley pots. I'm glad I've no call to be out in it ... nor poor Maisy, neither. I'm off to me daughter's in Crosby on Christmas Eve, but today we'll jest snug down an' 'ope for a decent day tomorrer.'

And next day, sure enough, the weather was better. It was still windy and very cold, and the gutters of Lavrock Street were choked with hail and snow, but the sky was clear and by the time Sean had said his goodbyes all over again it was plain that the ferry should sail.

So Sean, wrapped up well, walked down to the dock and was met by total confusion. The ferry which he and his friends had boarded the previous day, he was told, had been treated like a feather by the storm and had been crashed against the quayside, cracking the bows beneath the plimsoll line like an eggshell.

'She won't be sailin' for many a day,' another Irishman told him dourly. 'They're puttin' another ship on, but it won't holt the lot av us. It'll be divil tek the hindmost—an' she's more than half full already. I reckon they'll be chargin' twice over for tickets to try to sort the mess out somehow. They've already got every dock policeman an' a good few ordinary scuffers protectin' the gangplank.'

'Well, I'll be gettin' aboard if I have to murder every scuffer in Liverpool,' Sean growled. He was an even-tempered man, but the thought of being separated from his wife and family at Christmas was enough to turn a saint to violence. 'They'd better not try to stop *me*, I'm tellin' ye.'

The trouble was, every man present felt the same and it soon became obvious that no matter how hard they tried, the authorities could not let any more men aboard the ship, which rocked and swayed at its moorings, ready to depart.

'She'll come back for yiz,' the seamen shouted encouragingly to the disappointed crowds thronging the decks. 'Come down agin tonight an' we'll be back an' embarkin' passengers for Dublin agin.'

101

So Sean went back into the city to the telegraph office and sent his Eileen a telegram. *'Yesterday's ferry holed stop All unhurt,'* his message read. *'Next one sailed without me stop Look for me late this evening stop'*

Having done his best to put Eileen's mind at rest, Sean went back to his lodgings to explain the present state of play to Mrs Caldicott. 'So I should be in me own home for Christmas mornin',' he ended. 'But mebbe I'll be a day or so later comin' back than I t'ought.'

'Well, we'll be havin' a party in for Christmas, at me daughter's place in Crosby,' his landlady said cheerfully. 'So if somethin' else goes wrong, chuck, you just come back 'ere an' we'll tek you with us this evenin'. Only you'll be sharin' a bed wi' our Jack an' probably with our Fred an' all, 'cos me daughter's crammin' me 'ole fambly in like sardines so's we can all be together over the holiday.'

Mrs Evans, standing at the stove stirring something in a pan, turned and gave him a spiteful look, muttering something under her breath as she did so; Sean had no idea whether she was to share in her sister's party plans but he hoped not, for kind Mrs Caldicott's sake. However, he ignored the younger woman and spoke directly to his landlady. 'Thanks, Mrs Caldicott, but I'm gettin' back to Dublin even if I have to swim,' he said. 'I'm goin' down to the dock now an' I'm goin' to fight me way aboard if I have to flatten half the Irish nation to do it.'

'Good on you,' Mrs Caldicott said. 'I'm the same where fambly's concerned. They come first. Well, I'll say cheerio for the third time of askin'.'

So Sean went off again ... and this time he

caught the ferry. The men were packed in like sardines, but they didn't care. They sang, they drank beer, they laughed and joked—they were going home, what did it matter if they wouldn't arrive until the early hours of Christmas morning, so long as they got back to Dublin in time to share their families' day?

*   *   *

The telegram arrived at two in the afternoon, when Colm had cycled home for a few minutes to find out what was going on, and his mammy had shed tears of joy. 'Your daddy will be home for Christmas, though very late,' she told her children and, to his surprise, Colm felt a rush of pleasure and relief. Well, the man's me daddy, he told himself; we may not get on too well, but we don't hate one another. Naturally I'm relieved he's not drownded and pleased he's coming home. He's not so bad, after all. And now I'm working, things will be different.

'That's great, Mammy,' he said, therefore. 'Can I meet him at the Quay for ye? You'll want Caitlin to be in bed an' the quay at the dead of night's no place for a woman.'

'There's no point, Colm. You could be waitin' there, cold an' lonely, for hours an' hours,' Eileen said sensibly. 'Be sure your daddy won't expect to be met, he'll be home just as soon as he can, that'll be enough for him.'

But Colm, cycling back to Savage's, thought that he probably would try to meet the ferry. Now that he was a working man it might be good to have a better relationship with his daddy. And I've only got to be nice to him for a few days, so I have, he reminded himself rather guiltily. Then he'll be back across the water an' life here will be back to normal, wit' just the three of us, an' the mammy writing letters twice a week . . . but relyin' on *me* for a man's support.

'Well?' Mr Savage said as soon as his delivery boy put his nose round the door of the shop. 'Heard from the daddy, have ye?'

'He'll be comin' home tonight, late, on the last ferry,' Colm said. 'I've a mind to meet it . . . but Mammy says not, 'cos wit' the sailings all over the place, no one can say when she'll dock.'

'Your mammy's right, but I dare say you'll go your own way,' Mr Savage said shrewdly. 'You're all after havin' your own way, whether you go to the divil or no. You've only another two deliveries, then you can get off home. And your goose is a turkey, young feller.'

Colm had been putting away a small sum each week towards the purchase of a goose, so he stared, round-eyed, at his employer. A turkey was far too expensive for him and mammy had never cooked one. 'A turkey? But 'tis a goose I was puttin' me money away for,' he stammered. 'Whyfor d'you say a turkey?'

'Because I've a big bugger of a turkey left unsold an' you might as well have the benefit of it,' Mr Savage said. 'I'll holt on to your goose-money, then you can spend it on somethin' else after Christmas. A nice leg o'mutton or a saddle o'beef for the New Year . . . or for Little Christmas.'

'And you've sold me goose,' Colm said, grinning. 'Go on, Mr Savage, you've sold it, so you have!'

'I have so,' agreed Mr Savage cheerfully. 'The

104

woman who ordered the turkey needed it for a big party, an' now they aren't all comin', so she's changed her mind. But aren't you the lucky one now? The turkey's the size of an ostrich. Your fambly will be eatin' that turkey come midsummer day I tell ye!'

He produced the turkey, which was indeed enormous, and Colm had to agree that he was in luck, though there was a snag. 'It'll not go in me mammy's oven,' he pointed out. 'An' the baker will charge us more'n we can afford to roast it. If it'll go in their oven, that is.'

'Ah. Hmm. Tell you what, I'll cut it in two with me meat saw, an' your mammy can cook one half tomorrer an' the other half later. How's that for a solution?'

'What about the stuffin'?' Colm asked. 'I do like a nice helpin' o' stuffin'.'

Mr Savage sighed. 'Whyfor does a turkey have to have sage an' onion shoved up it's bum to mek it Christmas?' he asked rather plaintively. 'Your mammy will find a way ... she can stuff the half-cavity an' sew bacon slices over it. I'll put in half a pound o' streaky as well, an' never say I'm a mean man.'

'I never would,' Colm said, grinning at his large, red-faced employer. 'A turkey! Wait till I tell Caitlin she's goin' to taste turkey this Christmas.'

*   *   *

Sean sat on the ferry deck, wedged in, listening to the singing going on all around and smiling contentedly to himself. The sea was still rough after the storm of the previous day and the ferry pitched

105

and tossed, but nothing could spoil the contentment of men making their way home. On other trips, Sean recalled, there had been fights, arguments, quarrelsome voices raised. Not on this trip. The overall feeling of thankfulness that they would be getting their Christmas after all was too strong.

The ship docked at two in the morning.

'It's Christmas Day,' someone said as they began to pour ashore. 'Would ye ever have dreamed of startin' your Christmas Day on board a stinkin' ould ferry ship, now?'

'She's not a stinkin' ould ship, she's a quane, so she is,' someone else called out. 'She's a quane because she's brung me back to me ould wan an' me kids in time for Christmas. An' . . . an' the crew is saints, 'cos they come back for us though it were late an' dark, an' the sea were rough.'

'Let's give 'em t'ree cheers,' someone else shouted and the cheers—by no means the first of that voyage—were loudly given. Then Sean felt the gangplank beneath his feet and knew he would be on Irish soil in less than a minute, and felt unaccustomed tears in his eyes. He had so nearly not made it. He had seen the look on the faces of the few men who had been unable to get aboard and thanked God that he had not been one of them. To spend Christmas over the water, after a whole year of scrapin' an' savin' to come home. To be squeezed into a bed wit' Jack an' Fred, whoever they might be, instead of wit' his own lovely Eileen. To try to pretend jollity and Christmas cheer in a strange house amongst strange people, with the hated Maisy Evans grinning to herself to think him unhappy. It didn't bear thinking of, but it hadn't

106

happened and here he was—one foot fumbled for the ground and the other joined it—ashore in Ireland once more.

The whole crowd of them flooded across the quay and into the streets beyond, gaslit still, but unpeopled, quiet. Voices which had been raised were suddenly hushed as they got amongst the buildings. Folk were asleep here, kids as well as adults, all waiting for the morning; best not to wake them betimes.

Sean strode out and heard, from behind him, a voice: 'Daddy! Oh, Daddy, will ye wait on a minute? It's Colm, wit' Caitlin, too . . . Daddy, wait on!'

He turned—and there was his son, with Caitlin by his side. Both children wore broad beams and even as he turned they were on him, Caitlin leaping to hang round his back, her legs locked round his waist, Colm grabbing his hand and squeezing hard.

'Daddy! Oh Daddy, we've been waitin' hours, so we have, but isn't it worth it now, to know you did catch the ferry an' are home for Christmas?'

That was Colm, and the boy looked pleased to see him, for a wonder! Of course, meeting a ship is always an emotional moment, but . . . Colm, pleased? Perhaps the boy wasn't so bad, perhaps he'd wronged him. After all, he'd brought his little sister out at an ungodly hour in the pitch dark to meet the ship. That must mean the boy had some spunk—the girl had, he'd always known it. He squeezed Colm's hand back, then kissed his daughter's cheek and stood her down. 'What a great girl you are to be sure! Too heavy for me to carry now, I'm tellin' ye! Where's the mammy?'

'In the kitchen, asleep in a chair, tired out,'

Caitlin said importantly. 'She meant to stay awake to see you in, Daddy, but she just falled asleep. So we left her, me an' Colm, because she's had a busy day, so she has.'

'And a worryin' one,' Colm added, walking along beside his father. He's nearly as tall as me, Sean realised. 'She was desprit afeared you'd miss the ship, Daddy, an' that would have ruined our Christmas. She wouldn't let us come an' meet you, only she couldn't stay awake to stop us.'

'Hey, she'll wake up an' find you gone . . .' Sean began, worried.

But Colm shook his head. 'It's all right, Daddy, we left a note on the mantel, propped up behind the teapot. We told her we'd come down to the quay to meet the ship, but meself, I don't reckon she'll wake for a few hours yet. Worn out, she is, wit' work, an' worry, an' excitement.'

'Well, we'll mek this a Christmas to remember,' Sean said with deep contentment as they walked on through the darkness, drawing ever nearer to the only place to be at Christmas—home.

*   *   *

They had had a marvellous Christmas and a great New Year, Caitlin thought contentedly a week later, as she rejoined the Murphys in Marrowbone Lane, for school did not begin for another two days. Everything had been just grand, though at the start, when their daddy had missed the ferry, it had seemed doomed. But Daddy had got home in time for the big day, he had congratulated Colm on the enormous turkey and eaten his share of it, and his presents had been better, she was sure, than anyone else's.

Caitlin had got her sledge, though Daddy had sent the money over to mammy a while back, and mammy had bought it for him and hidden it at a neighbour's house. Colm had been right about Daddy not carting it all the way across the Irish sea, but that was the only thing he had been right about, for there had been other presents, all good. Naturally, she and Colm had longed for snow from the first moment they set eyes on the sledge, though Colm, of course, was too grown-up to admit it, but apart from the storm before Christmas there hadn't been enough snow to use it on yet.

'The sledge is more for everyone—the Murphys an' all, alanna,' her father had said when he gave it to her. 'This is for you yourself.'

'This' was a parcel done up in brown paper and string, which had come all the way across the Irish sea, and it was far more wonderful than Caitlin had dreamed. She opened it and there was a tiny doll, no bigger than her brother's hand. It was a baby doll, with a sweet baby's face, eyes that opened and shut although it was so tiny, and jointed limbs. It had no hair—babies didn't have much hair anyway—and it wore nothing but a scrap of towelling around its fat middle. 'Oh Daddy, Daddy!' Caitlin breathed, awed. 'It's the baby Tom Thumb, so it is. Oh, I love it and love it—I love it as much as Long Meg!'

'Well, it'll pop into your pocket, which Long Meg won't,' her father said tactfully. 'But I didn't buy it, alanna. Mrs Caldicott, me landlady in Liverpool, give it me. She said since I was the only feller livin' at her house wit' a daughter I could take it an' welcome. I'm glad you like it . . . would you write her a little letter, tellin' her so?'

'Oh *yes*, I'll write,' Caitlin said. 'Come along, Tommy Tiddler, you must meet me friend Long Meg.'

Mammy had made Long Meg out of old cotton stockings and bits of material which her ladies had thrown out, and embroidered a beautiful face on her and made her two lovely frocks, one pink and one blue. Long Meg had plaits of yellow wool and little soft shoes with cardboard soles and real leather uppers made, Caitlin knew, from the tongues of old shoes found by Colm on the rubbish tips. Caitlin would always love her best, but the baby doll was quite different. So tiny! So perfect! Tommy Tiddler would never ride in the pram or sleep in the shoe-box bed Mammy had made, but he would be with Caitlin always.

So those two presents made Christmas just perfect, and Colm was pleased with the leather flying-helmet, which Daddy had bought to keep his son's ears warm whilst on his bicycle, and the gauntlet gloves to match. Not many delivery boys had such fine clothes—or such weather-proof ones—and Colm had the share in the sledge, too.

He and Daddy had been very pleased with one another on Christmas Day, what with the enormous turkey and all the good things Daddy had brought. Mammy's present had been a beautiful woollen jacket and Daddy was given socks and gloves, which Mammy had knitted, and some pipe tobacco.

Caitlin loved it when they were nice to each other, and when she sensed that they were in good accord she relaxed and enjoyed herself twice as much as usual. And all through the time that

Daddy was home there was a fine feel in the house, a good understanding between father and son. Often, when Daddy was home, he and Mammy quarrelled over Colm and what Daddy called his 'gorlish, milksop ways', but this time the comfortable feeling that all was well only lapsed once to Caitlin's knowledge, and that was when they had walked to Phoenix Park and Daddy was watching Colm playing a game of Kick the Can with some friends.

'He's fifteen now, an' he's a fine specimen of a feller, so he is,' he said softly to Mammy, only Caitlin heard anyway. 'Next year there's no reason he shouldn't come wit' me, Eileen, an' earn hisself some dacint money, doin' a man's job.'

Mammy's face changed; grew cooler, somehow. But she said in her soft voice: 'He's doin' a man's job now, Sean. Deliverin' isn't aisy, not wit' that gurt old bicycle, an' he covers some ground, does our Colm. Don't put him down, there's a good feller.'

'He's earnin' seven an' six a week; ten bob if he's extry busy an' delivers late,' Daddy had said. 'That's not good money, alanna. Workin' till the sweat runs at a navvyin' job in England he'd bring home a lot more than that.'

'He'd be over the water wit' yourself, an' Cait an' me 'ud be left to manage as best we could,' Mammy said, her voice sad. 'He'd be livin' in lodgings wit' no one to care about him, see he was bein' brung up right. When he's a wife of his own he can choose to go away if he likes, but whilst he's just a young feller I'd rather keep him by me.'

Daddy had shrugged and turned away. 'If he sent more money home I'd be able to come back more

111

often,' he pointed out. 'And what are you sayin',
woman? That I'd not see the boy right?'

'Oh, you would, I know you would ... but I can't
let him go yet, Sean. Not yet. In a year or two ...'

But Daddy had turned away and was holding out
his hand to his small daughter. 'Come on then,
Caitlin, let's go an' tek a look at the fish pond, shall
us? It'll be dark soon an' your mammy will want to
be home, gettin' the tea.'

But apart from that one incident, Caitlin
thought, turning into Marrowbone Lane with her
hand held fast in Mammy's and little Tommy
Tiddler warm in her pocket, they had had a grand
Christmas altogether. They had gone to wave
Daddy off down at the quays, and for the first time,
as father and son stood a little apart, talking, it had
struck Caitlin how very alike they were. Sean was
taller of course, and sturdier, but apart from that
they both had thick black hair with a shine to it that
was almost blue, and they had the same sort of
face, with prominent cheek-bones, straight, thin
eyebrows and chins with a cleft. And they've both
got blue-grey eyes and their lashes are short and
straight, not curly like Mammy's and mine, Caitlin's
thoughts continued. Why, you'd know Sean was
Colm's daddy out of a thousand, so you would! Is
that why they don't always get on, then? Because
they're so alike that they could almost be twins?
She voiced the thought aloud as they turned into
Marrowbone Lane: 'Mammy, I was lookin' at me
daddy an' me brother Colm when they were
standin' waitin' for the ferry, an' they're just the
same, aren't they? Same hair, same eyes, same
faces, same way o' standin'. Even their voices is the
same, only Daddy's is deeper than Colm's. Is ... is

112

that why they sometimes argufy? Only I'd ha' thought they'd get on better, bein' so alike.'

Mammy laughed. 'They are alike, aren't they?' she said. 'And you're right, alanna, that's why they don't always get on good. But I don't t'ink either of 'em knows it! Never mind, eh? They were fine over Christmas, didn't you t'ink?'

'I did so,' Caitlin agreed. 'I hope they're always like that now, Mammy.'

'Oh well, we mustn't hope for miracles, alanna. But you never know, as Colm gets older an' wiser his daddy may find . . . may find t'ings easier.'

'An' Daddy may stop askin' Colm to go over the water wit' him,' Caitlin said. 'I don't want Colm to go, Mammy. But I wish Daddy didn't have to go either.'

They reached the Murphys' tenement and Eileen stopped and kissed her daughter. Her lips were warm on Caitlin's cold cheek. 'So do I, alanna. One day, perhaps he won't have to go,' she said. 'Mebbe he's right an' Colm should go as well, if that makes the day your daddy doesn't have to go come nearer. But . . . but not yet.'

'No, not yet,' Caitlin echoed fervently. 'Not until he's as big an' strong as me daddy. Not until I'm a woman growed.'

'That's it,' Eileen said, and giggled. 'Oh, Caitlin, you're a blessin', so you are! Run along in, now. I'll call for you when I come out of work.'

CHAPTER FOUR

January 1929 Liverpool

Rose woke long before dawn on Monday morning at once aware that something good was going to happen today, though she could not think immediately what it was. Her first thought was that she was still on holiday until Thursday, now that she was at the convent school, whereas her old playmates had been back at the grindstone for over a week.

Her second thought was that her room looked odd; no, not odd, *different*. The ceiling was dazzlingly white and there was more light coming in round the edge of the curtains, she was sure, than the hour merited. Had she overslept, perhaps? She could not remember why, but she knew it was important that she did not oversleep today.

She sat up and poked a toe out of bed, then hastily pulled it back in again. It was freezing! For a moment she sat there, hugging her knees and wondering, then she took a deep breath, pushed back the covers and took a gigantic leap out of bed, skidding on the lino so that she was at the window and wrenching the curtains back before she had thought, again, about the cold.

It was still very dark outside and the window-glass had been painted by Jack Frost in the night so she couldn't see through it, but she didn't have to; the dazzle of white told her that it had snowed last night. For a moment, excitement over the sudden

114

arrival of snow drove everything else from her mind. She squeaked joyfully, then breathed hard on the glass until she had made a round dark hole in the frost flowers and peered through it. The world was white. It was not just a scatter of snow which had fallen in the night but a great deal of it, enough to make slides, snowballs, snowmen . . .

She climbed back into bed, remembering that everyone except herself was back in school anyway and feeling rather deflated. Of course, snow was fun, but on your own? It wasn't quite the same. She wondered whether her father would be able to drive his tram, then concluded that unless he was on a long run, he almost certainly would. When points froze and the rails got iced up things were difficult, but the crews usually managed to keep their trams running somehow. And thinking of that brought the main excitement of the day back into her mind with a huge crash. Of course! Today was the day that her father had offered to take her on his tram for the whole of his shift, so that she could find out once and for all what a life of driving—or conducting—trams was like.

Immediately, the snow began to seem less like a blessing than a curse. Suppose Dad said he couldn't take her, not in such bad conditions? And then he worked until eight or nine at night quite often, which would mean missing any snow games the other kids might start when school finished. Ricky would come hammering on her door with one of his mam's biggest bar trays, to suggest that they should go up to somewhere like Havelock Street and career down it, two to a tray. And she wouldn't be there, so he would ask someone else and she knew what Dad and Mam would say if she suggested going out to play after Dad's return.

Still, she would rather have her day on the tram than any amount of games in the snow and anyway, there was nothing to say that tomorrow and the day after, for that matter, wouldn't be snowy too. So she collected her clothes, tipped water—she had to break the ice first—into her basin, and had a quick cat's lick and a promise wash. Then she dressed in her warm grey wool skirt with the matching jumper and set off downstairs.

There, in the cosy, lamplit kitchen, her mother was making breakfast. She smiled at her daughter as Rose took her place at the table, and put a plate with bacon, egg and fried bread down in front of her. 'Well, now, you're in good time,' she said comfortably. 'I' s'pose even the weather won't persuade you that there's more to life than drivin' blinkin' trams? Your dad'll be down in ten minutes.'

Rose grinned and began to tuck into her food. Of course she was no fool, she knew very well that the day on the tram was supposed to put her off them and not make her yet more enthusiastic. For as long as she could remember she had wanted to drive a tram when she grew up and, despite knowing that women were never thus employed, she simply could not think of any other job which would suit her so well. The convent school had been happy to take her in after her good examination results at St Anthony's school, and her parents hoped that she would remain there for another two years, maybe more. They desperately wanted her to better herself and education, they said impressively, was the way to do it. But when she thought of two more years' school, her heart

116

misgave her. However would she stand it, especially as everyone seemed to think it was about time she began to behave more like a girl! Boys had all the fun, she thought now, taking the cup of hot milk her mother offered with a word of thanks. Boys never got told to do housework, a good few of them wagged off school to play skippin' leckies or to muck around down at the Pier Head and, what was more, if they wanted to drive trams, then tram drivers they could be.

But on the other hand, they didn't get a whole day on their father's tram, either. Mam thought she would be bored, but Rose was sure she was wrong. She was to have her own carry-out, her own bottle of tea, and if she behaved and they didn't have an inspector aboard, she would be able to use the ticket machine and take the money whilst Georgie handed out the change.

Rose knew her mother did not fully approve of the day out, because she must have realised that far from damping Rose's enthusiasm it might make her worse than ever, but Mam never stayed cross for long. It was just that the convent school was expensive, and she truly thought that her daughter should have some more worthwhile ambition than the hopeless one of wanting to drive a tram. But after all, Rose reasoned, they said they wanted me to stay on at school; if they'd wanted me to grow up and be sensible they should have let me leave school, like Peggy will when July comes. But if they truly want me to get still more education then they shouldn't mind if I go on being silly and saying I want to drive a tram one day.

Because she knew it was silly that she, a girl, should persistently say she wanted to drive a tram

117

when she knew very well that it was one job that women never did. But that didn't alter the facts. Mam and Dad and other adults never said 'What will you settle for doing when you leave school?', they said: 'What do you want to do?' so they must expect a truthful answer—she wanted to drive a tram, like her dad did, so why shouldn't she say so?

Rose could have added truthfully that it was all part of wanting to be a boy, really. Mam thought it was peculiar and unfeminine to go on wanting to be a boy when you were fourteen, but that really was silly. A blind man could see that boys have the best of it, and who doesn't want to have the best of it, if they are honest? And then Kick the Can and other such games were a great deal more fun than skipping, or bowling a hoop, though Rose had done both in her time. And when careers were discussed at the convent school they talked about their girls becoming teachers, which made Rose's spine stiffen with outraged horror. Teachers, even if they weren't nuns, wore thick stockings and long skirts; they had their hair smoothed into unflattering styles and didn't get married or have kids of their own—she could think of nothing she would like less than being a teacher.

Her mam had suggested working in a shop or café but Rose, after giving it fleeting consideration, had decided against anything of that nature. It was boring work when compared with driving a tram, or even being a conductor, and until someone came up with something equally exciting, she would stick to her guns. They should have said that tram driving being impossible, she might turn to something else which meant she could work out of doors, such as driving a milk float, but they never did. Grown-ups had narrow minds, she thought sadly now, tucking into her delicious cooked breakfast. She had suggested that, or even selling flowers in Clayton Square or fruit down by the Pier Head and round the theatres, like the Mary Ellens did.

Mam had been outraged by the last suggestion, though unwilling, when it came to the point, to tell Rose why she was so horrified. Rose, who often caught the last tram back from the Pier Head when they had been on an outing, thought that the Mary Ellens were a jolly crowd and had a lovely life. On the last tram they were apt to sort out their fruit and hand the stuff that wouldn't sell on the morrow, the fades, to any kid standing nearby. And they held singsongs, carolling away until all the other passengers, no matter how inwardly disapproving, joined in. And sometimes one of them would befriend some lonely sailor, who knew no one in Liverpool, and walk off with him, arm in arm, chatting away as friendly as anything.

Dad had just laughed when Rose said she wouldn't mind being a Mary Ellen but Mam had tightened her mouth and sniffed. 'You'd be happy for Rose to join a bleedin' *circus* if she said she'd like to,' she had said sharply. 'You wouldn't care if she hung from a bleedin' trapeze showin' her drawers to thousands, you wouldn't.'

Rose had been quite shocked, for Mam never swore and there she was, using the word 'bleedin', twice in one minute. But Dad had just laughed and said Rose was only a kid, wasn't she, an' kids didn't know what they *did* want, apart from money for doin' nothin', an' wasn't their Rosie just like they'd been when they were kids?

119

That softened Mam, who got to remembering how she'd always wanted to be on the stage and had hung around the Rotunda on Scotland Road, waylaying the actors and actresses with offers of assistance, and how she had loved dressing up and acting out little plays with her brothers and sisters as audience.

Rose, who hated dressing up and didn't think working in a theatre or cinema would suit her at all—it wasn't outdoors, was it?—pretended to be interested, then said how about selling ice-cream from one of those little carts in Princes Park? Or what about the various stalls around the Bold Street area? Or a coalman might want someone to lead his horse, or she could help out at one of the Smithfields . . . the choices seemed endless to her.

'They ain't real jobs, queen, that's the trouble,' her father said when they were alone, her mother having taken herself off to make the tea, muttering about having a daughter who thought she was only capable of doing menial work. 'You wouldn't earn real money deliverin', or leadin' someone's horse even if they wanted you, which they wouldn't. Your mam's right when she says it's either shop work, factory work or somethin' better, like teachin'. Factories pay all right, but you gerra rough crowd in most factories, an' shop work's mortal hard. You'd be on your feet from early mornin' to late night, an' the take-home pay's poor. No, you'd be better off goin' on a teachin' course for a year— you'd like it, I dessay. An' think of the holidays, queen.'

'I wouldn't like teachin', I'd hate it. I been in school for years an' years already, I don't want to spend the rest o' me life in school,' Rose had

120

pointed out rebelliously. 'If I cut me hair an' wore kecks, would they let me try for a tram driver?'

'No . . . but tell you what, queen, it ain't that free an' easy, drivin' a tram. When's you goin' back to school?'

'In five more days,' Rose had said sorrowfully. 'That's the best thing about the convent, we get longer holliers than the other schools. But the work's harder, ever so much, an' the teachers nag more.'

'Right. Well, tomorrer why don't you come on the tram wi' me? You can come all day, I'll buy you a proper ticket an' all. You'll mebbe want to think twice after a whole day of tram drivin'.'

Rose had pounced on the idea, though she hadn't bargained on snow, of course. And her mam now reminded her of it as she took Rose's empty plate away and replaced it with buttered toast. 'You've seen the snow, of course. Dad won't know until he gets to the depot, but I've not known the trams to stop when the snow's barely two inches deep. No, I reckon you'll be with him today, though you'll find it mortal cold.'

'Don't sound so pleased, our mam,' Rose said, between mouthfuls of toast. 'Dad said to wrap up warm, so I shall. I'll be fine.'

'Oh, I didn't mean . . .' her mother began, to break off, with some relief Rose thought, as Jack entered the room. 'Ah, you're ready! I'll dish up your breakfast, then. Rosie's finished hers, 'cept for the toast.'

'Good girl, I knew you'd not mek me late,' Jack said, sniffing appreciatively. 'Eh, bacon! How deep's the snow, Lily? Ha' you been out yet?'

'Aye, I needed more coal,' his wife said, adroitly

121

sliding two eggs onto the slice of bread on his plate. 'It's a sharp one, but the snow's no more'n two or three inches at most, an' the sky's clear. It's my belief we'll have a sunny day, so mebbe most o' the snow'll be gone by evenin'.'

'Well, so long as we don't have trouble wi' the points an' the slopes,' Jack said equably, spearing bacon and carrying it mouthwards. 'Are you still on, queen? I won't mind if you'd rather stop at home today an' come wi' me tomorrer.'

But this Rose was not at all inclined to do. She shook her head and reached for another piece of toast. 'No, I'm comin' wi' you, Dad, like we said,' she insisted, spreading margarine and then plum jam. 'We're goin' to have a grand day, snow or no snow.'

Lily Ryder tutted and shook her head, 'Eh, I dunno, wharra girl, eh? I don't want you catchin' cold an' bein' laid up just in time for the start of term! S'pose the cold gets on your chest, chuck?'

'What? You've gorra admit, Lily luv, that my Rose of Tralee's as sturdy as any lad! I disremember her losin' so much as a day of school, except when she took the measles from young Ricky Elliott. Come to that, Ricky's uncommon healthy an' all. They may not be thoroughbreds nor high-steppers, but they're a pair o' right carthorses, those two kids.'

Lily laughed. 'It's the way we've brung 'em up, me an' Mrs Elliott,' she said. 'Plenty of good food an' a clack if they misbehave.'

'Oh yes, I've seen you handin' out smacks, time an' again,' Jack said sarcastically. 'The pair of 'em's spoiled rotten, it's a wonder they talk to the likes of me. Now where's me carry-out?'

122

'On the draining board, along wi' your flask o' tea. I've put Rosie up a box an' all, but her tea's in a bottle. I weren't goin' to buy another flask just for one day. Now, Rosie, go an' fetch your thick red jumper, your big coat, the red an' white scarf an' an extra pair o' socks. Oh, an' your wellingtons.'

'A couple o' blankets wouldn't come amiss,' Jack said wickedly, eyeing his wife. 'An' what's wrong wi' a pair o' long johns? She could wear 'em under that skirt, they wouldn't show much.'

'I've got an extra liberty bodice on now,' Rose grumbled, heading out into the hall where her coat hung beside her father's. Last night she had done the only household task she really enjoyed—she had got the button stick and the Silvo and she had polished the buttons on father's tramcoat until the little silver Liver birds shone like stars, and then she had got to work on all the rest of his equipment. His cap, which he wore all the time he was on duty, had his staff number round it above the shiny peak and the Liverpool coat of arms in the centre. Beneath his heavy coat Jack wore a blue shirt, a navy jacket and trousers with scarlet piping. Rose always polished his buttons and the Liver birds on his collar, and was proud to do so, as well as brushing away with the clothes brush until there was not a speck of dust or a hair to be seen on any part of the material, so she surveyed him with pride before leaving the kitchen. He looked marvellous, like a soldier decorated for outstanding bravery, she though happily. Dad had been a sailor in the war and he had medals, too, but privately she thought his present uniform the finest any man could wear.

Now, she obediently put on all the extra clothing

123

her mother had mentioned and added her thick school coat, a scarlet tam-o'-shanter and the wellington boots. Then she went back into the kitchen where her father was struggling into his own coat and perching his cap at an angle on his toffee-coloured hair. He turned when she came back into the room and whistled. 'Phew, Rosie, you're as broad as you're long! Never mind, queen, better warm than freezin' when you're in the old tram. Are you right? Then give Mam a kiss an' we'll be off, because it's a fair walk to Carisbrooke Road.'

'I'm ready, Dad,' Rose said. She kissed her mother and gave her a squeeze, suddenly sorry for her because Mam was too old to go gallivanting off on a tram for the whole day. 'What'll you do whiles I'm away, Mam?'

'Housework an' cookin', same's I do every day. An' mebbe after me dinner I'll walk round to Daisy's, see how she's goin' on,' her mother replied. 'Have a good day, queen, an' keep warm!'

'I will,' Rose said. 'Make us workers a nice hot dinner tonight, Mam!'

Her mother's laughter followed them as they left the house and turned into Netherfield Road.

*   *   *

It was a good walk to the tram depot and perhaps without the snow would have been a dull one, but as it was, Rose enjoyed every minute. She slid whenever she saw a puddle coated with ice, made snowballs and threw them at the gaslights and very soon shed her woollen gloves and the long scarf, though she shoved the gloves into her coat pockets

124

and wrapped the scarf round her middle. Jack Ryder, meanwhile, continued to walk onwards with the long, loping stride which he had developed over the years for covering a long distance at a fair speed whilst not arriving at his destination worn out.

As soon as they reached the depot, Rose became businesslike. She did not follow her father too closely whilst he clocked on and filled in his time sheets but seized a long, stiff-bristled brush and helped the men to clear the snow which had built up around the trams. And when Jack and Georgie came over to their tram—it was to be a number 19 today—she followed Jack as he did his checks and explained them to her.

'Always mek sure your sandbox is full,' he told her. 'Specially in this sort o' weather. Then I'll nip aboard and check me brakes whiles you give Georgie a hand to change the indicator.'

Rose watched as her father bent to the sandbox behind the huge front wheels and checked that it was full, then climbed up into the driving seat. Hastily, she followed him but turned right instead of left and walked along the wide central aisle between the long slatted seats to where Georgie was about to turn the handle of the object, similar to a roller blind, which would tell would-be passengers the number and destination of the tram.

'Oh Georgie . . .' she began, but Georgie was before her. 'Just linin' her up,' he said, grinning. 'Want to do it? Know where to stop? Can you read backwards, now? One o' the rules, tharris—all tram personnel must be able to read backwards!'

'I can, I can,' Rose said breathlessly, reaching up and beginning to wind. 'Ooh, I do love the 19,

Georgie, it goes to all the places that matter—
Kirkby, so's it's a nice long run, an' Eastbourne
Road—Dad'll use the sand on Eastbourne today, I
bet—an' when we reach the Pier Head we'll see the
river, an' the ferries, an' we'll swing round the
North Loop . . .'

'You know the route as well as your dad, I
reckon,' Georgie said admiringly. 'You want to ax
him if you can tek over, goin' along Easty. You'd
mek nothin' o' the hill, I reckon.'

They both laughed. Rose knew as well as
Georgie that it took a fair degree of skill to take a
tram down a steep hill, especially on a day when
there would be ice on the lines. 'Well, I wish I could
drive it a tiddy way, just a tiddy way,' Rose said
longingly. 'But if I did, that 'ud be the moment an
inspector jumped out, sure as sure.'

Georgie nodded. 'I know. Your dad does the
points sometimes, if I'm up to me eyes in
passengers inside, an' I'm always in a quake for
fear an inspector will come out of the woodwork,
but so far so good. Now if your dad's ready we'd
best be off. We're always crowded on a snowy day.'

'I don't see why. I should have thought folk
would have wanted to walk in the snow—kids do,'
Rose remarked, bringing the roller blind to a halt
at the right place. 'I'd best go and do the front one
now, hadn't I?'

'Your dad's done it. Can't hang about at this
time o' the mornin',' Georgie said kindly. 'Go an'
sit down now, where you can watch your dad.
They'll be queuin' up out at Kirkby for the first
tram, just mark me words.'

Accordingly Rose went up to the front of the
tram and sat down. The tram itself was partly

126

enclosed but the driver sat outside, warmly wrapped up against the cold. And in fact it was pretty cold in the front of the tram, too, so that Rose, mopping her streaming eyes as the tram moved off, thought that she would be quite glad when some passengers got aboard and warmed the atmosphere up a bit.

They reached the terminus and found, as Georgie had predicted, a considerable crowd waiting, mainly men. A good few of them, Rose guessed, would be travelling to the Pier Head to catch the ferry to work on the other side of the water. When you worked in Birkenhead you needed to catch the first tram to be at work on time. It was still dark, of course, but the tram was brightly lit and must, she thought, have seemed like a beacon of hope to all the would-be travellers waiting out in the cold.

But before Georgie would let anyone board he had to take the long hooked pole down from its resting place on a lamp-post and walk the tram-arm round so that it would go in the opposite direction. Then he would return the pole to its hook whilst Jack had to climb down and go round to the other end of the tram and drive from there, which was why, Rose knew, all trams had driver's cabs both at the front and rear of the vehicles. She supposed that had it been possible to put loops at every terminus the trams would have been made like buses and cars, always facing forward, but since it was not possible the conductors had the fun of rehooking the arm and the drivers had to leave a seat they had warmed and go round to drive the tram from the other end. Since it was still dark and no inspectors were about Georgie let Rose walk

127

the arm round, to her immense pride, though her father said gloomily that he just hoped no one noticed or, if they did, took her for a smallish man, in her long navy-blue coat.

As soon as Jack was settled his passengers, mainly men, scrambled aboard, some immediately making for the top deck, others cramming onto the long slatted seats, though the majority had to stand. Georgie came amongst them with his ticket machine and Rose, watching, longed to take the money, turn the little handle, punch and click, but knew it would be less a help than a hindrance at this very busy hour of the morning. She bought her ticket, however, with the money her father had given her, and wondered whether there would be an inspector brave enough to come out at this very early hour with the weather so bitter, and hold the loaded tram up on its rush down to the Pier Head.

They were stopped once, at the corner of Spellow Lane, but the inspector did not get aboard. He just checked Jack's number and time, and waved him on.

'Good thing he din't decide to check tickets an' all, or we'd ha' been late, an' missed the ferry,' Georgie bawled to Rose above the rattle of the tram. 'Ah, here comes the hill you're so keen on, queen—you can stand by your dad if you hang onto the post wi' both hands.'

Fascinated, Rose edged out of her seat and forward until she was just behind her father's broad, blackclad back. She watched as he spun the brake-wheel and turned the ratchet handle as far to the left as it would go, slowing the tram as much as possible. Then she saw his foot jabbing the brake and heard the slither and crunch as the tram wheels stopped sliding along the rails and ground the sand into powder when the brakes bit. The wheels shrieked a protest, a sound shrill enough to set your teeth on edge, but no one in the tram noticed. They came to work this way six days out of the seven and never, Rose was sure, stopped to consider whether the driver was doing a good or a bad job.

There was an altercation going on between two of the men standing; one had accused the other of *something*, but Rose was blowed if she could even guess what it was above the racket. When they reached level—or fairly level—ground once more she made her way back into the body of the tram to where Georgie leaned against the stairs. 'What were they quarrellin' about?' She shouted. 'I couldn't hear a blinkin' thing where I were.'

Georgie shrugged and bent to put his mouth close to Rose's ear. 'A woman, mebbe. Or a footie match,' he suggested. 'I don't try to listen, me. I got better things to do than listen to two dockies blindin'.'

'Yes, me too,' Rose said quickly, 'Coo, look at that! There must be twenty people standing there!' 'That' was a crowd of would-be passengers, stamping and shivering under the gaslight on Robson Street whilst their breath steamed round their heads.

'I see 'em, but we won't stop,' Georgie said. 'Unless someone wants to gerrof, which I hope very much . . . oh, that's done it.'

A burly man had reached up and tugged the leather strap once. Georgie sighed and Rose saw her father pull the handle to the left once more and begin to spin the brake-wheel. Georgie pushed his

129

way to the edge of the platform and addressed the crowd. 'One only,' he bellowed. 'Jes' the one this trip, mates! We're full, but one feller's gettin' down.'

The burly man pushed his way out and the crowd surged forward, but as soon as Georgie heaved the first man aboard he blew his whistle twice—he could not reach the bell from where he stood—and Jack obediently started up once more.

'Enjoyin' it?' Jack asked as they stopped at the Pier Head.

She had returned to her perch near his shoulder the better to look out across the sullenly heaving Mersey and at her father's question she nodded vigorously. 'It's great, Dad. Wish I could take her round the loop.'

Her father laughed. 'Oh yes, if I wanted to get me cards there 'ud be no better way.' He glanced back over his shoulder. 'Georgie finished unloadin' yet?'

'Yup. First new 'uns comin' aboard now,' Rose reported proudly. 'But a good lot o' these will get off in the centre, Georgie says.'

'That's it. You goin' to ring the bell when they're all aboard, chuck? Two for go, don't forget.'

'As if I could,' Rose said with mock indignation. 'Oh, there's someone running—do we have time to wait?'

'Just about,' Jack said. He spun the brake to 'off' and slewed round in his seat to watch the last passenger board. 'That it, queen? Go on then, pull on the strap!'

*   *   *

130

By the end of the day Rose had so much to tell her mother that she actually wanted to hurry home. It had been wonderful; even the weather had been kind to them. Very soon after the sky lightened the sun had come out and shone, palely but gamely, until it sank in a bed of crimson cloud in mid-afternoon.

When Jack's shift was over they returned to the depot in the tram, which was handed over to another driver who would take folk home from the various picture houses and theatres in the city, and she and Jack caught a Number 25, which took them along Netherfield Road to the corner of Cornwall Street.

'It's been the best day of me life,' Rose sighed as the two of them walked along Cornwall Street, Rose now kicking at the frozen slush as they went, for the pristine snow of earlier on had all but disappeared from roads and pavements, the sunshine had seen to that. 'I wish I could drive a tram really, Dad!'

'Yes, but you know you can't, Rosie,' her father said, trudging along beside her. 'And all days ain't like this one, queen. When it pours down wi' rain, or when there's a grey sky pressin' down on you an' a bitter wind, an' all your passengers is bad-tempered an' someone starts in to fightin', it's a diff'rent story, honest to God. You're goin' to be a young lady one o' these fine days, doin' a young lady's job. That's what your mam an' me want, queen. An' now you're fourteen it's a good time to start thinkin' serious-like about your future.'

'What if I marry?' Rose demanded. 'When you marry babies come, an' you have to keep house an' that. Then it wouldn't mek no difference what job

131

I'd been doin', I'd still have to give it up like Mam gave up shop work. As for tram drivin', acourse I know I can't, Dad. But there must be somethin' out o' doors that I could do.'

'Most out o' doors jobs is poorly paid,' Jack said. 'An' bein' out in all weathers don't do much for your complexion, Rosie. Mam doesn't want to see you wi' skin like an old brown gladstone bag afore you're twenty.'

Rose giggled. 'Like the old girls in Clayton Square, sellin' flowers? But they's a bit older'n twenty, Dad!'

Her father laughed too. 'Yes, mebbe,' he said. 'But I dare say they sowed the seeds of their leather skins when they was norra lot more'n twenty. Look, love, try to think! If you definitely won't go for teachin' . . .'

'Cousin Mona works out o' doors,' Rose said suddenly. 'I've not seen much of her or Aunt Daisy lately but I saw Mona carryin' a big bunch o' flowers, walkin' along Lime Street before Christmas, when Mam an' me caught a tram up to Lewis's, to do some shoppin'. I axed Mam what Mona were doin' an' she said she must ha' changed her job. Dad, if you're in a flower shop, that's as near out o' doors as meks no difference, I dare say. They keeps the big doors open so's the flowers can breathe, an' someone delivers all over the place from the bigger shops. What about that, eh?'

'That's a rare clever notion o' yours, queen,' her father said as they turned into the jigger which led along behind their house. 'It may not pay as well as some things, but if you'd enjoy it . . . you're right an' all, girls do deliver flowers more than young fellers do. Yes, I reckon you've hit on a good idea,

132

queen. We'll ask around.'

'You could ask Aunt Daisy, or better still, Mona,' Rose said, hurrying ahead of him down the jigger and opening the green wooden door which led into their tiny backyard. 'If she's working for a florist she'd tell us anythin' we wanted to know. Mona's all right—I like her better'n Aunt Daisy.'

'Yes but—but perhaps it's best to find out for ourselves,' Jack said. 'Come along in, Rosie, an' you can start tellin' Mam about your day at once!'

*   *   *

Later that night, when Rose had been long abed, Jack told his wife what Rose had said about seeing Mona with a sheaf of flowers in her arms, before Christmas.

'Oh, I know! I didn't mention it before, love, because I weren't too sure meself what she were doin'. Ever since Daisy an' I fell out I've not been goin' round there, so I couldn't ask, exactly, could I? But it's possible, ain't it, that Mona really is workin' for a florist? That she may have decided to—to be a sensible workin' gal? Except . . . well, she weren't dressed like a workin' gal an' that's the gospel truth. However, if Rosie really does want to work for a florist I'll have a talk around, ask a few questions. But I don't think I'll ask either Daisy or Mona! Better to let sleepin' dogs lie.'

Jack agreed fervently with this sentiment. Over the past few years, ever since he had first raised his worries about Mona and he and Lily and discussed their niece with complete frankness, they had not talked much about the Mullinses. And since the quarrel the mere mention of Daisy's name had upset his wife, so they kept off the subject altogether.

The quarrel had come about because Lily had decided at she simply must have a word with Daisy about Mona. 'You're right, folk are talkin',' she had told Jack worriedly. 'All them smart clothes, all that make-up, an' all them different fellers—well, what can you expect? I'm goin' to have a work wi' our Daisy, Jack.'

She had done her best to be tactful, but Daisy had been furious. 'What do it matter what folk say or think?' She had shouted when Lily falteringly began to explain why she had raised the subject. 'So they say she's no better'n she should be—well, what's wrong wi' makin' a bob or three on the side, eh? She's a pretty, lively girl, why shouldn't she use her looks to better herself? Eh? It's whar' I did you'll say next, an' what choice did I have, wi' a kid to bring up an' no feller? But I were just like our Mona in them days, so I took advantage of it, like. I went to dances an' it's surprisin' how generous a feller'll be in exchange for a few cuddles an' a kiss or two. You're not goin' to say I should have let me kid go hungry sooner than use me wits to make a bit o' extra?'

For some reason, this remark really riled Lily. She stared, open-mouthed, at her elder sister, then rushed into rash speech. 'Use your wits? It weren't your wits you were usin', Daisy Mullins, it were your . . . your . . .'

Fortunately, perhaps, words failed her at this point, but they had not failed Daisy. Rearing herself up to her full height Daisy fairly screamed at her younger sister, 'Why, you ungrateful little bitch! You was glad enough to be took to the picture 'ouse or to Seaforth Sands for the day, wasn't you? You held out your hand for any extrys goin', from whar' I recall, an' now you've got the cheek to go all prissy an' holy joe on me. *And* you're criticisin' me only daughter, sayin' she's no better'n she should be when she's done nothin' that I didn't do. An' wharrever I did I did *gladly* Lil, for the sake of me child.'

'Oh, sure,' Lily had said austerely. 'Well, no wonder your feller walked out on you, Dais, since as I 'member, you were bringin' in more money than you should've been right from the moment you left school. My, an' you've allus pretended it were him walkin' out on you for a younger woman, when all the time . . .'

' 'Course he walked out on me for a younger woman,' Daisy shrieked. 'I were a child bride, innocent . . .'

'Innocent my bleedin' foot! You was on the game, Daisy, an' well you know it. An' your precious daughter's the same. Why should I bandy words wi' you, eh? Jack said . . .'

'Oh aye, *Jack said, Jack said,*' Daisy mimicked savagely. 'It's never the fellers' fault in your book, is it, Lil? Why, my Mona's told me the number of times she's seen her Uncle Jack drivin' his tram real slow along Lime Street, whilst he eyes up the gals—an' her amongst 'em. Oh Jack's a saint, eh? Why, I could tell you . . .'

That had been the end so far as Lily was concerned. Describing the encounter to Jack she had admitted to flying across the short space which separated them and tugging out a considerable amount of Daisy's straggly, dye-streaked hair, whilst at the same time 'telling Daisy a thing or two'.

She had not elaborated, but Jack had seen the long scratch down one cheek and the incipient black eye. 'You were foolish to tek on a woman twice your size, queen,' he had said worriedly. 'She's hurt you. I've a good mind . . .'

'Hurt *me*? You should see her,' Lily had told him. 'Half her greasy, horrible hair's lyin' on the kitchen floor an' I had to scrub under me fingernails for hours to get her bleedin' skin out o' them.' She laughed grimly. 'That'll teach her to bad-mouth me husband, the best feller as ever lived.'

Jack had been touched by her faith in him, though none knew better than he how well justified that faith was. He had never looked at another woman since he and Lily had wed and what was more he was now so embarrassed over his niece's activities that he seldom turned his eyes from the roadway as he drove along Lime Street. 'Well, Lily luv, perhaps it's all been for the best,' he had said, taking his bruised and battered wife in his arms. 'At least you won't have to go rushin' round to Daisy's place wi' presents two or three times a month. And whiles we're on the subject, why *did* you feel you had to take her things?'

'I think it was because I felt guilty for not likin' her very much now she's a woman growed, even though she were good to me as a kid,' Lily said, her voice muffled against his chest. She was crying, too—he could feel her tears soaking into his thin shirt. 'I knew I should have liked her an' been grateful, but I just couldn't. So—so I give her presents, instead.'

Jack had nodded portentously. 'Thought so.

Well, flower, that's all at an end, I hope?'

Nod nod went Lily's head against his chest. 'I don't know as I'd *dare* go round Daisy's place agin,' she said with a rather watery giggle. 'I do hate quarrellin', our Jack, I'd rather steer clear in future.'

'Grand. Then good's come out of it, because I don't want our little Rosie mixin' wi' that Mona, an' I don't reckon Daisy'll be any keener'n you to be pals, after that quarrel. Now dry your eyes and blow your nose, and we'll get on wi' our own lives an' let Daisy an' her girl get on wi' theirs.'

So now, having raised the question of his niece again, Jack decided that it was best not to speculate. 'Mebbe she's workin' for a florist an' mebbe she ain't,' he said. 'But whichever, I reckon we're best to continue lettin' sleepin' dogs lie. Tomorrer, you tek Rosie round a couple o' florists an' she can see what she thinks. After all, she's goin' to continue at school for another couple o' years, come what may, an' you never know. In the meantime she may decide that teachin's just what she'd really like to do.'

He knew that Lily was still hopeful that Rose might change her mind and go for a teacher, but in his heart he doubted it very much. Rose was bright as a button, but she'd not be happy cooped up in a classroom when she could be out of doors. No, he agreed with Lily that she should continue her schooling and possibly go on after the convent to a business college, so that she could get an office job. And meanwhile the two of them ought to be able to keep Rose clear of Mona, particularly as the younger girl had very little time for the older.

So next day, despite the fact that the snow had

137

returned and with it, a nipping wind, Lily and Rose set off for the city centre, where they would enjoy themselves, Lily told her daughter, taking a good look at the dozens of florists in St John's Market and maybe get a spot of dinner at the Kardomah.

'There's Bees on Bold Street—they have lovely flowers,' Lily said as the two of them set off for the tram stop. 'They're worth a visit. An' . . . an' there's bound to be others what we'll come across.'

'If we go to the Kardomah we might as well pop into the Bon Marché,' Rose said slyly, knowing how her mother loved the shop. 'It's nice to have a wander round, Mam.'

'Right, we'll do that. And mebbe we'll nip into Cooper's an' get somethin' nice for your dad's tea,' Lily said comfortably. 'Poor Dad, he won't be sittin' at his ease sippin' tea at four, like we will, so we'll buy him somethin' really good.'

'An' there's a café on the second floor in Cooper's where we could have our cuppa,' Rose said hopefully. 'They have great cakes, too.'

Mother and daughter smiled conspiratorially at one another. They would have a lovely outing and enjoy, as much as anything, seeing Jack's face when they produced a treat for his tea.

*   *   *

Rose enjoyed St John's Market, but although she loved the flowers and thought the girls looked pretty in their smart overalls, she decided early on that this would not be the life for her. The customers were not always polite and the younger girls seemed just like skivvies to her. They were scarcely allowed to touch the flowers except under an older woman's instructions, and although the blooms smelled sweet most of them were greenhouse reared at this time of year and therefore very expensive, which meant that customers were few. What was more, they weren't particularly friendly to the shop assistants, giving their orders but not really being much interested in what was on show.

'But it'll be different when there's more flowers, more choice,' Lily said as they finished their tea. 'I know you thought the assistants didn't get much chance to handle the flowers, but I reckon you'd be makin' up bouquets an' bridal posies an' all sorts once the finer weather comes. Why, it won't be long before we're seein' the first snowdrops,' she added as they donned their outer clothes and headed reluctantly down the stairs once more. 'It'll soon be spring, you mark my words.'

'Oh, Mam, how can you say that?' Rose asked as they walked towards the street doors once more. 'We've got the worst of the winter to go ... all the winter term, in fact.'

'It cheers me up to think of spring,' Lily said, then stopped short as she pushed through the door into the chill of late afternoon. Outside, yellow fog swirled, thick with the scent of coal dust and river mud. 'Oh Lord, if there's one thing I hate it's a fog. I can't see across the street, never mind to the tram stop. There, an' I were goin' to suggest a walk up to Lewis's, but I think we'd better get ourselves home as soon as possible. It's thick enough now; just imagine what it'll be like be the time your dad comes home.'

'A pea-souper, I reckon,' Rose said gloomily. 'What'll we do, Mam? Go to the Pier Head? We'll have a good choice of trams down there. Oh, poor Dad, he's always late when it's foggy.' She seized her mother's arm and the two of them joined the jostling crowd on the pavement. 'Most folk'll be goin' home now the fog's down, so if we follow the crowd we'll probably end up at the Pier Head loops. What's for tea, Mam?'

'Well, I was goin' to have fried fish an' chips from Fred Morris, on Heyworth, bein' as how we've been on the razzle-dazzle all day. But seein' as the weather's turned bad on us and your dad'll be chilled to the bone, I think I'll make a stew. Warmed-up fish an' chips is no substitute for a good, hot meal, so we'll try for a tram which takes us up to Heyworth, then I can get stewin' meat at Sandon's an' veggies at Gaulton's. I like shoppin' on Heyworth, you always get good value, an' your dad dearly loves a nice stew.'

'Me an' all,' Rose said, licking her lips. They reached the loops and milled around with the others already waiting. Rose could hear the river sounds louder than the muffled traffic noises and somewhere a fog-horn boomed out its sad warning note. She took her mother's warm hand in hers and squeezed it, more to comfort herself than for Lily's sake. 'Won't be long now, Mam. A queue like this 'un means there's trams due quite soon.'

Rose was right, for within five minutes a tram approached, its bell ringing warningly because in a fog it was not possible to see the vehicles until they were almost upon you. Rose and her mother, used to the suddenness and the thickness of Liverpool fogs, had drawn their scarves up over their mouths and pulled their hats well down, but Rose spotted the tram's indicator board and gave a little crow of

140

triumph. 'It's a 31, that'll take us to Heyworth,' she said gratefully, for the cold was beginning to penetrate to the marrow of her bones, or so it felt, after the warmth of the shops. 'Come on, Mam, no point in hangin' back.'

Accordingly the two of them joined the pushing, shoving crowd of people trying to get aboard the 31 and presently Rose found herself crammed into the interior, with her mother right up at the far end whilst she herself was wedged between a small man who smelt of tobacco and kippers and an extremely large old lady, hung about with shopping bags and smelling strongly of onions.

'All aboard? Hold very tight, please,' the conductor shouted and began collecting fares, though there was scarcely room to move amongst the many standing passengers, or so one would have thought. But the conductor, used to the problem, managed to wriggle his way from one end of the vehicle to the other and mounted the stairs, shouting to the interior passengers the reminder that it was one pull on the strap to stop the tram and two to start it again when everyone who wanted to get off had disembarked.

'I ain't goin' to know when we reach Cabbage Hall, norrin this flamin' fog,' the old woman next to Rose remarked comfortably. 'Mind, I dare say someone'll tell me; folks usually does.'

'We're gettin' off on Heyworth, at Abbey Street,' Rose explained. 'Or we might get off at Hibbert, or Jefferson; it don't matter much. We've got shoppin' still to do, you see. I 'spect our mam'll tek a look in several shops before she buys.'

'Oh aye. I'm fond o' a bit o' shoppin' meself,' the woman said with considerable understatement

141

when you counted the bags, parcels and packages in her possession. 'But today I been gettin' stuff for me daughter. She writ me a list. I allus say there ain't no pleasure shoppin' from a list, but she jest don't see it. Now if I were shoppin' for meself I wou'n't go to all them posh shops on Ranny, I'd go along the Scottie, or Byrom, or even Heyworth. Oh aye, you can pick up a bargain like that, many's the time . . .'

The tram lurched to a stop and through the misted window Rose could see people surging eagerly forward. Several of them got on whilst the conductor took more fares and one, a slim girl who looked to be in her early twenties, was jostled close to Rose, apologising as the press of people pushed them together. 'I'm awful sorry, someone gave me ever such a shove and I've been footing it in the fog for what seems like hours. Did I hurt you?'

'No, I'm all right, I've got so many clothes on that bouncin' into me is like bouncin' into a football,' Rose said cheerfully. 'Why've you been walkin' in the fog, then? Mam an' me walked a good bit earlier, because I've been wonderin' whether I'd like to work in a flower shop, so we went an' took a look at some. But just about when the fog come down, I guess, we went into Cooper's for tea an' a cake. Were you shoppin', too?'

'No. Working.' The girl said briefly. She looked Rose consideringly up and down. 'So you're thinking of working in a flower shop! Well, it *might* be fun, of course, but I should think you'd be bored in a week. Still, you might really take to it I suppose.'

'I was beginning to see that it was pretty much like any other sort of shop work by the time we'd

142

done the first two or three shops,' Rose admitted. 'But it's so hard to find out what you would like to do when your mam an' dad just keep sayin' to stay on at school an' get educated. What do you do?'

'I'm a reporter on the *Echo*. I do all sorts, but today my first job was getting some copy for my fashion notes. I was interviewing the woman who's organising the mannequin parade at Lewis's in a couple of weeks, and then I went along to see another woman who's publishing a book of poems all about Liverpool. She lives down by the docks and I couldn't even *find* the house for the first half-hour, in this fog. Still, I'm finished for the day now, so I'm going to spend a nice evening with an old school friend. We'll have a cosy supper and then toast our toes by a decent fire and talk each other's heads off, I expect.'

'A reporter!' Rose said, much struck. 'You must be awful clever!'

The girl shrugged, then smiled mischievously at Rose. She was a pretty creature, with dark-red hair cut in a fashionable bob, reddish-brown eyes fringed with very dark lashes and a small, upturned nose, and when she smiled, a deep dimple appeared in one cheek. 'No, I'm not clever at all, just persistent. Oh, and I was good at compositions at school and wrote little pieces for the school magazine. I was lucky to get the job, though. Lots of girls fancy newspaper work these days, because they hope to get onto one of the glossies.'

'Yes, of course,' Rose said, wondering what on earth that might mean. 'I'm good at compositions, too, Sister's always readin' my stuff out. What's your name, then? I expect you'll be famous one day, and if I know your name I'll be able to say I met you when you worked on the *Echo*.'

'I'm Nancy Gregg, but I don't suppose I'll ever be famous, though you've a better chance in a newspaper office than in a florist's. What's your name, then?'

'Rose Ryder. Which school did you go to, Miss Gregg? Did they tell you to try for work on a newspaper? Only I'm at the convent school on Mount Pleasant and all they ever talk about is teachin', an' I don't want to be a teacher.'

Miss Gregg laughed. 'Typical! St Joseph's Select—my school—was just the same; all they could suggest was teaching, or staying at home and being a good wife to some chap. But I've an aunt in London who writes short stories and articles for the glossies and she said to try a newspaper first, so I did, and as I said, persistence paid off. Why, if I told you how hard I had to work to get the job it would put you off, but if you're really keen on writing, then get yourself trained as an office worker first off. Go on a business course and learn shorthand, typing, book-keeping, that sort of stuff. I had to, in the end, and I can tell you it's been useful. The reason that my boss sends me out on lots of stories is because of my first-class shorthand, so if you want to do my sort of work that's one good way to begin. Now I'd better start moving down towards the door or I'll get carried past my stop.'

'Oh, d'you live hereabouts then?' Rose said, very disappointed. 'I thought you'd be goin' a bit further than this.'

'I did tell you,' her new friend reminded her above the rattle and crash of the tram. 'I'm visiting a friend tonight, someone I was at school with.
144

Normally, I wouldn't be on the 31 at all, I'd be on the 10. I've a shared flat out at Prescott, because it's cheaper living out there than in the city, though it's a bit of a fag having to travel all that way night and morning. Still, at least it's on a tram route. I was determined not to live right out. The trams are so convenient and very much cheaper ...' Miss Gregg reached up and tugged on the strap. Despite the fog she seemed to know very well when the area she wanted came in view. 'Well, Miss Ryder, it's been interesting talking to you and I wish you the very best of luck in your future career. Stick to your guns and maybe you and I will work together one day. Good-evening.'

'Good-evening,' Rose said, wishing fervently that she could hop off the tram and question her new friend further. But at least she knew her name and where she worked. It would not be impossible to get in touch with her again.

The tram stopped and several people other than the young reporter surged towards the doors. Rose moved obediently up towards the front as her mother beckoned and they managed to find a fairly comfortable perch against the glass panel which separated the driver from his passengers.

'You all right, Rose?' her mother asked. 'Who was that gal, then? I saw you chattin' to her—pretty thing, weren't she?'

'Yes, and ever so friendly. She was tellin' me about her job ... she said she went to St Joseph's Select ... where's that, Mam?'

'Dunno, but the Sisters of Mercy teach there. It's rather posh, I think ... costs a deal, I dare say. Not that your fees are exactly cheap, but ... '

'Fares please! Move further down the car, ladies

145

and gents all! Now come along, madam, if you want to gerrof you've gorra move a bit faster'n that.'

The tram was stopping again and though the conductor's remark was good-natured, the lady so addressed was not. 'I can't see a bleedin' thing out there,' she said plaintively in a strong Irish accent. 'I don't know whether we're at the Landin' Stage or John o' Groats, an' there's no one willin' to say for sure, so naturally I'm lingerin', so I am. I don't want to find meself lost in weather like this.'

'We's on Shaw Street,' shouted a man who had just climbed aboard. 'Come on, missus, if it's Shaw you want.'

'All right, all right, I'm after getting' off, then,' the woman said hurriedly, beginning to push through the passengers again. 'Sorry, chuck, was that your toe?'

'No, it was me whole bleedin' foot,' the trodden-on one, a man in stained overalls sucking an ancient pipe, said cheerfully, 'Never mind, queen, there ain't room in 'ere to tell your arse from your elbow, lerralone a foot from the floor.' He grinned across at the conductor. 'If you get all them lot out there on, we'll sink widout a trace, like the good ole *Titanic.*'

'She hit an iceberg,' Rose piped up. 'Trams don't hit icebergs much.'

'Ah, anything's possible in a fog,' the conductor said genially, then turned to address his would-be passengers. 'Only five more inside ... full up on top. Sorry, mate, I'm full up now, I dussen't tek another soul else I'll gerra black mark on me time-sheet from the next inspector.'

'It's perishin' hangin' about in this bleeding' fog,' the disappointed passenger wailed as the conductor disengaged his clutching hand frin the pole and blew his whistle for the driver to start. 'When's the next one due, friend?'

'Any minute,' the conductor bawled cheerfully as the tram drew away. 'They'll be queuin' up down at the Loop any minute now.'

The tram lurched onwards, and Rose saw with some dismay the fog swirling, yellow and thick as phlegm, past the glass. Even the brightly-lit shop windows were no more than a blur and landmarks which were normally a part of every route were impossible to spot. But there is always someone aboard who recognises something.

'We're turnin' into Heyworth,' a man remarked. 'I'm gerrin' off here. Anyone else for Hibbert Street?'

Lily jogged Rose's arm. 'Come on, Rose, we might as well get down, it's handy for the butcher,' she said rather breathlessly. 'Follow that feller—he'll mek a way for us.'

And very soon they found themselves on the slippery wet pavement, with the street lamps' glow scarcely visible above their heads. Indeed, Rose found the greengrocer by walking slap-bang into his display of cabbages.

'I'll be glad when me shoppin's done,' Lily said as he poured potatoes, onions and carrots into three brown paper bags and pushed them into her string shopping carrier. 'Just Mr Sandon for the stewing meat an' we can make our way home.'

'Don't fog make everything wet!' Rose grumbled as the two of them, sharing the shopping, headed for home at last. 'That feller weren't so far out when he said the tram were like the *Titanic*. At least, I'm as wet as if I'd been paddlin' off Seaforth

147

Sands.'

'Clammy more'n wet,' her mother contributed, walking sturdily along, one arm hung about with shopping bags, the other linked in Rose's. 'An' we hardly talked about the flower shops at all! What did you think? Would you like to work in one, chuck?'

'I'm not too sure. I don't know as they're much different, really, from other shops,' Rose admitted. 'But I think mebbe you an' me dad are right when you say wait an' see what's on offer when I'm older. Mam, you know the girl I were talkin' to in the tram when we first got aboard? She's a reporter on the *Echo*. She said women can get real interestin' jobs on newspapers an' things like that. I've always liked writin' compositions, an' Sister Therese says I'm good at 'em. Mebbe I wouldn't mind workin' for a newspaper. Or . . . or a magazine, even. I do love readin' all the stories an' articles in me *Girl's Own*, so I guess I'd like writin' 'em too.'

'Oh Rosie, that 'ud be rare good,' Lily breathed, stopping in her tracks for a moment to stare at her daughter. 'All them magazines have women editors an' col-columnists an' so on. Oh, your dad an' me 'ud be so proud!'

'I'd like you an' me dad to be proud of me,' Rose admitted a little sheepishly. 'I allus knew, Mam, that I couldn't drive a tram, not really. So we'll talk about it tonight, shall we? When Dad comes home.'

'Oh, Rosie,' Lily said, beaming at her daughter through the thickening fog. 'Just wait till we tell your dad what you just telled me!'

*　　　*　　　*

148

Thinking about it later that day, Jack decided that he must have been brewing a chill ever since he had left for work, but it didn't really make itself felt until noon, when he and Georgie were eating their carryout. Then, because Georgie, shivering, remarked on the cold, Jack realised that far from feeling cold he was hot—extremely hot.

'Cold, la?' he said incredulously, mopping his brow with his large white handkerchief. 'I'm like a turkey half-way through the Christmas cookin'. I'm awright when I'm in me cab, but sittin' here wi' you I'm fair on fire.'

'You do look hot,' Georgie said after staring at him for a moment. 'I reckon you're in for one of them feverish colds, old son. Or mebbe the flu. There's a lorrof it about.'

'I never get colds or flu, Lily reckons the fresh air keeps me clear o' infections,' Jack said positively. 'No, I'm just warm, like.'

But by mid-afternoon he knew he was by no means all right. His nose was streaming, as were his eyes, his mouth seemed gummy and unpleasant, and he felt as though someone with a very large drum was beating it just behind his eyes. By the time the fog came down, indeed, he told Georgie he thought he ought to report sick. 'Because I ain't safe, not bein' able to see for the fog in one way an' through me flamin' eyes in another,' he explained. 'Besides, the timin's are all to hell 'cos o' the fog so they'll likely prefer us off an hour or so early to us havin' an accident. Though it go agin the grain to tek time off, when I've never done such a thing before,' he added. 'I feel as though I'm lettin' the company down.'

'Load o' nonsense,' Georgie said breezily. 'Look, we'll do the run out to the terminus, then I'll change the boards to "out of service" an' we'll head for the depot. You can't help bein' ill, old son, so don't worrit yourself about it.'

Which was how Jack found himself heading for home, on foot, a good deal earlier than he had expected to. As he walked slowly and increasingly unsteadily down the road, he became aware again of how very ill he felt. In fact, what with the fog and his increasing sickness, he scarcely knew whether he was heading for home or not. He decided to catch a tram but couldn't find a stop, finally realising groggily that he had probably turned a corner without realising it and was on a side road. Pulling himself together momentarily, he forced himself to stand still and listen for several moments, and even through the blanketing fog he heard sounds of people and traffic to his right, so when the opportunity came he turned towards the noise.

Soon he came to another road, upon which he could just about see the gleam of the tramlines, and after walking for what seemed like hours it suddenly occurred to him that far from getting busier and more populated, this road was growing quieter and lonelier as he walked. He must have turned in the wrong direction and be walking away from the city not towards it.

He wondered about turning round and retracing his steps, but he felt so ill. The fever was doing odd things to his sight, too. Houses wavered as though under water and the pavement undulated beneath his feet, whilst sounds were gradually receding. Even his footsteps were silent now, and he could no longer catch the faint roar of the traffic nor hear the drips and tricklings caused by the fog. Jack leaned against the wall of what he took to be a warehouse and stared around him. This road seemed to have been going on forever, he had been on the same pavement for a long time, or so it appeared. When he came to a corner, or a side road, instead of merely crossing it he would find the street name and orientate himself by it. God knows, being a tram driver teaches you to know your city streets, he thought thankfully. If he knew roughly where he was he could find his way to a tram stop and ask the conductor to put him down as near Cornwall Street as possible.

Accordingly, he walked on, slowly and stumblingly, but with more purpose. At one point he heaved his watch out of his pocket and gazed at its wavering face. It showed five minutes past seven, which was a nasty surprise. He had left the depot getting on for two hours ago and had he been walking in the right direction he would have been home by now. But he dared not turn round and retrace his steps until he had a fix on his present position, so he tucked the watch away, pulled his muffler up to cover his mouth and set off once more.

He found a street sign at last and knew, more or less, where he was. He had indeed been heading in the wrong direction but if he continued on until he came to the next road junction he would be back on a tram route. Because he would now be heading for the centre instead of away from it, he might not come across a group of people waiting for a tram because most folk were leaving the city at this time of night and heading for their homes in the suburbs, but he would certainly find one of the tram stops. He would stand by it—well, lean against it was likelier—and wait. There was bound to be a tram along soon, because at this time of night, with the huge crowds of would-be passengers, trams were frequent on all routes.

The trouble was, the fog was so thick! Looking upward now, Jack realised that even when standing directly under a lamp-post, all he could see of its light was the faintest of glows. Would he be able to recognise a tram stop sign or would be simply walk straight past it? He pulled out his handkerchief and blew resoundingly upon it and, for a moment, felt better. His head and even his ears cleared, though the faint buzzing that had troubled him for the best part of an hour was still there. And he realised that he should retrace his steps and head towards the city once more. He knew he was on a tram route and in order to get back to Everton he should be on the other side of the road.

Nevertheless, he stood very still for a moment, listening. Yes, that sounded very like a tram approaching right now—thank God! The driver was sounding his bell, the noise bouncing off the terraced houses on either side, which was good, Jack thought approvingly. Clearly, rescue was at hand, and since the sounds seemed to be coming from his right, he should hurry across the road and wave the driver down. If he stood on the very edge of the kerb . . .

He was half-way across the road, peering anxiously to his right through rheumy and fog-dazzled eyes, when the tram came. It arrived from his left, the driver concentrating on ringing his bell warningly and peering ahead. Jack, realising his mistake at the last minute, tried to hurry, leapt for the kerb, and somehow got entangled in his own feet and his long overcoat. He felt something hard clout him on the shoulder, then the world exploded into a thousand brilliantly-coloured stars, before darkness abruptly descended.

* * *

'He come out de fog, starin' in a wrong d'rection, but he was off de rails, headin' for de kerb, an' I thought no danger,' the driver wailed, climbing laboriously out of his seat and running towards the still figure half on and half off the pavement. The conductor, carrying a big electric torch, swung it across the silent, greatcoated figure. 'Oh my Gawd, I would ha' sworn I din't touch him!'

'Nor you did,' the conductor said comfortingly. 'I were hangin' out to see where we was, an' I seed everything. The poor bugger din't see us till the last minute—you know how confusin' fog can be for sounds, I reckon he thought we was comin' from t'other direction. Now, let's tek a look ... Gawd, it's old Ryder!'

'Who? I thought it were a uniform coat.' The driver bent over the man still sprawled across the pavement kerb. 'Aye, you're right, its Jack Ryder. Wonder what he were doin' here, walkin'? He's a fair way from home—he's from Everton, ain't he?'

'That's right. Look, ole feller, I'll go to the house here for help, you stay wi' him. I don't know as I'd dare to move him, not wi'out someone as knows a thing or two about first aid. He's given his head a rare hard bang, there's quite a bit o' blood.'

'Right you are,' the driver said. 'Pity we've no

one aboard, but ain't that always the way of it? I'll put me coat over him an' all, he feels mortal cold.' He looked nervously at his conductor. 'He ain't . . . he ain't *dead* is he, Claude?

'Not him,' the conductor said cheerfully, 'I'll be back before you know it.'

*   *   *

By eight o'clock the stew was cooked and Lily was extremely worried. She and Rose sat down and ate their own meal, but without much appetite. Jack should have been home an hour ago and although in a fog one could be held up for hours, he had not been on one of the longer routes and should, Lily felt, have made reasonable time. The trams were still running, though the timetables, she realised, would be in tatters. And folk would not be eager to leave their homes on such a night, so Jack should be back soon.

At nine o'clock there was a knock on the door. Lily jumped to her feet but Rose was quicker. She dashed across the hallway and tugged at the solid old front door. Swinging it back, she coughed as the fog surged in and then said uncertainly, 'Mr Brownlea? Is it you?'

'Aye, it's me, chuck,' the figure on the doorstep said through his scarf. 'I wondered if your dad would lend me his spirit level. I'm rehangin' our pantry door an' I'd like to gerrit straight.'

'I'm sure he would, but he's not home yet,' Rose said. She glanced uneasily over her shoulder, at the kitchen behind her where she knew her mother would be listening, hoping for news. 'He's awful late, Mr Brownlea. He should've been back a

154

couple of hours ago.'

'Aye, but fog's thicker'n pea-soup, it's more like blind scouse,' Mr Brownlea said and chuckled at his own joke. 'Your dad's probably got purron another route 'cos someone's gorra dose o' this flu that's going around, an' he's mekin' his way back home this very moment.'

'I dare say you're right,' Rose said, very relieved. 'I'm sorry about the spirit level, Mr Brownlea, but I don't know rightly where it's kept. I'll tell me dad though, an' I'm sure he'll fetch it out an' bring it round as soon as he's home.'

'Oh, no hurry tonight, queen,' Mr Brownlea assured her. 'Tomorrer will do. Now no more worryin'. Promise?'

Rose was about to reply, mendaciously, that she would not worry any more, when her mother came down the hallway and stood at her shoulder, answering for her. 'No, Mr Brownlea, we shan't worry no more, 'cos we're goin' to walk down to the depot an' see what's happenin', if he ain't home in the next thirty minutes,' she said quietly. 'I know my Jack, an if everything had been awright an' he was just goin' to be late he'd ha' let us know somehow. You're right, worryin's pointless, but action isn't, an' action it will be, very soon now.'

Rose turned and beamed at her mother. 'You're right, we'll both feel no end better if we *do* something. There's nothin' quite so horrible as standin' an' waitin'.'

So when Mr Brownlea had made his way back along the pavement to his own house, Lily and Rose heaved at the ropes which attached the airing rack to the kitchen ceiling and brought it down. A critical feel of their coats, scarves and gloves showed them to be, if not dry, at least a good deal drier than they had been earlier. Boots which had been carefully stuffed with scrumpled-up newspaper were likewise emptied, felt and pronounced wearable.

'We'll have a hot cuppa, then we'll wrap up warm an' leave for the depot,' Lily told her daughter. 'I'm not one to imagine things, but I'll feel a whole lot better when I see your dad for meself. It ain't like him, say what you will, to leave us worryin' in weather like this.'

For outside, the fog was thicker than ever. Richly yellow now and smelling of coal dust, industrial fug and the turgid reek of the river, it pressed against the windows as though it wanted to join them round the kitchen fire and when at last, fully dressed and with the hot tea drunk, they opened the back door, it flooded in like a river breaking its banks.

'I'll lock up because the spare key's always on the lintel in the privy, Jack knows that,' Lily said, suiting action to words. 'Now hang onto me arm, queen, an' we'll pur' our best feet foremost. Only we'll stick close to the houses, an' check at every street corner, an' if it gets too thick we'll just have to try to catch a tram.'

'Can't see the stops, nor can't they see us—the tram drivers, I mean,' Rose pointed out, clutching her mother's hand firmly. ' 'Sides, a long walk'll do us a power o' good. I'm that tired o' frowstin' in the kitchen, Mam. To be honest, I just want a sight of me dad, then I'll be grand.'

'Me too,' Lily sighed. They reached the corner of the street and turned into the main road. 'Eh, Jack'll gi' me the rough side of his tongue when he

156

sees you dragged out on a night like this, queen, but I dussen't leave you in the house alone. No, I reckon you're best wi' me.'

'I reckon so too,' Rose said loyally. 'Hello, Mam, someone's comin'. Best stand still till they're past— it might be me dad, it's a feller at any rate, I can hear a man's voice.'

The two moved to stand against the nearest house wall but the men were audible long before they became visible and Rose suddenly realised that they were talking about an accident of some sort. She tugged at her mother's arm. 'Mam, there's been some trouble . . . I wonder . . .'

' . . . couldn't ha' done a blind thing,' the voice was saying, the words echoing eerily around the small, compact houses. 'Me driver's always careful, you know that, Georgie, but he never touched him, only made him jump for the kerb to get out o' the way . . . an' he went down an . . .'

The two men loomed up beside Rose and her mother and promptly found themselves seized by Rose. 'Georgie! I—I mean Mr Allen—what's happened to me dad? He's not come home an' Mam an' me's awful worried.'

Georgie Allen cast a glance at the man with him, then turned back to Lily and her daughter. 'Rosie, Mrs Ryder, I'm glad we bumped into you—we was just headin' for Cornwall Street, me an' Mr Edwards here. Perhaps we'd best go back to your place . . . we don't want you hangin' around in this cold whiles we talk.'

Rose turned obediently for home but her mother was made of sterner stuff. 'No, Georgie,' she said sharply. 'Tell what you've got to tell, an' tell it quick. It's Jack, ain't it? He's hurt. Where is he? I
157

knew, when he din't come in for his meal that somethin' bad must ha' happened, only you keep hopin' . . . What's happened? Ah, dear God, don't tell me Jack's . . .'

'Jack's in hospital, Mrs Ryder,' Georgie said gently. 'He left off early, 'cos he seemed to be goin' down wi' either flu or a feverish cold, an' I got a replacement driver an' continued me work. But when I were clockin' off at the depot Mr Edwards here spotted me an' came over. He telled me Jack had had a bit of a knock in the street, an' that he'd been took to Mill Lane Hospital, that being the nearest. So we thought we'd come along an' tek you up there, bein' as how the fog's thrown everything into total confusion, an' there's no sayin' when the trams will be runnin' to time again.'

'A taxi! We'd better get a taxi,' Rose said wildly. Her mouth had gone dry at the mere mention of the word 'hospital' and her heart was pounding. 'Is—is he very bad, Mr Allen? Oh, me poor dad, me poor dad!'

'No use searchin' for a taxi in this, Rose,' Georgie Allen said kindly. 'You're better on your own two feet, where you can see pavement edges an' such. The trams have stopped now, too, so it's Shanks's pony for the lot of us. Mrs Ryder, this is Teddy Edwards, what fetched help for Jack. Teddy, this is Mrs Ryder, Jack's wife.'

Greetings were exchanged as they walked, for Georgie was clearly anxious to get them to hospital as soon as possible. 'Likely Jack'll be conscious by the time we reaches the ward,' he said. 'Why, once them doctors an' nurses get to work on him, he'll be right as ninepence in no time. Still, he'll be eager to see the pair o' you, so's he can reassure you both that he's awright.'

Georgie had a torch which he flashed occasionally, telling them, when he knew himself, what area of the city they had reached, but apart from that they simply continued on their way through the fog, scarcely speaking. Rose was aware of the tense urgency with which the two men hurried them along, though she did not remark on it, simply clinging to her mother's hand and praying in a muttered gabble beneath her breath that her dad would be all right, that they would arrive at the hospital and find him pale but grinning, teasing them for the worries.

'Here we are, ladies,' Georgie said at last. 'I'm to take you straight up; Sister said so. Are you comin', Ted, or will you wait down here?'

Mr Edwards elected to wait and the other three hurried along through quiet, shiny corridors until they reached the ward where Jack Ryder lay.

'He's in the third bed on the left,' the conductor told them as they slipped quietly in through the swing doors. 'If he's asleep you'd best not wake him. Go over there; I'll find the Sister or one of the nurses.'

Having pointed out the bed Georgie hurried away and the other two stole over. Jack lay on his back, his head wreathed in bandages. He looked grey and old and very stern, and despite herself, Rose felt her eyes filling with tears. She sniffed, then took a deep, steadying breath. She would not cry and distress her mother further, she would not! But Lily had pulled a stool from under the bed and sat herself down on it. She began, very gently, to stroke Jack's forehead and suddenly Rose felt that she should not be here, not now, watching her parents at such a private moment. She moved back a bit and glanced anxiously towards the doorway, where Georgie Allen had disappeared. Would he fetch a doctor as well as a nurse? Her dad looked so ill and strange, she wished that a doctor would come. But no one appeared and her father's eyes remained closed. Quietly, Rose found herself a stool and sat down on it. All round her, men in other beds slept, snored, mumbled in their sleep. Only her father, it seemed, lay so completely still.

*   *   *

Jack had only come round once after the accident when they began to work on his injuries. He was suffering from the most appalling headache, too bad to be called a headache really; it felt as though someone with a great trip-hammer had got into his head and was laying about him, striking delicate body parts with enormous force, indifferent to Jack's pain. But even in his anguish he had tried to ask where he was, what was happening, because in the back of his mind he knew that he must be overdue at home, that Lily would be worried. But all he could do was murmur disconnected words and phrases beneath his breath, and presently he plunged back into unconsciousness once more.

The second time he came round someone was stroking his face. Very gently, very tenderly, soft, familiar fingers caressed his cheek, smoothed round his brow, descended across the other cheek. For a moment even the terrible pain in his head seemed less all-embracing, so that he tried terribly hard to move, to get nearer the source of his comfort.

160

There was a lovely smell, too. Hyacinths? No, not exactly, it was more like a bluebell wood in May with the sun on it—and Jack hadn't smelled bluebells like that since he had been a small boy of nine or ten, staying with an old aunt in Ireland. She had lived on a farm and had enjoyed having a little city boy to visit as much as he had enjoyed visiting her. Remembering that magic time he tried to move his head on the pillow, but it was too difficult, and opening his eyes didn't help much. It was night, there were shadows round him, that was about all he knew.

After a bit, though, he realised that the soft buzzing hum that he was hearing wasn't just the awful noises in his ears which had haunted him most of the day. It was someone singing under their breath, a song that he loved, sung by a voice he trusted. He knew the song, and the words.

'The pale moon was rising above the green
      mountain,
The sun was declining beneath the blue sea,
When I strayed with my love to the pure crystal
      fountain
That stands in the beautiful vale of Tralee.'

A voice sang, a small, sweet little voice. Rosie's. Rosie, his own dear little daughter, his own Rose of Tralee. Which meant that Lily was here too, the woman who meant more to him than life itself. He heaved a deep breath and, with enormous effort, spoke. 'Lil? I'm sorry, my dear love. I didn't mean for to leave ye.'

He didn't know why he had said that; he wasn't leaving . . . was he? His head hurt terrible, to be

sure, and his eyes weren't seeing so good, but . . .
he wasn't leaving his lovely Lily, his dear little girl,
to manage without him? He could not, must not,
do that!

Panic struck him. He tried to sit himself up in
bed, or he thought he tried, though it had no result
whatsoever. But he shouted—only it came out as a
whisper—that they must come nearer, so he could
speak to them.

He felt their presence, though he could scarcely
make them out, shadows amongst shadows. But it
didn't matter because suddenly a little strength
returned to him. He said, 'Tek care of each other.
Rosie, help your mam. Lil, dearest, tek care o' the
kid. I'm—I'm not feelin' so good.'

There was a choked sob and he felt a small hand
slide gently into his. He tried to grasp it but could
not. No strength, no strength. He, who had once
been so strong that he had lifted a poor dead horse
out of the path of his tram, could now not
command sufficient strength to hold his little
daughter's hand.

'Dad? It's Rosie. Can you hear me?'

He tried to nod and made a buzzing murmur of
assent. He thought she understood.

'Dad, I'm goin' to stay on at school an' try for
work on a newspaper! How about that, eh? Mam
says you'll be proud of me if I do that, really
proud.'

He made another little buzz. He wanted to tell
her he was proud of her anyway, proud of his
bright, sweet-natured little tomboy of a daughter,
even if she settled for working on a market stall or
in some obscure little shop. But now he heard
Lily's voice and smelled the most wonderful

162

scent . . . lilies and roses, he thought confusedly, the flowers of paradise, lilies and roses.

'Jack, we loves you so much, Rosie an' me. You won't leave us? You'll stay wi' us, get better, come home to us?'

He wished he could answer, but the darkness was deepening even as the smell of the flowers became stronger and stronger . . . and suddenly the scene changed and he was in a meadow, the grass studded with flowers and the scent of them heavenly. He saw that the sky above was blue and the sunshine fell golden upon the scene then he was jumping to his feet, running through the grass which swished gently against his bare, sunburned legs and shouting with pleasure as he ran. He was ten again; his aunt's dog, Floss, ran ahead of him, her brown eyes beaming with pleasure because she had someone to play with at last. He ran and ran, and felt the wind of his going in his soft, child's hair, and shouted with delight because, presently, he would go back to the farm for tea and see his gentle mother waiting for him.

For a moment the thought of his mother disturbed him; where was Lil? Where was Rose? For a fleeting second he was back in the dark, with the two of them pressing close to him, the tears of one falling on his forehead, of the other on the back of his hand. It's all right, he wanted to tell them, we'll be all right, all of us. You have each other and I have . . .

But he was back in the meadow, picking daisies and buttercups, the lingering sadness disappearing as the bouquet of summer flowers grew between his small, rather dirty hands.

'Come on, queen, we can't do any more here,' Lily said quietly, taking her daughter's hand as they made their way out of the ward and down the stairs. 'Internal injuries the doctor said ... there was nothin' they could do.' She heaved a sigh and squeezed Rosie's small hand. 'Oh, Rosie, I don't know how to go on without your dad and that's the truth.'

'I don't know either, Mam,' Rose said sadly, her face white and tearstreaked. 'But Dad's gone to heaven, hasn't he? Because everyone loved him, and he was so ... so *good*, me Dad. Why, just before he ... he went he was smilin', I saw him smile. He knew we was there, lovin' him, didn't he? He heard me sing "Rose of Tralee", I'm sure he did.'

'That's right, Rosie,' Lily said steadily. 'He knew we loved him all right, same as we know he loved us. An' it's love that matters, in the end.

Outside, the fog had disappeared completely. It was a different world from the one they had left hours earlier. The sky was clear and black, the stars very large and bright against the darkness. The moon swung high above them, turning the city into a black-and-silver enchantment. Rose peered upwards, trying to see whether heaven was visible on such a night, whether the soul of her father, flying towards the moon, could be glimpsed, just for a second or two.

But she knew she was just being foolish, because she could not, right now, bear to be sensible. To tell herself that she would never see her father again, that she and her mother were on their own

164

now. Earlier, she had been so happy, longing for him to come home so that she might surprise him with her news. Now, the bright day had died on her; triumph, excitement, pride in herself had all died with him. Now all she wanted was to go home and go to bed ... and wake up to find it was a horrible nightmare, that he was alive and well, and whistling as he shaved in his bedroom, before the cracked little mirror which hung above the washstand. 'Mam? It—it still don't seem real, somehow. I don't want it to seem real.'

There was a long silence, then her mother's voice came, low and choked with tears: 'Nor do I, queen. Nor do I.'

CHAPTER FIVE

1930 Dublin

It was a gloriously warm day in June and Colm, Caitlin and their parents were sitting down to a good tea. Sean had come home for a whole week and Eileen and Caitlin were incandescent with joy, Colm less so, because Sean had made it plain from the moment he stepped into the house that he thought it was time his son came over the water with him, to earn 'dacint money', as he put it.

Colm had been with Switzer's for six months, his mother having heard that the job was coming up, so that he had applied in good time and got it, he knew, partly because his mother herself was such a reliable worker. He was a delivery boy and helped out in various departments when he was not actually delivering, and so far had found the work enjoyable and better paid than his previous job, for a small butcher could not afford the wages that a very large department store could.

So Colm had no desire meekly to go off to England with his father and had prepared a series of arguments which, he had hoped, would convince Sean that Dublin was the best place for his son. Fortunately, Colm thought, helping himself from the round dish of pink shrimps in the middle of the table and beginning to head and tail them, his mother was of the same opinion and right now he was not having to say a word, because she was saying them all for him.

'Sean, me love, it's grand, it is, havin' the boy here to keep an eye on Caitlin when I'm busy, to give a hand in the house. And there's his money comin' in regular ... oh, I know you send yours regular too, acushla, but sometimes the post's not all that good and we have a bit of wait, so we do. And then there's no sayin' where he might end up now he's workin' at Switzer's. They're a good company and he's already caught attention— several of the floor walkers started as delivery boys, just t'ink of our boy a floor walker! And there's little Nell, a smart girl if ever there was one and very fond of our Colm ... very fond. She'll put in a good word for him, you can be sure of that, when there's a job goin' that he might do. So you see our boy's got a future at Switzer's, whereas if he came over the water wit' you, who can tell whether he'd ever rise higher'n navvyin'?'

This would have been dangerous talk six months before, but not now. Now, Sean was driving a great thing called an earth-mover—well, that was what he called it—digging out the beginning of the Mersey Tunnel and earning, as he pointed out, very good money indeed.

So, having listened to his wife, Sean scooped more shrimps onto his plate and took a thick slice of bread and butter. Sighing, he glanced across the table at Colm. 'Well, if you're content to do that sort o' work, son, I suppose there's nothin' I can say. But to be stuck indoors . . .'

'I'm not, not yet,' Colm said quickly. He was a delivery boy most of the time and hoped that once he was old enough Switzer's would promote him to driving, or at least being driver's mate, on the big wagon which carried furniture and other large items. He had no desire to be a floor walker, despite his mother's fond hopes, and thought that he would be as desperate as his father would be over such a stuffy, confining career. The floor walkers wore dark suits and stiff white collars and gloves, and strolled gently round their departments chiding the assistants or giving the customers lordly advice. Their hair—when they had any—was Brylcreemed flat to their bony skulls and their fingernails were short and white. As a race, all the delivery boys hated them . . . but it would not do to say so to Mammy. She revered floor walkers and could see no higher calling for a son of hers. 'I'm out most o' time Daddy, not stuck in the shop at all at all. But I don't think I'd be right for floor walkin' Mammy. Me daddy's right, I'm not an indoor feller, I like to be out an' about. Indeed I'd like to drive the big furniture wagon, so I would.'

'You never know,' his mammy said immediately. 'If you stick wit' Switzer's you just never know. It 'ud be a grand job drivin' the wagon, an' the money

167

would be good, too. More bread an' butter, Sean?'

'Yes, please,' his father said, having cleared his plate of both shrimps and bread and butter whilst his wife and son talked. 'These shrimps are prime, so they are. Did you an' Caitlin catch them all yourselves?'

'I got most of 'em,' Caitlin said importantly. 'Colm was too busy wit' that stupid Nell MacThomas. He was showin' her how to skim stones—as if she cared!'

Colm turned a reproachful glance on his small sister. She was a cheeky young wan if you liked— she should have been grateful to be took to the seaside by himself and Nell, when they would so much have preferred to be alone. But he did not intend to take such a remark from Caitlin without fighting back, not he! 'Sure an' your opinion's carved in stone is it, then?' he said scornfully. 'The sort of opinion that folks t'ink worth listenin' to? An' you a gorl as goes around wit' Cracky Fry, an' t'inks he's the cat's pyjamas? I could say a t'ing or two about Cracky if I'd a mind, but I wouldn't demean meself.'

Caitlin snorted. 'Cracky may be a bit rough, but he's me friend, so mind your tongue, Colm O'Neill. An' I tell you one t'ing, he's more fun on a beach than that Nell MacThomas!'

Seeing the scarlet in her cheeks, Colm felt ashamed of himself. Cracky Fry was a skinny, underfed urchin of about twelve, one of a huge family, who had taken to hanging around with Caitlin lately. He was always dirty and in rags, and his arms and legs were covered with flea bites, but for all Colm knew he might be a decent enough feller and anyway, it was silly to draw comparisons

168

between his friendship with Nell and Caitlin's with Cracky. So he reached across the table and rumpled his sister's hair affectionately. 'Sure an' you're right, a pal is a pal, an' no one can gainsay that. Will you pass me the loaf?'

Caitlin, mollified, said she was sorry she'd been nasty about Nell. 'For she's pretty, I'll grant you,' she said magnanimously. 'I dare say she's awright really, Colly.'

Colm grinned at her and went on with his tea whilst his thoughts returned happily to Nell. She was a real catch and he just loved her. Though whether that was how Nell felt he did not truly know, for Nell, bless her, liked a bit of company and had shown no more favour to himself that she had to other young gentlemen who had asked her out. There had been Tim Docherty in Gents' Outfitting and Ralph Meyers from Hardware, and they were only the ones that he, Colm, knew about. But Nell was beautiful and sweet, and he was head over heels in love with her, so he had to prove himself the better man, did he not? Tim was a gadabout, had taken several girls from the store dancing or to the flicks, and Ralph was a dull dog, always neatly dressed and well groomed but with no conversation and no get up and go, either. It wouldn't take Colm long to show Nell that he was worthy of her, and once he had done that he was sure pretty little Miss MacThomas would give the other fellers the go-by and concentrate on him.

'She's a real little lady, is Nell,' his mother said anxiously now. 'She's very well thought-of, so she is. Of course they aren't serious yet, but . . .'

She left the sentence unfinished, not sure, Colm supposed, whether his having a young lady would tempt his father to let him stay in Dublin or not. Colm knew it wasn't Nell's charms that his mother had in mind so much as how lonely she would be in the city without her son. Having a husband who was absent for more than eleven months out of the twelve was bad enough, but having a son over the water too ... well, it didn't bear thinking about. And now that he was almost a man, she relied on him heavily not only to keep an eye on Caitlin but in a thousand different ways.

'Hmm,' Sean said. He folded a slice of buttered bread and took a big semicircular bite out of it. 'Well, it's up to you, of course, young feller, but when I was your age I'd have wanted a bit of adventure, so I would. I've a good landlady in a dacint house, we're well fed, the place is clean ...'

'Give him another year or two, see how's he's progressin' wit' Switzer's,' his mother pleaded. 'No point in movin' the boy when he's happy where he is—an' doin' well.'

'It was only a suggestion, alanna,' Sean pointed out gently. 'You mek more of it than I'd intended. Now come on, tell me what'll we be doin' tomorrer?'

'Seaside—more shrimps,' Caitlin squeaked. 'You'll come wit' us, won't you, Colm?'

'Can't,' Colm said briefly. 'Haven't been wit' the firm long enough to take a proper hollier. I'll come on Sunday, though.'

That was a big concession, because Sunday was the only day he could tempt Nell into a proper day out and he knew, grinding his teeth at the thought, that either Tim or Ralph would jump in if he failed to suggest a suitable outing. Briefly, as he finished off his tea and reached for the fruit-cake, he wondered whether a family trip to the seaside might tempt Nell, then decided hastily that it would not. Nell wore the latest fashions and had her hair first shingled, then permanently waved. It was the colour of waving corn and her eyes were as blue as the skies over that waving corn, but she was not overfond of country pursuits and the day at the seaside, with Caitlin in tow, had not been an unqualified success. He had spent most of it, he remembered, in promising Miss MacThomas that they would go to the cinema that evening, and that he would purchase, for her delectation and delight, one of the specially splendid boxes of Switzer's chocolates for them to share.

'What are you doin' this evenin', Colm?' his father enquired, more out of politeness than interest, Colm supposed. 'I t'ought we might take a stroll in Phoenix Park an' listen to the band. You comin' along?'

'Can't. I'm taking Nell to the Pillar on O'Connell Street,' Colm said briefly. 'I promised.'

'He's bought choccies,' Caitlin said enviously. 'A big box.'

'I hope your young lady isn't a gold-digger, now,' Sean said, only half-jokingly. 'I never could afford chocolates when me an' your mammy went to the flicks, but you never minded, did you, Eileen? A quarter of a pound of aniseed balls between the two of us suited us fine, eh alanna?'

'It did so,' Eileen admitted. 'But times change, Sean. Nowadays the girls expect more, so they do.'

'Well, I hope the fellers don't,' Sean said, giving his son a knowing look. 'Because even the biggest box of chocolates won't buy more than a few kisses from a dacint kind of a girl.'

171

Colm grinned sheepishly. 'It's makin' up to her for takin' Caitlin to the beach wit' us I am,' he admitted. 'Besides, Nell's a smart city lass, she doesn't usually get took to the seaside. So now I'm makin' me smart move, an' the choccies an' the flickers . . . an' a seat in the back row.'

His mother pursed her lips in pretended disapproval, but Sean grinned, then stood up and slapped him on the shoulder. 'You'll do, young feller,' he said. 'Now go an' put on your best, so's you don't disgrace the name of O'Neill, an' your mammy an' your sister an' meself will clear this lot away an' get ready for our own evening. But don't be too late back, because we'll expect a progress report, Mammy an' meself.'

Colm, immensely relieved at the friendly, teasing tone his father was adopting, replied in kind and decided that he would try to have a quiet word with the daddy some time. It wasn't that he wouldn't have liked to go over the water with the ould feller, there was a part of him which would have enjoyed the adventure just as much as Sean had supposed he would. But he knew his mammy and the young wan would miss him something cruel . . . and he was that hopeful of getting Nell MacThomas to agree to be his girl. His daddy would surely understand that whilst there was a chance of getting Nell to take him seriously and agree to drop all the other lads he'd not go gadding off anywhere?

Accordingly, he went up to his room, changed into his one and only best suit and tie, Brylcreemed his hair with the very last little smear in the jar, pinched some of his mammy's lavender water which he rubbed cruelly into his newly-shaven chin, and at last set off for Goldenbridge, because Nell lived, unfortunately, on the other side of the city from himself, in a neat little house with a square of garden before and another behind. Her father worked at the brewery, in the offices, and was clearly a person of some importance, though he seldom did more than grunt at Colm in a rather threatening way. Colm had tried chatting to him whilst he waited for Nell to appear, but Mr MacThomas, it seemed, did not chat lightly.

This evening, Colm was hopeful that Nell might be ready when he arrived, so he did not hurry himself and got to the MacThomas house at the hour appointed instead of thirty or forty minutes early.

Nell wasn't ready, exactly, but he didn't have to run the gauntlet of her father's grunts this evening; her mother took him through into the kitchen, explaining that Mr MacThomas had a friend in the front room. She was a very pretty woman, rather like her daughter to look at, but she wasn't easy to know, like his own mammy. She talked to him to be sure, but in a rather cool, offhand way which meant that most of his replies were mumbled and embarrassed, so it was with real pleasure that, a mere five minutes after being ushered into the kitchen, he heard Nell's light step on the stair. Mindful of his manners, Colm got hurriedly to his feet and stared towards the kitchen door. He was just in time.

Nell pushed it open and smiled at him as though there was no other feller she would rather have been with, which was enough to make him forget her grunting father and rather offhand mother. 'Colm, how smart you look. Where's you takin' me?'

'Where *are* you taking me, if you please,' Mrs MacThomas said sharply, causing Colm to give her a surprised glance. So far as he could recall he had never promised to take Mrs MacThomas anywhere—what was she on about?

But Nell took the reprimand in her stride. 'Sorry, Mother, but I was speakin' to Colm, you know. Well, Colm? I know it's the flicks, but which picture house? And what's on?'

Colm always took girls to the Tivoli on Francis Street, but he knew better than to suggest such a venue to Miss MacThomas. He had indeed done so, before he realised how very superior she was, but she had made it plain that she did not intend to spend an evening in what she rudely condemned as a 'common fleapit'. Accordingly, he said with some pride, 'Oh, the Pillar of course! An' they're showin' a romance, wit' Mary Pickford. Will that suit you?'

'A romance!' Nell breathed. She held out her light coat so that Colm could help her into it. 'Oh, I do love a nice romance. An' Mary Pickford! She's the most beautiful of 'em all. What did you say, Mother?'

Colm had distinctly heard the older woman mutter something as soon as the words 'a romance' had passed his lips but now she said, 'Nothing, my dear. Off you go then and don't be late. Don't bring my daughter home late, Mr O'Neill.'

'We'll catch a tram, Mrs MacThomas,' Colm said eagerly. 'There's always a tram when the flicks comes out. Don't worry, I'll tek good care of her.'

'See you later, Mother,' Nell said as they went out of the back door. 'Don't worry if we're a bit late, though. You know how crowded the last tram

174

gets. And it's a nice night; walkin' wouldn't be so terrible.'

Colm was about to say, loyally, that he would not dream of letting her walk when she dug him in the ribs with a sharp elbow and hustled him out of the house and across the tiny back garden to the small wooden gate. As they started along the back lane, heading for the main road, she said sharply, 'I've no doubt we'll be back in good time, Colm, but I'm not a child any longer and me mammy must learn that I'll please meself as to the time I get in. Come along now, we don't want to miss the beginnin'. Where's the chocolates?'

'Here,' Colm said, producing the box from his raincoat pocket. 'They're all soft centres; you said you liked them the best.'

'I do,' Nell said. 'An' we'll have ices in the interval.'

' 'Course,' Colm said loftily, reflecting that he would have to borrow from his mammy for the rest of the week. Still, it was worth it to get Nell in the dark beside him . . . and in the back row! And, he hoped, in a good mood when primed with chocolates and ice-creams. But time would tell, time would tell. Proprietorially, he took her elbow to steer her across the road and to his delight she leaned a little against him. 'We're goin to have a lovely evenin',' she announced. 'When shall we open the chocolates, Colm?'

'As soon as you please. Right now, if you like,' Colm said recklessly. He only hoped she wouldn't eat them all up by the time they arrived at the picture house. 'Will we get a tram at this stop?'

'All right. And we'll open the chocolates when we get on the tram,' Nell said. She hugged his arm.

'Oh, I do love the flickers, Colm! We're goin' to have a great time!'

And Colm, watching her gobbling chocolates on the tram, thought rather apprehensively that if he could continue to afford it he would try to see that his pretty Nell had lots of chocolates and lots of trips to the picture house. He was almost sure, now, that she must have serious intentions towards him. After all, a girl who was wooed with chocolates and seats at a posh cinema would surely respond by . . . by . . .

Colm dreamed of kisses and cuddles, and of a future which contained Nell as his acknowledged girl, and decided he could do without carry-outs for a few weeks. He wondered about doing another job in his spare time to earn more cash—but what spare time? Switzer's employed him from eight in the morning until eight at night, though he did get Sundays off.

'Colm? Do have one . . . they're delicious.'

Colm, eyeing the shrinking chocolates, said tactfully that chocolate always made him thirsty, so it did, and refrained from indulging.

'It makes me thirsty, too,' Nell said. She helped herself to another. 'But if we have ices in the interval . . .'

Colm decided not to bother with an ice for himself. Not if they wanted to catch a tram home, that was. But what did it matter? Once Nell was his girl, they would have to sort out the chocolate and ice-cream situation, but in Colm's experience girls realised that a feller had to live and didn't demand too much of him once they were acknowledged to be going steady. It was just in the early stages of a courtship, whilst you were 'makin' an impression',

176

that you needed to lash out all your cash on special treats.

'Last one,' Nell said, taking it out of its little paper cup and tucking it into one rosy cheek. 'Never mind, I dare say there'll be some more for sale in the foyer.'

'I expect so,' Colm said rather gloomily. 'But we don't want to miss the beginnin', do we?'

* * *

Much later that night, foot-slogging it across Dublin from Goldengate to his own home, Colm felt so happy that he could have burst into song—did, in fact, whistle piercingly until it occurred to him that not everyone wanted to hear a whistler just before midnight, when they were snugged down in bed.

He had been richly rewarded for his generosity. Nell had kissed, cuddled, snuggled—in fact, her enthusiasm had been so great that Colm had feared an usherette with a waving torch might well get the wrong idea and turn them out—until he was hot as fire and filled with an urge to fight her battles, slay dragons on her account and generally to be her champion.

Even when they came out of the picture house she had been loving. They had walked slowly to the tram stop, his arm round her waist, her head on his shoulder, and talked of the film, of the following day, of other people at Switzer's.

'Will you come dancin' wit me, Saturday evenin'?' Colm asked at last as they got down off the crowded tram and walked with delicious slowness towards her home. 'There's all sorts of places we could go—I know you didn't much enjoy the beach the other day, but . . .'

'I want to be with *you*, not your family,' Nell crooned. 'Let's go round the back an' have a cuddle, shall we? We can stop out in the lane, where the privy'll hide us from the house.'

Colm was all for it, but wondered aloud what would happen if her mother or father happened to pop out into the yard for the usual purpose and saw them hiding round the back of the privy.

Nell, however, had informed him that he was worrying unnecessarily. 'They'll be gone to bed,' she assured him. 'I'd ask you in, so I would, but the mammy 'ud come down if she heard your step. She's so *suspicious*, Colm—as if I'd misbehave, an' me her own daughter!'

She had not exactly misbehaved in the quiet little back alley behind the privy, but she had done a lot of clutching and kissing and a certain amount of moaning. Colm, striding out through the cool darkness, told himself stoutly that he had enjoyed every minute, of course he had, but he'd been mortal afraid that someone would hear, that a voice would shout at him, that Nell would be wrenched from his arms by an indignant parent.

It had not happened, though, and at last Nell had torn herself away from him and gone indoors, promising to see him at work tomorrow to arrange their next outing.

And now he was planning it, for wasn't it plain as the nose on your face that he'd made a great hit with her? No girl would do all that cooing and cuddling and canoodling, particularly a nice girl like Nell, unless she intended going steady with a feller.

So when at last he got into his bed, and wound his alarm clock and pulled the covers over his head, it was with the pleasant sensation of having done pretty well, by and large. Soon Nell would be his acknowledged young lady and his father would see that it was quite impossible to part the young lovers, and he and Nell would save their money and soon it would be a white wedding, a little house . . .

Colm went happily to sleep.

*   *   *

Next day, of course, he was up betimes. Polishing his shoes, singing softly, making porridge for himself and Caitlin, because his parents would be up later and would probably have a proper cooked breakfast.

Caitlin needn't have got up because she was on school holidays, but she had. She came into the kitchen looking frowsty and unbrushed, and began hacking away at the loaf. 'I'm makin' your carry-out, amn't I?' She asked in an injured tone when he wondered what the dickens she thought she was doing to that loaf. 'Mammy's havin' a lie-in, so she is, so I thought I'd come an' do it for you, Colly.'

'Well, thanks, Cait,' Colm said, touched by his sister's thoughtfulness. 'But a couple o' slices wit' some cheese between 'em will suit me just fine. Don't cut no more.'

'An' Mammy said you was to have an apple,' Caitlin said, mercifully leaving the torn and lopsided loaf alone and turning her attention to the pantry. 'An' some o' the gur cake, too.'

'Grand. Thanks, colleen,' Colm said again. 'Put it in me box then an' I'll be off. Got a deal to do

179

today.'

Caitlin sniffed. 'You mean you're goin' to go chasin' after that stupid girl,' she said. 'I don't know what you see in that Nell MacThomas, she's stuck up, an' stupid, an' . . .'

'We're goin' steady, Cait,' Colm said warningly. 'She's me young lady, so don't you go bein' rude about her. Anyway, you'll love her when you get to know her as well as I do.'

Caitlin sniffed again. 'Shan't,' she declared roundly. 'I like jolly girls who run on the sand and play in the sea, not them who squeak when a wave comes up the beach and keep askin' to "tek a wee look at the shops", the way your Miss MacThomas did.'

'Can't discuss it now, Cait,' Colm said diplomatically, grabbing his carry-out. 'See you tonight . . . oh, and have a nice day now.'

But leaving his small sister ladling herself out more porridge, he forgot her as soon as she was out of his sight. All he could think about was Nell—his Nell!

*   *   *

He arrived at Switzer's just as the cleaning women were leaving, and made his way first to the basement with the other delivery boys and then, as soon as he could, up to the main shop floors. It was too early for customers to be wanting his services yet, but he would do odd jobs, run errands and so on until the time came for the first deliveries. Accordingly, he made his way up to Hats, Gloves and Accessories, where Nell worked, and was soon busy carrying boxes from the store, so that the staff

180

could replace items which had been sold the previous day.

He looked round hopefully, of course, but of Nell there was no sign and he had just resigned himself to the fact that she, too, must have been sent off on an errand to another department when he noticed that the end changing cubicle still had its curtains drawn across instead of being looped back. And what was more, there was someone inside—and it could not be a customer since at this hour the floor was given over to staff, all making last-minute preparations for the day ahead.

Colm walked over to the cubicle, then hesitated. Suppose Nell was inside, changing a laddered stocking, for instance, for a new one? He ought, perhaps, to knock, but how could one knock on a curtain? If he just took a peep . . .

To think was to act. Colm lifted the curtain a tiny way from the wall and peered though the gap.

*   *   *

The sight that met his eyes chilled his marrow to the bone. There was Nell—*his* Nell—apparently struggling in the arms of the floor walker, Mr Molloy!

Colm had never liked Mr Molloy, who was a sneering sort of man, with thick black hair set in uniform waves across his narrow skull and a high, superior voice. But on the other hand he had never considered Mr Molloy a man at all, thinking him more like one of the wax models with which Switzer's decorated their windows. What was more he was *old*, probably as old as forty, and ugly as well, with his long white face and fleshy red mouth

181

beneath a horrid little moustache.

But now it was clear he was being all too masculine and not in the least like one of the unoffending wax models. Sweat glistening on his dome-like forehead and his hands, grasping Nell's upper arms, were large, hairy and workmanlike.

Astonishment kept Colm still for perhaps two seconds, then indignation, fury and even jealousy flooded in, causing him to bound across the cubicle and grab Mr Molloy by the shoulder, swinging him violently against the free-standing mirror, which, in its turn, cannoned into the wall.

'What the hell d'you t'ink you're doin'?' Colm gasped, as Mr Molloy, now very red in the face, swung round to face him, gobbling like a turkey cock. 'That's my young lady you're—you're maulin' like a floosie, Molloy!' He had never expected to address the floor walker in such terms, but then he had never dreamed of finding him in such a compromising position. Now, with one hand still on the older man's shoulder, he measured up the distance between his own clenched fist and Mr Molloy's long, spadeshaped chin. 'Take your choice . . . hands off or a biff which you'll not forget in a hurry.'

Nell gave a stifled shriek and Mr Molloy hastily took his hands from her shoulders. 'There's no need for talk like that, young O'Neill,' he said breathlessly. 'Get out of here at once or you'll find yourself on the street wit'out a character, I swear it. As for Miss MacThomas, if she wishes to make any sort of a complaint . . .'

'I don't, sir, indeed I don't,' Nell squeaked. She scowled at Colm. 'Mr Molloy was kindly gettin' a smut from me eye, so he was, when you burst in, shoutin'. I think, Mr O'Neill, that you'd best apologise to Mr Molloy for what you've been sayin'.'

'Apologise?' gasped Colm. 'Nell, alanna, I saw you strugglin' . . .'

'You did no such thing,' Nell snapped. Her cheeks were fiery red and her eyes flashed with what looked like real indignation. 'Haven't I just told you Mr Molloy was takin' a smut from me eye, an' me in real pain with the feel of it?'

'And what right have you got, O'Neill, to interfere between meself and this young lady?' Mr Molloy said, clearly gaining confidence from Nell's attitude. 'What's she to you? Eh?'

'She—she's me young lady . . . we're walkin' out,' Colm stammered. 'Isn't that so, Nell?'

'No, it is not,' Nell said firmly. 'As if I'd take up with a delivery boy!'

'So you'd best apologise and I'll see if I can forget what's happened today,' Mr Molloy said smoothly. He flattened down his hair with both hands and turned towards Colm. 'Because if I hear one more word from you on the subject, young feller-me-lad, it'll be your cards, I promise you that.'

Colm must have looked positively dumbstruck for Nell suddenly giggled. 'Oh, run along, laddy,' she said dismissively. 'An' in future, don't interfere with your betters.'

Colm turned away, then back, feeling the good, cleansing heat of true rage burning within him. He would not let the nasty little slut have the last word, not he! 'Me betters?' he said scornfully. 'Well, I've learned one lesson this mornin', so I have, and it's not that either of you are me betters. You're

183

nothin' but a flirt, Nell MacThomas, an' your *friend* is just a dorty ould man, so put that in your pipe an' smoke it.'

He turned away just as Mr Molloy came at him, a fist upraised. Colm guessed that the older man meant to push him or shoulder him out of the cubicle, or something of that sort, but he did not give him the chance to do more than take a couple of steps. His young fist slammed into that long, blue-shadowed jaw and Mr Molloy thumped, like a felled ox, into the pale-pink carpet of the changing cubicle.

For a moment there was a stunned silence, then Colm swung round to face Nell, certain that now she would not be afraid to admit that Mr Molloy's attentions had not been welcome, for surely it had been fear which had caused her to turn against him, the feller who had taken her out only the night before.

But Nell was bending over Mr Molloy, shaking his shoulder, all but crying. 'What have you done, Colm O'Neill?' she shouted. 'Oh, poor Mr Molloy—just you get help, or I'm goin' to tell everyone in Switzer's that you attacked him for no reason at all at all!'

'But Nell ... he was carryin' on wit' you, an' you're me gorl,' Colm said, his voice low and bewildered. 'Why only last night ...'

'Last night? A bit o' fun an' you start thinkin' you're someone special,' Nell said sneeringly. 'Oh, I do believe you've killed him stone dead, so I do.'

'He's movin'. He were only dazed, like,' Colm said. 'Nell, I t'ought ...'

But Nell was pulling and heaving at Mr Molloy to get him in a sitting position, crooning softly the
184

while, 'You're all right, sir, so y'are! Come on now, sit yourself up straight, you'll be right as rain in two minutes . . . lean on me, sir, lean on your Nell.'

Colm about-turned and left the cubicle. He walked through the department in a daze of disbelief. That his Nell could turn on him like that! But surely she would see reason when she realised Mr Molloy was not badly hurt? He ought to report the older man.

He would do nothing immediately. He would let tempers cool, then try to see Nell by herself so that they could work out what best to do, for she would not want, any longer, to work close to Mr Molloy.

Colm went back to his own department and was given orders to take parcels to various parts of Dublin. He set off on a round which meant he would not be back in the store until lunch-time. I'll ask Nell to come out with me so's we can eat our carry-out together, he planned. Then we'll talk through the whole miserable business and see what's best to do.

*   *   *

But by lunch-time Colm was walking the streets of Dublin with his cards in his pocket and despair in his heart. What a cheap little jade Nell had turned out to be. She and Mr Molloy had dreamed up a fine story between them, in which the only vestige of truth was that he had punched the older man on the jaw and put him out for the count on the changing-cubicle floor. According to Nell, it had been he, Colm O'Neill, who had been pestering her there with unwanted kisses, when Mr Molloy, attracted by her distressing cries, had come to her

185

rescue. And what had Colm done when Miss MacThomas had been wrested from his grasp? He had gone berserk, refusing to listen to Mr Molloy's gentle reprimand, and had hit his superior, knocking him down and rendering him unconscious.

The Head of Department had told Colm crisply that not only would he leave the store forthwith, without claiming any of the wages due to him, but he would do so without a reference. 'Young fellers who behave so bad don't get references from *this* firm,' he had said, glaring coldly at poor Colm across the big, polished mahogany desk. 'Your mammy will be much distressed, since it was she who persuaded us to employ you, but that you must explain to her yourself. You're lucky, so you are, that Mr Molloy has decided not to take you to court for assault. Miss MacThomas urged him not to do so, to be sure, but it was his own generosity which carried the most weight. Indeed, you have reason to be grateful to the gentleman, because we ourselves could have prosecuted you for causing an affray, but Mr Molloy said being sacked without a character would be sufficient punishment.'

By now, Colm knew better than to try to defend himself. He did say, 'What were other members of the staff doin' whiles I were layin' waste in the changin' cubicle, sir?' only to be told, not gently, that they had been unaware of the fracas since it was first thing in the morning and they were all at the opposite end of the room, setting out their wares for the day.

'But no doubt if called upon to give evidence against you, they would remember seeing you both entering and leaving the cubicle . . . and would also remember poor Mr Molloy staggering out of there, with a black bruise on his chin, some two or three minutes later,' the Head of Department said frostily. 'Now go, O'Neill.'

Colm had left and now he walked along Grafton Street, deprived even of the bicycle, since that was Switzer's property, wondering rather desperately what on earth he should do. It would be useless to try to pretend to his parents that he was still in work. For one thing, his mother would be back at Switzer's the following week and would soon be told, if not the truth, at least the version that was going around, and for another, he had always been straight both with the mammy and the daddy and did not intend to change now.

He was sure, however, that his mother would believe his version of the story, and knew with equal certainty that Caitlin would, too. She had never liked Nell, never trusted her and, being a loyal little sister, would accept his word on what had happened in that changing cubicle without a moment's hesitation. But his father was another story. Daddy doesn't know me so well for one thing, Colm reminded himself, and he doesn't know Mr Molloy at all. But surely he'll believe me when I tell him what really happened?

Aw, janey, but it'll ruin his holiday, having me on his hands all the time and no money coming in.

There was nothing he could do about it but try his best to get a job in the meantime, so he could at least show that he had alternative employment. And where would a strong and sturdy eighteen-year-old find work in Dublin at a time when such strong, healthy young men were eight a penny and jobs were so hard to find?

Still, there must be something. Delivery boys were always wanted. But not, of course, those who had been sacked from Switzer's for bad behaviour without a character.

Slowly beginning to realise the predicament he was in, Colm continued, morosely, to pace the streets.

*   *   *

'Well, lad, it's not the end of the world! Aren't we after findin' a silver linin' to every cloud, then? I wanted you to come over the water wit' me, to find yourself a well-paid job, and hasn't Switzer's played right into our hands, like? No one over there is goin' to ask whether you've socked a floor walker on the chin, are they? They'll know you're my lad, so you're reliable, an' they'll see for themselves that you're strong. What d'you say?'

Caitlin, sitting at the table eating rice pudding, stared from her father to her brother as the daddy spoke. She had finally taken it in that there was nothing they could do to help poor Colm over the dreadful calumny which that wicked Nell and horrible Mr Molloy had put upon him and now, she could see, there was equally little they could do to prevent Colm being carried over the water by their daddy. It was even fair, she acknowledged it, that he should have Colm's company, for did not she and the mammy have each other, as well as all their friends here in Dublin? But she had listened when Daddy was explaining to Mammy that almost the only recreation for a man on his own in the big city of Liverpool was the drink now, and wasn't he eager to keep away from pubs and the sort of bad
188

company that spent all their spare time drinking? So it would be a big help to the daddy if he and Colm were together.

Nevertheless, she knew that she and Mammy would miss Colm dreadfully, and wished there were some way that the wicked Mr Molloy and the wickeder Miss MacThomas could be brought to book for their sins. Then and only then would Colm be able to go back to his job in Switzer's, where he had been so happy. But Colm was answering his father now, so Caitlin, still spooning rice pudding, listened. Would Colm simply give in and agree to go over the water with the daddy? Or would he come up with some brilliant idea so that he would be able to stay?

'You're in the right of it, Daddy,' Colm was saying, far less morosely than might have been expected. 'Sure an' me faith in women has reached rock-bottom, so it has, for wasn't I convinced that Nell was fond o' me? And didn't she turn me over to the enemy, so to speak, and dive into the arms of that ugly ould feller wit'out a t'ought for meself?'

'She's a wicked girl, indeed she is,' Eileen said mournfully, putting her pudding spoon down in her empty dish. 'I never t'ought it of her . . . a liar is bad enough but to deliberately get me innocent son into trouble . . . I tell you, Miss MacThomas had better rue the day she lied about me son, for there's them as know me for an honest woman and I shan't hesitate to tell the trut' an' why should I not? Oh yes, Nell MacThomas will be known for the lyin' little whore she is be the end of the week.'

'What's a whore?' Caitlin asked, when no one said anything. 'Is it another word for a liar, mammy?'

189

'It's a nasty word, a word I never would have used but that I'm so upset,' Eileen said quickly. 'Oh, Caitlin, alanna, 'tis a wicked ould world, an' the sooner you know it the better.'

'Well, mammy, if you can tell folk the trut' of it, why must Colm go over the water wit' me daddy?' Caitlin asked composedly, stowing away the word 'whore' in the back of her mind for future investigation, for if it didn't mean 'liar', then what exactly did it mean? 'For there's the trut' about Mr Molloy too—why should you leave him out, when it was as much his fault—more—that our Colm got his cards?'

'Mr Molloy's a powerful man, though an outrageous wicked one,' her mother said. 'Still, never fear, the word'll go round about him, too. But the bosses, they don't listen to what ordinary folk say. We'll mebbe reach a stage or two above Miss MacThomas so that she's known to the staff for a liar with a wicked tongue, but a floor walker— well, I don't reckon we can do much there, save to make sure that the ordinary folk know that he's lied for his own advantage. And that everyone knows he's not above havin' a bit o' slap an' tickle wit' one of the shop assistants,' she added thoughtfully. 'He's a married man ... yes, mebbe Mr Molloy will regret the day he lied about me son an' all.'

'But it won't get our Colm his job back,' Sean said. He reached for his mug of tea and took a long draught. 'Never fear, alanna, your brother may feel uneasy about leavin' home, but he'll soon settle down in Liverpool. There's friendly folk there, an' plenty of entertainment for a man an' his son, an' pretty girls ...'

190

'Pretty girls? You've never said nothin' about pretty girls before,' Eileen said with pretended indignation. 'The last t'ing I want is for me only son to take up wit' an English girl.'

'Most of 'ems Irish livin' in Liverpool,' Sean assured them. 'Their grans an' grandas came over at the time o' the great famine an' stayed on. Oh, our Colm will do very well in Liverpool ... I've dacint lodgings, so I have, wit' a good sort o' woman ... an' you needn't worry yourself over her, Eileen me dote, for she's not a young woman. No, pushin' seventy is Mrs Caldicott ... an' she'll mek him as welcome as she's always made me. Shall you be after cuttin' that cake now, alanna? I can't wait to sink me teeth into it!'

*   *   *

That evening, whilst her elders talked over Colm's future, Caitlin went over to Cracky's tenement. He lived at the very top of a tall and tottery building, with a great many brothers and sisters, a good-natured, rather feckless father and a thin, wispy little mother who had once, Caitlin knew, been remarkably pretty. But now she was worn down by the wickedness of Cracky and by the good-natured indifference of her husband, who liked a quiet life and would not get one, he said frankly, if he interfered with his youngest son.

It was a pity, Caitlin considered, that Cracky was such a bad boy. Not just naughty or high-spirited, but downright bad. He stole from market stalls and from any shop that didn't guard against him, he knocked at doors and ran away, threw stones at passing carriers, jeered at girls—other than

191

Caitlin—and always denied all wrongdoing, not being above blaming anyone handy for his sins.

Caitlin could not count the various wickednesses into which he had dragged her. Not reluctantly, but sometimes ignorantly. When autumn came, all the chisellers took themselves off into the countryside around Dublin and boxed the fox in the orchards. Only Cracky raided the orchards with a 'borrowed' cart and sold the subsequent mound of apples in the nearest market. Only Cracky mitched off school whenever it suited him to do so, in order to sell his ill-gotten gains or simply to enjoy himself. Lately he had taken to wriggling through the small downstairs windows at night in order steal anything which he could lay his hands on and, though he only attacked the big houses, Caitlin believed her brother, who had said that Cracky would end up in the Joy for his sins and then, perhaps, he would realise that crime truly did not pay.

But Caitlin liked Cracky and knew he would never get her into more trouble than she could cope with. The problem was, his parents never told him off and when he wanted, or needed, something or other, expected him to provide it for himself. So he did and got an undeserved name, Caitlin thought, for being a bad lot.

Certainly the Brothers who taught him had a low opinion of their pupil. 'Born to be hanged, so y'are,' Father O'Halloran said, applying the stick to whatever part of Cracky he could get at, for Cracky had never yet stood still to be beaten. 'If we have any more complains of ye, young Fry, I promise ye'll not live to be old.'

A fat lot Cracky cared! So now he had another good reason for bunking off school and didn't

192

hesitate to use it. He frequently invited Caitlin to share his expeditions during school hours, but so far she had declined. Her mother was not as easygoing as his and would very likely beat her to a pulp if she missed school. Besides, Mammy would never expect her to provide food for the family or a new pair of shoes for herself, so she had no reason to steal.

But right now she wanted Cracky for a discussion and speedily found him. He had tied a rope to the arms of a lamp-post and was selling a dozen swings for a farden, and not doing too badly out of it. No one could get you up in the air like Cracky could, because most chisellers would be afraid you'd break your neck if they swung you round at that speed. But Cracky never considered things like that and was making a mint. Not, admittedly, of fardens, but he was reaping a couple of bites of apple, a length of good string, a chunk of soda bread and so on. He would end up richer in one way or another, Caitlin knew. 'Hey, Cracky,' she called, cantering along the pavement and skidding to a breathless stop beneath his chosen lamp-post. 'You know that girl I was tellin' you about, that girl me brother Colm likes?'

Cracky gave his present customer an especially vigorous twirl, causing the child to shriek with excitement, then raised his brows at her. 'That one what works at Switzer's? Aye, I 'member her. What's she done?'

'She's give our Colm the go-by an' got him the sack an' all,' Caitlin said indignantly. 'He's goin' across the water wit' me daddy an' it's all her fault, so it is.'

'Wait on. Last push, Jimmy,' Cracky said, giving the child an almighty heave which caused the rope to swing out almost level with the lamp. 'I've just about finished here. When the lampie comes round he gets in a rare takin' if I'm still givin' rides. Us'll go a walk, shall us?'

'Oh yes, then we can talk about doin' somethin' to that Nell girl,' Caitlin said with deplorable viciousness. 'It'll break me mammy's heart, havin' both me daddy an' me brother off over the water. I know where she lives an' who her daddy is, so mebbe, if we t'ink real hard, we can work out some way to mek her sorry.'

'Aye, we could do that,' Cracky agreed, shinning up the lamp-post and untying his rope. He wound it over his shoulder and dropped lightly onto the pavement beside her. 'But that won't stop your Colm goin' over the water, will it?'

'It might, if he got his job back,' Caitlin argued. 'We can have a go at the floor walker what give him the sack an' all. He's a hateful man, Mammy says as well as Colm.'

'A floor walker! I reckon we might do somethin' really good to a floor walker,' Cracky said. 'I niver could stand them stuck-up eejits, it 'ud do the feller good to tek him down a peg or two. Now you tell me all you know about the whole business as we walk an' we'll see what we can do.

CHAPTER SIX

May 1931 Liverpool

Rose came out of the house in St Domingo's Vale and brushed under the lilac tree which stooped low over the path, releasing its perfume in a great, heady gust. A year ago today, she reminded herself, we were moving into this house, hoping against hope that we were doing the right thing, worrying that we might have spent Dad's insurance money unwisely . . . and yet it's been a good year, the best since he died.

Rose could not look back on that first year after her father's death without an inward shudder. They had been so unhappy, so bewildered! Jack's death had been so sudden, so totally unexpected, that neither Rose nor her mother could believe that he had gone, that he would never come whistling into the house again to ask about their day and tell them about his, and this lent a nightmarish unreality, it seemed to Rose, to everything they did.

But oddly, the arranging of the funeral had helped, firstly by taking up a great deal of time and energy, then by involving them with relatives, friends and colleagues, though their first impulse had been to hide away and hug their grief and disbelief. The funeral itself, when it took place, helped even more. Seeing Jack, pale and stern in his coffin, brought home to them as nothing else could have done, that he had really gone, truly left them, and the great throng of people attending at St Anthony's church and coming back to the little house in Cornwall Street afterwards, showed how sincerely Jack had been both loved and respected.

In the crush, Rose thought that her mother had not realised that Aunt Daisy was not present, but she was wrong. Lily had noticed and was both astonished and hurt by her sister's absence, though she whispered to her daughter in a quiet moment that at least her niece Mona had come to her

195

uncle's funeral. 'Try to have a word wi' her, find out why Daisy hasn't come,' she hissed, presiding over a barrel of beer, for she had been determined that the wake should not be a miserable, mean affair, and Jack had been well insured. 'Me own sister . . . I can't for the life of me understand why she should be so cruel.'

So Rose had approached Mona, who was looking very smart in a black coat and skirt with a little black hat tilted over one eye, and the cousins had kissed spontaneously, and Mona had hung on to Rose for several moments. 'Where's your mam, Mona?' Rose asked as soon as she decently could. 'My mam's ever so upset she isn't here. She does know Dad's gone, I suppose?'

'I dunno,' Mona admitted. 'Look, you're goin' to be needin' more glasses . . . shall us go an' wash a few up? It'll be easier to talk.'

So the two girls had made their way into the kitchen, where they found a great many neighbours already tackling the huge pile of dirty crockery and glasses. 'Come up to me room for a moment,' Rose hissed. 'We'll be alone there.' So up the stairs the two of them hurried and sat down on Rose's small bed.

Mona had turned to her immediately. 'I'm sorry about Uncle Jack,' she said, and Rose saw her cousin's big blue eyes were swimming with tears. 'He were ever so kind to me when I were a kid. And your mam was good to me an' all . . . it's only these last few years things have been difficult, but you an' me's always been pals, wouldn't you say?'

'Ye-es, only you're a good bit older'n me,' Rose said guardedly. She had been aware that her parents wanted to keep her away from Mona,

196

though she had no idea why. Indeed, now she supposed it was because Aunty Daisy had not liked her father, though she could not understand why. 'But Mam and Auntie was always such good pals; then something happened . . .'

'Yes, they had a real old fight over something,' Mona said with some relish. 'Just like me an' Mam did, I'spect. But look, I come up here to explain, then I want to have a word wi' Aunt Lil, so we'd berra gerra move on. Me mam's took in a feller, Rosie love, an' him an' me don't see eye to eye. In fact, I moved out a few weeks back, only I don't like me lodgings much. So you see, I don't even know if me mam knows Uncle Jack's dead.'

'I see,' Rose said thoughtfully. 'Well, that'll cheer Mam up for sure, Mona, 'cos she were mortal upset that her own sister could treat her so bad. But if Aunt Daisy doesn't know . . . Only how couldn't she? She'd have heard, surely?'

'She's moved out of Prince Edwin Lane,' Mona explained. 'The feller said no point in keepin' two houses goin', so they both moved into his'n, and that's way out Fazackerley way. You put a notice in the Echo, but if she don't gerra paper out there . . .'

'You mek Fazackerley sound like the end of the world,' Rose said, laughing for the first time in what felt like years. 'I daresay they have newspapers there just like we do here.'

Mona laughed too. 'Aye, but I don't like to think of me mam missin' Uncle Jack's funeral on purpose, queen. I'd much rather think she didn't know what had happened. Any road, that's what I'll tell your mam if she asks.'

'Fair enough,' Rose said, standing up, 'We'd better be gettin' back downstairs or me mam'll

197

wonder what we're up to.'

'Sure,' Mona said, getting up as well. 'But wait a sec, Rosie, I want to ask you somethin'.'

'Fire away, only be quick. Folk is beginnin' to leave.'

'Right. Do you think . . . is there any chance Aunt Lil might be wantin' a lodger? Only I'd sooner be far live wi' you an' your mam than wi' strangers, an' if she's short of a bob or two I'm in a fairly decent job . . . What d'you think?'

'You'd have to share my room,' Rose said, beginning to smile. 'Did you think o' that, now? Two of us in the one room, an' it's only small. But if you wouldn't mind, I wouldn't either. Only I don't think Mam's got round to wonderin' where the money's goin' to come from yet.'

This proved to be no more than the truth. Later that evening, when everyone had gone, Rose had asked her mother about taking Mona in, but Lily was clearly undecided. The two of them were tidying away the last remnants of the wake and now Lily wrapped half a loaf in paper and popped it into the big, old-fashioned bread-crock which had belonged to Rose's grandmother. 'Oh queen, I don't know. She's me niece and she told me she'd got a decent job . . . I asked her straight out if she hung round Lime Street with them other gals still an' she swore on the Bible that she don't do that no more, but sharin' a house—and a small one, like this—well, it takes some thinkin' about. She's right about money, though, so we'll have a word wi' Mr Exeter. He's dealing with the insurance money, and a pension and that.'

'I wouldn't mind sharin' wi' our Mona,' Rose had admitted. 'She's all right. But I'll be leaving school now, Mam. You can't afford to go on paying fees now.'

'You're not leavin' school unless things are desperate,' Lily had said firmly. 'There'll be money, all right, Mr Exeter said so—mebbe you can go to college after all, queen.'

But of course it had not been possible. She had been forced to leave the convent before Jack's affairs had been sorted out since ordinary day-to-day expenses soon began to prove more than her mother could manage and school fees were out of the question. It had not helped, either, when her mother's solicitor, Mr Exeter, had called them in to his office over six months after Jack's death and told them that Mr Ryder's savings and insurance money would not be enough to last them for the rest of their lives.

'You are young and your husband died young, Mrs Ryder, so the money cannot be expected to cover all your expenses for the many years that, I trust, lie ahead of you,' he had said kindly. 'Like everything else, however, money can be made to work for you and not simply allowed to lie idle in a bank account. Unless, of course, you intend to start a job of work?'

'I don't think I could earn a great deal, Mr Exeter,' Lily said in a low voice. 'I was only a shop assistant before . . . before we wed, Jack and me.'

'I see. And your daughter is . . . ?'

'Just fifteen, Mr. Exeter. I'd hoped to finish her education—it's what her father would ha' wanted—but it may not be possible.'

'I don't think the sort of wages Miss Ryder could earn would be a great deal of use to you, Mrs Ryder,' Mr Exeter said. 'But I don't want you to dip into your capital, even for school fees; it is most definitely not to be recommended. However, I have a suggestion to make. Have you ever considered taking lodgers, Mrs Ryder? There is sufficient money to pay a deposit on a neat house and set yourself up with the right sort of furniture, bedding . . .'

His voice had trailed away under Lily's doubtful glance. 'Well, I'm a fair cook, Mr Exeter,' she said after a short pause. 'And running a house is something I *do* understand. But there's no room for a lodger, not unless . . .'

'I quite understand that your present home would be unsuitable,' Mr Exeter said quickly. 'But if you were to put the money into bricks and mortar . . .'

'Buy a *house*?' Lily squeaked. 'Or did you mean rent?'

'I meant buy, with a mortgage, because that way your outgoings would be small and your income sufficiently generous, if you bought a large enough house, to cover your expenses and leave you with a nice little sum every week,' he said soothingly. 'The house would be yours when the mortgage was paid off and meanwhile you would be able to complete your daughter's education, if necessary in evening classes, which would mean that when she did find employment, it would be commensurately more rewarding.'

Lily and Rose both shot him enquiring glances. Rose was glad to see that her mother, too, was puzzled by the expression.

'If Miss Ryder completes her education then her salary would be larger,' Mr Exeter said patiently. 'But perhaps the thought of running a lodging house is repugnant to you?'

'No-oo,' Lily had said thoughtfully, having given the matter some thought. 'Tell me more, Mr Exeter.'

So Mr Exeter had told them more and mother and daughter had left his office rather excited and no longer quite so cast down. It had been, Rose remembered now, a summery September day with a brisk, salt-laden wind blowing off the Mersey and the streets crowded with girls in bright cotton dresses and young men in shirtsleeves. She and her mother had gone into a Lyons and had tea, discussing with great excitement what sort of house would suit them, and in which neighbourhoods they should start their search.

It had not been that easy, of course. In fact there had been times, during the following six months, that they had very nearly despaired of ever finding anywhere which they could afford. If they had not insisted on a nice neighbourhood they could have had a fair choice, but Lily was firm on that point; she did not want a good house in a run-down district, because that would not attract the sort of lodgers she needed. As house after house proved to be too small, too large, needing too much money spending, or simply far too expensive, the Ryders' hope had begun to fade. Rose had left school and had taken an ill-paid job in a small dress shop. It was run by a mean, sharp-tongued woman who believed in getting her moneysworth out of her staff and many a night Rose toiled until ten or eleven o'clock, to return home to drop exhausted into bed, only to be awoken by the alarm clock going off at seven so that she could be back in the shop by eight-thirty.

And then, out of the blue, Mr Exeter had come round to tell them that he knew of a house for sale on St Domingo Vale which would, he thought, be within their means. 'Oh, but that's such a good neighbourhood,' Lily had said wistfully. 'We'll never manage to buy there, Mr Exeter. We've gone after property around there before, but it's always been far to pricey for us.'

'This one's different,' Mr Exeter said. He named the price, which seemed far too reasonable for St Domingo Vale to the Ryders. 'There's—there's a reason for the price being lower than is usually asked, but I'll leave you to find that out for yourselves. Mrs Ryder, please go and look at the house—and take your daughter with you. I really think it may be the answer.'

So Lily and Rose had set out on Sunday morning, and had taken one look at the house and fallen in love. They had expected to find it badly run down, in desperate need of repair, but though the paintwork was flaking and the gate had a hinge missing, it looked neither run down nor in need of expensive alterations.

As for the small front garden . . .

'It's got a tree, and lovely big flower beds, an' bushes . . .' Lily said. 'Oh Rosie, I've always wanted a garden real bad! An' it's so tall an'—an' gracious, somehow. I just hope Mr Exeter didn't get the price muddled in some way.

So they trod up the neatly bricked path, taking in the gleaming windows, the brass knocker on the door and the redded steps. Lily knocked at the door which was answered by a middle-aged woman with black hair parted in the middle and pulled back into a bun on the nape of her neck. She was dark-eyed and olive-skinned and as soon as she spoke Rose realised she was a foreigner, though her English was excellent. 'Mrs Ryder?' she said. 'I am Mrs Kibble, Mr Exeter told me to expect you. Do come in and I will show you around.'

And throughout the examination of the house, Rose could see Lily's eyes growing brighter, her smile more natural. It was wonderful, just what they had been searching for, with a pleasant hall, a parlour, a big kitchen and a tiny scullery on the ground floor, two large bedrooms and a bathroom on the first floor, three bedrooms on the second floor and an attic up a rickety flight of stairs with two tiny windows set in the tiles and marvellous views.

Having gone all over the house, Mrs Kibble took them down to a large, warm kitchen where she sat them down at a table and provided them with cups of tea and a selection of biscuits. Rose had crunched a biscuit immediately but she could see that her mother was too nervous to do more than sip her tea. Then Lily put the cup down, took a deep breath, and asked the inevitable question: 'Why are you selling up, Mrs Kibble? And—and why's the house so cheap? 'Cos it's—it's awful nice, and very large.'

Mrs Kibble stared at her. 'But did they not tell you? This is not my house, Mrs Ryder. It belonged to a dear friend. And the reason that it's not been taken before is, I believe, because I live in the basement flat. I am, dear Mrs Ryder, what they call a sitting tenant, which means I cannot be evicted.'

'Well, I don't see nothing wrong wi' that arrangement,' Lily said, after a pause. 'Did Mr Exeter tell you that I'm going to take lodgers? An'

I take it you pay rent?'

'Yes, but it is a very small rent,' Mrs Kibble said almost apologetically. 'The previous owner, Mrs Rivers, was a dear friend, you see, and I helped her in the house as sort of part payment I suppose you could say. Not everyone cares for that sort of arrangement.'

'Well, I should like it very much,' Lily said calmly. 'Would—would you be prepared to continue the arrangement, Mrs Kibble? My daughter is working so won't be able to give me much help around the house so I had intended to get someone in for a few hours each week once the house is full. Why should it not be you?'

From that moment on, the Ryders felt that their future, if not secure, was at least settled for them. Rose gave up her job to help Lily with arrangements and purchases and exactly a year ago today, they had moved in. Rose could still remember the thrill of it, the excitement of possession.

It had lasted, too, in that they both loved the house and Lily and Mrs Kibble got on extremely well. Together, the three of them cleaned down, stripped wallpaper and hung new, painted skirting boards, picture rails and window frames. Mrs Rivers' furniture was to be sold at auction, so Mrs Kibble and Lily went along and bought the few items they could afford and that they thought would be suitable for a lodging house. Rose wrote advertisements and put them up in the local shops and took them in to the *Echo* offices so that they might also appear in the newspaper. Curtain material was bought and made up on Lily's old sewing machine, carpets were frowned over and linoleum replaced that which was too worn, Lily felt, for respectability.

The first few months had been a trial, however, because Lily was so nervous about taking in men who she did not know that they did not manage to fill all their rooms. And they had so many rooms! A front parlour, a living-kitchen and a scullery on the ground floor, as well as a small cloakroom leading off the hall where Lily kept her cleaning materials, two big bedrooms on the first floor, with the bathroom over-looking the back garden, three decent-sized rooms on the second floor, and a big attic room, which was Rose's special domain. Many a decent-looking man turned up at the door, only to be regretfully turned away by Mrs Ryder, because the chap could not immediately satisfy her with impeccable references.

What kept them afloat were commercial travellers, who tended to stay only a night or two, which meant, of course, that the Ryders' house was never full, and they never knew with any real certainty what the next few weeks would bring in the way of rent-money.

And then there were men who thought they would settle down in the pleasant house in the Vale, where Mrs Ryder made them so welcome and proved to be an excellent cook.

'It's being a seaport,' Lily said gloomily, when nice, respectable Mr Truelove gave in his notice only ten days after nice, respectable Mr Ellis had done exactly the same thing. 'They've had enough of the sea and think they'll settle down ashore, but they don't, they're too used to moving on. What we need, Rosie, is someone who'll stay with us for a year or two.'

'Well, I'm going to get a job, Mam,' Rose had told her mother a couple of months earlier. 'I've done a year of night classes and me shorthand and typing is really good. I know the money was poor when I was in the gown shop, but now I'll get an office job an' that'll be better paid, you see.'

So she had done just as she had said; gone out and got herself a job. She was the junior in a block of offices on Dale Street and was expected to arrive there before the rest of the staff so that she could open up. She was happy there, settled, and although her salary was not marvellous, it was almost twice that which she had been getting in the gown shop.

But the lodger situation was still not as good as it might have been, and she had just written out yet another advertisement, which she would take round to the *Echo* offices in her lunch-break. But you had better get a move on, girl, she chided herself as she turned into Tythebarn Street and glanced up at the clock above the chemist's shop. You don't want to be late and give Mr Lionel a bad impression or he might decide he'd rather have an office boy than you after all!

'Rosie! Hey, Rosie!'

Rose turned round. Behind her, her cousin Mona waved frantically, then cupped her hands round her mouth and shouted, 'Come back here a mo, our Rosie. I've got suffin' to tell you.'

Rose had not seen her cousin since they had moved into the new house, and it seemed rude to continue on her way now, particularly as she was well aware that Mona wanted to lodge with them. 'What is it?' she asked therefore, as soon as Mona was close enough to hear.

'I'm on me way to work, Mona, and I daren't be late.'

Mona cast her eyes up to heaven and heaved a sigh, but grabbed her cousin's arm as she did so. 'I won't keep you a moment, queen, it's just that I've gorra lodger for you . . . as well as me, I mean.'

'Oh? Well, look, chuck, you'd best go round an' have a word wi' me mam, she's the one . . .'

Lily had told Rose that she suspected Mona of taking money from men and Rose, though she thought this very shocking, was still rather fond of her cousin and did not want to get involved in a terrible row, like the one Mam had had with Aunt Daisy. Besides, Mona had said she was out of all that, or so Mam had said, so why not take her at her word and let her lodge with them? It would be fun, she thought, but knew she could not go against her mother. If Lily's mind was made up . . . but might not the temptation of a second lodger, if she accepted Mona, change even the sternest mind? Lodgers were thin on the ground at the moment, though Rose knew that her mother was still hoping to get answers from her advertisements in the newspaper and from the neatly-lettered card in the window. But until she did so they would be on short commons and Rose could tell, from the neat little line between her mother's brows and the tightness of her mouth, that Lily was truly worried.

'Your mam's not 'ere right now, chuck, an' you are,' Mona said quickly. 'Besides, I feelin' she ain't too keen. But I'm out o' the game all right an' tight, I'll tell you all about it when we meet, honest to God I will. If you can persuade her it's gospel truth, an' that I'm as decent a girl as yourself, surely she'll lerrus share?'

207

'Look, walk alongside me if you've got to keep talkin',' Rose said desperately. 'Me job ain't much, but it's all I've got. I'm goin' to evenin' classes to improve my shorthand an' typin', so's I can be someone's secretary, but that takes time an' while I wait we've got to eat.'

'You ain't the only one,' Mona pointed out, panting along beside her. 'My boss is a reg'lar slave-driver, won't give me five minutes I ain't earned. Look, how about if I meet you this evenin'?'

'Can't. I'm at the tech,' Rose said thankfully. 'Go an' see me mam, she'll be glad to see you, gi' you a cuppa.'

'Wharrabout your dinner hour? Don't they give you no time off for your dinners?' Mona said desperately, still trotting along beside her. 'Oh, if I'm caught out 'ere by me boss there'll be 'ell to pay!'

'Ye-es . . . all right, meet me at twenty to one by Sainsbury's caff in Imperial Buildings,' Rose said. 'Don't be late!'

'I'll be there,' Mona promised, turning back. 'Don't you be late either, you cheeky young cow!'

Giggling, Rose hurried on her way and reached her office just as another office junior arrived. She greeted him cordially and whipped up the long flight of stairs to her domain, which was the outer office and the small kitchen. She filled the big iron kettle and stood it rather precariously on the gas ring. Then she got out the cups and checked the sugar and biscuit supply. She looked at the clock in the outer office; time to get the milk.

There was a shop on the corner which sold tins of milk but Mr Edward, the oldest of the three

Evans brothers who owned and ran the business, did not approve of tea or coffee made with tinned milk, so one of Rose's first tasks in the morning was to hurry along to the dairy with her enamel jug to get fresh milk. She usually put the kettle on before she went and because she ran most of the way it was generally about to boil when she got back. Then she made the tea, let it brew whilst she went into the outer office and made sure that everything was ready for the rest of the staff and such customers as might call upon them in person, and returned to the kitchen so that she would be ready to pour out the freshly made tea when Mr Edward, Mr Lionel or Mr Garnett might put in an appearance.

The firm was called Patchett & Ross, though so far as Rose knew there was no one of either of those names on the staff, and they were import-export agents, which meant, for Rose, that a good few of the incoming and outgoing letters were addressed to strange names and stranger places, and that Mr Edward wrote a great many letters to various shipping lines which, if they were urgent, she delivered by hand, sometimes waiting for a reply, at others simply turning round and returning to Dale Street with all speed.

But now the weather was fine, she was back with the milk, Mr Edward and Mr Lionel had come in together in a pleasant frame of mind and gone though to Mr Edward's large office, and she had the tea steaming in the pot and the milk standing in the sink to keep cool.

In the old days, before they had employed Rose, the firm had had an office boy called Rufus who had made the tea and—she assumed—typed painful notes on the huge, old-fashioned typewriter in the outer office. But Rufus had gone to sea as soon as a berth was offered and since he was the third office boy to do so in three years the brothers had decided to try a girl for a change.

So far, everything had gone well. Rose had been told she made far better tea than Rufus, typed, when she had to, with fewer mistakes and was very much quicker to return after her errands. She worked as hard as she possibly could, smiled at both customers and staff—and why should she not, when she was happy with them?—and dreamed of the day when she might take over as private secretary to one of the brothers, thus trebling or quadrupling her wages and her importance to the company.

But unfortunately, as Mr Lionel kept stressing, these were not good times for import-export agents. 'A Depression means no one buys or sells as much, and since we need both buyers and sellers we're bound to suffer more than most,' he was apt to say gloomily, when a would-be customer went elsewhere or a shipping line could not find a space for their goods. 'But we'll soldier on, eh Ryder?'

Being a mere office girl, Rose did not get a handle to her name, though all the typists and clerical workers were called Miss this or Miss that. Not that she minded. It was a job when work was scarce, it was a happy office, and although fourteen shillings and sixpence a week might not be very much, it was a deal better than she would have got in a small shop somewhere. Even Mona, who had worked in the flower shop for a number of years and was past twenty, only got eighteen shillings a week, though she sometimes got tips from grateful customers when she delivered a particularly fine bouquet. She had once told Rose that she trebled her wages on Valentine's Day each year and did almost as well in the pre-Christmas period, when folk ordered wreaths and Christmas trees and fancy table arrangements.

But right now she should be taking the tea through. She poured two cups, added a china plate upon which she laid out three plain biscuits and two gingernuts, then popped her head out of the kitchen. By squinting sideways she could see the half-glazed door of Mr Edward's office. Through it the figures of the two elder brothers could be seen dimly. She was about to go back into the kitchen for the tray, however, when Mr Garnett came loping across the outer office. He was a good deal younger than the others, taller and thinner and less substantial, as though their parents had used all the good material making the first two and had had to water Mr Garnett down a little.

Hastily, Rose poured a third cup of tea, added more biscuits and set off with her tray. She would deliver the tea and then go into the typists' room and see whether there were any early deliveries for her. Breezily, she crossed the room with her heavy tray, bumped briefly on the door and flung it open. She carried it across to Mr Edward's lovely big desk with its pink blotter, its silver ink-pots and the trays for pins and paper-clips and stood the cups carefully before him. 'Mornin', sirs,' she said cheerfully. 'Nice one today, isn't it? We've run out o' custard creams but there's plenty o' rich tea.'

'Morning, Ryder,' Mr Edward said, whilst Mr Lionel muttered something about the typists eating the biscuits and Mr Garnett sat down on one of the

211

revolving leather armchairs and began to make a chain with the paper-clips. 'Get some petty cash from Miss Fielding and buy some more custard creams, would you? We've got several customers coming in later ... don't want to offer 'em plain biscuits.'

'Right, sir,' Rosie said. She hurried out of the room, then slowed to cross the outer office. She was thinking about her interview with Mona later. What on earth could she say to her cousin which she'd not already said? There was absolutely no point in Mona appealing to her, when it was Mam who held the purse strings and said who lodged with them and who did not. Of course, Mam was getting worried, there was no doubt of that. And why should they not take Mona in, after all? Dad wouldn't have turned her away, Rose decided. Yes, that was the tack to take. Lily would want to please Dad, whether he was here to speak for himself or not and she was suddenly certain that Dad would not have turned Mona away, whatever she had done.

'She won't do wrong whiles she's under *our* roof,' she could hear his deep, calm voice saying, inside her head. 'Gi' the gel a chance, our Lily. If things was diff'rent, an' it was Rosie wantin' a roof over her head, I hope someone 'ud give her a chance.'

Yes, that was the way to go about it, Rose decided, especially if Mona really did come clean and tell her why she'd decided to change her ways. Mam was as soft as a brush, really, always ready to give someone a second chance, but the reminder of Dad would clinch it. Happier now, she headed for the typists' room.

Rose met Mona in her lunch-hour and agreed to sound out her mother about the Irishman, Sean O'Neill, who urgently wanted what he called 'dacint, homely lodgin's' for himself. According to Mona the man, whom she described as elderly and respectable, with a wife and small daughter and a son in his twenties back home in Ireland, had lodged for some years with a woman in Lavrock Bank and had been perfectly happy there.

But then his son had accompanied him back from Ireland and had taken a job in the city, and the woman in Lavrock Bank had resolutely refused to have the son as a lodger too. And though Mr O'Neill had found the son a place in a terraced house only a couple of miles or so off, he did not like being separated and wanted to be nearer.

'Then might that be two lodgers?' Rose asked hopefully, but Mona explained that the son was not at all keen to move, personally.

'He's wi' a lorra younger fellers, an' likes it right well,' Mona explained. 'But he wants to meet his da for a meal now an' then, mebbe to go for a drink in a pub, an' two miles is a bit far of an evenin'. What's more, when Mr O'Neill suggested his son might come in for dinner of a Sunday, his landlady said she'd not allow it, not even if he paid extry, like. So Mr O'Neill thought it were time for a move . . . an' he don't like the Lavrock place above half any more, 'cos the woman who first took him in moved away, an' Mr O'Neill can't see eye to eye wi' the new landlady. There's been bad feeling afore this, he telled me.'

'D'you think he'll care for us?' Rose asked rather

doubtfully. He sounded a difficult tenant to her.

But Mona was reassuring. 'You'll like him an' he'll like you,' she said. 'He's a nice ole feller, honest to God, Rosie. He'll be no trouble, an' who knows? You might get the young 'un an' all, in time.'

'How did you meet him?' Rose said at last. It was, she knew, the first question her mother would ask.

'I've gorra pal at work, a gal called Janet Feeny,' Mona said. 'We was goin' off for a day to New Brighton an' I went to her house to fetch her out. She lives next door to Mr O'Neill's lodging house an' as we came out, so did Mr O'Neill. He was meetin' his son, as they was goin' for a bit of an outin' too, takin' the ferry an' all. So naturally we started to chat, an' next thing we knew, we were discussin' his situation, so far from where his son lodged, an' were sayin' I'd an aunt wi' a big old house up that way an' I was hopin' to move in meself when you was settled. An' then Mr O'Neill mentioned as he was searchin' for digs, an' I remembered you'd said you'd got plenty of bedrooms . . . the rest you know, as they say.'

'I see,' Rose said. 'So you don't really know this feller all that well yourself?'

'No, but Janet does an' she told me all about him, an' his son, an' why Mr O'Neill wanted to move.' Mona leaned over and tweaked Rose's nose playfully. 'Any more questions, Miss Nosy?'

'No, I reckon I know as much as you do, now,' Rose admitted. 'Come on then, let's buy a penn'orth o' chips, then I've got to get back to the office.'

So Rose returned to Patchett & Ross hopeful

214

that her mother would agree to the two lodgers and that presently she and Mona would be living together, for much though she liked the new house and the new neighbourhood, she sadly missed her pals, who had gone to school with her and knew her so very well. So far, she had met a couple of girls who lived nearby, but though they were friendly enough they were not really interested in her, so Rose welcomed the thought of having her cousin to share her home. Mona will be able to give a hand in the house, too, she told herself as she bustled around the office in the four o'clock tea-break, pushing her battered trolley into the typists' room and on to where the clerical staff worked. I expect, once we've got a full house, there'll be work in plenty.

Then Mr Garnett called her in to his office and asked her to take a letter to a ship which had just docked. 'Ask for the first mate, Mr Simpson,' he said. 'And give the letter to him. We sailed together once and as m'brother says, there's nothing like the personal touch in business.'

'Right, sir,' Rose said automatically, taking the long brown envelope. 'Do I wait for a reply?'

'Ask Harry . . . that is, Mr Simpson,' Mr Garnett said after a moment's thought. 'He may not be able to reply at once, but if not, tell him we'd appreciate a reply within twenty-four hours. All right?'

'All right, Mr Garnett,' Rose said, taking the two steps necessary to reach the doorway of Mr Garnett's tiny cubicle. It seemed unfair, she thought, in view of his size, that Mr Garnett had drawn the short straw, or the tiniest of all the offices, but she supposed that the size of the office was more a question of seniority than size of

215

inhabitant. Still, seeing Mr Garnett trying to double up his long legs under the small desk, and knocking his elbow on the wall every time he forgot the restrictions of his room and tried to write without cramping up his arm, was enough to make a cat laugh. 'I'll go right away.'

'That's a good girl,' Mr Garnett said. 'I'll be here until six but then I'll have to get a move on. I've got a date with an angel, y'know. So mind you're back by then.' He hummed the tune of the song he had just quoted and Rose turned and smiled, though the thought of Mr Garnett making love to a young lady was more comical even than seeing him squeezed behind his desk. He reminded her of one of those crane-flies, all legs and loosely-jointed body, which buzz around in the summer evenings, bumping into faces and lights, and making girls scream, and she thought that being hugged by him would be a horrid experience. His arms would go round a girl twice, she pondered as she ran down the stairs. Still, he couldn't help being so long and thin, she shouldn't make a mock of him, even in her head. I'm no oil-painting, she reminded herself. Oh, don't I wish my hair were smooth and shining, like Greta Garbo's, or a lovely dark red, like Norma Shearer's! And it would be nice to have a pert little nose like Clara Bow's and a wonderful figure, like Marlene Dietrich's. But since she was unlikely to become a film star, she supposed that it didn't really matter and continued to dash out of the offices.

The walk to the Queen's Dock, where the ship she was to visit was moored, was a pleasant one on such a mild and sunny afternoon. Rose hurried, because she could not amble once she got going and anyway she knew it would be a protracted business to find the right ship, then the right man and either get permission to go aboard or ask someone to bring him ashore, but even so she thoroughly enjoyed the walk. The wind was blowing onshore and brought with it the salt tang of the sea, a sort of wild freshness which suited Rose's mood. No wonder so many of the firm's office boys had run away to sea, she thought. All the glamour and excitement of a life on the ocean wave was perpetually being brought home to them—and the wages at Patchett & Ross, though sufficient for a girl, could not have compared well with what a midshipman or a cabin boy—Rose was vague about ships' crews—could have made. Still, she could not imagine going to sea herself. She loved the land too much, her home, her mother, even her job.

Presently she turned right onto Sefton Street and after slowing to wave to some small boys travelling on the overhead railway and slowing again to cross the swing bridge at a decorous pace, she reached the Queen's Dock. The ship she wanted was moored in Number One Dock, so she headed there.

The gangplank was down and the sailor guarding it called to another seaman, who went and fetched Mr Simpson, who proved to be the absolute opposite of his friend Mr Garnett, being short, broad and round-faced, with his skin brown from the salt breezes, and small, twinkling eyes.

He took the envelope, opened it and read the contents quickly, then turned back to Rose. 'Hello . . . you're new, aren't you?'

'Yes, sir,' Rose said. She had no idea how one

217

should address the first mate of a cargo ship, but decided to play safe. 'The office boys keep running away to sea so Mr Edward thought a girl might be safer.'

Mr Simpson grinned. 'Well, in one sense I agree with him, but knowing my old pal Spidy Evans ... still, mustn't tell tales out of school, eh? How d'you enjoy the work?'

'It's grand,' Rose said. 'Is—is there a reply, sir? Only Mr Garnett said most particularly that he wanted me to go straight back to the office. He's got a date wi' ... well, an appointment I should say.'

Mr Simpson laughed. 'A date? Not a real date, with a real girl? Not old Spider Evans? What girl would look twice at a beanpole like him?'

'I wouldn't know, sir,' Rose said rather woodenly. She did not think it nice of Mr Simpson to refer to his old friend in such terms. 'Is there a reply, then?'

'No, not ... hang on a mo. You're the messenger, right?'

'That's right,' Rose said cautiously. 'If you write a note I'll tek it back to Mr Garnett.'

'Well, it's not exactly ... hang on here for a sec.'

And before Rose could say again that she could not linger he had turned and run back up the gangplank and onto the ship. Sighing, Rose sat down on a bollard. No point in getting in a state— you could not expect the feller to write a note standing on the quayside. Naturally he would go back into his cabin or whatever they had aboard ship and write it properly there.

After five minutes, her new acquaintance reappeared. Furthermore, he had what looked like a largish box swinging from one hand and Rose's heart gave a disbelieving thump. Surely he did not expect her to carry that great thing back to the office with her? She was a messenger, not a dockie.

But Mr Simpson had anticipated objections. 'It's light as a feather,' he said cheerfully, handing over the box. 'Tell old Spider that I knew he'd want the old feller really, but just didn't have time to take him when he last visited me. And here's the reply,' and he thrust a sheet of paper, folded into a square, into her right hand and the box into her left.

'I'm not meant to carry bleedin' great packages,' Rose said indignantly, then almost dropped the box, which, she now realised, was not a box at all but a cage of some sort with a green baize cloth draped over it. 'Hey, what's in here? Ooh, it moved . . . it's alive!'

She set the object hastily on the ground, staring at it with widening eyes, but Mr Simpson stepped forward at once and lifted a corner of the green baize, so that she could see what was within. It was, she saw, a large, many-coloured parrot with scaly grey legs and white patches around its remarkably bright and intelligent eyes.

'Don't worry, it won't bite,' Mr Simpson said, snorting with laughter. 'It's Mr Garnett's parrot, Gulliver. The bird never left his side whilst he was afloat and when he decided to stay ashore he left it with me, promising to pick it up next time we docked. Only what with one thing and the other, with him always being busy and myself the same, I've not got round to handing over the bird. But you turning up . . . well, it suddenly struck me that it was a heaven-sent opportunity, see? Now you get back to good old Spidy and tell him you've got Gulliver there and he'll be so pleased he'll probably throw up his date tonight and take you out instead.' He looked her over. 'He could do worse,' he added with a chuckle. 'Pretty little thing like you, he'd have a grand evening, I'm sure.'

But Rose scarcely heard the compliment, far less heeded it. 'Will it sit quiet or will it try to fly round and overset me?' she enquired worriedly. 'I don't know nothin' about birds, Mr Simpson. Suppose it flaps an' breaks a wing or a leg? Mr Garnett won't be too pleased wi' me then, will he?'

'Keep the baize cover over him and he'll think it's night, and night's the time for quiet sleep,' the first mate advised. 'He won't flap around in the dark, got more sense. As for breaking a leg or wing, just think, girl! In the wild, that bird would roost in a tree during one of the hurricanes common in his native country, and the branches would whip around far more than just swinging from your hand.'

'Well, I don't know as how . . .' Rose began, but she was speaking to Mr Simpson's back; he was mounting the gangplank, calling out to someone at the head of it. Rose, with a sigh, adjusted the big wicker hook on top of the birdcage which accidently tipped the cage at an odd angle and she heard an ominous thump; clearly, regardless of what Mr Simpson might say, the bird had forgotton about clinging to the branch of a tree in a tropical gale and had simply dropped off its perch. Accordingly she pulled the cage until it was swinging freely alongside her and set off.

*　　　*　　　*

220

It was a fair journey after all, though once or twice, when she tripped over a manhole cover or turned a corner a little too sharply, strange sounds issued forth from under the baize. Indeed, when she was forced to stop rather abruptly at the junction of Victoria Street and John Street, an old lady waiting at the kerb to cross behind her began to tut indignantly at the dreadful, raucous words which she plainly thought were coming from Rose's lips. Rose gave the cage a quick kick and the mutter died away into low grumblings—clearly Gulliver realised that night or not, retribution was at hand if he misbehaved.

'Sorry, missus,' Rose said humbly, as the old woman told her she ought to know better, a neat-looking lass like her. 'It ain't me, though, it's this blamed parrot I'm carryin' home for ... for a friend. I never knowed a bird could ... hey up, off we goes!' For a large wagon had trundled past at last, leaving a clear road behind him for herself and her bothersome burden. She smiled placatingly at the woman and marched off thinking with some amusement that Mr Garnett must have been quite a lad, once—fancy teaching a bird to say things like that!

She reached the office and plodded up the stairs. A glance at the clock in the outer office confirmed that it was just on six o'clock but she would have known anyway since the typists were issuing forth from their room like a swarm of ants, eager to return to their own homes as speedily as possible.

Mr Garnett, however, true to his promise, was still in his room. He jumped to his feet as she entered and smiled hopefully. 'Ah ... did all go

221

well, Ryder? I take it you saw Mr Simpson? Is he able to find space for . . . oh my God, what on earth . . . ?'

For Rose had crossed his office—two steps—and thumped the cage, still baize-covered, down upon his desk. 'From Mr Simpson,' she said firmly. I've got to go now, Mr Garnett . . . oh, an' there's a note. Here.'

She thrust the square of paper at him and would have left the room, except that he seized her arm and prevented her from moving a step. 'No you don't, Ryder,' he said firmly. 'Not till I've read the note and you've explained just what you mean by banging objects down on my desk and trying to run off! What *is* it, for God's sweet sake? It looks like . . .'

With his free hand he pulled off the baize, blinked incredulously, then groaned, staring first at the bird and then at Rose whilst his long face paled. 'My God, it's Gulliver! I *told* Stinker Simpson that my mama wouldn't hear of my keeping the bird at home, I *told* him to give it to one of the seamen if the old man wouldn't hear of the bird going to a pet shop or suchlike but not to try to hand it back to me. Well, I won't have it— you can just turn round and take it back.'

'I can't . . . but read the note, sir,' Rose urged. 'Mebbe it says somethin' to the purpose. Only he seemed sure, Mr Garnett, that you'd want the ole feller.'

'Want it? Me, want Gulliver, after all the trouble the wretched bird caused when I took it home the first time?' Mr Garnett laughed grimly. 'No, no, he knew very well I wouldn't want it! This is his idea of a joke and a very poor one at that.' However, as

222

he spoke he let go of Rose and unfolded the note, then gave a shout. 'Ha! He says the bird makes such a racket that even the captain's got tired of it and since I bought it in the first place they thought it ought to come back to me.'

'Well, that seems fair, sir, if you bought it,' Rose said in the pause which followed. 'Besides, you could always sell it again . . . there are pet shops all over the Pool, you know, there's a lovely one on Heyworth Street, they'd probably give you a bob or two for this feller.'

'Ye-es. But I'd not like to think of him being ill-treated,' Mr Garnett said slowly. 'To tell the truth, Rose, I'd have him like a shot if it wasn't for Mama. But she won't stand for it and says so. I keep meaning to move out, get a place of my own, but until I do I have to abide by her rules, don't you know.'

'I didn't know you still lived at home, sir,' Rose put in, since some comment from her seemed expected. 'Doesn't your mam like birds then?'

'No, she has an aversion to feathers,' Mr Garnett said quickly. A little too quickly, Rose thought suspiciously. 'And there are other reasons . . . she has a very active social life . . . but what about your mother, Ryder? You live at home, don't you?'

'Yes, I do. Me mam's a busy woman too, she takes in lodgers,' Rose said quickly. 'There's no way she could give a home to a bleed . . . I mean a perishin' parrot. Well, Mr Garnett, I'd best be off, I've an evenin' class tonight an' if I don't get on me way soon I'll not have time for a bite o' tea afore I leave.'

'Don't go!' Mr Garnett said sharply. 'Look, you say your mother takes in lodgers and couldn't give

223

the parrot a home. Well, how much would she charge me to have the parrot as a lodger?'

'The *parrot*?' Rose squeaked. 'You want to know what she'd charge for a *parrot*?'

'That's right,' Mr Garnett said patiently. 'Look, Ryder, I've tried to explain that my mama won't let me take the parrot home and from what it says in this note, if I try to take it back to Stinker Simpson he'll see to it that I can't send any more shipments aboard his craft, which could be tricky, particularly at the moment. On the other hand, your mother's a businesswoman. I provide this nice, roomy cage and a sum to cover his keep and whatever space he takes up. After all, it's not for ever, just until I get a place of my own or find a friend who'll hang on to him for me. What about it?'

'Mam won't like it,' Rose said cautiously. 'How much was you thinkin' of, sir?'

'Two bob a week,' Mr Garnett said. 'Just to keep a parrot, a bird which would cost you a fiver at least from a pet shop. It's money for old rope, Ryder, money for old rope.'

'There's a snag here somewhere,' Rose remarked, though without rancour. Two bob for looking after a bird did seem like money for jam. 'That bird talks, it said a few things when I was crossing the road. Is it that your mam don't like?'

'We-ell, he's lived aboard ship for most of his life so he can be a trifle coarse,' Mr Garnett admitted. 'Come on, Ryder, say you will! Look, I'll make it three bob, I can't say fairer than that, can I? I can't just abandon the poor old fellow to some wretched pet shop. He has all sorts of odd likes and dislikes ... tell you what, I'll come as far as the shops with you, in a taxi, and I'll buy his first week's

224

food so's you know what to get.'

'No need for that,' Rose said hastily. She had no desire to be shut in a taxi with her spider-like boss, nor to have folk seeing them walking along the street together and drawing all the wrong conclusions. 'Gi' me a list, sir, an' I'll shop on me way home. Only I really must get a move on, or I'll be so late mam'll throw me out, parrot or no parrot.'

So it was agreed. Mr Garnett gave Rose five bob on account and a list of Gulliver's likes and dislikes. He enjoyed grapes, peanuts and a handful of little pink shrimps as a special treat, and was very fond indeed of sunflower seeds, but for the most part he lived on the seed which pet shops sell especially for parrots.

'Buy some cuttlefish bone, he likes that, and let him out of his cage for at least half an hour each day,' Mr Garnett instructed her as he walked beside her down the stairs and out of the now deserted offices. 'Don't worry that he'll attack you or try to escape, but don't leave windows open or he might get out by mistake. He's a fine fellow, you'll have no trouble with him.'

'I hope not. But if me mam won't have him, he'll be back tomorrow, I'm warnin' you, Mr Garnett,' Rose said frankly. 'Me mam wants a nice little kitten to keep the mice down, not a perishin' parrot!'

'But a kitten won't bring in any rent,' Mr Garnett said craftily as they reached the roadway. 'And a parrot which chatters away can be quite an attraction in a lodging house, I should think. Are you sure you won't come part of the way in my cab? I don't want to get you into trouble with your mama.'

'It's all right, I'll walk fast,' Rose said. 'G'night, Mr Garnett.'

＊   ＊   ＊

Rose walked along the crowded pavements, trying not to swing the cage too much and gazing hopefully ahead. In fact the collision, when it occurred, was as much her fault as anyone's, since she was trying to spot the pet shop and thus walked slap-bang into a heavily built man with a ditty bag over one shoulder and a suitcase in his hand. The disaster occurred because the suitcase struck the cage, which flew out of Rose's hand and landed against the wall with a crack which caused the cage door to fly open.

'Oh Gawd, look what you done,' Rose squeaked distractedly as the parrot sidled out of its cage and flew to the lintel above the nearest shop. 'Come down here, Gulliver ... oh, you bad bird, whatever will Mr Garnett say if I lose you?'

Gulliver, peering down at her, did not seem particularly interested in her fate and, when Rose held up her hands imploringly, showed no disposition to descend. The man who had collided with her said, 'That your bird? Give 'im a call, gal, that'll fetch 'im, they'll usually come to the sound of a voice they knows.'

Rose turned on him, eyes flashing. 'If you'd been lookin' where you was goin' this wouldn't have happened—and I'm ... I'm lookin' after the bird for me boss, he don't know me voice. Oh Gawd, what'll I do if he flies further off?'

'Who owned 'im last?' the man asked, and Rose

226

turned and looked at him properly for the first time. She could not guess his age, though his dark hair was streaked with grey at the temples, for his skin was smooth and tanned and his light-blue eyes were steady, though creased at the corners. He was wearing navy trousers and a seaman's jersey, and despite the fact that he had been the cause of Gulliver's escape, he did not look like a trouble-maker or an unreliable person. But looks, Rose thought, were not everything.

'What the devil does it matter who owned him last?' she said impatiently and turned back to the bird, who promptly deserted the lintel and made for the nearest gas-lamp, where he sidled up and down on the cross-piece, turning his head to look at her with one bright, wicked eye. 'Come on down, Gully,' she begged. 'Come to Rosie an' she'll give you . . . give you . . .'

The man beside her dug a hand into his pocket, then addressed the bird in a calm, conversational voice. 'What's in me pocket, Gully? What d'you think I've got for a good feller, eh? Come on, Gully, come an' see what's in me pocket.' He drew his clenched fist from his pocket and held it out, palm uppermost, curling and uncurling his fingers in a way which clearly intrigued the bird. 'Wharrav I got, then? Good bird, who's a good old feller, then? Give us a kiss, Gully, then you'll get your bit o' summat nice.'

The parrot continued to stare suspiciously down at them and Rose was about to make a biting comment when he gave a brief squawk, flapped off the lamp standard and came down onto the man's outstretched wrist. The stranger opened his hand, displaying a few peanut kernels, and whilst the

227

parrot was investigating them the man's other hand descended gently but firmly onto his back. He lifted the bird then popped him back into the cage, not forgetting to thrown in the peanuts first, then latched the little door securely once more and turned to Rose. 'Awright now, Miss? Sorry I knocked into you, but you wasn't lookin' where you was goin' either, you know.'

'Nor I was, but that don't matter, now he's back in his cage. Thanks ever so much, mister,' Rose said fervently. 'How did you do it, though? You don't know Gulliver, do you?'

'Never met before this moment, but I know parrots; used to 'ave one of me own,' the man said cheerfully. 'That's why I asked you who owned it last, because they respond to a voice, you know. I took a guess that the bird 'ad been owned by a seaman—most of 'em's brought back by sailors—an' I hoped me voice might fetch 'im down, which it did. As for the peanuts, a shipmate o' mine's gorra monkey an' it's mortal fond of peanuts. But look, I'm searchin' for somewhere called Oakfield Road, you wouldn't know where it is, would you? Someone telled me I should tek a turnin' off St Domingo Road and it ud lead me through, but I misremember the name o' the cut.'

'Oh, so you are a seaman,' Rose said, satisfied that she had guessed right earlier. 'An' your pal's got a monkey! I'd love to see a monkey, I've never seen one up close, 'cept in the pet shops now an' then. An' I do know Oakfield, I'm goin' that way as it happens. Come along o' me . . . and thanks again, mister.'

'Me name's Pete Dawlish,' the man said, falling into step beside her. 'Here, let me tek the cage, you don't want to carry it.'

'I'm Rose Ryder and you've got quite enough wi' that suitcase an' the ditty bag,' Rose said firmly, however. 'Why d'you want Oakfield Road? D'you live there?'

Pete Dawlish laughed. 'No, Miss Ryder, but I'm hopin' to do so. The fact is, I've had enough o' the sea, for the time bein', at any rate, an' a pal of mine—not the one wi' the monkey, one o' the other fellers—tipped me the wink that they was lookin' for a clerk in the Ocean Line offices, so I went in there and they've took me on. I worked for the P&O shipping offices before I went to sea, so I know what I'm about. But when I lived in the pool afore I was wi' me parents, an' they moved on years ago, so now I'm searchin' for lodgin's, an' there's a woman in Oakfield Road what's got a room. See?'

'Well, there's a coincidence,' Rose said. 'This here parrot's a lodger in a manner o' speakin'. He belongs to me boss, but Mr Garnett can't tek him home on account of his mother, who don't like birds, so he's comin' to live wi' Mam an' me until Mr Garnett gets a place of his own.'

'Oh? Does your mam take in lodgers, then?'

'That's right,' Rose said. 'We live in St Domingo Vale, that's between Breckfield Road an' Oakfield, so you'll be passin' me door to get where you're goin'. But first I got to go into the pet shop an' buy some grub for this feller.' She jiggled the cage and the parrot muttered tetchily, 'Mind me feet, you fool,' which made Rose jump. 'I've got a list,' she added. 'Peanuts is on it, an' grapes, but for tonight I'll just get 'im nuts an' some bird seed.'

'That's the ticket,' Mr Dawlish said heartily. 'Sunflower seeds—my ole feller loved sunflower

229

seeds. An' you'll need to fill 'is water jar as soon as you gerrin. Birds drink quite a lot, or my parrot did, anyroad, an' your water spilled out o' the pot when the cage overturned.'

'I'll do that,' Rose said. 'Could you hold the cage for me while I go in the shop please, Mr Dawlish? I'd be ever so grateful.'

Mr Dawlish complied and when she got back, complete with parrot provender, he was squatting on the pavement, conversing with the parrot through the bars whilst scratching the bird's raised poll with a finger through the wicker bars.

'Thanks, Mr Dawlish,' Rose said, picking up the cage and starting off along the pavement once more. 'Lor', I'm goin' to be late tonight. It's me night for me evenin' class but small chance I've got of makin' it there, what wi' Gully here, an' Mr Garnett keepin' me late.'

They turned into Mere Lane as she spoke and her companion looked pensively at the road sign.

'It weren't a lane I were lookin' out for,' he said. 'Still, I dare say this way's quicker.'

'Well, I had to buy the parrot food so I stayed on Heyworth Street a bit longer than I might have and besides, this way's just as quick if you want the Walton Breck end of Oakfield,' Rose explained. 'You aren't goin' out of your way though, honest to God.'

'Don't mind if I am,' Mr Dawlish said comfortably. 'It's nice to 'ave company, Miss Ryder. Where's your evenin' class held, then?'

'Oh, a way from here,' Rose said vaguely. Nice he might be, but she did not intend to make him a present of her entire life history. 'Is the lady in Oakfield Road expectin' you, Mr Dawlish?'

'No, I don't think so,' Mr Dawlish admitted. He swung his suitcase from his left hand to his right as they reached the pit on the corner of Mere Lane and Breckfield Road, crossed it, and began to descend the long hill on which St Domingo Vale was situated. 'I say, these are nice 'ouses! Did you say you lived here?'

'That's it,' Rose said proudly. 'The one wi' the lilac tree . . . see?'

They reached the garden gate and Rose paused. 'I hope you find everything all right, Mr Dawlish, then we'll be neighbours,' she said. 'It's nice round here, though to my way of thinkin' Oakfield's a good deal noisier than the Vale. Still . . .'

'There's a sign in your front window,' Mr Dawlish said, as though Rose could not possibly be aware of it. 'Rooms to let. Could I ask . . . I wonder if I might . . .'

' 'Course you could,' Rose said heartily, swinging the gate open. 'Come in, Mr Dawlish, an' if the room an' the terms aren't to your satisfaction . . . well, at least you'll see where Gulliver's goin' to live for a while.'

The two of them went up the path and climbed the neatly redded steps to the front door.

*   *   *

It was a strange old world, Lily told herself a week later as she and Mrs Kibble cleared up the breakfast things and began to wash up. Eight days ago she had had no lodgers and had been beginning to worry. Now she had three, for the evening Mr Dawlish had arrived, Lily had agreed, albeit grudgingly, to have Mona if her acquaintance proved suitable. She also had a parrot, though Gulliver, she felt rather confusedly, had come into her house under a false flag and, having entered, was proving difficult to evict.

The truth was that when she had seen Rose entering the house with Mr Dawlish, and explaining that her companion had come ashore after several years at sea and was looking for lodgings, she had leapt to the conclusion—who would not have done?—that Gulliver was his property. And Mr Dawlish was so nice; quiet, dependable, humorous. And of course she thought—who would not have done?—that he would look after his parrot in his room and would keep him there unless invited to bring him down, in his cage, to be with him in the sitting-room of an evening.

So she had showed him up the stairs to the best front bedroom; double windows overlooking her pride and joy, the garden, and beyond that the quiet road. She had named her rent, deciding to stand out for a decent sum since it was the best bedroom, and knowing that she could agree to ask for less but could scarcely, should he prove amenable, ask for more. Mr Dawlish agreed unhesitatingly to the price, only enquiring if it included breakfast in the morning, a main meal at night and lunch on Sunday, when he would be at home all day.

'That's right; and a supper and cocoa before you go to bed,' Lily had said and had seen, by the slight widening of her companion's blue eyes, that this had been well beyond his expectations but had not cared in the least. She had a lodger!

And when he was in his room, unpacking, and

she, Rose and Mrs Kibble were in the kitchen, cooking up the evening meal of sausages, bacon and black pudding which Rose had been hastily dispatched to buy from the nearest butcher, Rose had broken the news to her that her cousin Mona had found her another lodger, a middle-aged Irishman. And that Mona herself would be happy, now that her aunt and cousin were settled, to come and share Rose's room and to pay her aunt a reasonable rent.

'We-ell . . .' Lily had said cautiously. 'It's awright, is it, Rose? She won't go misbehavin' herself?'

'I'm sure she won't,' Rose assured her mother. 'That was why she and Aunt Daisy fell out—because Mona wanted to stop meetin' up wi' fellers an' Aunt Daisy wanted her to go on. Mona said it was a fool's game an' she was quittin' while she still had her health an' strength, an' Aunt Daisy told her the only fool was her an' that if you wanted good money you had to tek chances. Imagine, Mam, a woman sayin' that to her only daughter!'

So Lily agreed that they would give Mona—and Mr O'Neill—a trial, and gone happily down to her kitchen to prepare a meal and to tell Mrs Kibble the glad tidings.

And now, a whole week after settling her new lodgers into their rooms—Mr Dawlish in the best front, Mr O'Neill on the floor above in what she called, to herself, the second-best front, and Mona sharing Rose's nice attic room—she had discovered that Gulliver, far from belonging to Mr Dawlish, was not actually owned by anyone in the house.

'He's stayed in Mr Dawlish's room because Mr Dawlish said he'd give an eye to him while I were workin',' Rose had explained. 'But really, he's a

233

lodger, just like the others. Didn't you wonder why I give you that three bob, Mam, last week? It were his rent money.'

'But I don't tek parrots,' Lily had wailed. 'Oh, Rosie, how could you? You deceived me, that's what you been an' gone an' done. An' you mean that now Mr Dawlish has started work at the shippin' office I'm to look after that bleedin' bird day an' night? I don't know nothin' about birds an' what's more I'm scared of 'em. Look at the beak on him—it's curved like one of the Turkish dagger things you see on the fillums. He could tek me finger off wi' one bite!'

'He's all right, Mam, honest. And if I'd gone on sayin' "no", I'd likely have lost me job,' Rose said. 'An' as for deceivin' you, I did no such thing! I thought you'd guess when I gave you the three bob, honest I did.'

'Oh come on, Rosie, how could I guess?' Lily had said, staring with loathing at the parrot in its cage which now stood in the middle of the kitchen table. 'Mr Dawlish seemed real fond o' the crittur, an' you never said a word about Mr Garnett, or ... or ...'

Rose was a truthful girl, however, and in the end she had admitted that she had not wanted to tell her mother the truth straight out. 'I knew it 'ud come best after you'd got to know Gully,' she said. 'Only ... only it were difficult for you to get to know him, him bein' in Mr Dawlish's room most o' the time. An' when Mr Dawlish brought him down you never so much as offered the ole bird a peanut!'

She had sounded injured and Lily, despite herself, had laughed. 'Oh, go on wi' you,' she had said. 'I s'pose I'll get to like it, in time. An' three bob a week ain't to be sneezed at.'

But now, she and Mrs Kibble were clearing up in the sunny kitchen with Gulliver, in his cage, sitting on the Welsh dresser, and Lily was trying to accustom herself to the idea of letting him out of the cage once they had finished their work. He normally spent his time in the bow window in the front room where he could watch passers-by and comment, in peace, upon anything which occurred to him. But today, when she had gone in earlier to take the cover off his cage, he had said: 'Poor ole Gully, gi's a kiss, pretty Gull, pretty feller!' all in a gabble, which had ceased abruptly as she opened the door to leave the room. Glancing back, she had seen him ruffling up his feathers and turning back to the window, and somehow he had looked so lonely and about half his usual size . . . so she had gone back and carried the cage into the kitchen, where he had danced on his perch, shouted and catcalled and generally made it clear that he was happier with company. Or so Lily felt, at any rate, and Mrs Kibble had agreed with her.

'If he gets too noisy I'll carry him back to the front room,' Lily said as the two of them finished clearing away. 'Rose says Mr Dawlish lets him out for an hour or so every day, only he's workin' late tonight an' won't be able to do it, so since she's goin' straight to her night class after work I s'pose I oughter lerrim free for an hour or so. If I keep the door an' winders tight shut it should be awright.

She hadn't said that to Rose this morning, mind. She had been quite clear where she felt her own duties towards Gulliver stopped. 'I'm sorry, Rose, but I can't abide birds, so it's stayin' in the cage,'

Lily had said firmly. 'One day without an airin' won't kill it. Chances are I'd lerrit out an' we'd never see it again, an' then what would your Mr Garnett say?'

Rose had agreed, reluctantly, that it would not harm the bird to stay in its cage for a day and had promised faithfully to let it out for an hour after her class, and Lily had been content enough with that. But seeing the parrot hunched up on its perch, she had begun to feel mean. After all, it wasn't such a huge bird and it had been good all morning so far, even shouting out 'Cheerybye, Rosie' as her daughter had left for work. And it sounded a bit like me, an' all, Lily told herself, secretly very impressed with the bird's quickness. And Rose had said that it couldn't fly very far even if it wanted to, as its wings had been clipped. She said all it seemed to do when let out of its cage was to potter about, sometimes going for a short little flight, at other times investigating the furniture and fittings of whatever room it was in. So surely she could let it out just for an hour? Rosie would be so pleased with her, would be able to go straight to bed after her supper, instead of having to stay downstairs with the parrot for an hour.

Having almost made up her mind to take the plunge, Lily approached the cage. It was still on the kitchen table, but she could carry it back to the front room—it would be safer there since tradesmen would simply bang on the door and enter, not having the time to hang about and wait for a housewife to come running. She thought about calling Mrs Kibble down—but decided against it. She would take Gulliver through to the front room, check that the windows were closed, shut the door and open the cage. And then she would do all her usual cleaning work in the room whilst the bird pottered about. But first she would fetch some vinegar and her soft cloths, since it was her day for cleaning the bow window-panes, and she would also bring the duster and the beeswax so that she could do the furniture, and the carpet sweeper to pick up any bits on the small square of carpet, and the feather duster to clean the picture rail and to swish down any spiders daring enough to make their webs at ceiling height.

She brought through all her cleaning equipment and fetched the cage. She stood it on the small window table, then she and Gully stared at each other doubtfully through the wicker bars. Gully said: 'Gi's a kiss!' in a creaking, old-man's voice, then, in her daughter's very tones, he added, 'D'you want a peanut, Gully? Gi's a kiss then!'

You had to give it to him, Lily decided, approaching the cage and gingerly unfastening the door. He was a first-rate mimic and he learned like lightning. She had heard Rose talking to him as she gave him peanuts or raisins or the little pink shrimps that he loved, but she'd not realised he could pick up a couple of sentences so quickly.

The door open, she pinned it back and waited, with some apprehension, for the bird to flap out, but nothing happened. Gulliver sat on his perch, eyes half closed, muttering something beneath his breath, and after a few minutes, satisfied that he was not about to do anything untoward, Lily began her work. And presently, turning back to the window for a moment, she saw that the bird had left his cage and was, as Rose had described it, pottering about. Indeed, he was behind her

237

aspidistra and when he peered at her through the branches he looked so comical that she had to laugh.

'Pretty Gully,' he said contentedly, and Lily said: 'You'll have to learn to say "pretty Lily", me boy, if you wants to keep in my good books!' and then got on with her work.

The front room was her favourite place, and she always cleaned it herself and presently, carried away by the sheer enjoyment of waxing the round mahogany table in the window embrasure, she began to sing softly to herself beneath her breath, *'Bobby Shaftoe'e gone to sea, silver buckles at his knee, he'll come back and marry me, bonny Bobby Shaftoe!'* The sun fell in syrupy golden slabs on the new carpet and on the table, polished until it shone like dark water, and on the empty cage, turning its wicker bars to gold. And Lily realised, with a tiny stab of guilt, that she was feeling happy, really happy, for the first time since Jack's death.

But Jack would be glad for her, she knew that. There was no more generous man than Jack. And she went on flicking with her feather duster and presently began to sing once more.

*　　　*　　　*

When the door opened an hour later and Mrs Kibble came into the room, Lily had lost all her fear of Gulliver and was treating him like an old friend. They had sung a chorus together—he did not know *'Bobby Shaftoe'*, it appeared, but was familiar with *'Fifteen men on a dead man's chest'*, which he roared out in a convincingly seamanlike voice—and exchanged a good deal of light banter.

Indeed, at one point Gulliver had proved that he wasn't quite as bright as Lily had thought him by making advances of an amorous nature towards her feather duster. But Lily had poked him with it and knocked him off the picture rail so that he had flown, squawking, right round the room, coming to rest again on the top of his cage and imitating her subsequent laughter with great aplomb.

In fact, so at ease with him did she feel that it never occurred to Lily to shout to Mrs Kibble to shut the door and before either woman had done more than open her mouth to speak it was too late. Gulliver, perched on the picture rail and making his slow, sideways way along it, had dived for the opening and disappeared.

'Oh Gawd!' Lily squeaked, truly dismayed. 'Is the back door open, Agueda?' She used the older woman's Christian name for the first time in her panic.

'I do not know, it may be,' Agueda replied. 'The butcher has just delivered ... oh, let us pray he shut the door again, Lily, or we shall be in very great trouble.'

It was the first time, too, that the Spaniard had used Lily's first name, and in the hunt for Gully which followed both women abandoned formality for ever and became real friends.

'Look out, he's makin' for the door—grab him!' Lily shouted, when they had followed the bird into the kitchen where the back door was still a couple of inches ajar. Agueda was tall and still carrying a duster; she flailed with it, diverting Gully from his intended route, and Lily hurled herself at the back door, slamming it almost on his beak as he dive-bombed towards it once more.

239

'Lock it, lock it,' shouted Agueda. 'Oh, shut the kitchen door . . . too late! Where has the evil one gone?'

The evil one had made for the stairs . . . the bedroom windows would be open at this time of the morning to air the rooms. Lily tore up them at a speed which her daughter, twenty-five years younger, could not have bettered, but it was all right. Agueda had closed all the doors and the parrot, having zoomed twice round the hallway, made for the next flight of stairs.

It was a merry chase and lasted all morning. At first, they merely endeavoured to catch Gulliver, then they tried to trap him by laying a trail of peanuts as far as the door of the front sitting-room.

But at this point something struck Agueda. 'If we open that door and he flies through it, he might go straight for the chimney and disappear up it?' she asked, wringing her hands. 'Oh, heavens, Lily, and it's not been swept since last autumn—he'd be black as the ace of spades by the time he got out of the chimney pot, and we'd never catch him.'

'No, 'cos he'd look just like a bleedin' crow, which wouldn't mek it easy since there's dozens o' crows around here,' agreed Lily with a giggle. 'Oh, now I dussen't go into the front room at all for fear he meks a dive for the chimbley! Oh, Agueda, what the *devil* are we to do?'

'We'll go into the kitchen and make ourselves a bite of lunch, which I really feel we deserve,' Agueda said, fanning herself with the feather duster. 'When we can trap him in the kitchen . . . we'll lure him with some peanuts . . . then one of us can fetch his cage through . . .'

'An' purrit on the kitchen table wi' some peanuts

scattered inside, an' mebbe that'll work,' Lily said hopefully. 'If it don't, I'll fair roast Rosie when she comes home tonight.'

CHAPTER SEVEN

Later the same day found Colm walking along the pavement with his shoulders hunched against the light summer rain and wondering, not for the first time, what his father's new lodgings were really like. Sean had been delighted with the change and had praised St Domingo Vale and the Ryders to the sky, but Colm had not been deceived. His mother wanted them living in the same house and his father was ashamed to write home yet again admitting that the two of them were still apart, albeit close. Colm didn't see why he should move just because his mammy worried about him, and him man enough to send money home and take care of himself, so when Sean had suggested that he, too, should move to this place in St Domingo Vale his first impulse had been to say that he was happy where he was and wouldn't be movin', thanks very much. But in fact it wasn't really true. Sure, there were other young fellers of his age sharing the cheap dormitory-style rooms, with a dozen men all sleeping on mattresses on the floor, but the main reason he couldn't move was money. He hadn't been earning enough to go for more palatial surroundings; he simply had to be content with what he'd got.

But as time went by he had started to long more and more for a bit of privacy and a decent hot meal

241

of an evening, instead of whatever rubbish old Mr Backhouse served up, and the company of working men whose main preoccupation was to get to the pub and begin gargling down the ale. Colm was beginning to dream, not of home nor of palaces, but quite simply somewhere to wash his clothing, which wasn't crowded with other fellers all doing the same, and a yard that wasn't hard up against the railway line so that nothing you washed ever came indoors again clean. And, of course, a decent meal when you came in hungry after after a long day's work.

Now, with his new job, it was a possibility. Although navvying had paid better here than many a job in Ireland, it still didn't pay well enough to afford decent lodgings, and though Sean had made it plain that he would help his son financially, Colm wasn't having any of that, not he. He valued his independence now and didn't want to have to ask his father before he went out to the pub for a few beers, or to the cinema with a girl, nor did he want his every doing reported to his mammy and little sister. But he'd recently changed his job and was making a bit more money, so why not at least go round and see what he thought of the room in St Domingo Vale? It was a small room, but wouldn't he be pleased and happy with any room if it meant a bit of privacy and a good meal of an evening.

Sean was a quiet man who did not interfere with his son, but Colm knew how very pleased his father would be to have him in the same house. Pride and a lack of the means to change might have kept Colm in his miserable dockside digs, but now he could afford a decent place, so felt he could give his father the satisfaction of sharing the same house. After all, it was because of Sean that he was earning a better wage, and it would be thanks to his father that he had a chance of these good lodgings. Why continue to turn his face against a move merely because he felt he should not be beholden? After all, if a man could not be properly grateful to his own father, to whom could he be grateful?

So Colm continued to walk through the rain, letting it soak into his thick thatch of curly black hair and trickle down the sides of his lean face, as he reflected that he hardly ever thought of his old life at Switzer's now. It hadn't been much of a life, running errands for a bunch of old women and looking up to a smarmy feller simply because he had stuck at the one dead-end job for what seemed to him now like centuries. He didn't even regret leaving Dublin, far less the pert and unreliable Nell. He was, he considered, well out of that, for since his arrival in Liverpool he had gone out with one or two girls and had enjoyed their company without once wanting to make it a permanent relationship. Nell, he occasionally considered, had done him a good turn when she had let him down the way she had.

Not that he thought about her, or his old life, often. Indeed, working as he was, he didn't have much time or energy for introspection. As his father had predicted, he enjoyed using his strength, though it had left him worn out at first. It was only as time went on that he began to look around for amusement in the evenings and on Sundays, when his time was his own. There were cinemas, museums, the seaside and the country, but best of all were the dance-halls. There were quite a few of them in Liverpool and they were not frequented by

243

many of the large army of Irish who lived around the docks, but Colm and one or two of his friends loved to dance, and to meet the bright, neatly dressed local girls.

'Never tell 'em you're Irish until they've got to know you,' his friends advised. 'Sure an' isn't every one o' the little darlin's huntin' for a feller wit' a pocket full o' money to spend on 'em. An' don't they believe, the little darlin's, that us Irish send all our wages home? So do like the rest of us an' tell 'em you're from the Isle o' Man, or the Shetlands . . . most of 'em seem to t'ink 'tis true.'

'What? An' you wit' a brogue on you as broad as Delaney's donkey?' Colm had said incredulously. 'They're coddin' you, Paddy!'

But codding or not, he performed well enough to find plenty of partners at the dance-halls and told himself, as he paused to cross Heyworth Street, that he did not intend to stop going out of an evening and at weekends even if he was in the same house as his father.

'Colm! Hey, hold on, feller! And aren't you the one to rush away now? Waitin' for you, I was, be the entrance, only Mac said he t'ought you'd left earlier.'

Colm turned and grinned self-consciously as his father strode towards him. 'Sorry, Daddy,' he said. 'I was later than I expected so I thought you'd have gone on. Well, we'll walk together.'

'A good thing I hurried, an' caught you up,' Sean grumbled as he drew abreast of his son. 'What would Mrs Ryder think, wit' you turnin' up ahead o' me, an' me not there to introduce you?'

Colm bit back the words *She'd think I was a man growed, an' what more natural than that, Daddy?*

244

and sighed instead. 'Never mind, we're together now,' he said diplomatically. 'Only ... s'pose I don't like the room, Daddy? Or ... or the house. Or s'pose Mrs Ryder doesn't care for me at all at all?'

His father laughed shortly. 'She'll say the room's took,' he said promptly. 'An' if you t'ink it won't suit you'll go away sayin' you'll be in touch later an' I'll have to mek up some cock-an'-bull story to fit. Awright?'

'Sure,' Colm said humbly. 'T'anks, Daddy.'

'I wish it weren't rainin',' Sean remarked as they crossed another road and turned their feet towards a pleasant-looking road ahead. 'I'd rather you'd seen it in sunshine, but you wouldn't come when I asked.'

'That's right,' Colm said. 'But I'm here now, Daddy. An' I don't mind the rain. I like it. It reminds me of home, so it does.'

Sean laughed. 'Oh well,' he said resignedly. 'What d'you t'ink o' the road? We're half-way down.'

Colm looked carefully round him, realising for the first time that this was a good neighbourhood, with nice houses. They were three storeys high and they all had small gardens—and the road was wide and quiet—with a sort of clean and tidy brightness about many of them which Colm did not associate with lodging houses. He said as much to his father, who nodded seriously.

'You're right there. So far as I know, we're the only lodgin' house in our part o' the Vale, most o' the others is still occupied by families. D'you know which one is ours?'

Colm felt like saying *none of 'em; we live in*

Dublin but again he swallowed the unwise words. It was nice, in a way, that his father felt so comfortable with the Ryders that he thought of it as home. And he knew very well where Sean's loyalties lay. It was just that because the two of them spent so much time here in Liverpool and so little in Dublin, they were bound to develop a kind of affection for their Liverpool surroundings. So he didn't voice his thoughts but said: 'No, Daddy. Shall we have a guessin' game, see which one I'd like the best?'

'No contest,' Sean said. He sounded smug. 'I'll let you guess if you like, but it's the best house in the Vale, so it is. Go on ... we're getting' close now.'

'The one wit' the tree?' Colm asked. 'No, it can't be that one, it's far too grand, it must be ...'

'You're right, young feller, the one wit' the tree,' Sean said. ' Aren't the steps the reddest you ever did see? But we'll use the footscraper, or they won't be red but covered wit' mud! Close the gate behind yous.'

Colm gaped, then obeyed. No wonder his father had been so keen for him to share his good fortune! But there was bound to be a catch, of course. The place would be all cold linoleum and peeling paint-work inside, with an overpowering smell of cabbage and a chill like death. And Mrs Ryder would be old and cross, and would wear black—she was a widow woman, his father had told him that—and she would hobble on bunioned feet and grumble if he laughed aloud or talked above a whisper.

They trod carefully up the steps and his father turned the doorknob and the heavy door with its

246

multi-coloured glass panel swung open. 'It's never locked at this time o' the evenin',' Sean said, stepping over the threshhold. 'Not wit' most of us comin' in from our work around now. So . . .'

He stopped speaking. A shriek of remarkable intensity had rung out and a girl shot into the hall, yelling as she ran, 'Shut the bleedin' door, will ya! Oh Gawd, here he comes . . . quick, quick, shut that bloody *door*!'

There was a flash of colour above their heads and instinctively, as his father slammed the front door shut, Colm jumped and grabbed. There was a shriek even more shrill than the previous one, a scattering of coloured feathers and Colm's hand closed around a soft and yielding object even as something sharp and painful jabbed into his whitened knuckles. 'Ouch!' he roared. 'Stop bitin' me, ye spalpeen, or I'll pull every feather out of your ugly body!'

'Don't hurt him!' shouted the girl. 'Don't you go squeezin' him or I'll drag every hair from your bleedin' head! He's Mr Garnett's, an' Mr Garnett's comin' this evenin' to see him! Don't you go let 'im go, either!'

Even in the heat of the moment, Colm thought that such contradictory instructions were a little unfair, but he hung onto the bird, which presently stopped hacking away at his knuckles and said, in a lugubrious voice: 'Poor ole Gully wants a peanut . . . Shut that bleedin' door!'

The girl giggled. She was a slender, curly-haired kid of about sixteen, Colm guessed, a mere child, but she'd a nasty tongue on her, nevertheless. Swearing away like any old navvy, he thought, horrified. Why, if his little sister had behaved like

247

that his mammy would soon have washed out her mouth with soap.

But someone else had now erupted into the hallway; a pretty woman in her forties, Colm judged. She said in a trembling, scandalised tone: 'Was that you I heered swearin', Rosie Ryder! I'll give you a slap you won't forget if . . .' Her eyes had moved past the girl now and seen Colm, and her face was transformed by a beaming smile. 'Oh, you've got him! Oh, thanks ever so . . . that bird's been on the loose since ten this mornin' an' I've been out of me mind wi' worry! Here, we've put the cage in the front window again, hopin' to get him back in it, only Agueda remembered the chimbley, an' every time we went towards the kitchen door, he'd leave the peanuts we'd scattered an' zoom across as if he couldn't wait to escape. I tell you, Rosie, we've had the devil of a day wi' the ole . . . ole bird.'

'He only went for the kitchen door because he wanted to go back into his cage, I expect, Auntie Lil,' another voice broke in and Colm, turning, beheld a vision. Tall, slim, golden-haired, the prettiest young woman he had ever seen stood in the kitchen doorway. She was wearing a navy-blue macintosh with a cheeky little Robin Hood hat on her head and she was shaking out a scarlet umbrella and smiling in his general direction. Colm smiled back and nearly let go of the parrot, but not quite. He had not forgotten the fearful threats uttered by young Rosie . . . but who was this? Sean had said two girls lived there, he had not said that one of them was a vision!

'That's as maybe, Mona,' the woman addressed as Auntie Lil said. 'But we've got this young feller to thank for catchin' him. Could you bring him in here an' put him in his cage, please?' She flung open a door and gestured into the large and comfortable furnished room within, then turned to Sean. 'Oh, Mr O'Neill, me wits have gone beggin' . . . this'll be your son Colm, what's thinkin' of takin' a room here. Oh, whatever will he think of us, actin' like mad things an' our Rosie screamin' like a fishwife an' swearin' like . . . like nobody's business!'

'It's awright, anyone would swear—an' scream— over a parrot on the loose,' Colm said, smiling forgivingly at the youngster. He had been annoyed with her for speaking to him as though he, and not she, were the younger, but the mere presence of the vision had made such things of no significance. He had already made up his mind that come hell or high water he would take the room. The vision had taken off her macintosh to reveal the sort of figure normally only seen in advertisements or on the silver screen.

She was really something—to live in the same house as her would be—well, it would be really something as well!

'Oh well, Gully's awright now,' the girl Rosie said, as Colm put the parrot carefully into the cage and as carefully shut and latched the small wickerwork door. She had accompanied him into the room, presumably feeling some responsibility for the bird and for his handling of him, and now she looked quickly down at her feet and up at Colm. 'I'm sorry if I were a bit sharp, like,' she said grudgingly. 'I lost me rag back there. An' I'm sorry he bit you an' all; I don't think he's ever bit anyone before.'

'Sure an' that doesn't matter,' Colm said mildly. 'For I've not been bit be a parrot before. But I don't bear a grudge.' He bent over the cage and put a finger through the bars, rubbing the bird's colourful red-and-blue head. 'T'was fear which made him strike, not wickedness.'

Sean, who had not opened his mouth whilst all this was going on, said deprecatingly: 'Gully's a nice bird, so he is. Him an' me's gettin' to know one another, eh Gully?' The bird, seeming to notice him for the first time, cocked his head on one side and sang, in a deep, cracked baritone which Colm recognised at once as his father's voice, 'Cockles and mussels alive, alive-o!'

Everyone laughed and Sean pushed a peanut through the bars and turned to the small group standing in the doorway. 'Well an' hasn't it been a meetin' an' a half, now?' he enquired. 'An' me son simply wantin' a quick look at the room, so he does.'

'And so he shall,' Mrs Ryder said at once. 'And he'll stay to supper an' all, him havin' saved our bacon so to speak over Gully here. What I'd ha' done if he'd gorrout of that door . . .'

'Well, he didn't, Mam,' the girl called Rosie said. She spoke rather pertly, Colm thought. 'Shall I tek Mr O'Neill—Mr Colm O'Neill I mean—up an' show him the room for you? Only you'll be wantin' to get the supper on the go, what wi' Mr Garnett poppin' by later an' all.'

'Thanks, Rosie,' her mother said with obvious relief.

But the older girl spoke up at once, taking the younger gently by the arm and holding her back when she would have begun to mount the stairs.

250

'Don't you bother yourself, Rosie. I'm goin' up to change out of me shop stuff, I'll show Mr O'Neill the room.'

'Thanks, Mona,' the younger girl said at once, and followed her mother out of the hallway and into the kitchen, but Sean came up the stairs in his son's wake, much to that son's disapproval. He did not think he would be able to make much headway with the beautiful vision whilst his father was about. But then, if he was going to live in the same house he need not rush, nor show his hand too soon.

Accordingly, the two men followed the swinging bob of golden hair up the first and second flights of stairs and into a pleasant room, then glanced about them. The window was uncurtained, but the panes sparkled with cleanliness and the walls, though bare, were whitewashed icily bright. The narrow bed was covered by a gaily coloured patchwork quilt and there was a washstand complete with ewer and basin in blue-and-white china, a white-painted wooden chair, a chest of drawers with a square of mirror on the top and a line of hooks on which, presumably, one hung one's jacket and trousers.

'Sure an' isn't it a dacint room now?' Sean said, glancing at his son. 'Look at the view, Colm!'

To avoid having to say anything Colm went over and stared out of the window. It was a view, too—he could see hundreds and hundreds of patched and vari-coloured roofs and, away in the distance, the faint blue line of distant hills. 'It's a grand view,' he said obediently and meant it. 'And it's a good little room an' all, Miss Ryder.'

'I'm not Miss Ryder, I'm Mona Mullins,' the

251

young woman said. 'Me an' Rosie's first cousins—
our mams are sisters. An' you'd best call me Mona,
anyways, 'cos we's goin' to have to call you Colm.
Can't manage wi' two Mr O'Neills, you know!'

'Colm's just fine,' Colm said at once. 'So you
don't live here, Miss . . . Miss Mona?'

'I do so,' Mona said at once. She fluttered
enticingly long lashes at him in a wink whilst Sean
was still admiring the view. 'Right above you, that's
where me room is. Me an' Rosie share the attic,'
she added quickly, as Sean turned back towards
them. 'Me mam moved away an' Auntie Lil took
me in, so I live here along o' the Ryders now.'

'Aye, don't you remember me tellin' you that a
young leddy as lived nearby had recommended me
to her aunt?' Sean put in. 'I told you when I moved
in, so I did.'

'Yes, probably,' Colm said vaguely. The truth
was that he often didn't listen when his father was
talking to him, going off into a dream as the gentle
brogue went on and on. 'But anyway, 'tis a grand
room for me, an' I'll be glad to take it.'

'You haven't asked the rent,' Mona said
demurely, casting him another of those exciting
glances beneath her sooty lashes. 'Don't be *too*
eager, Mr Colm.'

'I know the rent,' Colm said at once. 'Me daddy
told me when your aunt said she'd a room ready.
I can move in at the end of the week if that's
awright wit' Mrs Ryder.'

'We'll go downstairs an' tell her right away,' Sean
said. Colm could hear the muted excitement in his
father's voice and was glad that he had been able to
give pleasure so easily, for now that he had met
Mona Mullins he felt sure he would be extremely

happy and comfortable in St Domingo Vale. And from what he could remember of his father's talk he approved of the family. Indeed, the girl had greatly taken his fancy; Sean had said she was hardworking and sensible, so surely he could only be delighted when he saw where his son's inclination was leading him?

They went downstairs—just the two of them for Mona went up to her own room to change—and into the kitchen. The youngster was cutting a large loaf of bread into generous slices and buttering them, whilst her mother drew from the oven a meat pie topped with wonderfully fluffy, crisped mashed potato. She saw Colm and straightened, pushing the hair out of her eyes with one hand and deftly angling the pie onto the kitchen table, which was covered with a checkered tablecloth.

'Seen all you want o' the room? Good, then you're just in time for tea. It's shepherd's pie, bein' as we had roast mutton last night, with green peas, an' a nice suet puddin' wi' treacle sauce to follow. I know how hungry you fellers get, though, so we allus do a pile o' bread an' butter.'

Colm smiled blissfully whilst his father looked smug. A real meal and served decently, not just slapped down for everyone to help themselves. Oh, his father had been right to persuade him to come over and take a look for himself. He and Sean washed their hands over the sink and as they finished and turned away the kitchen door opened and another man came in. He was very dark-haired, of medium height and had a ready smile, which he turned enquiringly on Colm.

'This is Mr O'Neill's boy, Colm, Mr Dawlish,' Mrs Ryder said. 'He's thinkin' about the little

room. Colm, this is another of me gentlemen ...
Mr Dawlish works down at the docks in shipping.'

'I told you me son were thinkin' of makin' a
move, so I did,' Sean remarked as the three of
them seated themselves at the table. 'Well, he likes
the room, do you not, Colm?'

'Rosie, go an' call your cousin, tell her I'm
dishin' up,' Mrs Ryder interposed. 'I might tell you,
Mr Dawlish, that poor Colm walked into a
desperate situation when he come round here.
That Gulliver had gorrout of his cage an' was
shriekin' an' divin' round our ears like an eagle.
Indeed, if Colm hadn't collared it, I don't know
where it 'ud be by now.

'Oh, you'd ha' got the ould feller safe,' Colm said
easily, watching the spoon dig into the richness of
the crisped potato topping to reveal the hot,
golden-bubbled meat below. 'What wit' your
daughter keepin' nix on the kitchen door an' your
niece about to come in, you'd ha' caught him soon
enough, so you would.'

'He bit you, though,' Rosie remarked, coming
back into the room, closely followed by the vision.
Mona was wearing a pink dress with a cream lace
collar and very shiny black patent-leather pumps.
She looked like a girl who was going dancing and
Colm's heart sank a little. Did she have a young
man, then? Was she spoken for? But the glance she
shot across at him as she sank into her place
heartened him. It was a teasing look, the sort, he
now knew from experience, given by a girl to a
young man who interested her. 'Did you put
somethin' on them bites, Mam?'

'He barely grazed me knuckles,' Colm lied,
keeping his hands below table level. 'It 'ud tek
254

more than a wee bird to get t'rough skin as tough as mine I'm after t'inkin'! Thanks, Mrs Ryder.' This last as a well-piled plate was put before him. He turned back to Mona. 'Are you goin' dancin'? That's a rare pretty frock.'

Mona smiled and thanked him, and Rosie said, with an edge to her voice: 'Not in the middle of the week, she isn't! We're both goin' to our evenin' classes to try to better ourselves.'

'Rosie's doin' a business course,' Mona said. 'I'm studyin' modelling gowns.' She tossed her golden bob and took a large forkful of shepherd's pie, then spoke rather thickly through it. 'I'd like to work in Lewis's, showin' their dresses an' that, but so far I'm only a sales assistant in Gowns.'

Colm opened his mouth to say he'd a friend who had worked in Gowns over in Dublin, then thought better of it. Mr Dawlish was telling Mona what a fine mannequin she would make and how she'd out-earn them all once she got onto a commission basis and Rose was asking if anyone wanted more bread and butter, whilst Sean ate solidly, his eyes going from face to face as the conversation progressed. It occurred to Colm, taking another slice of bread, that this was like being at home; people helped themselves, his father, seeing Mrs Ryder's cup of tea empty, had earlier simply got up and refilled it for her. An easy household and one he very much wanted to join. He knew, now, that even had Mona not been living here he would have wanted to become a lodger in St Domingo Vale.

Satisfied, he finished his shepherd's pie and passed his plate along the table to Rose, who was clearing. Then he watched with delighted anticipation as the suet pudding was brought out of

255

the pan of boiling water, untied from its cloth, tumbled onto a serving plate and cut into generous slices. Mr Backhouse, Colm knew, would be serving his own idea of a pudding about now. It would probably be a large slab of bought cake, stale, of course, because if he waited until it was stale he got it cheaper, covered in custard made with water. And everyone would be so hungry that they would dive eagerly for the bit left over.

'Awright for you, Colm?' Mrs Ryder had gently placed before him a very large slice of the pudding and Rose, standing up, pushed a steaming jug towards him.

'Help yourself to treacle sauce, chuck. It's easier than me askin' you to tell me when I've poured enough,' she said, as though she were forty and he a mere stripling. 'Anyone want another cuppa?'

*　　　*　　　*

'D'you like him? That Colm O'Neill feller?' Rose asked later that evening, as she and Mona made their way to their evening classes in the Kirkdale Senior Evening Institute on Walton Road. She chuckled. 'I didn't half bawl him out when he come through the front door, but I said sorry after. An' he caught Gully, acourse,' she added. 'Mebbe if I'd not shrieked he'd not ha' caught the ole feller.'

'Oh, I like him awright,' Mona said with somewhat studied casualness, Rose thought. 'Good-lookin', but then a good few of the paddies is that. But he's a sight too young for me—bet he's no more'n twenty.'

'Well, you're only twenty-two,' Rose pointed out. She wondered whether to tell her cousin that she

256

suspected Colm was, in fact, rather less than that, but decided not to do so. It would make her sound as though she was trying to put Mona off him. He *was* good-looking, though, with his father's deep-set blue eyes, a strong, jutting chin and the dark hair which curled crisply about his well-shaped head. But, Rose reminded herself as they crossed Sandheys Street and headed for the building, exchanging greetings with other class members as they went, she was not interested in acquiring a young man, especially not one who lodged with them. She wanted to be able to apply for Miss Rogerson's job as Mr Lionel's personal secretary when she left to be married in a year or two, and that meant studying hard at both shorthand and typing, always being on time, forever being obliging and never forgetting her goal for one moment. Sometimes Rose remembered wistfully that she had once yearned to become a journalist, but such ambitions had been impossible once her father died. She had had to get a job, and she realised how lucky she was that she had found work with Patchett & Ross, which suited her so well, with advancement perfectly possible. Now, she enjoyed both typing and shorthand, knowing that her mastery of these skills could take her to the very top of the secretarial tree—and that could mean good money and security, too.

She and Mona went dancing occasionally, and of course they met young men and spent the evening with them, but for her own part Rose was always careful to keep such things on a merely friendly footing. Mona was clearly looking for something or someone a bit more permanent, but Rose told herself firmly that she wanted a life, not a feller, and continued to flit from flower to flower. Besides, she was a great deal younger than Mona, not quite seventeen, and what with evening classes, her work with Patchett & Ross and helping her mam in the house, life was quite full enough without the additional complication of a young man.

But sitting before her typewriter, fingers just above the keys, as the gramophone ground out '*Tea for two*' and the girls endeavoured to type a page of script to its rhythm, she could not help thinking rather wistfully that Colm O'Neill was just the sort of bloke she would have gone for, had she wanted a boyfriend. But seeing as she did not, as how she wanted a life first, she had better put him out of her mind. And she stared ahead of her and typed in rhythm, and wondered whether Mr Garnett had completely forgotten to come round and visit Gulliver, or whether he had only been teasing and had not meant to visit them at all.

*   *   *

Autumn was almost over before, more by luck than judgement, Lily Ryder got her last lodger. Advertisements had availed her little because, rather belatedly, she had realised that lodgers could not all be trusted.

She herself had been very lucky with the O'Neills and Mr Dawlish, but a woman on Oakfield Road had had one who had flitted, not only owing her money but taking everything portable he could carry with him. 'An I never suspected a bleedin' thing,' she had said indignantly to a friend on the tram, when Lily was seated right behind them. 'Oh,

258

'e seemed respec'able enough, 'ad a good job, so 'e claimed, so I never did no checkin' up. An' now 'e's pawned all me little bits an' bobs, no doubt, took the cash I kep' in the brown teapot above the mantel, to say nothin' o' other little savin's what I were keepin' for me old age, an' probably gone off to fool some other poor bugger. Oh, if I could lay me 'ands on 'im . . .'

Lily might not agree with the language, but she was totally at one with the sentiments. She grew nervous of any would-be lodger who was not personally recommended, though she had taken both the O'Neills and Pete Dawlish entirely on trust. But I'm a fair judge of character, she told herself consolingly as she worked around the house. *They're* all right, I'm sure of it. It's just that I don't fancy some stranger livin' in me house.

'Mr Dawlish was a stranger once and it were only Mona what knew Mr O'Neill,' Rose pointed out, but it was no use. Lily had realised there were bad people about and she didn't intend to be landed with any such under her roof. She only had one remaining room, on the first floor, next to Mr Dawlish's and didn't want to make a mistake.

Other than that, though, things were going well. Everyone was settling down nicely. The three young people grew used to one another and a good deal of teasing went on, though anyone with half an eye, Lily considered, could see that poor Colm O'Neill was dotty about Mona and that she was merely flirting with him.

Rose, on the other hand, seemed to have no particular preference for anyone and went about her work and play with calmness and apparent indifference. Sometimes her mother thought she

259

saw a slight wistfulness in her daughter's eye when it rested on Colm, but that was surely unlikely? Rose, in her mother's eyes, was a great deal prettier than Mona; clearly, if Colm was indifferent to her it was because she had given him no encouragement, whereas Mona played up to him whenever she felt inclined.

Pete Dawlish was a quiet man with a predilection for long country walks. He was off most weekends, walking in Wales, or up in the Peak District, and when he was at home spent a good deal of time planning his next excursion. The Ryders both liked and trusted him, and found Sean O'Neill to be a solid family man who wrote long letters home every weekend and talked about his wife and small daughter non-stop. He did not go out much, but Colm made up for this by spending almost none of the daylight hours in St Domingo Vale. He went dancing, to the cinema or theatre, out with pals to New Brighton or to football matches or dog races. He hung around Mona, it was true, but so far as Lily knew, had never actually asked her out.

And as the autumn days advanced inexorably towards winter, Lily began to feel a little guilty over her sister Daisy. She had taken the child Lily about with her, bought her presents, played with her. Perhaps I ought not to have spoken to her the way I did, the soft-hearted Lily told herself as she scrubbed and polished, cooked and cleaned, in her lovely house. Perhaps she and Mona only fell out because I'd been critical, Lily thought worriedly as she knelt in the autumn garden, taking out the weeds and gathering up the mounds of dead leaves to carry round the back and put into her compost pile. Perhaps she never did hear of Jack's death—if she never heard it was no wonder she'd not been to the funeral. And worst of all, of course, was the fear that Daisy was really unhappy. She had taken up with a feller and he had not liked her daughter. Who was to say that he still liked Daisy? Without her daughter's money coming in and with no feller to support her Daisy could be in deep trouble. So, having thought it over for a number of days, Lily decided to go and visit her sister.

She had to ask Mona where Daisy was living, of course, and Mona, it turned out, did not actually know.

'She ain't back at our old place, that I *do* know,' Mona said, when asked. 'But I met a neighbour weeks back, an' she said Mam an' her new feller had fell out. But I dunno where they went. I never asked.'

So Lily put on her tidy coat and a hat which, she thought privately, made her look like a Welsh coal miner, and sallied forth.

She was successful. 'She's nobbut a couple o' miles away,' the neighbour said cheerfully. 'She's fell on 'er feet, your Daisy. She's 'ousekeeper in a 'ouse in Rodney Street owned by an old chap what used to 'ave one o' them posh shops on Lord Street in Southport. Made a mint o' money be all accounts, an' retired a year or so back, only when 'is wife died 'e cou'n't manage, so 'e put an advert in the *Echo* an' your Daisy answered it. I met Daisy in Lewis's, buyin' a couple o' dark dresses for best, she said, an' she told me what 'ad 'appened an' where she was now. She were right pleased wi' 'erself I can tell you.'

'What happened to the feller what she moved in

wi' after she left here?' Lily asked. She had not wanted to admit she knew how Daisy had behaved, but things had clearly changed. It was best, she felt vaguely, to go armed, with knowledge at least, into her sister's possibly enemy camp.

'Oh, 'im.' The neighbour sniffed 'Fly-be-night, that one. Lef' her high an' dry, an' young Mona gawn an' almost no money comin' in . . . Well, she were lucky to gerra decent job after . . . Still, there you are, it's a funny ole world.'

Lily said that it was indeed and left, heading for the new address. She knew Rodney Street and made her way there, found the number and, with some trepidation, knocked on the door.

There was quite a long delay, then a small maid came to answer it. She wore a dark dress with a frilled white pinafore over it and when Lily asked for Mrs Daisy Mullins she said that at this time of the afternoon Mrs Mullins would be downstairs, in her basement sitting-room, and would Miss like to follow her?

Lily had followed her, and had been much impressed by the gardens of the house and by the little sitting-room, with a bright fire burning in the grate, everything neat and clean, and knick-knacks on every available surface. The room was lit by electric light and the curtains and the covers on the comfortable-looking chairs were in a pleasant autumn-tinted chintz. It looked like no room the slatternly Daisy had ever owned, but Lily was at once aware that there was an even more amazing change in her sister. Daisy, spotlessly clean in a black dress and shawl, with her hair pulled back into a bun and a pair of gold-rimmed spectacles on a chain around her neck, had invited her to take

262

the chair on the opposite side of the hearth and had then hissed at her that she'd got this job by being respectable, and she'd thank her sister to see that no idle rumours got around about her for she, Daisy, had suffered from idle rumours in the past and knew what she was talking about.

It was not a good beginning. Lily, however, had bitten her tongue and said in a placatory tone that she could see things had changed.

'Aye. They had to, an' that's the truth, for never was a woman so mistook in a feller as I was in Rolly Matteson,' Daisy had said bitterly. 'When I moved into 'is house he was all charm an' wi' a purse full of' money, an' within six months he'd pawned just about everything I owned an' flitted wi' the young gal what lived on the corner. I'd been givin' him me rent money, seein' as 'ow I'd had to take a bit of a job to make the money go round, an' he'd not paid over a penny of it, not he! So I were evicted . . . on the street, Lil, wi' not a pal in the world, an' me own daughter shunnin' me—to say nothin' o' me sister.'

'You should have come round, Dais, an' explained,' Lily said awkwardly. 'I dare say I'd ha' let bygones be bygones an' give you what help I could.'

Daisy snorted. 'Well, I di'n't think there were much chance o' that,' she said roundly. 'As for that gal o' mine . . . least said soonest mended. But I'm awright now, Lil, in fact I'm in the pink. In clover. I get me keep, all me clothes, a couple o' maids an' a scrubbin' woman to do the dirty work, all I have to do is cook, keep house an' mek sure the ole feller gets wharre wants. I was allus a good cook when I took the trouble, an' believe me, Lily I tek the

263

trouble now. It's worth a bit o' trouble to have a good wage, an' a nice room of me own an' no worries.' She leaned forward and pulled the kettle over the flame, where it began to hiss comfortably. 'And it's all me own efforts what 'ave got me where I am today and I won't 'ave no one messin' it up. So if you've that in mind . . .'

'Why would I want to do that, Dais?' Lily asked, honestly shocked that her sister could even think such a thing. 'But I come round to say as how your Mona's wi' us, sharin' a room wi' Rosie, so if you ever want to see her . . . ?'

'I can't think I shall,' Daisy said, narrowing her eyes. 'Wharra daughter, when her mam's in trouble she just turns away! No, I can do very well for meself without no interference from me so-called family.'

'Mona di'n't turn away, exactly, Dais. She said your feller turned her out, wouldn't let her live with you. And . . .'

'Oh, "Mona said, Mona said",' Daisy mimicked. 'I won't 'ave no one comin' round 'ere tellin' a lot o' lies about me. You di'n't say you was me sister, did you?'

'No, is it lies like that you're afraid of, Daisy?' Lily said, beginning to feel the first stirrings of real annoyance. 'Because they're what other people call truths, you know.'

Daisy reared up in her chair and tightened her lips. Her nostrils flared and her eyes sparked dangerously. 'Truth, lies, wharra you on about? I won't 'ave folk spoilin' wharr I've found for meself, that's wharr I mean; not Mona, nor you, nor anyone else. Well, I'll mek us a cuppa, then I'll have to go about me business, gerrin' the tea for

264

the ole feller, an' you can mek yourself scarce. I dunno why you come, truth to tell.'

'I told you I came because Mona's livin' with us an' I thought you oughter know how to gerrin touch wi' her,' Lily said in a dangerously quiet voice. 'As for you doin' well for yourself, that's grand, that is. But I'm alone now, since Jack was killed the best part o' three years ago. I' s'pose you di'n't know?'

'Jack, dead?' Daisy said, but there was that in her eyes which told Lily that she had known all along, had even, in her spiteful way, not been displeased. 'Oh well, that means we're both widders—though I've told Mr Clitheroe as I've neither kith nor kin of me own, which is another good reason for neither you nor Mona comin' round 'ere an' spoilin' things for me.' She must have seen the look on her sister's face for she added in a more conciliatory tone: 'Not as I'd deny you're me sister, if it come to the crunch, but I don't want to be made to look a liar, now do I?'

'I don't know why not, since you are one,' Lily said, taking the cup which Daisy held out and standing it down on a small side table. She got to her feet and Daisy followed suit. 'Thanks for the tea, but I can't drink it, Dais, it 'ud choke me. Well, I won't tell Mona where you are if you'd rather I didn't, but if you end up dyin' in the workhouse, wi' no one to give an eye to you, you'll only have yourself to blame.'

Daisy snorted scornfully. 'Nasty. You're the one as'll end in the work'ouse, givin' a roof to a gal like Mona, what's no better'n she should be. Oh aye, you warned me about her, now I'm warnin' you. She'll batten on you now you're widdered an' needin' her help no doubt, 'cos you allus was a fool, Lily. But me, I'm featherin' me nest so good I'll be in clover even after the ole feller pops 'is clogs, I shan't need no one, don't you fret. An' by the same token, don't think you can come spongin' off me when things go wrong.'

'Well, you nasty, spiteful crittur!' Lily said, throwing caution to the winds. 'Talkin' that way about your own daughter, what's norra bad gal when she's in decent company. As for spongin' off of you, it's allus been the other way about from wharr I can remember.' She turned on her heel and stalked across the room, heading for the front door once more. 'I'm off, an' rare glad to go I tell you!'

Apparently this was more than Daisy could stand, for she hissed: 'That's right, you go, an' don't you come round me again, Lily Ryder! You thought yourself better'n me me when your Jack was alive for all he were only a bleedin' tram driver, but now he's dead you're just dirt beneath me feet, not worth botherin' with! Get out, go on, get out!'

Lily hurried back along the dark corridor, through the green baize doors and across the marble-floored hall. She tugged the big door open and ran out, glad to be in the fresh air once more and about to leave her sister's spiteful tongue behind her. To her considerable astonishment, however, as she descended the steps Daisy said, behind her: 'Thank you for callin', Mrs Ryder, and if I have a place vacant be sure I'll let your daughter know.'

Lily turned and saw that the maid who had let her in had come hurrying across the hallway and now stood at Daisy's elbow. Lily filled her lungs and shouted. 'I dunno who you stole them fancy gold spectacles off of, Daisy Mullins, but it's clear you aren't seein' so good! If you have a place vacant you can stick it up your . . .'

The hastily slamming door, with a last view of Daisy's suddenly horrified face in the narrowing gap, sent Lily off down Rodney Street in a paroxysm of giggles, but she suddenly realised that tears were running down her cheeks and stopped at a tram stop to collect herself, realising that the encounter had upset her considerably. Just then a tram drew up beside her and Lily hopped aboard, not even stopping to consider whether it went in her direction or not. She took a seat inside, for though it was getting on towards evening it lacked a few minutes to leaving-off time so the vehicle was comparatively empty, and asked the young conductor for a ticket to the terminus. Better take a hold of myself before I go home, she thought, dabbing her eyes with a small handkerchief and then blowing her nose vigorously, because there's no point in tellin' the girls where I've been nor what's been said. And no point in dwellin' on what that evil Daisy had said about Jack—*just a tram driver*, indeed! But if she went home now, all red-eyed and upset, she'd go and spill the beans to someone just to get it off her chest and that would never do.

It was a nuisance, of course, that she had not noticed the tram number, so she had no idea where she was about to end up, but she had always enjoyed a tram ride. It reminded her of Jack and the many times she'd ridden with him so that they could walk home together, or have a bit of a talk whilst he waited in traffic queues or watched the time at the terminus.

So now she sat contentedly enough, watching the city unfold before her eyes, trying to guess where she was going. And when at last the tram stopped and the driver got down to stretch his legs, his big gunmetal watch in one hand, she realised that an old friend had been driving, only she had been too preoccupied to notice. Accordingly, she got down and walked round to where he stood, shuffling his feet, whilst the conductor strolled up and down, stretching his legs. 'Hello, Mr Sutton! How are you keepin'?'

'Well, if it ain't Mrs Ryder,' Mr Sutton said, carefully tucking his watch back in his pocket and beaming at her. 'What are you doin' right out here, queen? You've not moved out to Dingle, have you?'

Lily laughed. 'No, though we're livin' in a different area, me an' Rosie. Do you know St Domingo Vale?'

'Oh aye, a tram driver gets to know most parts o' the city,' Mr Sutton said. He drew a cigarette paper out of an inside pocket and a small tin of tobacco. 'Mind if I roll meself one, Mrs Ryder? How are you managin', you an' the gal?'

'Pretty well, thanks, Mr Sutton,' Lily said. 'I'm takin' lodgers, which keeps me busy, an' Rosie's gorra job with a company on Dale Street.'

'Right,' Mr Sutton said, carefully licking along the edge of the thin white paper and then with equal care spreading the tobacco along its length. 'You'll not have met me conductor before, though, 'cos he's new to the job. He's from the Pool originally, but he's been workin' down south, in London, for a couple o' years. When the chance came he moved back up north—sensible feller.

268

Hey, Tommy, come over here, an' meet Mrs Ryder. Jack Ryder an' me worked together for years.'

The conductor approached. He was young and fair-haired, with light-blue eyes and a curving, amused mouth. ''Ow d'you do, Mrs Ryder?' he said affably. He pulled a bag out of his pocket. 'Wanna humbug, chuck?'

Lily Ryder chuckled and took the proffered sweet, then turned her attention back to the train driver.

'Tommy was on the trams down south,' Mr Sutton explained. 'He's conductin' for now, but he's hopin' for a drivin' job in a year or so. He wanted to come home, so he's been stayin' wi' me an' the missus whiles our Andy's been workin' up in Scotland. Andy's comin' back home in a month or two, though, so Tommy's on the look-out for somethin' else—somethin' where they don't mind shift work, I reckon.'

He stared hard at Lily, who looked limpidly back, but her mind was racing. A tram man! It would be grand to have one in the house again, whether he be driver or conductor, and a tram man was bound to be trustworthy. She turned and looked at Tommy.

He grinned at her, one cheek distended with the humbug. 'You gotta room goin' beggin', Miz Ryder?' he asked affably. 'I'm 'ouse-trained, ax anyone!'

'We-ell, I don't know . . .' Lily said doubtfully, but she did, of course. She thought that Tommy would fit in very well—and because he was a tram man he would have had to supply references when he came up to Liverpool in the first place or he would never have been taken on. 'Tell you what,

269

tek me back to the Haymarket so's I can get me proper tram back to Everton an' I'll mek up me mind.'

'Thanks, Mrs Ryder,' Mr Sutton said. 'He's a good lad, Tommy. We've had no trouble wi' him, the missus an' me.' He turned to his conductor. 'Back aboard, ole feller,' he said. 'Who knows, you may be fitted up wi' lodgings before our Andy gets home!'

*　　　*　　　*

Rose came out of Mere Lane and set off across Breckfield Road, heading for the Vale. She was feeling pleased with herself. She had got excellent marks in both shorthand and typing during the recent examinations and Mr Lionel, the most difficult of the brothers, had said, albeit grudgingly, that the firm was pleased with her. She had been using the spare typewriter in the typists' room whenever they were extra busy and had actually taken dictation a couple of times, managing to read her shorthand outlines back to everyone's satisfaction. She was still doing the office girl's work, but already Mr Edward had suggested that the firm employ a boy with a bicycle, who could get errands done faster than Rose could manage on foot, and she could still deal with the post, make the tea and do various other odd jobs when not actually engaged in typing up the lengthy documentation needed for their work. It would mean a higher salary, better prospects and less time spent, Rose thought guiltily, in plodding through the wet and dirty streets, delivering light packages and letters. Furthermore, Christmas was only a matter of weeks off and other members of staff said that the brothers rewarded good work with generous Christmas bonuses. So Rose was feeling pleased with life despite the fact that autumn was clearly over and the wind which blew the leaves around her feet was a chilly one, with winter on its breath.

Mr Garnett had not found time to visit the parrot despite frequent promises, but it seemed to her that the bird was settling in and was, in fact, very little trouble. Indeed, they would miss him when he did leave, for his squawky voice and amusing ways were becoming a part of their lives. Now that he was used to them, indeed, he was friendlier towards everyone, even Lily, who still regarded him with some suspicion. He loved to have his head rubbed and would close a chalky eyelid over his wicked eye whilst this was being done, and when Mr Dawlish was home he would let Gully out of the cage and the parrot would sit on his shoulder, nibbling gently at the lobe of his ear and shouting with pretended surprise and swaying exaggeratedly whenever Mr Dawlish moved.

And it was marvellous having Tommy Frost actually lodging with them—a tram man and eager to talk about his work, too! It was for that reason that she liked him, Rose told herself; it had nothing to do with curly fair hair, light-blue eyes and a smiling mouth. And he'd been a driver down south—so he hoped to be put onto driving during the winter, even if only as a stand-in when the regulars were off. He was good fun, was Tommy, Rose thought now, he always had plenty to say for himself, unlike Colm, who seemed quite content to sit at the table during meals and eat and listen. But although Colm continued, when he thought no one was looking, to gaze in a very sloppy sort of way at Mona, Rose no longer minded. Let him! He was nice-looking, she would give him that, and a pleasant enough fellow, but he wasn't a tram man and Rose had decided that, if she could never drive a tram herself, at least as a tram man's wife she would be a part of it all, the way her mam had been.

So Rose danced along the pavement, well pleased with life. And it wasn't only that the lodgers were fitting in so well and seemed part of the family, nor that the parrot had settled down too and was generally accepted by everyone, which caused Rose's light step. It was because she was going dancing at the Daulby Hall ballroom with her friend Ella from work, which was a rare treat. Before she and Ella had started studying in earnest they had gone weekly to one or other of the city's dancing classes and dancing had speedily become a favourite pastime, but ever since she had realised that certificates were her best hope of getting the better jobs, Rose had slogged away most evening at her shorthand outlines and on the cardboard keyboard which had been given to the class in order that those without machines might practise at home.

So since she and Ella were determined to do well in examinations and must, therefore, study constantly, Rose had not been to the dancing classes nor the cinema for weeks and weeks, and even the bright summer weather had, in the main, seen little of her. Only the crisp certainty of her teacher's voice, reading out the results of the recent examinations ('certificates to follow'), had

272

persuaded Rose that she might now relax a little, and Ella's suggestion that they should behave like normal girls for once, instead of prigs and bluestockings, had met with only token resistance.

'We never did,' Rose had protested. 'We just worked hard while it were necessary; that isn't what a bluestockin' does. An' there's more exams to come, you know. Though not till after Christmas, acourse.'

'Maybe there are,' Ella had said. 'But tomorrer's Saturday night so what say we go on a spree? An' not to classes, either, but to a real, proper dance wi' an orchestra an' all. Why, if we go to the Daulby Hall, near the Majestic, there'll be sailors there off the ships down in the docks. Me big sister goes an' she says there's a lorra men go there, though they're mostly foreign. Still, I like dancin' wi' men better'n wi' other gals.'

'Aye, you've a point there, 'cept I don't much like dancin' wi' fellers what can't speak English,' Rose said. 'There's a feller what lodges wi' me mam, he's always off dancin'. Wonder if he'll be there? Tommy Frost, his name is—I might of mentioned him once or twice.'

'I dare say you have,' Ella said, giggling. 'But I thought it were the Irish feller you were sweet on— the one what's workin' on the tunnel.'

'Oh, him!' Rose said scornfully. 'He's always makin' moon-eyes at our Mona. Tell you what, though, shall we ask her to come wi' us? Then you'll be able to tek a look at Colm for yourself. An' if Colm comes to the Daulby, then Tommy might, too. He goes dancin' quite often, I believe.'

'Do you want your Mona to come?' Ella had asked doubtfully. 'After all, if she's as pretty as you say she'll cramp our style a bit. We want the fellers buzzin' round us, not round her. As for that Tommy you mentioned, he'd probably come to the Daulby an' dance wi' you if he lodges wi' your mam, even if Mona don't come. Only you'd have to tell him where we was goin', an' suggest he comes along,' Ella added.

But Rose immediately vetoed such a forward suggestion. 'It 'ud look as if I were bleedin' desperate,' she said, feeling her cheeks growing hot at the mere idea. 'But if I wait till we're all round the table, havin' our dinners, an' then ask Mona if she'd like to come wi' us to the Daulby ... well, I wouldn't have cheapened meself, but they might easily come along wi' us. Don't you think that's more ... more casual, like?'

'If you wan', then do it that way,' Ella agreed. 'Right, chuck. Best frocks an' silk stockin's an' we'll meet in the foyer at half nine.'

So Rose rattled along in high good spirits, singing 'On the sunny side of the street' beneath her breath as she went, already looking forward to her night out. It would be so nice to wear something pretty and whirl beneath the coloured ballroom lights and chat to girls she'd not seen since the previous winter. Even to herself, Rose did not admit that the thought of Tommy coming to the dance, asking her to waltz or quickstep, was what really excited her.

Rose hurried round the back and burst into the kitchen, to find her mother and Mrs Kibble engaged in the preparation of the evening meal, whilst Mr O'Neill leaned against the draining board, cap in hand. Gully, in his cage, gave her a squawk of greeting, and put his head between the wicker bars of his cage and speared a curling piece of apple peel, which he then proceeded to bang against the side of the cage as though he believed himself to be killing a worm.

'Mam, I've got me results and you'll never guess what I got in the shorthand tests an' the typing speeds . . .' she was beginning, when she realised that Colm's father was speaking. She stopped short, turning a guilty face towards him. 'Oh, I'm so sorry, Mr O'Neill, I didn't realise I was interrupting you.'

'It's awright, Rose,' Mr O'Neill said placidly. 'I was just tellin' your mam here how meself would be away for two weeks over Christmas. It's a week proper leave an' a week unpaid, but I t'ought I'd tek it, seein' as how Mrs O'Neill's been poorly wit' a cracked wrist, and' young Caitlin's acting a part in the Nativity play, an' she's fair des'prit for meself an' her big brother to see her in it. Colm won't come as well, not this time. He was lucky to get the job at his age and knows it, so he won't risk comin' back and findin' himself out of work. Of course I told your mammy I'd pay me room just the same, but she says . . .'

'I won't tek money for a room that's not being used, Mr O'Neill,' Lily said firmly. 'It ain't my way. Particularly as Mrs O'Neill's not been too brave lately. Besides, a fortnight's norra long time; it'll soon be gone.'

'I t'ink, meself, I'd be happier payin' a retainer,' Sean said, and Rose saw Mrs Kibble, who had been frowning, give a satisfied nod. 'You name the price, Mrs Ryder. I know you'll do what's right.'

'Tell you what,' Rose said suddenly. 'It 'ud be nice for me an' Mona to have a room each for a change, just over Christmas, an' I'm goin' to get a

275

Christmas bonus from Patchett & Ross.' Rose turned to her mother. 'Suppose we ask Mr O'Neill here to put his things in his son's room, just whilst he's in Ireland . . . wouldn't that be fairer, Mam? And I could pay a bit—I wouldn't mind at all.'

'That's fine by me, so it is,' Mr O'Neill said at once. 'But you've no need to pay for a room in your own house, Rose. Others pay a retainer, a smaller sum which the landlord names, surely that 'ud be fairer? So what d'you say, Mrs Ryder?'

Lily hesitated, then named a small sum in an even smaller voice. Rose smiled to herself. Mam was a nice person, she would never take more than her due and, much though she enjoyed having Mona in the house, there were times when the two of them were both dressing for work in the small room that she could not help thinking wistfully of the days when she had not had to share. But now, everyone was smiling, even Mrs Kibble, and Mr O'Neill, in a relieved voice, said that he would hand the money over before he left for Dublin.

'For we'll be busy till then,' he said, walking over to the kitchen door. 'We'll want to get presents for those at home . . . an' somethin' a bit special for the star o' the nativity play I'm t'inkin'.'

'And we'll make sure that Colm gets a good Christmas, though it won't be the same as seein' his little sister in her play an' giving his mam a big hug an' a kiss,' Mrs Ryder added reassuringly. 'Still, no one can risk his job these days, work's too scarce. Well now, Rosie,' she gave her daughter a hearty hug whilst Gulliver screamed excitedly and swung the apple peel harder against the bars. 'You've passed, eh? Your Dad would ha' been proud.'

276

Over the supper table, generously laden with a great tureen of savoury stew and another of mashed potatoes, Colm listened with interest as Rose told Mona that she was off to the Daulby Hall with her friend Ella and would Mona like to come along? Colm liked dancing; if Nell had done him any favour it was to teach him to dance, and he had been along to various ballrooms since he arrived in Liverpool and had danced with a number of pretty, light-footed young women. But he'd never been lucky enough to choose the same dance-hall as Mona and now it looked as though he might find out where she went—or at least, where she might— or might not—be going tonight.

But he pretended indifference, continuing to eat the delicious stew—Mrs Ryder was a wonderful cook, as good, in her way, as his mammy—whilst listening closely. What would Mona say? Would she agree to go the the Daulby? Even if she did not, she might easily name the ballroom of her choice, and then . . .

'Dancin', our Rosie? Wharrever next!' Mona's thin, darkened eyebrows rose dramatically. 'I thought you was too busy wi' your books an' exams for such pastimes!'

Rose giggled. 'I was. But I passed, didn't I? So now I want some fun. Are you goin' to come along wi' us, Mona? We're goin' to the Daulby, an' I thought I'd wear me pale-blue linen. It 'ud be the first time I've had it on, an' Mammy made it months ago, didn't you, Mam?'

'I did,' Mrs Ryder agreed placidly. 'But it were for parties, not the office, an' you've been too busy

for parties, chuck. Still, you should go about more.'
She turned to her niece. 'Why don't you both go,
keep an eye on each other?'

'We-ell, I might,' Mona said, cocking her head
on one side. 'I've gorra coffee-coloured lace dress
I'm longin' to wear. Only why the Daulby? You get
all them foreign seamen . . . they jabber on so, an'
they squeeze an' all.'

'The ones off the Argentinian boats?' Mr
Dawlish put in. He laughed. 'But they dance well,
I'm told.'

'Oh, no one dances like an Irishman,' Sean put
in. He grinned at his son. 'You oughter go along as
well, Colm, let 'em see how a feller from Dublin
can leap like a leprechaun an' show a clean pair o'
heels to the best of 'em.

'You're right there, Mr O'Neill,' Mona said,
forking in more stew. 'The Argies can dance, I'll
give 'em that, but they smell of cattle boats, so I
still prefer our local fellers.' She looked under her
lashes at Colm, making his heart skip a beat, then
glanced at Tommy's fair head, bent over his plate
as he industriously ate. 'Though I always thought
Irishmen had two left feet, to say nothin' of clods of
earth on their boots!' Colm and his father laughed
and protested, and Mona, dimpling at them,
addressed Tommy, who was sitting opposite her.
'Wharrabout you then, Mr Frost? Why don't the
pair o' you come along to the Daulby? As soon as
all the girls realise you ain't foreign they'll be all
over you! Why not, eh?'

'I wouldn't mind,' Colm said, 'As for boots,
you're doin' me a rare injustice, Miss Mona, for
I've got me a good pair o' dancin' pumps and foot
it wit' the best, though it's not certain I am of the

tango, or the foxtrot. But I can charleston up a storm I'm tellin' ye. An' anything I can't dance I'll watch till I pick it up. I'm a quick study wit' me feet, so I am.'

'Well, I'll see how me cash is holdin' out,' Tommy said. 'If I'm in the money I'll certainly give you girls a treat an' come to the Daulby. Seein' as 'ow I'm a boy scout at heart it'll be me good turn for the week,' he added in a mock-righteous tone. 'Mekin' sure the pair of you ain't dragged off to the white slave trade by some sleazy, hip-swivellin' Argy.'

'The three of us,' Rose reminded them. 'Don't forget me pal Ella's comin' along an' all. We're meetin' in the foyer at nine thirty an' we were goin' to the upstairs ballroom, although we aren't beginners. Most o' the Argies stay downstairs for some reason.'

'I might as well come wit' you, Tommy,' Colm said. He did his best to sound casual, uncaring, but feared that his voice let him down by its evident cheerfulness. 'If we go in at half-time it's cheaper and I'm savin' up for Christmas—aren't we all, now?—but it's a dacint evenin' out for threepence, and havin' a few dances an' soft drinks is cheaper than spendin' an evenin' in the pub punishin' the hard stuff.'

'Don't they sell alcohol at the Daulby, then?' Mr Dawlish said, grinning. 'Oh well, don't you go tryin' to persuade me to join you—I'd rather tek a few pints an' have a bit of a singsong any day than prance around wi' a lot of fancy Argy fellers a-watchin'.'

'I'm wit' you there,' Sean said. He wiped a piece of bread round his now empty plate and heaved a

279

satisfied sigh. 'Sure an' you're a wonderful cook, Mrs Ryder. My Eileen won't be knowin' me at Christmas, so fat I'm after becomin' on your good food.'

'Get along wi' you, Mr O'Neill,' Lily Ryder said, beaming. 'Rosie, if you clear the crocks Mona and meself will fetch in the pudding.'

Colm watched the two girls gathering up the plates and hugged himself inwardly. At last he was going to hold the delectable Mona in his arms, murmur into her ear—and be extra careful not to stand on her size fives! He had a shrewd suspicion, though, that Mona might prove expensive company. Nell's depredations had made their mark on him; he fought shy, now, of girls who demanded expensive drinks or wanted only the best seats in cinemas and theatres.

On the other hand, though, he told himself as he watched the arrival of the apple pie and custard, no one gave anything away for free in this world and he had a pleasant suspicion that Mona would prove generous in other ways if he stumped up for the largest box of chocolates, the best seats. So there you had it. If you wanted a first-rate looker and a chance to cuddle in the dark you had to be cheerful and part with your hard-earned cash. A pity Christmas was coming up ... but he'd manage, somehow. He would work overtime, get some work clearing leaves up in one of the big houses on the outskirts of the city. Oh aye, and Mona would be worth it, lovely girl that she was.

'Colm, have ye gone deaf, son? That's the second time Mrs Ryder's asked you if you'd like custard. What're you t'inkin' about, boy! Stop dreamin' about the dance or there'll be none left an' I know how you love apple pie.'

Colm felt his cheeks grow hot. 'I weren't . . . I were t'inkin' I might take on some odd-jobbing in me time off, so's I can buy me mammy a better Christmas present.'

'Good idea,' Tommy said approvingly. 'We might go together, Colm.'

Mrs Ryder cut into the pie and passed it, and the jug of custard, up the table to Colm.

'Don't tease the boy, Mr O'Neill,' she said kindly. 'It's the girls dream about dances, not young fellers. Help yourself, Colm, an' then pass the jug along.'

*   *   *

Although it seemed rather strange when Rose thought about it, there had been no suggestion that the four of them might make their way to the Daulby together and probably it was as well. It was generally accepted that if a feller was serious he would pay for you to go into the dance, but for a casual friendship like theirs it was fairer all round to meet inside. And besides, Mona's toilet, when she was going dancing, was somewhat elaborate. She tugged out every good dress she possessed— and she possessed many—before agreeing with her cousin that the coffee-coloured lace was the nicest.

'Ella'll be wonderin' where I've got to,' Rose grumbled, as at last Mona, with a final dusting of powder on her small nose and a last brush at her shoulders to make sure no loose hairs remained on the lace, finally pronounced herself ready. 'We said half-nine, not half-ten!'

'Don't exaggerate, flower,' Mona said, setting off down the stairs at a trot. 'We may not make half-

281

nine—well, we won't—but we'll be there by twenty to the hour if we gerra move on.'

'I hate being late,' Rose grumbled as they let themselves out of the house with her mother's reminders not to go missing trams or arriving home at midnight ringing in her ears. 'Still, I bet the fellers won't be on time.'

'Stop moaning and run!' Mona shrieked suddenly. 'There's a tram, our Rosie; if we miss this 'un it'll be a while afore the next at this time o'night.'

They tore down the Vale and onto Oakfield Road, and really sprinted to the tram stop.

'But there's a bloomin' crowd aboard,' Mona said as they inched towards the doorway. 'I don't mind standin', but I do mind bein' left behind. I bet half o' these kids is goin' to the Daulby.'

But they weren't left, because Rose plunged impetuously forward, getting foot on the step and heaving herself aboard, then turning to help Mona. There were some good-natured squeaks and growls from passengers shoved even further down the car, but the conductor rang the bell and the vehicle moved ponderously forward. The movement shunted everyone towards the front and a good-natured railway worker, still in his overalls, pushed the two girls behind him and put a muscular arm across the entrance, effectively penning them in.

'Where're you goin', gals?' he asked. 'This tram's always crowded an' I'm off at the next stop.'

'Daulby Hall,' Mona told him. She tossed her golden curls and showed him the brown paper bag under her arm. 'Can't you tell, mister? Them's me dancin' pumps in there, an' I'm wearin' me best dress.'

The man chuckled and told Mona that she was lookin' rare smart an' didn't he wish he were ten years younger, and Mona said something about many a good tune being played on an old fiddle, which made Rose feel uncomfortable. She thought uneasily that her cousin was being very friendly considering she had never met the man before this moment, but it probably didn't matter since he was an old man of at least thirty-five. Now if he had been younger she would have thought Mona was being flirtatious and egging him on. But before she could say anything someone else shouted 'Tickets, please! Come along now, tickets, ladies and gents!' and the conductor, a small, rosy-faced man, pushed and wriggled his way out of the crowded interior of the tram.

The girls turned away from the railwayman and handed over their pennies, and it was no time at all before the tram stopped at their destination and what looked like the majority of the passengers got down and made their way towards the hall, though some of them, Rose guessed, were heading for the Majestic cinema, where they would be meeting friends who had watched the film and would go dancing later, perhaps at the Daulby, or possibly at one of the other popular venues in the city.

'Dear God, wharra crush,' Mona said crossly as they went towards the foyer of the dance-hall. 'I'm glad I brought me pumps in the bag, at least all those clodhoppers only trod on me workin' boots. Now, Rosie, can you see your Ella anywhere?'

'No, I ... oh yes, there she is,' Rose said. She clutched her cousin's arm. 'Come along, we'd best grab her before she disappears. Is Saturday night always like this, I wonder?'

283

'Bound to be. Folk come dancin' on a Saturday 'cos they can lie in on a Sunday,' Mona said wisely. 'Is that Ella, in the orange dress? She's a bit showy, ain't she?'

'It's not orange, it's flame. It's a very fashionable colour,' Rose said stiffly. She thought, herself, that the dress was a trifle bright, but Ella was her friend and Mona had no call to question her taste. Rose had noticed some very odd clothing in her cousin's wardrobe this evening. 'Come *on*, Mona, or we'll lose her.'

She ignored Mona's mutter of 'Norra bad thing, to my way of thinking,' and continued to wriggle through the crowd until she reached her friend's side. 'Here we are, Ell,' she said breathlessly. 'Got your joey?'

'Aye. An' a bit over for a drink an' some chips, after,' Ella said. 'Is this your cousin? Hello, Mona, I'm Ella Thompson. Me an' Rose work in the same office, an' we're at night-school together an' all.'

'Glad to meet you,' Mona said. 'Come on, lets gerrin before all the best places are took.'

*   *   *

Rose was enchanted with the ballroom. She had been dancing before, but always at one of the establishments where it was taught. She saw the soft but brilliant lighting, the orchestra and the assembled dancers as though they were a marvellous sort of stage set and had to work hard not to show how impressed she was before Ella, who had obviously frequented such places before, and Mona, who seemed entirely at home

There were some chairs and tables, but mostly

the girls stood on one side of the ballroom in small groups whilst on the opposite side the young men congregated, laughing and chaffing one another, and pretending not to notice the girls, although their eyes roamed speculatively across the room whenever they thought themselves unobserved. Rose scanned the young men as they made their way to the cloakroom to leave their coats and walking shoes but she could see neither Colm nor Tommy. Still, it was early yet and they'd probably have coats to hand in as well.

They emerged from the cloakroom clutching the tickets the girl on the counter had given them, Rose smoothing her skirt nervously and glancing rather self-consciously down at her new dancing shoes. She felt sure everyone must be staring at her, but when she glanced around she saw at once that people were too busy with their own friends to worry about strangers. The band had left the platform and were nowhere to be seen, and the dancers were queuing at the bar for soft drinks, crisps and biscuits.

Rose peered around her, then clutched Ella's arm. 'Ella, I thought I saw someone from work! You know, the office boy, Reg. Is it him, over there by that pillar?'

'Come on!' Mona said. 'There's a table . . . first one there grab it!'

Rose followed and the three of them sat down quickly on the chairs then relaxed and looked around them.

'I bet Tommy an' Colm turn up after ten o'clock and you made me rush meself like a mad thing,' Mona complained. 'Everyone else has gone into the ladies to do their hair and powder their noses again—will you save my chair if I just pop off for a moment?'

'Oh, you go then,' Rose said. 'Though why you want to put more stuff on your face I can't imagine. It's a good thing Mam didn't take a hard look at you, me girl, or you'd ha' been sent up to our room to wash it all off again.'

'I'm older than you,' Mona reminded her. 'Besides, you can't work in a flower shop an' not make up nice. Nor you can't come to a dance wi' your face all bare, like a schoolgirl.'

'She don't half slap it on,' Ella said as Mona, with a flick of her blonde hair, disappeared into the crowd. 'My mam would say there's a bit o' make-up an' there's paintin', an' your cousin paints. Not but what she's very pretty,' she added quickly. 'In fact, she's downright lovely—I doubt we'll gerra look in wi' the fellers tonight.'

'She dresses lovely, too,' Rose said rather wistfully. She had been delighted with her blue merino dress with its neat waist and the cream lace which edged the V of the neckline. She had bought a piece of matching blue ribbon to tie up her curls in a knot on top of her head, and had felt modern and grown-up . . . until she saw Mona in the coffee-coloured lace with its deep décolletage, the way it clung to her body until it frothed out into fullness just above her cousin's silk-clad knees.

'Yeah. That lace thing must have cost a packet,' Ella agreed. She looked down at her flimsy, flame-coloured dress with its myriad little pleats and uneven hemline. 'I was real proud of this 'un, until I saw your cousin's. Now . . . well, it looks a bit—a bit bright, like. An' you can see it wasn't bought at Lewis's, or Blackler's.'

286

'Nor were mine, chuck,' Rose said ruefully. She looked over her friend, from the top of Ella's soft, toffee-brown hair down across the peaky, elfin face to the slender body in its bright dress. 'But I tell you what, you've gorra sort of fresh, young look. Mona looks more—oh, more *used*, like.'

They were still chuckling over it when Mona came back and sat down, thumping her small evening bag down on the table between them. 'I just seen the fellers,' she said. 'Tommy an' Colm, I mean.'

'Oh, good. I thought I saw one of the fellers from work, too,' Rose said. She giggled. 'I can't imagine dancing wi' Reggie, can you, Ella?'

The band had taken their places once more and the conductor announced they were to play a waltz and could he have all the young ladies and gentlemen on the floor, please? Ella leaned forward. 'Reggie's awright, but . . . oh, Lor'!'

'What? Don't say Reggie's goin' to join us, I think . . .'

Someone loomed over the table. Someone very tall and very, very thin. Someone familiar. 'Hello, Miss Ryder, Miss Thompson. Are you enjoying yourselves? And now are you going to introduce me to your friend?'

It was Mr Garnett, and he was staring meaningfully at Mona.

*   *   *

Much later that night, curled up in her bed with the sound of Mona's snuffling little snores sounding in her ears, Rose, hugging herself, went over her very first official dance. She had enjoyed it so much and

287

at first it had seemed positively doomed. Mr Garnett was her *boss*; how could she possibly feel at ease with his eyes on her all evening? And if he felt it was only polite to join them ... well, it was just too awful to contemplate.

But it hadn't happened like that. To be sure, Mr Garnett had danced first with Mona and later, rather punctiliously, with herself and Ella, but he had not spent the intervening time at their table. He had gone back to the group he was with and, so far as Rose was aware, had not so much as glanced at them since.

It hadn't been too bad dancing with him, either, although because of the difference in their heights and the length of his legs—Rose had found herself whisked around the floor, lapping the other dancers several times, and had ended up breathless. She had half expected him to talk about work, or Gulliver, too, but instead he chatted inconsequentially about the dance, the dullness of the refreshments and the fact that he hoped the rain would hold off for the journey home.

And as soon as he had done his three duty dances—that was how Rosie saw it, thankfully— Colm and Tommy had appeared, looking very smart in dark suits, white shirts and sombre ties, and bringing with them a short, square young man called Max who had immediately endeared himself to the girls by proving to be an excellent dancer and an amusing companion. It transpired that he was also a tram-worker, though only a mechanic, and had not been invited along by Tommy, as the girls had at first supposed. The three men had met up in the foyer and when Colm had admitted that the two of them were meeting three young

288

ladies . . .

'Well, after that there were no gettin' rid of him,' Tommy had admitted, grinning. 'Specially when he saw what stunners you was.'

The girls had snorted at that, but nevertheless it was a good start to the evening, and the fun had been fast and furious, with Max and Ella, Tommy and Rose, and Colm and Mona taking to the floor for the next dance.

After that they had all taken turns and danced with each other, and though, when dancing with Colm, poor Rose knew that he had spent the entire time trying to keep an eye on Mona and Tommy, she had still managed to enjoy herself immensely. She was a good, neat dancer and actually performed the tango, with Tommy, as though born to the elegant, swooping movements, though she thought, privately, that Mona would probably have done it better. Since neither Max nor Colm felt sufficiently self-confident to undertake an attempt, however, the other four stood on the edge of the floor and applauded whenever Tommy and Rose swooped past, making Rose feel positively like a film star, she told her partner.

But the best time of all had been the walk home. They emerged onto the pavement outside the Daulby to find the sky clear and star-spangled overhead, the weather just sufficiently frosty to make them thankful for their warm coats, hats and sensible shoes. And when Ella and Max had left them, the four of them joined arms and strode out briskly, Rose trying to match her steps to the longer ones of her companions, for even Mona was three or four inches taller than she, and this seemed very amusing and, when they occasionally broke into a run, downright funny.

They had entered the kitchen as quietly as they could, of course, but Rose's mother had sat up for them. Rose thought this was awfully kind, especially as her mam had made a big jug of hot cocoa and provided a platter of her own shortbread biscuits and some ginger cake, but she did notice that the young men looked a little glum.

She had mentioned this to Mona as they undressed for bed, and Mona gurgled and said that of course the fellers had been disappointed. ' 'Cos I reckon they'd meant to have a nice . . . a nice kiss an' cuddle in the warm kitchen, instead of on the back doorstep, like they usually do,' she had explained. 'Fellers don't tek you dancin' just for the pleasure of treadin' on your toes, you know. They buy you some drinks an' refreshments, an' you're supposed to pay 'em back in kisses.'

'Really?' Rose had said, considerably fascinated. 'D'you mean they'd have kissed both of us, or would it have been one each?'

Mona, dabbing half-heartedly at her make-up with a damp flannel, stared at her through the mirror on the washstand. 'Gawd, you don't know nothin', you,' she had said with affectionate disgust. 'One each, acourse!'

'Oh! Then . . . then which?'

'Which d'you think?' Mona had asked aggravatingly and then refused to discuss the matter further. Only Rose knew, of course, that Colm would have grabbed Mona and she herself would have been grabbed by Tommy. It stood to reason—Colm had been staring goggle-eyed at Mona all evening, including the times he had danced with Rose. She had felt happy and comfortable in his arms, until she had realised why he had answered her at random and kept turning his head and twiddling her around. Indeed, Rose's toes had gone uncrushed chiefly due to her own nimbleness, but Colm, she thought bitterly, would scarcely have noticed had he trodden on her head, so anxious was he not to miss a movement of Mona's.

It had spoiled her dances with him; of course it had. No girl likes to know that the man who holds her in his arms is not only thinking of someone else but manoeuvring her so that he can look at that person as well. Still, Tommy was handsome, charming, good fun . . . and a tram man, to boot. What was more, he was driving now, not just conducting. And he'd been wearing his uniform overcoat and the familiar smell of the serge was enough to turn Rose's knees to water. She had always thought trams romantic, even when it was just her dad who worked them. Now, she thought, she might have a husband of her own who drove a tram . . . a giddying thought.

So she curled up in her bed and decided that, should they go dancing together again, she would tell Tommy that she did not want to dance with Colm. It was a shame, because she had liked him very much, once, but a girl had to be practical. The very thought of wanting a boy who didn't want her was repugnant to Rose. All that silly talk of unrequited love could easily be avoided if one kept one's head. Colm was, so to speak, 'taken'. Therefore it behoved her to look around for someone else and to treat him simply as someone who lived under the same roof as herself and who would be appreciated only as a friend.

Having made her decision, Rose put the thought of dancing and young men firmly out of her mind and thought, instead, about waves curling down on a sandy shore, trees stirring in a spring breeze, sheep jumping over fences.

After a while, it worked and Rose slept—and dreamed confusingly of Colm and Tommy attempting to drive a herd of sheep into the waves whilst she, in the guise of a sheep-dog, barked at their heels and tried to make them see the error of their ways.

*   *   *

Colm had enjoyed the dance, the walk home through the darkened streets ... even the cocoa and biscuits. He washed, undressed and got into bed with the delicious memory of Mona in his arms, prepared to stay awake all night, if necessary, so that he could relive those magical moments.

But oddly enough, when he returned in his imagination to the ballroom, it was not Mona who snuggled softly in his arms but Rose. He knew it was her, he could smell the delicate scent she used, feel the slender firmness of her waist and looking down, see the rich, dark-brown curls of her hair and the whiteness of her parting. He could even see the curve of her cheek, the smooth, creamy skin, the lashes, so black and thick, which swooped over the blue of her eyes.

Odd! He had spent most of the time whilst dancing with Rose in twisting her around so that he could watch Mona. Ah Mona, with her golden curls, her generous curves, her low-cut and clinging dress! He tried to visualise her mouth, her skin ...

and found himself visualising, instead, Rose's gentle lips, her damask cheek.

This is a nightmare, so it is, he informed himself indignantly, opening his eyes on the darkness until he was sure he wasn't dreaming. Then he replaced the young and pliant Rose with the highly desirable Mona and allowed his hopeful hand to slide from her waist down onto the clinging curves of . . . of another part of her. She was smiling up at him, quiescent . . . only it didn't work, that was the trouble. In his dreamlike state he asked Mona to dance, held her firmly, whirled her round . . . and found himself holding Rose and watching Mona as she quick-stepped with Tommy, or Max.

'Damnit!' Colm thought crossly, sitting up in bed with the promptitude of a jack-in-the-box. 'I'll dream what I bleedin' well want, so I will!'

He lay down again, but sleep was inexorable now and would not be denied. He plunged into its depths, trying to hold a vision of Mona before him . . . but he couldn't do it. He simply slept, deeply and dreamlessly, until morning.

CHAPTER EIGHT

1931 Dublin

Caitlin couldn't wait for Christmas, as she kept saying every time there was an opportunity, and now she and Cracky were wandering along the pavement under the hissing gas-lamps, planning how they would spend the holiday. Cracky intended to spend it with her, he had just said so, but Caitlin didn't think he ought to be allowed to cherish false hopes. 'It'll be all right until me daddy comes home, and me brother Colm, Cracky. Only once they're back in Dublin you won't be seeing much of *me*, Cracky,' she said half apologetically. 'They'll mebbe want to do dull things now and then see; and if so, I'll sneak out an' come round to your place, an' we'll go off together.'

'I don't see why I can't come round to Cloddagh Court an' be wit' you, Cait,' Cracky said. 'It ain't as though me mammy 'ud mind. She'd be tickled to get shot o' me for an hour or two, so she would.'

'Ye-es, but I don't know whether Daddy an' Colm would want you hangin' around,' Caitlin said with unconscious cruelty. 'It's their own home an' their own family they'll be after wantin', after so long away.'

'They won't mind me,' Cracky insisted. They were running along Grafton Street, jumping the paving cracks, and his voice came out in short jerks. 'They'll want to do *old* people's t'ings. They'll be glad to see the back of ye from time to time I guess.'

'They will not so!' Caitlin said immediately, stopping short to glare at Cracky. Unfortunately since he didn't realise she was going to stop he continued to bound along and so missed one of her most furious and aggressive glares. 'Cracky! I said they would not want to see the back o' me, not after so long across the sea, in that old England.'

Cracky stopped and wandered back to her. In the lights from a nearby shop window Caitlin could see he was scowling. 'Well, if that's how you feel, I'd better not be runnin' round after ye now. I'll see you when they've gone back, if I've a moment to spare,' he said gloomily. 'I was comin' back to your place to help you wit' your messages an' that, but if I'm not wanted once your brother gets back . . .'

'Oh well, mebbe I'm wrong,' Caitlin said. It was another week and more to the Christmas holidays and Cracky was a great feller for giving a hand and keeping her company. 'Mebbe youse can be wit' us, come Christmas.'

Cracky grinned and fell into step beside her. 'I'll make meself useful,' he promised. 'Besides, your mammy likes me well enough now. Why, didn't she give me Colm's old trousers, an' mend 'em an' make 'em smaller to fit? I bet if you axed your mammy she'd say, "Bring Cracky along, for he's a great little feller, so he is," he added complacently. 'Your mammy likes me to keep you out of mischief whiles she's workin', Caitlin O'Neill.'

It had not always been so, but it was true now and Caitlin acknowledged it. Cracky never came round to their place with a dirty face or with mud caked on his bare feet. Indeed, he had even let Caitlin's mammy cut his hair and give him some old clothes, and because she didn't mind mending she was always willing to do the odd repair job for Cracky. In return, he kept an eye on Caitlin and if he didn't always manage to get her out of scrapes, at least he stayed with her, no matter how tempted to fly away and disown his little friend.

For as Cracky had improved, Caitlin had grown more ingenious and naughtier. Not that she meant to be wicked; she started off each new day with a vow that today she would be as good as gold. Only things happened and opportunities occurred . . . but as her mammy said, she didn't always have to *take* the opportunies; she could sometimes think

295

first—and not act.

But I'm a reformed person, she reminded herself as she skipped along the pavement. It's *weeks*—well, days—since I was last in trouble, because if you want Santa to visit you have to be good near Christmas, and in the New Year I'll make a real resolve for to be entirely changed and always Mammy's little helper. She could just imagine herself dressed in a clean pink dress with a snowy pinafore over it and shiny black-button shoes on her feet, gently soothing the sick and making soup for the old street beggars, and was rehearsing what Daddy would say when Mammy told him how wonderfully helpful and grown-up she had become, when she saw, ahead of them, Cracky's sister, Roisin. Roisin was a real, grown-up lady now, working in the jam factory on Parnell Street, and she had money, too. So Caitlin nudged Cracky and the two of them broke into a sharp trot. Roisin was generous to her smaller brothers and sisters, and she was lively and loved to tell them stories of her friends—and enemies—at work, so it was worth a run to catch her.

'Roisin!' Caitlin panted, grabbing her by the arm. 'Where's you goin', eh? You aren't headin' for home, that's for sure.'

Roisin stopped and smiled down at them. 'I'm goin' Christmas shoppin' for a little somethin' for baby Timmy,' she said. 'I t'ought I'd mebbe get a little wooden horse. He'd love a wooden horse, would me laddo.'

'Can we come?' Caitlin asked eagerly, all thoughts of going home and having tea temporarily forgotten. 'We'll help you choose the best, won't we, Cracky?'

'We-ell . . .' Roisin began dubiously. 'I'd love to take youse both, but your mammy will worry if you're late, an' it's dusk already. Better not, alanna.'

'Oo-ooh,' Caitlin moaned. The difficulties of being good. But if she went with Roisin and took her time, Mammy would have made the tea and laid the table, and she might get just a little cross . . . or even very cross indeed, since Caitlin's only job after school was the table-laying and a bit of a hand given towards their tea. 'Oh, well, if Mammy's cross I could say I forgot the time . . . an' I do love the big shops, so I do!'

'Yes, but if your mammy gets cross she'll mebbe tell your daddy an' Colm that you're a bad spalpeen, an' they won't take you on outings,' Cracky put in craftily. He was thinking of his sharing their tea, Caitlin thought, and gave him a light kick on the ankle. It looked like a mistake, but Caitlin was cunning at 'accident on purpose' kicks, as Cracky well knew.

He swung his own leg and got her right on the kneecap, and she couldn't even holler, since she'd started it, so instead she said defiantly: 'Me daddy may tell me off, but Colm won't. Colm will know I'm good at heart; he was always sayin' just that when I did somethin' Mammy thought I shouldn't.'

'Oh, but Colm isn't comin' home this year,' Roisin said confidently. 'Still, alanna, he'll be back next summer I've no doubt. No, you'd better not come shoppin' wit' me, I don't want you to be in trouble at home.' And before Caitlin could put her right, Roisin had smiled, waved and disappeared in the direction of the big shops on Grafton Street.

Caitlin stood for a moment, whilst a tide of fury

washed all over her. Just what did Roisin mean by that? Did she think she knew more about the O'Neills than Caitlin did, by any chance? How *dared* she say that Colm wasn't coming home for Christmas, when Caitlin was looking forward to seeing Colm even more than Daddy!

But Cracky, unaware, caught hold of her arm and pulled. 'Come on, your mammy may want us to run a message,' he said urgently. 'An' it's hungry I am for me tea! Don't worry about old Roisin, we can go wit' her another day . . . she might give us a penny to spend at the week's end, when she's paid.'

Caitlin shook him off. She was so angry she didn't care what Cracky thought, or what he said to Roisin when he got home, either. 'Your b-bloody old sister's a wicked l-liar, so she is,' she stuttered. 'Of *course* Colm's comin' home wit' me daddy. Fellers always come home wit' their re-relatives. Oh, I'd like to t'ump your Roisin on the nose for sayin' untrut's about me brother.'

'Aw, don't go on,' Cracky said, giving her shoulder another tug. 'Your mammy told you she didn't know for sure about Colm yet. I 'spec' another letter's come. Your mammy gets a lot of letters, don't she?'

'But how could horrible Roisin know before me?' Caitlin demanded, standing with legs apart and hands on hips, determinedly refusing to let Cracky move her so much as an inch along the pavement. 'She's a bad girl, to tell lies to a young wan like meself! I'm . . . I'm a holy innocent, you know.'

Cracky gave a rude shout of laughter. 'Holy innocents wear haloes an' they don't have no bodies, just little wings where their necks oughter

298

be,' he said mockingly. 'You're a holy terror, that's what you are.'

'An' you're as big a liar as your . . . your *damned* sister!' Caitlin shrieked. 'You're twice as naughty as me! And you can't come to me home for tea, nor at Christmas, either, so sucks to you.'

Unwarily, Cracky put his hand on her arm, beginning to say penitently that he was sorry, that he'd not known . . .

But to be touched, when she was in a rare temper, was fatal. Caitlin aimed a small clenched fist at Cracky's nose—and hit her mark. Cracky roared and, forgetting his resolve to take care of his little friend, hit back. In less than two seconds the two of them were fighting in earnest, swapping mighty blows which occasionally even connected. Through a red haze Caitlin thumped, dodged, kicked, scratched . . . and to keep her temper blazing she occasionally let forth a shriek of 'Frys are liars! *All* Frys are liars!', scarcely hearing Cracky's breathless retort that all O'Neills were soft in the head and wasn't that a well-known fact now?

Indeed, when the interruption came she was actually sobbing with rage, and her first inclination was to fight on and ignore the voice which was raised in a scandalised shout. But then firm hands seized her and dragged her off her opponent, and a soft voice said in her ear: 'And what's all this, then? I come out lookin' for my little girleen because it's gettin' dark an' I'm worried she might be in trouble, an' I find her engaged in a street brawl an' fair raisin' the roof wit' her screechings. Why, you sound worse than the banshee herself—an' you look worse, too, Caitlin Maria O'Neill! What's the meanin' of it? And if it isn't Cracky, your best pal, wit' blood runnin' from his poor nose an' his poor shins kicked into pieces! You should be ashamed, young lady!'

It was her mother, of course. Naturally, when you're being really specially bad and wicked it's always the person you most want to impress who sees you. Caitlin gulped, knuckled her eyes—she had been crying hard, what with the knocks and her temper—and looked up into Mrs O'Neill's stern face. 'Mammy, tell Cracky me brother's comin' home for Christmas, just like you said. Oh tell me he's wrong, an' me dearest Colm will be home wit' me daddy.'

*   *   *

Eileen O'Neill looked down at her small, dirty, tear-streaked daughter and repressed a smile. Poor kid, she was always vowing to be good and gentle, just the sort of little daughter her parents wanted, and she'd had a good long stretch of being good, too—it must be all of ten days, Eileen told herself. But the fact was, they'd spoiled her rotten, she and Colm and dear Sean, when he was home, and now she'd got a temper on her when she was crossed and a wickedly inventive mind, and it was a full-time job looking out for her. Indeed, she valued Cracky's help and the last thing she wanted was for the two children to fall out. So she didn't smile, but turned her daughter around to face Cracky. 'Look what you've done to your friend's nose, you wicked wretch! Well? What do you say to Cracky?'

'He hit me too, though not nearly as hard,' Caitlin muttered, chewing her knuckles. 'But ...

300

but I did start it.' She looked across at Cracky and although Eileen could only see the top of her head, she could tell that Caitlin was smiling. 'It was a good punch that first one,' she said. 'I'm real sorry, Cracky. If you'll come home wit' the mammy an' me I'll make it better wit' warm water an' a key down your back. An' I'll give you first go at the cake,' she added generously.

'Oh . . . well, it's all right,' Cracky mumbled. 'I didn't know you was goin' to go *mad* or I'd ha' dodged, so I would. An' I know I shouldn't hit a girl, Mrs O'Neill,' he added. 'But she'd ha' kilt me stone dead if I'd not fought back. She's a terror when she's roused . . . an' I did laugh at her over somethin' or other,' he finished.

'Right. Well, we'll go home and clean you both up an' I'll start the tea in earnest,' Eileen said. 'But before we move a step from here, Caitlin, let us get one t'ing crystal clear. I *told* you that Colm wouldn't be here for as long as Daddy, did I not?'

'Yes, Mammy,' Caitlin said. She gave a disgusting snort and wiped the back of her hand across her nose. Eileen closed her eyes but said nothing. Kids never carried handkerchiefs and the jumper Caitlin was wearing had been through too much to be ruined by a runny nose. 'But I t'ought, . . . you never said . . .'

'I told you he'd not been wit' the tunnelling long enough to take a proper time off,' Eileen said remorselessly. 'He only has the two days. An' he's writ home—there's a letter for you too, alanna—to say it's not worth the ferry fare to come all the way home one day and leave the next. So it'll just be your daddy who comes home this time.'

'Oh. Well, why did you tell Roisin afore meself?'

301

Caitlin said piteously, more tears starting. 'I'd never have clacked Cracky only Roisin said . . . she said . . .'

'I met Roisin earlier in the day, when I'd just opened the letter,' Eileen said. 'I was disappointed meself, there's no denyin' it, but I t'ink your brother's showin' good sense. The summer's more fun an' he'll have longer then if he stays in England now. So how about tellin' Cracky that all Frys speak the trut', now?'

'Well, Roisin spoke the trut',' Caitlin muttered. She cast a black look at Cracky. 'But when I said I were a holy innocent he said I were a holy terror and that weren't true, Mammy. I'm pretty good, aren't I?'

'Sure an' you do your best, but I'm bound to confess you're no holy innocent,' Eileen said, repressing another smile. 'Say you're sorry to your pal now, an' we'll get back to our teas.'

But astonishingly, when Caitlin, with rather an ill grace, did apologise to Cracky, and when Eileen repeated her invitation to tea, Cracky turned them down. He refused nicely, with a smile, but nevertheless he said he had better go home, his mammy would probably need him . . . he might catch up with Roisin and help her to carry her parcels.

Eileen watched him go uneasily. She realised that she relied upon Cracky more than she had ever acknowledged, even to herself. When Caitlin was with him, Eileen knew that no harm would befall her daughter. Oh, she might—probably would—get into all sorts of scrapes, but she would come home intact, or almost so. Sometimes her knees might be grazed, her cheek scratched, her school jumper unravelled, but she would have been as well guarded, Eileen knew, as she would have guarded the child herself. So the thought of Cracky being suddenly unavailable was a frightening one. When Colm had been here he would be at the flat before Eileen herself got back from work and he had kept an eye, but with Colm gone and Cracky standing on his dignity, how on earth would she manage? Asking another child to keep an eye on Caitlin would be useless, she knew that. Caitlin could be led but not driven and how many older children would understand that? Cracky wasn't far out when he had called her daughter a holy terror.

'Awright, Cracky Fry, go home then, why don't you?' Caitlin squeaked. 'I don't care—me daddy's comin' home an' we'll go out, go to the Mayro an' . . . an' buy presents from all the big shops an' we'll go wit'out you, what's more.'

Eileen slapped across Caitlin's legs, hard and quick, leaving a red mark, and saw Cracky wince even as Caitlin let out a howl any tom-cat would have envied. 'Mammy, Mammy, that hurt, so it did! I'll tell me daddy you're a wicked woman who smacks good girls,' Caitlin whimpered. Then she turned on Cracky. 'It's all your fault, Cracky Fry! Go on, go away, like you said you would.'

'Cracky, I'd be honoured if you'd take your tea wit' us,' Eileen said desperately. 'An' the biggest, best present under the Christmas tree shall be yours. And when we pass the bakery you shall have a sticky bun for puttin' up wit' Miss No-Manners here. Now then, what d'you say to that?' She gave Caitlin a little shake. 'What'll you do after school wit' no Cracky to give an eye to you? For I'd not have you alone in the flat, creatin' havoc the way you would if there was no Cracky to keep you in check. So what d'you say to your friend now?'

'I'm really, truly sorry,' Caitlin gabbled. Eileen was sure her small daughter had suddenly realised what her life would be like without Cracky to mind her. 'Do come back to tea, Cracky ... I never meant what I said.'

Cracky grinned at them both. 'Well, I will then,' he said magnanimously. 'Lead on, Mrs O'Neill!'

*   *   *

It was a good tea. Thick slices of fatty pork fried until it was frizzled golden brown, a pile of golden potato cakes cooked in the pork fat and a plateful of bread and margarine to fill in the chinks. Then there was tea, and a hefty slice each of tea brack.

'I'm stuffed tight,' Caitlin said happily, if inelegantly, as she drained her teacup. 'Me an' Cracky'll wash up for you, Mammy, 'cos I was too late to lay the table or help. An' if we do a good job, could you read us Daddy's letter after?'

Her mother agreed to this and the two children got on with the work, so Eileen settled down in front of the fire with her knitting and began to turn over in her mind how she would manage Christmas, now that she knew for sure Colm would not be coming home. It was a shame that the boy should miss his family holiday but Sean had promised that their landlady, the Mrs Ryder whom both the O'Neills had frequently mentioned in their letters, would make Colm very welcome and see that he had a good time. 'What's more there's other young folk in the house. Two very pretty girls and a young feller not much older than Colm,'

Sean had written in his neat, slanting hand. 'So I wouldn't be weeping for your son. Likely he'll have a better time in the Vale than he would have at home.'

Eileen did not believe for one moment that a Christmas spent in a foreign land could possibly equal one spent by your own fireside, but Sean was just trying to cheer her up very likely. Already she had planned to send some special Irish dainties across to England for her boy—a harsh mother she would think herself if she did not do her best to make his Christmas a good one—and Sean had said Colm would be sure to go to Mass, along with the Ryders, on the day itself.

Presently, their work finished, Caitlin and Cracky clattered away from the sink and came and sat on the rag hearthrug before the blazing fire. They were the best of friends once more, all their former animosity forgotten. Caitlin said, with assurance, that since Colm would not be coming home after all there would surely be room for Cracky, even on Christmas Day, and Eileen agreed that if Mrs Fry could spare him . . .

'It'll be one less to feed,' Cracky said briefly and Eileen, sighing, wished that other families were as happy—and lucky—as her own. Poor Mrs Fry had a dozen kids to feed, a husband out of work more often than he was in it, and a tiny, filthy room in which to cope with them all. Two of the older boys and one of the girls were working, but they had moved out as soon as they got jobs, no doubt anxious to keep some of their own money, and though Mrs Fry had told Eileen that Roisin, Pat and Declan were good kids and the apple of her eye, paying up as they did at the end of each week,

305

Eileen did not blame them for moving out.

'Mammy? Are ye goin' to read us Daddy's letter?' Caitlin coaxed presently, eyeing the envelope on the mantel above her head. 'We've done a good job; the crocks are all put away, an' the washin' bowl rinsed out an' dried up. An' you *did* say . . .'

'Right, then,' Eileen agreed, reaching down the letter. 'And when it's done I'll play for you and you can sing a carol, then we'll walk Cracky some o' the way home, because a breath of air before you go to sleep is good for you. Ready?'

Once the letter had been read aloud, Eileen handed the small enclosure to her daughter. 'And this is a line from Colm to yourself, alanna,' she said. 'You read it this time, to Cracky an' meself.'

Caitlin sat up importantly and read the short note aloud.

Dear Caitlin,
Mammy will have told you I'll not be home this Christmas, but me job's a good one and I don't want to lose it. However, I'm buying you a nice gift for to make up for me absence, and Daddy will pop it into his case, so you'll not go short, alanna.

I wish I could have come just for a few days, but I'll be back for the summer and we'll have a grand time then, so we will. Take care of Mammy and be a good girl and who knows, I might send you an Easter gift, too!
With love from your brother
Colm.

'Well now, a present from your brother,' Eileen
306

said. 'Sure an' aren't you the lucky one, Caitlin O'Neill? And now let's sing that carol—which will you choose, Cracky, for 'tis your turn.'

Cracky chose 'The Holly and the Ivy' and Eileen went to the small piano which stood against the wall and played, whilst all three of them sang lustily. On Christmas morning they would all go to Mass, but on Christmas afternoon Eileen would invite some neighbours in and they would have a good old singsong, because the O'Neill piano was the only one in the neighbourhood and was much appreciated. Indeed, in the summer it was not unusual for neighbours to come to the door and ask if they might carry it downstairs to the courtyard, where a celebration of some kind—a wedding, a christening, or a birthday party—was being held. Some of the other women could pick out a tune on it but no one else played it properly, as Eileen could, and she gave Caitlin piano lessons two or three times a week, though she thought privately that her daughter would never master the art. Caitlin had a sweet singing voice, but no patience with the chore of learning to read music, let alone to practise.

Mrs Monahan, who lived in the flat above their own, told Eileen that she should give up her various jobs and play the piano for profit, but Eileen just laughed. She knew she was a very ordinary performer—and was aware, too, that she worked for a definite purpose, though no one knew how close that purpose was drawing except Eileen herself.

For both Sean and Eileen O'Neill were saving up so that, when the opportunity occurred, Sean could come back from across the water and the family could move out to Finglas, to a cottage near the River Tolka. Long ago, when she and Sean had been courting, he had taken her out to Finglas and showed her the cottage in which his father had been born. At present it was inhabited by a very old man and his ancient, almost blind wife, but the day would come when the owner would be looking round for new tenants, Sean had told the pretty young girl he was planning to marry. 'It's me dream to move back here one o' these days,' he had said wistfully. 'See what a big garden there is wit' the cottage? A man handy wit' a spade could grow enough vegetables for his family an' more, an' he could keep a goat for its milk an' a donkey wit' a cart behind to drag seaweed from the shore to make the soil rich, an' the wife could pick the fruit from the trees ... see there, plums, apples, cherries ... an' make jam an' sell it in the Dublin markets ... Oh, Eileen, I'd dearly love to live out here.'

Ever since that day, Eileen had saved in private for the means to make this dream come true. The rent for the cottage would be higher than that for their flat, but it wasn't the worst of it. It was losing Sean's steady wage—and her own—which worried her and made her put away every penny she could towards that happy day.

Neighbours often wondered aloud why she continued to work so hard when her man brought in good money and now her son, too, was earning. Eileen smiled, but never told them. It was a secret, private dream, between herself and Sean, and she would tell no one, for suppose they never managed it? Suppose they lived out the rest of their lives in Dublin, in the crowded tenements? She would rather folk did not know that they had tried, and failed, to escape.

'Can we have another carol, Mammy?' Caitlin pleaded. 'Just a wee short one, before we walk Cracky home.'

'No, for it's late, thanks to you not comin' in for your tea on time,' Eileen said, but her smile robbed the words of their sting. 'Put your warm coat on, alanna, and we'll set off . . . an' if there's a chestnut seller by the market we'll buy a bag for to keep our hands warm an' for the lovely country smell of 'em.'

'And for the taste,' Cracky said longingly. 'We should ha' gone nutting ourselves last mont', Caity me gorl, then we could ha' lavished a grosh o' nuts on your mammy wit'out her payin' out her farthin's.' He went and fetched Eileen's coat from the hook on the back of the door and courteously helped her into it, then he wound his own long woollen scarf several times round his neck and tucked the end into his trousers. The scarf was his only concession to winter, though later, Eileen reminded herself, she must pick up some more boots for him at one of the markets. They liked the kids to wear boots to school and indeed, Caitlin never went barefoot. With three of them working there was no need; they could afford them. And Mrs Fry never put her nose up when Cracky came home with boots, or a warm jacket, or a scarf. Eileen did not imagine that Cracky told her where the clothing came from, he was too careful for that, because when the two girls had been at school, Cracky's mammy had been further up the school than Eileen, who was still in the babies class. Now that she had a bit of money to spare, Eileen was happy to spend some of it on a young lad as useful as Cracky, but she was too tactful to allow the Frys to believe they were accepting charity and always 'paid' Cracky for various services in warm clothing or food.

And soon the three of them, with Caitlin in the middle, were making their way down the street, with a farthing bag of chestnuts apiece, blowing on the hot nuts, eating and laughing as they went, with Christmas beckoning ahead of them, a bright glow in the darkest night.

CHAPTER NINE

1931 Liverpool

Rose bounced through the back door, so excited and pleased with herself that she felt like proclaiming her news from the housetops, but instead she looked round the kitchen, made sure that her mother and Mrs Kibble had both turned towards her, then played a blast on an imaginary trumpet. 'Tan tara! Guess what's outside, in the backyard. No, don't look, see if you can guess.'

'Some holly an' mistletoe? We're goin' to decorate the front room an' the paper chains is up already,' her mother said placidly. 'Oh, norra bigger cage for Gully, chuck? His old 'un's fine, he teks up quite enough room as it is.'

Rose heaved a sigh. 'No, not a bigger cage, mam. Nor holly an' mistletoe, though I wouldn't mind gettin' a bus out into the country an' pickin' some, if Tommy an' Mona would like to come along. What about you, Mrs Kibble? Have a guess, go on!'

'Santa Claus, in his red coat and beard,' Mrs Kibble suggested, smiling. 'And the reindeer, too, of course.'

'Well, you aren't far off at that.' Rose withdrew for a moment, pushing the door wide, then came in through it once more, this time grasping the handlebars of a bicycle. 'Tan tara!'

'Rosie, where in the Lord's name did you get that?' Mrs Ryder said in a gasp. 'You've not saved up enough yet, you said so only yesterday.'

'No, I know. Look, I'll put it in the shed, then come in and explain,' Rose said, having smoothed her hand along the saddle as though the bicycle would appreciate a bit of petting. 'It's not new, but it's just what I wanted.'

'It's a decent-looking machine,' Mrs Kibble remarked, as Rose disappeared once more, and walked over to push the door to, for it was a windy evening. 'Looks as though your gal's fallen on her feet again, Lily.'

'Aye; it 'ud have took her another year to save up enough for a new 'un,' agreed Mrs Ryder, going over to the stove and jiggling the pan of potatoes to make sure none had stuck to the bottom. 'But that'll be all her Christmas money gone, I reckon.'

As she spoke Rose reappeared in the doorway and, entering the kitchen, slammed the door behind her, shed her heavy coat and hat, and stripped off her woollen gloves and scarf. Then she kicked off her wellingtons and put on her old slippers, finally walking across the kitchen and running her finger along the bars of the parrot's cage.

'How you doin', Gully?' she said cheerfully. 'Did

311

you see me bike? All I need now is someone to teach me to ride it.'

'Oh, one o' the young gentlemen'll teach you,' her mother said, pulling the potatoes slightly to one side of the hob and bending to remove a roasting tin, complete with a large piece of sizzling pork, from the oven. 'I seem to remember Mr O'Neill tellin' us once that his son had been an errand boy, so Colm could probably show you.'

'I reckon I'll practise by meself first,' Rose said at once. 'Tommy an' Colm would only laugh when I fell over. But aren't you goin' to ask where I got it? An' what I paid for it?'

'You'll tell us whether we ask or not,' her mother observed. 'But whiles you talk, queen, you might lay the table. The men will be in quite soon and Agueda and meself are a bit behind.'

'Oh. Right,' Rose said, going to the dresser drawer and getting out a checked tablecloth. 'You know Mr Garnett?'

'Aye,' her mother admitted. 'Since he's come round here three times this last week to see his dratted bird you could say we know him, more or less.'

Rose grinned. Ever since the night of the dance, Mr Garnett had been more interested in his parrot than one could have believed possible. He had told her next day at work that he was ashamed of himself for not visiting earlier and in due course he came, laden with various gifts—food for Gulliver, flowers for her mother, chocolates for what he called 'Your family, Mrs Ryder'.

'He's got his eye on Mona,' Rose's mother had remarked. 'Well, she could do worse; he's a nice young gentleman and clearly he's gorra good

312

future. Oh aye, she could do a deal worse.'

'My dear Lily, he may not intend marriage,' Mrs Kibble had pointed out. 'He's going to inherit that firm one of these days, his family is an old, proud one. Mona is a pretty girl, but . . .'

'I'm sure he don't intend marriage,' Rose's mother had said briskly. 'But he'll take her about, introduce her to his friends . . . there's no harm in that, I'm sure.'

'So long as he doesn't turn your niece's head,' Mrs Kibble had said rather gloomily. 'It would not do to raise her hopes, Lily.'

Rose had said nothing, but she thought that Mona was safe enough. She was always extremely polite, indeed charming, to Mr Garnett, but she hadn't actually been out with him, far less back to his home, wherever that might be. Indeed, she was still showing far too much interest in Tommy for Rose's peace of mind, particularly as Colm continued to eye Mona as keenly as the pigeons in Williamson Square eyed anyone scattering corn.

'Well, besides his interest in his dratted bird, it seems he's got a sister. She's a bit younger than him but she's still quite old. Twenty-two I think he said. Her name's Penelope, an' she's gettin' married next spring to some feller who lives down south somewhere.'

'Oh aye?' Lily said absently. 'Wants a parrot, does she, queen?'

'Oh Mam, you'd be real upset if anyone took Gully off of us,' Rose said reproachfully. 'You only say that to mek me feel bad. But if she don't want a parrot, she don't want a bicycle, either. She's goin' to have her own little sports car—imagine that!'

'I can't,' her mother said, lifting the pan from the

313

stove and carrying it over to the sink, where she began to strain the potatoes through a blue enamel colander. 'What's more, I don't want to. Women didn't oughter drive cars, that's for the fellers, Why, they'll be havin' women drivin' trams at this rate.'

'Oh Mam, you're so old-fashioned an' set in your ways,' Rose said, irritated. 'Well, to cut a long story short I was tellin' Mr Garnett as how I were savin' up for a bike, an' he said how about his askin' his sister if she'd like to sell her old rattler, so I said smashin', sir, but I didn't think anythin' would come of it. He said that a week ago an' I thought he'd forgot all about it, and then, this very mornin', he come into the office an' said Penelope said I were welcome to it, only I'd have to buy a new pump, an' mebbe get a bit o' work done on it, so he'd got a servant to walk it in, an' he took me down to the yard at the back an' handed it over there an' then.'

'That was real generous, real nice o' the gal,' her mother said. 'An' she wouldn't tek no money, queen? Well, that's a right good Christmas box if you ask me. It looked awright, from what I saw.'

'I offered to pay but Mr Garnett told me no need, she were glad to be rid of it,' Rose said happily. 'It's what I've wanted most, as you know. Oh, I know it had flat tyres an' no pump, an' the brakes was a bit rusty, but the fellers in the office give a hand in their dinner-hour an' now it's fit to ride. Or would be if I *could* ride,' she amended.

'Well, you're young and you'll learn easily,' Mrs Kibble said. 'Ah, I hear footsteps.'

'They're back!' Mrs Ryder said, beginning to mash the potatoes with some butter and a dash of

314

milk. 'Mek the gravy in the pan, Rosie me love, then we'll eat as soon as the fellers have washed up. An' after, you can see about lessons on that there bicycle. Pity it's dark, but they may be able to rig up a light in the yard. Or you could try the street—the gaslights mek it bright enough for bicycling, I dessay. But let's get this meal on the go, ladies!'

*   *   *

Colm thought afterwards that you never knew what fate had in store for you. Certainly, when Mrs Ryder had been telling them about the bicycle, which had been given to her daughter, it had not occurred to him that his life would be changed by it. Far from it, in fact. He had only volunteered to help Rose to learn to ride because, shamingly, he thought that Mona might come along too, either to learn as well or to watch.

Well, he had been right about her joining them, because on that first evening the four of them, himself, Rose, Tommy and Mona, all assembled, with the bicycle, in the road in front of the house. They had tried the jigger first, but it was too narrow, too uneven and also too dark, so they had gone round to the Vale, guessing that there would be neither traffic nor people around on such a cold night. However, though it was windy still, the rain clouds had cleared and a moon lit the scene with its frosty light. Furthermore, of course, the gas-lamps cast their warm glow, so when he began to instruct Rose in the art of mounting the bicycle it was possible for her both to hear his words and to see his actions.

'Show her yourself, Colm,' Mona urged, so Colm

315

lowered the bicycle seat with one of his own spanners so that Rose could sit in the saddle and still not lose contact with the ground, and showed her how to mount the female way, how to lean the bicycle so that she could get into the saddle without losing control and how to coast, with her toes touching the road surface, to give herself a sense of balance.

Rose was all excited, pink-cheeked and smiling. Like a very nice child, Colm found himself thinking as he hung on to the carrier above the back mudguard to prevent her from falling to one side or the other. She was a quick learner, too, and though he intended to keep the saddle down until she was more expert, he could see that, with help and practice, she would soon be cycling to work.

The lesson turned out to be fun, too, and though it was indeed a cold night, they both began to warm up very nicely, Colm by running alongside the bicycle keeping Rose upright and Rose from the exertion of pedalling, swaying perilously and occasionally, despite Colm's best efforts, falling off.

After a bit, however, the audience tired and sloped off indoors—or Colm supposed that was where they had gone. But strangely enough, he found that he no longer cared at all whether they stayed or left. He was having fun! Rose was sweet, falling off the bike several times into his very arms and clinging round his neck, laughing, panting and thanking him breathlessly as he hoisted her back into the saddle, until Colm suddenly realised that he was quite looking forward to her next tumble. She was a cuddly armful, with her breath soft against his cheek and her laughter trembling on her lips, even as she exclaimed over the various pains of a pedal in the calf, a cracked ankle or a grazed knee.

So when she suddenly managed to pedal a few feet without falling off he was quite sorry and put the saddle up, telling her with mock severity that if she insisted on being so good at bicycling he'd have to make it more difficult for her.

'You're mean, Colm O'Neill,' Rose said, smiling up at him, her eyes very blue in the soft lamplight and her lips very rosy. 'You want to see me take a real tumble, don't you.'

'No indeed, nothing is further from me thoughts,' he assured her. 'Tell you what, Rosie, let's make it easier for you. If you can ride along as far as the next lamp-post without falling off, you're safe, but if you fall you'll have to give me a great big kiss, so you will.'

She had been laughing; now she stopped, looking up at him consideringly. 'If I fall I've got to kiss you; is that the bargain?'

'Yup,' Colm said, secure in the knowledge that, between the two lamp-posts, a grid in the gutter would make at least a wobble a certainty. 'That'll keep you on the straight an' narrow.'

'It will,' Rose said, hoisting herself back into the saddle with great determination. 'Gi's a push to get me goin', then.'

'Well, I don't know whether I should . . . that's helpin' you, which isn't in me best interests,' Colm said, then helped her into the saddle—she still could not mount alone now that the saddle had been hoisted higher—and held her against him for a very enjoyable moment whilst she got her balance. 'Still, one little push . . . off wit' you now!'

The bicycle wobbled furiously, then righted itself

317

and Rose began cautiously pedalling towards the next lamp-post.

'It's grand you're doin', me little darlin',' Colm said encouragingly, trotting along behind her. 'Oh, was that a wobble, now? Are ye goin' to tipple over sideways just to please me?'

'You'd be best pl-pleased if I showed you I could do it, then you could go in an' . . . an' sit by the fire wi' Mona,' Rose said in a breathless and wobbly voice. 'Only another couple o' yards . . . there! What about that then, me friend?'

She had reached the lamp-post just as the bicycle swerved, bucked like a horse seeing a dog under its feet and tipped her unceremoniously onto the pavement.

Colm ran forward, plucked her from the paving stones and, with her snug in his arms, bent his head and fastened his lips on hers. Rose gave a mutter of protest, a wriggle like a landed fish . . . then she was responding, kissing him back, her arms winding themselves sweetly about his neck even as her body swayed closer against his.

Carried away, Colm lifted her off her feet and kissed her once more, long and hard, then stood her down. They gazed at one another in the lamplight, both more than a little breathless. Finally, after a moment, Rose said in a small voice: 'You cheated, Colm O'Neill. You said I'd have to kiss you if I fell off before I reached the lamp-post and I got there!'

'So you did. An' didn't I make it plain that if you *did* get there, wit'out fallin' off, then I'd kiss you, so I would? Surely you realised?'

Rose giggled and punched him on the arm. Colm hissed in his breath and pretended to clutch his muscle, though he had scarcely felt the blow. 'You're a trojan,' he declared. 'Well, since there seems to have been a . . . a misunderstandin', I'll say it clear as clear this time. If you can cycle back to the other lamp-post wit'out fallin' off, then I'll kiss you. But if you fall then you'll kiss me. Is that fair or isn't it?'

Rose giggled again and picked up the bicycle, then prepared to mount. 'That seems fair enough,' she said, and Colm heard the little shake in her voice and saw the way she looked at him, shyly but with a sort of trembling anticipation, and realised that he was seeing her as if for the first time. She had shed her heavy coat and thick scarf, and in the lamplight her dark curls framed a rosy and delightful face. How could he ever have thought her less than beautiful, he marvelled, with that creamy skin and those big, dark-blue eyes? And what had got into him to look past her to Mona, with her peroxided hair, her bold glance and her painted lips and cheeks? Why Rose was the prettiest, sweetest girl in the world and he . . . he was the luckiest feller alive.

'Off I go then . . . gi's a push, Colm,' Rose urged, and Colm launched her and then trotted alongside until she stopped, triumphant, under the lamp-post. 'Well? How'd I do, Colm? I'll be ridin' to work after the weekend, I betcha.'

'You will so,' Colm agreed. He took the bicycle from her and leaned it against the lamp-post, then stood close, gazing down at her, and found himself breathing heavily. 'Now was it me to kiss you, or you to kiss me? I can't remember which way round it was for the life of me.'

'Does it matter?' Rose said. She looped her arms

319

round his neck and held up her face, the lips slightly parted, looking as tempting and delicious as anything Colm had ever seen. 'I'm almost sure you're goin' to kiss me, whichever way round it was.'

'So I am, alanna,' Colm said. He pulled her close and slowly, slowly, lowered his head until their lips met—and clung, he thought wonderingly, as though they had been lovers for years. She was wonderful, this Rosie Ryder—why in God's sweet name hadn't he realised it weeks and weeks ago?

When, presently, they pulled apart, he said as much. 'We've been wastin' our lives, so we have,' he told her. 'When we could have been doin' this every night o' the week. Well, I hope you don't t'ink that now you can ride a bicycle you're safe from me kisses, for you are no such t'ing, Rose Ryder. Will you come to the flickers wit' me tomorrer night, an' sit an' cuddle in the back row of the stalls?'

'Certainly not,' Rose said with dignity. 'Well, I'll come to the cinema wi' you, Colm, an' thank you kindly, but . . . but . . .'

'But what?'

'Well . . . you don't *arrange* to kiss and cuddle, it either comes . . . comes natural, or it doesn't happen at all. And you . . . you're awful, that's what you are!'

'I'm sorry, alanna,' Colm said penitently. 'Sure an' you're right. I'll put it another way. Will you come wit' me to the flickers tomorrow night? I'll buy you chocolates an' treat you like a queen, so I will.'

'Well, I don't know,' Rose said slowly. 'It's one thing to learn me to ride a bicycle an' quite another to go to the cinema together. How do I know you really want to, and aren't bein' . . . bein' carried away, sort of?'

She was trying to appear offended, but all she sounded was very young and very sweet. 'Put your coat on, and your scarf, or you'll catch your death now that we're not leppin' up and down,' Colm said, and helped her into it, then donned his own, which he had laid carefully down on top of hers on the low garden wall. Then he put a casual arm round her and began to wheel the bicycle along the pavement, turning into the jigger when he reached it, and reflecting that the hour must be late and he had no desire for Mrs Ryder to pop out to see how they were getting along, and surprise them kissing instead of cycling demurely up and down.

Rose turned in his arm and smiled up at him, a grin full of mischief. 'But I thought it was Mona you were after,' she said innocently. 'She was tellin' me only last week . . .'

Colm had his arm round her waist; now he squeezed her and also gave her a playful shake. 'She's a fine-lookin' girl, your cousin. I t'ought she was a real dazzler, but that was before I'd really looked twice at yourself, you see. Sure an' havin' had you in me arms, I'd no sooner go out wit' another girl than fly to the moon. I'm wonderin', now, whether the eyes in me head have been lookin' inward 'stead o' out, these past weeks.'

'Pretty talk,' Rose said as they crossed the jigger and Colm had to let go of her whilst he opened the back gate and pushed her bicycle through. 'But pretty talk butters no parsnips, as me dad used to say. Besides, you've only seen me by lamplight. Wait till you see me proper, in the kitchen, wi' me old brown coat an' me shabby boots. Then you'll likely think again.'

Colm wheeled the bicycle into the small shed, locked the door and offered her the key. 'Think again, would I so?' he said scoffingly. 'For it's not your old brown coat nor your shabby boots that I'll be lookin' at, alanna. 'Tis your pretty face and lovely lips that hold my attention.'

'Oh, cream-pot talk,' Rose said. 'Last one in makes up the kitchen fire an' brews the cocoa.' And she set off across the yard without waiting and shot through the back kitchen door as though the devil were after her, Colm thought, pursuing, and grabbing at the collar of her coat so that they entered the kitchen together, laughing and breathless.

There was no sign of Mona or of Tommy, but Mrs Ryder and Mrs Kibble were sitting one on either side of the fire, comfortably knitting. They both looked up as the young people appeared and Mrs Ryder put her work down and rose to her feet. 'Has me daughter broke your neck an' her own knees, or are you still both in one piece, Colm?' she enquired cheerfully. 'For 'tis no easy thing to ride a bicycle when you start in to learn by gaslight. It must be rare cold out there, too. Will you have a cup of cocoa and some biscuits before you go off to bed?'

'We're all in one piece, Mam,' Rose said, a little self consciously Colm thought. 'And I'd love cocoa and biscuits; what about you, Colm?'

'That'll be grand, Mrs Ryder,' Colm said gratefully. 'As for your daughter, she'll be ridin' to work in a week, so she will.'

'Not if there's frosts, or snow,' Mrs Ryder said firmly, pulling the kettle over the fire. 'Nor fog,

322

neither.'

'No, not if the weather's bad,' Rose allowed. 'But when the spring comes I'll be able to bike every day and save me tram fare. To say nothin' of the time I'll save hangin' about at tram stops.'

'I t'ought I might get me a bike too, wit' the money I've been puttin' away,' Colm said thoughtfully as the steaming mugs of cocoa were placed on the table by the open biscuit tin. 'For there's more to a bicycle than savin' time an' tram fares. You can have a deal o' fun, so you can. Trips into the country, further down the coast ... if there's two of you, that is,' he finished.

Mrs Ryder looked at him and at Rose. Then she smiled, 'Well, well!' she said. 'Wonders will never cease.'

'What d'you mean, Mam?' Rose said suspiciously, with heightened colour. 'Why are you grinnin' like that?'

'Oh, nothin', just me thoughts,' her mother said airily. 'Another biscuit, Colm? No? Then it's about time I got me hot-water bottle an' made for me bed.'

'Oh, yes, me too,' Rose said. 'As soon as I've finished me cocoa I'll foller you, Mam.' The two older women got up and began fussing with the kettle and under cover of their conversation Rose smiled at Colm over the rim of her mug. 'Thanks for teachin' me to ride, Colm,' she whispered. 'I'm goin' to tek me cocoa to bed wi' me. See you in the mornin'.'

*   *   *

Once in bed, Rose lay in the dark, warm as toast

323

despite not having made herself a hot-water bottle, and smiled and smiled. Fancy, after all her heart-searchings and the way she'd felt when she realised that Mona and Tommy were a bit interested in one another, and all the time it was Colm! Of course he had muddied the waters by appearing to be interested in Mona himself—well, he *had* been, Rose told herself with ruthless honesty—but now that they had realised . . . she could not imagine enjoying anyone's company more than Colm's. And his kisses . . . her warm cheeks grew warmer at the thought . . . surely nothing could have exceeded the sweetness of them! He was going to buy a bicycle so that they might go out on trips together. He had not said that, exactly, but he had made it clear enough. She still liked Tommy, of course she did—he was a tram man, wasn't he?—but it was, she realised now, just the normal friendliness a girl might feel for a handsome young man.

In the next bed, Mona gave a gurgling snore and brought Rose's mind round to her cousin and Tommy. Mona liked Tommy, she could tell, and she rather thought he liked her. So where did Mr Garnett fit into the picture? Because, though Rose might not be as knowing as her cousin, she was no simpleton, either. She knew that Mr Garnett had shown no interest in his poor old parrot until he had bumped into Rose at the dance—and consequently, had met Mona. Now he came round to the house . . . but so far as she knew, he had not invited Mona to go out with him. Queer! He was not slow in coming forward where girls were concerned, so the typists at work said, and his shipmate Mr Simpson had implied as much as well. And Mr Garnett had a car, which Mona would certainly like. She was sure—well, almost sure—that Mona would take up with Mr Garnett even if she liked Tommy ever so, because Mr Garnett would be a person of importance one day and Tommy, though he was handsome and very nice indeed, would surely not seem a better 'catch' than Mr Garnett.

For Mona had made no secret of the fact that she intended to marry someone who could keep her in the style to which she wished to become accustomed. When Rose said that this seemed a bit cold, slightly heartless, she had said, tartly, that it was all very well for Rose, with her mother and the boarding-house behind her. 'I've only got meself to rely on,' she had said. 'And I don't want to have to scrape and scrat all me life. It isn't even as if I'd gorra decent job, wi' prospects, like you've got, our Rose. So if I get the chance to better meself by marriage I'll do it, even if he's old an' ugly.'

'You never would, chuck,' Rose had gasped, filled with repugnance at the thought of having to marry an ugly old man. 'Oh Mona, nothing would be worth that.'

'It would, because if he was old enough he'd die quite quick an' leave me a rich widder,' Mona had said, and laughed. Rose had joined in the laughter, but the conversation had made her uneasy. Was that why Mona never went out with Tommy alone? Was she waiting for Mr Garnett to declare himself? And would he? Rose quite liked Mr Garnett, who could be a laugh when he wanted and sometimes came into the typing pool and chatted very pleasantly. But there was no getting away from it, he was built like a clothes prop and his face was long and knobbly. His lank, pale-brown hair always

325

looked as if it needed a brush, and his skin was sallow and pimply around the chin and hairline.

But Rose was becoming gloriously warm and comfortable, and she could feel sleep stealing up on her. I hope I have nice dreams, she told herself, snuggling down. What she meant was she hoped she would dream of Colm, but even to herself that seemed rather too bold, so she just closed her eyes, ignored Mona's snuffles and grunts, and willed herself to sleep. I'll see him at breakfast, she thought, and a pleasant tingle ran through her. Her last thought, before sleep claimed her, was to wonder whether, in his turn, Colm might dream of Rose Ryder.

*   *   *

Mona, having tired of watching the bicycle-riding lesson, had come indoors when Tommy had left to go down to the pub for a couple of beers. He had suggested she might go as well, but Mona had declined; her aunt, she knew, would not approve of a female going into the bar, though a visit to the Jug and Bottle was of course quite permissible. But she declined wistfully. She would have much enjoyed a visit to the pub with Tommy—indeed, she would have liked to go with him anywhere. However, she had herself well in hand. Tommy was fun, but she doubted that he was steady husband material. Better to enjoy his company when she could do so without anyone raising their eyebrows, and at other times steer clear. For Mona had decided that if she wanted a decent future, she must become the sort of girl that Rose was and forget that she had ever been—well, flighty.

Flirting with Colm, who was so good-looking, was fun, but she did not intend to wreck her future for an Irish navvy. Besides, she was well aware that with her looks she could easily make a very good marriage, and that would mean no more toiling at the flower shop and no more helping out in the house, either. The sort of future, in fact, that girls dream about. She might not marry Mr Garnett, there were better fish in the sea, she told herself, but if she got involved with Tommy God knew what would become of her.

So instead of going down to the pub with Tommy she had spent a quiet hour or two chatting to her aunt and Mrs Kibble, whilst she embroidered cream-coloured roses on a fine white silk underslip which she meant to give her cousin for a Christmas present. She was a good needlewoman and enjoyed the work, but had gone up to bed some time before Rose and Colm came in, since she had worked late tonight and would be in late tomorrow, too, because of the date she had made earlier that day. She had been drowsing when Rose came in, but had woken some while later, to find her cousin comfortably asleep and had then, annoyingly, been unable to return to her earlier slumbers.

Wakefulness, she suspected, however, had come to her because she was elated and excited by what had happened to her earlier in the day—and God knew she had worked as hard as she knew how to make it come about. She had spotted that Mr Garnett was the sort of feller she needed the first time they'd met, at the Daulby Hall, but of course it wasn't her part to make a move. Infuriatingly, a girl couldn't approach a feller and suggest a date—

not unless she wanted to be thought a right little wanton, anyway—but there were ways. A couple of times during Mr Garnett's visits to the house she had mentioned casually that she now worked in a florist's shop in the Exchange Station arcade and after watching for two whole days—and being told off by Miss Ellis for absent-mindedness—she had decided that despite Mr Garnett's car, money and position, he was none too bright, and had not taken any of her hints. Irritably, she had begun to plot once more how to manage to meet him outside the house in the Vale, but before she could put any of these plans into action, it became unnecessary.

Just when she had given him up, while she had been in the back room surrounded by flowers and making up wedding bouquets, he had marched boldly into the shop, asking the price of the chrysanthemums which stood in deep green buckets, scenting the air with autumn.

Miss Ellis, the manageress, had served him. He had chosen the most expensive blooms, buying gold, bronze and dark-red chrysanthemums and told her to wrap them in fancy paper and all, since, he said, mysteriously, they were a present.

Hovering in the background and listening with all her ears, Mona's heart had nose-dived—a present? Did this mean he had a young lady and had merely come into the shop by a strange coincidence? But then he had turned, with the bouquet in his arms, and begun to try to pick up the parcels which he had stood down on the floor whilst he chose the flowers. Clasping them all, he had looked round rather helplessly. 'I say, I wonder if someone could give me a hand out to the car? I couldn't bring it into the arcade, of course, so it's a dozen or so yards down Tithebarn Street, a five-minute walk away. Only otherwise I'll be bound to drop something and, with my luck, it'll be the flowers. They're for my mother, and she's most awfully fussy . . . Could you . . . ?'

Mona knew Miss Ellis and decided that Mr Garnett wasn't as stupid as he seemed. The manageress was far too high and mighty to stagger out into the roadway with an armful of parcels . . . and what was more, with only the two of them in the shop, she wouldn't be likely to leave Mona by the unguarded till. Not that I'd dream of takin' owt that weren't mine, Mona told herself, stepping forward at Miss Ellis's gesture. I'm far too keen to keep me job—for the moment, at any rate.

'Miss Mullins . . . ah, there you are! Would you carry the bouquet out to the gentleman's car please? And come straight back, of course.'

'With pleasure, Miss Ellis,' Mona said, in the refined voice she kept for the flower shop. 'Ay shan't be more than a few minutes, Ay'm sure.'

She took the flowers and went out to the arcade ahead of Mr Garnett, only turning once to enquire which was his vehicle—not that she needed to ask. It was a blue sports model, very dashing, the only expensive car in sight.

'It's the blue one,' he had replied and had overtaken her to unlock the passenger door so that he might begin to pile his parcels in the space behind the two front seats. 'I say, Miss Mullins, fancy me choosing the shop you work in! What a bit of luck, eh? I've been hoping to meet you alone, some time.'

'Alone?' Mona said, giving him a coy glance beneath her lashes and glancing round the crowded street. 'This ain't exactly a quiet spot, Mr Garnett.'

'No, but ... I mean without y-your cousin and aunt and so on. I wondered ... what time do you finish work this evening?'

'Not till eight or even later; it's the run-up to Christmas, you see, an' we've a load o' wreaths an' such to make,' Mona said gloomily. 'I'm doin' a weddin' now ... but tomorrer, now ... I'll be off be six tomorrer.'

'Ah! Well, how would you like to come to the theatre with me? Or for a run in the car? It's new ... I wouldn't mind taking her for a spin, we could eat first ... there are several good places near here ... what d'you say?'

'We-ell,' Mona murmured. 'I dunno ... you're me cousin's boss ...'

'I know what you mean, but we needn't tell anyone, need we?' he said, turning and taking the bouquet out of her arms. 'Tell you what, I'll keep mum if you will. You can say you're working late again, making more wreaths.' He gave her what he no doubt imagined was a suggestive smile and patted her head rather as if she were a large and possibly dangerous dog, Mona thought. 'Well, what d'you think?'

'It would be lovely, Mr Garnett,' Mona said quickly, before he could change his mind. 'It would be real nice to go out with ... with a young gentleman.'

He raised thin brows. 'Oh? Don't try to tell me you're not in the habit of going out with chaps, Miss Mullins, for that I won't believe! You're far too pretty to stay at home alone, night after night.'

'I used to go out a bit,' Mona said, looking soulful. 'But now I'm livin' wi' me aunt an' me cousin, she likes us to go around together. I'm awful fond of our Rosie, but there's times when I'd enjoy a bit more freedom. She's ever so sweet, but only a kid, you know.'

'Very well, then. Mum's the word, hey? And I'll meet you ... let's see, shall we say outside that newsagent's? And would five past six suit?'

'Yes, it would be grand,' Mona said, handing him the bouquet. 'Tomorrer night, at five past six then, Mr Garnett. I'll look forward to it.'

'And you can call me Garnett; they only use the "mister" in the office because we're all Evans and it would be a bit confusing otherwise, eh, what?' He laughed, then walked round the car and opened the driver's door. 'Until tomorrow evening then, Miss Mullins.'

So now, Mona began to make her plans. She had her eye on Tommy, as a sort of back-stop, so he mustn't find out that she was seeing Mr Garnett, and she dared not let Rose or Aunt Lily know. They wouldn't like it. She did not quite know why, but she knew that disapproval would follow an announcement that she was going out with Rose's boss. Never mind, though. If it got serious, if it looked as though Mr Garnett was going to pop the question, then she could always move out, or brazen it out, whichever seemed the better. And what was more, if she said she had a feller, sort of introduced him slowly, then it was just possible that Rose and Aunt Lily would not only approve, but would see, as clearly as Mona did herself, that she was doing the right, the sensible thing.

Though there was no denying he was a plain feller. His long, thin face was miserable-looking, and he had long, thin hands too—damp hands.

Mona had always disliked damp hands. And then there were the pimples; folk said fellers grew out of pimples but that Garnett must be in his mid-twenties and his chin and brow were fair pitted with the things. And he had that voice so many of his type had ... the sort of voice, Mona thought, that Miss Ellis and she both tried to imitate when they were serving important customers. Well, imitating it was all very well, but to have to use it always ... and to have it sounding in your ears from across the breakfast table—heavens, from the next pillow—would be a trial, to put it no stronger. I wonder if I can stand listenin' to it, Mona thought crossly, let alone do it meself always, not just on special occasions.

But she comforted herself with the thought that she needn't try to talk posh herself, not when she was out with Garnett. It wasn't like work, when you needed to impress people. Mr Garnett wasn't interested in her accent, he was interested in her—well, in her body. And personality an' brains an' that, Mona reminded herself hurriedly. Once she'd got him there'd be no need to crack her jaw trying to sound like someone she wasn't.

In the other bed, Rose gave a muffled snort and turned over. If I don't give over worryin' an' get to sleep soon, it'll be mornin' an' I'll be no manner o' use in the shop, Mona reminded herself despairingly. So I better stop thinkin' about that long streak of misery and concentrate on his sports car, his handmade shoes an' the money he brings home each week. Wasn't it just like fate, now, that Tommy was good-looking, fun, amusing ... and a bleedin' tram driver, whilst the other ...

With a muffled groan, Mona heaved the bedding

up over her shoulder and began to think about Tommy, to imagine that he was suddenly rich, that he had come into a fortune which some old geezer had left him for ... for stoppin' the bleedin' tram right outside his door an' savin' him a long walk. It was a good day-dream, for Mona had recognised in Tommy something—she could not for the life of her have said what—which spoke to something in herself. And very soon it was no longer a day-dream. Mona slept.

*   *   *

Sean watched the sudden change in his son's attitude to Rose—and Mona—and was delighted. He could see that it would make life much easier for Colm whilst he himself was enjoying his Christmas in Dublin, but it was not only that. Anyone with half an eye, Sean had been telling himself for weeks, could see Colm was always making calf's eyes at Mona. She was very like that Nell MacThomas who had made such mischief at Switzer's and had actually been responsible for getting Colm the sack. Why he should gravitate to another blonde good-time girl Sean could not understand, for his son was bright enough in other ways. He had good friends at work, all of whom Sean liked, and over the months that they had toiled on the tunnel together he had grown to trust Colm as a fellow worker who pulled his weight, could be relied upon, and was polite and tactful to those in command. It was, Sean thought now as he made his way to the tram stop, just the female sex who seemed to put his son in a flat spin.

But a few days ago he had begun to realise that

333

Colm had changed. He no longer talked about Mona as though she were a mixture between a saint and a film star. And what was perhaps better, he did not speak of Rose as though she were anything but a pretty, sensible young thing. But his eyes gave him away. They softened when they fell on Rose, into a completely different look from that which Colm had been wont to give Mona. When he had regarded Mona there had been hunger, apprehension . . . but never a hint of the sort of glow which filled Colm's eyes now when Rose came into the room. You could see he liked Rose, respected her and regarded her as someone very special. But you could also see that he wanted to be with her; he had taught her to ride the bicycle and that, Sean thought now as he made his way towards the tram stop, had just been the start of it. Since then they had been to the cinema together, and spent a couple of happy evenings shopping for Christmas extras in Paddy's market and also—the opposite end of the scale—in Lewis's.

Sure an' I'll have so much to tell me darlin' Eileen when I get home that I'll not stop talkin' for the fortnight, Sean thought contentedly, climbing onto the tram and giving the conductor his money. She worries about her boy—it's only natural—but now I'll be able to reassure her. She's said, over and over, that a dacint girleen would be the makin' of him and though I know very well she had an Irish rose in mind, she'll like the English rose when she meets her. Indeed, he intended to give such a glowing report of their landlady's daughter that Eileen would fall for her at once, and long for nothing more than that Colm and she should find their happiness together.

He had felt desperately sorry for the lad as they had realised that Colm would not be able to go home to Ireland when his father did. They had plotted how he might come home just for Christmas Day itself, taking the ferry back on Boxing Day, but had decided it was too expensive—and too unsettling—for the bare day. And now he could see that Colm was very well content and would not want to go back to Dublin even had the foreman changed his mind and told him to buy his ticket and stay until his father returned. He wanted to be with Rose, and Sean knew that both Ryders would see that his son had a good time and did not spend the day moping.

It's a weight off me mind, Sean told himself, beginning to stand up and make his way to the exit, for his stop was approaching. Now I'll be able to go home without feeling mean and selfish, because I'll know that Colm's where he wants to be and is having a great time. Why, they might come to a proper understanding over the holiday, which would be best for everyone. It wasn't that he thought Colm would suddenly begin to turn to Mona again, but he would be happier when young Rose and his Colm had actually committed themselves. At the moment they tried to pretend that they were seeing more of each other because they were both at a loose end, but Sean knew it wasn't that. Oh, Mona seemed to be out most evenings and had disappeared for the whole day the previous Sunday and Tommy, who Sean considered was just the sort to lead a girl up the garden path and leave her in the lurch, had also been off somewhere most of the time. But Colm would have gone out with Rose regardless, Sean

335

was sure of it, only he realised it was all new to them and they wanted it to be their secret for a little longer, until they felt sure enough to admit a certain fondness.

The tram stopped and Sean swung himself off the platform and set off towards William Brown Street. He and Colm were on different shifts now, though usually they went to work together. But because most of the Irish would be taking the full two weeks off, Colm had been put on a late shift, so Sean was by himself this morning.

As he turned down into the mighty beginnings of the tunnel, with the huge machinery clattering and men shouting, Sean thought happily: not long now and I'll be out of it. Back with my darlings, handing out the presents Colm and me's took so long in choosing . . . and then it'll be big fires and good food, and a bed warmed by the prettiest woman in Dublin . . . and herself in my arms, soft and tender and giving, the way she's always been.

'Why's youse got that soppy look on yer fizz?' someone shouted and a huge navvy, even taller than Sean himself, grabbed his shoulders and twirled him round. 'T'inkin' about your woman, Paddy? An' what you'll be doin' a week today?'

Sean felt his cheeks grow hot and ducked under the other man's guard to give him a sharp poke in the stomach. 'It's all very well for you, Scouser. Wit' your bed warm each night an' your own woman to cook your vittles, you've got not'in' to dream about!'

The large man guffawed and pretended to clutch the stomach, hard as iron, which Sean had just punched. 'Don't you go knockin' me about, Paddy, or youse won't be home for Christmas after all, 'cos

336

if I'm off work, who's to keep the others at it, hey?'

'They'd probably manage well enough wit'out either of us,' Sean said. He and the big man did the same job though on different shifts. 'Anythin' to report, have ye?'

'There's been a blockage in one of the drainage headings, but there's men clearin' it now. You'll not need to worry about it. What's it like above?'

Once you got down into the main tunnel, the weather above was a matter of guesswork until someone came down to start his own shift. Grinning, Sean said, 'It's rainin' ink, feller,' and then, when the big man growled warningly, added: 'Well, it's what I'd be callin' brass monkey weather if I was as foul-mouthed as the rest of ye! I'd call it bleedin' chill, though. I'm wonderin' if we'll be havin' a white Christmas?'

'Nah! Never 'appens,' the big man said. 'Right, now you're here I'm off. See you tomorrer. Don't do nothin' I wouldn't do.'

*   *   *

'Rosie! Come here a tick, queen.'

Rose had been about to leave the kitchen for her bedroom, where she meant to wrap parcels, but at her mother's words she stopped in full flight, with the reel of string, the coloured paper and a quantity of ribbon in her arms. 'What is it, Mam? Only I want to get these things wrapped up and out of the way tonight, if I can. It's just lucky that Mona's out, an' Colm, an' Tommy, too, so I can get on quietly for once.'

'I won't keep you long, chuck,' Lily Ryder said. She had been making pastry and cutting it into

337

rounds, but now she put her cutter down and signed deeply. 'The fact is, Rosie, I wanted a word wi' you whilst there weren't no one else around, so seeing as the place is quiet, for once, it seemed a good opportunity. Where's Mr O'Neill, d'you know? Mr Dawlish won't be back in port for another two or three days so he's not likely to come walkin' in on us.' As Lily had guessed, Pete Dawlish's decision to come ashore and do an office job had not lasted. He had missed the sea terribly and as soon as the opportunity presented itself once more he had signed on and gone back to his ship.

'Mr O'Neill's gone to the shops wi' Colm,' Rose said a little impatiently. 'I wanted to go too, but I got to get these things wrapped. Fire away, Mam, do.'

'Well, I will, though I wish ... Rosie, did you take some money from my dressing-table yesterday?'

'Money? No, 'course not. How much?' Rose said without undue concern. Just lately, her mother had been awfully absent-minded and indeed careless about money. She had put eighteen and sixpence in the old teapot on the mantel in the kitchen and when she went to get it, it had gone. There had been a bit of a hullabaloo, until Mrs Kibble had come in from the front room and said it was neatly piled up on the window-sill. Then there was the milk money, which her mother had stood ready by the back door, or thought she had. Only it wasn't there when she wanted it, and so she'd had to borrow off Rose and really scrat around to pay her back. The trouble was, the back door had been open for most of the day, since she and Mrs Kibble had been going in and out with armfuls of linen. It was a fine day and they had decided to wash and—hopefully—dry the loose covers from the front room, hence the open door, so anyone could have picked up the money and walked off with it.

Whatever had happened to it, it had not been found in some spot where her mother might absently have laid it, and certainly Mrs Ryder trusted her boarders absolutely . . . but the money had gone somewhere, there was no doubt about it.

'Are you sure, queen? You know I wouldn't mind if you had—it would be a relief, honest to God. You see, it were on the dressing-table when I come back from Paddy's market, yet this mornin', when I went to put it back in me purse, it weren't there.'

'Oh, Mam . . . are you *sure* you put it there? Remember the teapot money that time. As for takin' it meself, of course I didn't, an' if I had, wouldn't I have told you? It's not as if you're ever mean wi' me, or take too much off me, like some mams do.'

'Thank you, queen,' Lily Ryder said, turning from the sink and crossing the kitchen to give her daughter a hug. 'No, but you've got to ask everyone . . . Agueda says she's gettin' suspicious that there's a thief hereabouts.'

'A *thief*? You don't mean one of the boarders, do you, Mam?'

'Gracious no, I'm sure they're all decent fellers,' Lily said hurriedly. 'And yesterday afternoon the window-cleaner came an' when Agueda checked, the window weren't properly latched. But . . . well, I've known old Shifty Smith twenty year, an' I can't believe he'd thieve from me.'

'No-o, but what about them lads who help him?'

339

Rose put in. 'Suppose one of 'em saw the money an' slid his arm through the window? Could he have reached it from outside?'

'I dunno. Depends whether I stood it on the left or the right an' to tell you the truth, Rosie, I just can't somehow 'member exactly where I put it. Only this time I'm certain sure it were there . . . and it ain't now! So you see . . .'

'Was it much money?' Rose asked practically. 'Or just some loose change, like?'

'It were quite a bit . . . almost two quid,' Lily said, sounding guilty. 'Agueda scolded an' said I were careless, which I suppose is true, but I never thought I'd have to be careful in me own house, Rosie. I like all me boarders, I can't believe any of 'em would tek money, but . . . well, there's no gettin' away from it, it's gone, honest to God it has. An' I've been a lot more careful since the milk money went missin', so I know it *were* there, even though it was gone this mornin'.'

'I'd put money on the window-cleaner's lad,' Rose said, remembering the number of different young boys who had come scrambling up the ladder to give the panes a final rub with a dry chamois leather. 'He's always gettin' new ones, how can he say whether they're trustable or not? He never knows 'em long enough.'

'I suppose it's the likeliest answer,' Lily admitted. 'The trouble is, I've never been careful where I put things down, an' we've never been short by so much as a penny . . . not when your dad was alive, that was.'

'No, but then we didn't tek boarders so there wasn't so much comin' an' goin',' Rose pointed out. 'What's more, you an' Dad cleaned our windows, didn't you? An' tradesmen didn't call like they does here. And . . . well, you didn't have money to leave about careless-like, did you. Because you were the only one who paid folk an' you kept your cash in your purse. Now, when you're busy, Mrs Kibble or meself or Mona will pay at the door, so you leave the money where it's easy seen. Oh Mam, don't worry yourself over it, but latch the windows in future when Mr Smith comes callin'.'

'I expect you're right,' Lily said. She began to fit her rounds of pastry into a bun-tin which she had standing by. 'Anyway, chuck, you go off an' wrap your parcels and I'll get on wi' me mince pies. I'm doin' some extra so's Mr O'Neill can tek 'em home wi' him when he goes.'

'How about two each for after our tea?' Rose asked hopefully. The lovely warm smell of baking was making her hungry already. 'How about a couple for me to tek up to me room, come to that?'

Her mother laughed, but shook her head. 'No, you'd only go gettin' grease marks all over that nice paper. Well, I'll give you one when you come down agin, 'cos you've relieved me mind. I wouldn't like to think that old Shifty had took advantage o' me an' that's a fact.'

Glad that she had put at least some of her mother's fears to rest, Rose hurried upstairs. She had agonised over whether to buy a present for Colm, not because he might not have bought anything for her—that would be fair enough—but because getting a gift from her might have embarrassed him. She'd already got a nice tortoiseshell comb for Mrs Kibble to put in her iron-grey hair, a tablet of scented soap and some talcum powder for Mona and a brooch for her

341

mother. She was especially pleased with the brooch, which she had saved up for ever since she had seen it in Paddy's market, and was sure that her mother would love the tiny white enamelled lilies of the valley nestling amidst their green-enamelled leaves.

But finally she had decided that if Colm bought her a present she would produce his and if he did not she would wait until they were alone and hand hers over anyway. After careful thought, she had spent her money on a blue muffler which, she told herself, would keep him warm—and smart—all through the winter.

So now she chose a piece of bright wrapping paper and began to fold the muffler up in it, using blue ribbon to fasten the rather bulky parcel. Tomorrow, she thought joyfully as she put the wrapped parcel in her dressing-table drawer and turned her attention to the next present, tomorrow Mr O'Neill would go off for his Irish Christmas—and Mona would move into his room until he came back once more. Rose was naturally an early riser, Mona liked to lie in until the last minute and though Rose tried to tiptoe round as silently as she could she knew she usually woke Mona long before her cousin wished to greet the light of day. And Rose herself would have liked a lie-in sometimes on a Sunday morning, but if they both got up late then one of them would be hanging around waiting to use the washstand, and secretly cursing the other for her tardiness. So Rose got up early and washed first, then Mona, groaning, would drag herself out of bed and splash water around, whilst Rose brushed her hair, put on the clothes she had selected, ironed and hung up the night before, and gave her shoes a rub with the cloth she kept especially for that purpose in the pocket of her pink-and-white-checked overall.

The two girls got on well enough, but sometimes Rose missed the quiet of her own little room and felt that the two of them, dressing to go out of an evening, were always on top of one another, elbows banging, heads together to share the mirror at the last moment before rushing downstairs. Rose loved and admired many things about Mona, but knew she would enjoy Christmas all the more for the additional privacy which Mr O'Neill's absence would give them.

Just lately, she and Mona, though they got up and dressed at roughly the same time each weekday morning, seldom went to bed at the same hour. Rose had been out with Colm several times, but they were usually home by eleven o'clock at the latest—often earlier. Mona, however, had taken to coming in well after midnight, though Rose had to admit that her cousin crept into the room and undressed so quietly that she, Rose, never woke.

But it meant, of course, that Mona got into bed still fully made-up and had to do her hair by guess in the dark. Rose had naturally curly hair—which she hated, because curly hair was not fashionable— but Mona tied her hair up in rags each night. Not into curls, it was true, but into the smooth, swooping style which she favoured. The result was that Rose felt guilty because, although she tried, she simply could not stay awake until her cousin came in, and while she apologised fervently and begged Mona to put the light on and bustle about all she liked, Mona would not. 'Don't worry, Rosie, I'm gettin' a dab hand at undressin' in the dark an' puttin' me hair into rags by touch,' she had said consolingly, when Rose talked to her about it. 'As for not washin' before I gerrin to bed, what does it matter? I wash in the mornin', don't I?'

But mornings were always a rush, and Rose knew that the cat's lick and promise which Mona gave herself when she had the use of the washstand, before re-applying her make-up, was not the sort of scrub, from top to toe, which she should have had.

But at least from tomorrow we'll be in our own rooms for a couple of weeks and we'll have all the time in the world in the mornings, she told herself now, finishing off the packing of her last parcel and heading for the stairs once more. Only because it's Christmas, I dare say we'll both be going to bed pretty late. Isn't that just how things always work out, though? But at least we'll have a basin and jug each instead of sharing the one, and whoever wants a lie-in can have it without being disturbed by the other.

Having finished her parcels, she glanced thoughtfully about the room. She must hide the presents—particularly Mona's—because her cousin must not spoil the surprise by seeing what she had bought her before Christmas Day, but where to put them was a puzzle.

In the end, she put them right at the very back of her underwear drawer and crossed her fingers that Mona's curiosity would not lead her to snoop. She did not think it would, but she knew that if Mona needed clean knickers and did not have a pair to hand, she would borrow a pair of Rose's though she would always ask, of course. But sometimes she doesn't wait for me to answer, Rose reminded

344

herself. Still, the parcels are at the back—and I can tell Mona they're there and warn her not to look. I'm sure she won't if she knows.

Downstairs in the kitchen her mother was still cooking and, when Rose appeared, smiled rather wearily and pointed to a clean pink china plate upon which reposed a number of mince pies. 'Help yourself to any o' them,' she said. 'I'm onto sausage rolls now—how I hate the dratted things! All that roly-polying . . . why can't they be an easier shape, eh?'

Rose laughed and took a mince pie. 'Oh Mam, you're daft,' she said, biting into the rich, crumbly pastry. 'How about if I finish the sausage rolls then, while you make us both a mug of cocoa?'

'Bless you, Rosie,' Lily said gratefully, laying down her rolling pin and going over to the sink to wash her hands. 'A change is as good as a rest, they say. And I reckon another dozen will see us through the festive season. Where's your cousin gone tonight, then? Out wi' Tommy?'

'Dunno,' Rose said briefly, curling her pastry round the sausage meat and cutting it off, then brushing the two long sides with water and sticking them firmly together. 'She worked late, that I do know, but what she's doing after that I'm not sure about. She likes Tommy, doesn't she, Mam?'

'So do we all,' her mother said, then took the big black kettle from the fire and began to fill it at the sink, raising her voice to combat the gush of the water. 'We're a happy little crowd, ain't we, queen? We're awful lucky, you know. Not everyone who takes in lodgers gets along like we do. And as for Mona liking Tommy, I'd say they was just friends. Still an' all, it's best to be friends, wouldn't you

345

say?'

'Yes, sure,' Rose said absently. She chopped the two-foot sausage roll she had made into four-inch pieces and began to place them on the greased baking tray her mother had prepared. 'Ah, there's someone comin' through the yard. If it's Mona, she's early for once.'

But when the back door opened presently it proved to be Colm and his father, rosy-faced from the cold and sniffing the warm cooking smell appreciatively.

'That's a grand smell, so it is,' Mr O'Neill said, eyeing the mince pies. 'Don't they look beautiful, sittin' there on that plate just waitin' to be et? Only I suppose they're for Christmas,' he added mournfully. 'And there's me an' Colm wit' our bellies flappin' against our backbones an' all our money spent on Christmas presents.'

'Oh get along wi' you, Mr O'Neill,' Lily Ryder said, laughing. 'Them mince pies is a bit of a supper for us all—an' there'll be some sausage rolls too, only you'll ha' to leave 'em to cool. Hot sausage meat can scar a feller for life.'

'I'll chance it,' Sean O'Neill said, taking off his coat and hanging it on one of the hooks on the back door. 'And wouldn't you know it, now, young Rosie's got the lead on us, Colm, she's gobblin' one already. Come on, let's show these Ryders what an O'Neill can do in the way of appreciatin' good food.'

*   *   *

The theatre trip had been exciting and enjoyable, despite Garnett trying to cuddle her for most of the performance and Mona, who wanted to concentrate on the play, having to be quite nimble at times, but now, sitting beside Garnett in his car as he drove her—he said—to a special and excellent restaurant, she began to feel the first stirrings of disquiet. Would they end up at a hotel with a meal—and a room—prebooked? God knew, Mona pondered, several times she had thought him keen as mustard, but he had always drawn back at the last moment. In a way this suited her, he was so long and thin and miserable-looking and so incredibly inept and clumsy—he usually managed to tread on her toes at least once every dance and to shut her coat in the car door, or to leave one of his own gloves at the cinema, dance-hall or theatre they had been frequenting—but she told herself that if—*if*—he tried to take liberties she really should let him go at least a bit further. She was doing her best to prove to him that she was a decent girl, the sort of girl who wouldn't allow 'that kind of thing', yet she also had subtly to encourage him or he might simply lose interest and move on to some other, easier girlfriend.

So she had not stopped him kissing and caressing, within reason that was, and usually he would draw the car to a halt in some quiet spot and begin to cuddle, always stopping, however, when she made it plain that he must do so or earn her considerable displeasure. Yet, so far, he had not suggested that their friendship might go further, had not taken that final step into intimacy, and Mona guessed that Garnett somehow knew that she would want more than a few expensive outings before she would even consider giving him her all.

In fact, she had made no secret of her rules, if

347

rules you could call them. Kissing was all right, cuddling was fine, too, so long as too many liberties were not taken, but the ultimate prize was being saved, she told him righteously, for a real commitment. An engagement ring and a promise of wedded bliss had to be at least in view.

Of course she had not put it quite so bluntly as that, but Garnett was no fool and had clearly realised what she meant, and the moment she gave her 'desist' sign—a kick in the shins or a french burn of the wrist proving a common language a good deal plainer than a 'that's enough!' had proved to be—he stopped whatever he was doing and returned to the straight and narrow.

Mona's difficulty came because she had a shrewd suspicion that Garnett would want at least to sample the goods before he bought, to put it plainly. However, she was none too sure of how far he needed to go before deciding whether he wanted to burn his boats and settle for an engagement at the very least. And she did not intend to agree to a word-of-mouth engagement sealed by some trumpery piece of jewellery, either. A solitaire diamond ring with the stone the size of a sixpenny joe would, if the marriage did not actually come off, prove a consolation, she thought.

So if he had booked a hotel bedroom, what should she do? If she went upstairs with him, she realised shrewdly, she could scarcely act the injured innocent when he started to make the obvious moves. But if she refused . . . oh Lor', would she lose him altogether? He was her best chance so far of a good marriage, and the fact was, the more she got to know him the more she liked him. Despite what she believed Aunt Lily thought, she had only ever made love to one man during her time treading the pavements outside Lime Street station, and that was because she had honestly believed she had found herself a proper husband at last. They might have married, too, had not her mother made mischief. No, Mona had always played fair, at least by her standards. Right from the start she had known what she wanted and made it clear to any man who approached her that she was just a companion, a dancing partner, someone to be seen around with, and would never hop into bed on a mere acquaintanceship.

She had very little trouble, either, because she froze the wrong sort off with a threat to call the scuffers if they pestered her again, an' what sort o' a gal did they think she was, then? And even then she had had a shrewd eye for the right sort and had allowed them a little more licence. But she could scarcely pretend she didn't know Garnett, after three weeks or so of constant outings and treats. He had bought her pretty things—a silk scarf, a gold charm bracelet and some charms to hang on it—and there was no denying his generosity in other ways too. Always the best seats at the theatre, the most delicious chocolates, the grandest and most expensive meals in restaurants which she had not known existed—at least, not from personal experience.

The trouble was, she was no longer as single-minded as she had once been and that was because of Tommy Frost. She really liked him; his wonderfully neat and experienced dancing meant that she danced wonderfully too, when in his arms. His gaiety was a tonic and it never mattered what she said to him—she had to watch her tongue with

Garnett—because he was her own kind. And his kissing simply set her on fire, made her long to throw her rules to the wind and let him go on ... except that he never did. He seemed to know by some instinct what was the right moment to stop. It's my misfortune, Mona thought miserably now, that he stops just when I least want him to, when I'm all on fire for more.

He understood her meetings with Garnett, too. Without a word of reproach he hung around the house or sat in his window until he saw her come in, then he would steal down to the kitchen in his socks and they would make their cocoa and get out the biscuit tin and talk and talk. Tommy intended to make his fortune in some unspecified fashion before he was thirty and they discussed the sort of car he would drive, the house he would buy and the way all his old colleagues on the trams would envy him. Then, when the time came for them to go to their own rooms, he always gave her a kiss and a cuddle, though he never overstepped the mark. He did take her out occasionally, but so far as that went he couldn't compete with Garnett Evans, though she found him pleasanter and easier company.

Me and Tommy, we're two of a kind, she reminded herself now, as the car's headlights lit up the white country road. We're both determined to make our fortunes—oh, how I wish we could make them together!

'You're very quiet, Mona, my dear.'

She had been thinking about Tommy so ardently that the sound of Garnett's voice came as a real shock; she jumped, then laughed rather breathlessly and turned to face him. 'Sorry,

Garnett, I were a thousand miles away. Where are we goin'? You didn't say it were way out from the city—you don't mean to make me lose me beauty sleep, I hope?' The coquettishness of her tone was enlivened by a little genuine worry—had she sounded cheap?

But if so, Garnett did not appear to mind. 'We're going along the coast, my dear, to an excellent restaurant where I've booked us a corner table in a quiet spot by the log fire—you'll love it. As for missing your beauty sleep, don't fret your pretty little head. I'll see you get home in good time—don't I always?'

'Yes, always,' Mona said, and spoke no more until they drew up outside a large comfortable-looking house with a number of smart cars already parked before it. Garnett saw her out and into the hall, where he spoke to a man in tails about their table, whilst Mona went to the cloakroom and divested herself of coat, hat and long leather boots. She had brought her court shoes in her bag and popped them on, then checked herself in the large, pink-tinted mirror which hung on one wall. Her hair was tousled and she was rather pale, but a comb and a quick flick with her little rouge pad soon cured that, and out she went to join Garnett in the hall.

'Ah, lovely as ever,' Garnett said gallantly. 'Mona, I've just discovered that the confounded manager has made a muddle and our quiet table has been double-booked. But I've hired a private room and our meal will be served there. How does that suit you?'

Mona stared. A private room? Did he mean a . . . a bedroom? But he was not looking guilty or

351

shifty or anything like that, just enquiring, with his rather bulging pale eyes fixed on her face and one long pale hand fingering the bow tie at his neck.

'Umm . . . I suppose it's all right,' she said at last. One good thing—she was not in the least afraid of Garnett. If necessary she firmly believed she could scream louder, scratch harder and run more swiftly than her companion. 'Let's take a look.'

The room proved to be a small sitting-room with the promised log fire, a table and two chairs set temptingly close to the lovely warmth, and a comfortable-looking couch. It was not a bedroom nor a boudoir, whatever a boudoir might be. Mona did not know, but she believed it was a very compromising sort of room.

'Well?' Garnett asked. 'Shall I tell the fellow to bring our meal in about ten minutes? Give you a chance to have a drink of something warming and to settle yourself.'

'All right,' Mona conceded graciously. She crossed the room and sat on one end of the couch, then patted the cushion beside her. 'Do sit down, Garnett, and stop fidgeting about like that.'

Garnett had been poking at the fire one minute and standing up to peer at the contents of the bookshelves which flanked the fireplace the next. Now he looked across at her and grinned. 'You sound just like my mother,' he said cheerfully. 'She's always telling me to sit down and stop fidgeting.'

'Well, do it then,' Mona demanded. 'Then you can tell me what we're goin' to have for our supper.

'I ordered asparagus soup, roast duck and all the trimmings, and a raspberry Pavlova to follow,' Garnett told her, taking his place beside her and putting an arm round her waist. 'And now that we're on our own at last, I've got a proposition to put to you.'

'We're often on our own,' Mona said rather uneasily. 'What d'you mean, Garnett?'

'I've told the waiter not to serve dinner until I ring the bell,' Garnett said, his long face flushing. 'I . . . I've been wanting to ask you something for weeks, Mona, but somehow I never seemed to get the opportunity. So just listen to me for once and don't interrupt or I'll take the whole evening to come out with it. It's like this . . .'

CHAPTER TEN

It was Christmas Eve, and the two girls were rearranging their rooms, for Colm had carried his father's case down to the docks earlier in the day and seen him off for his two weeks at home with the family in Dublin. Then he had gone to work, because tunnelling did not stop for anything, not even for Christmas Eve, though Colm would be off work for the following two days.

'Here, you'd better take your apricot jersey coat and skirt,' Rose said, taking the garments from their shared wardrobe and offering it to her cousin. 'It's so pretty that if you left it behind I wouldn't be able to resist wearing it.'

'Sorry, I didn't see it what with the door an' all the other gear,' Mona said. 'Can you bring it down, then? Oh, and you can keep that rose-pink lipstick; it don't do a thing for me.'

'Oh, Mona . . . are you sure? Thanks ever so

much,' Rose said with real sincerity. She had coveted the rose-pink lipstick for a long time. 'And if that's the last lot, we'd better go downstairs as soon as we've settled them in Mr O'Neill's room. Mam's ever so busy; we could give her a hand.'

'She can't still be cooking, can she?' Mona asked, tottering under her load. 'But I don't mind helping.'

'All women seem to do in the run-up to Christmas is cook,' Rose observed, following her cousin down the steep attic flight. Her arms were full of clothes and she was wearing two of Mona's hats on her head and looking very strange indeed, but at least it would save another trip up and down the narrow stairs. 'Unless they work for Patchett & Ross, of course, in which case they have to type out huge great sheets of goods dispatched and goods delivered until their fingers nearly fall off.'

'Or unless they work in the Exchange Station arcade, like me,' Mona said, clattering down the steps and raising her voice to be heard above the noise. The main stairs were carpeted but the attic ones were not. 'Now I've been makin' wreaths an' bouquets an' Christmas arrangements until me hands nearly fruz off it's been that cold.'

'Isn't it funny how men seem to want every bleedin' job done before Christmas, and make you go grey and insane doin' it?' Rose said idly. 'Even Mr Garnett's got all naggy about his work bein' up to date before the holiday. Still, it's over now for another year. They can't follow us home an' force you to make holly wreaths an' me to type invoices. So from now, we're safe to enjoy ourselves.'

'Mmm,' Mona said. She reached the landing and crossed to Mr O'Neill's room, where she began to hang her clothes in his now empty wardrobe. 'You goin' out tonight, Rosie?'

'Yup. We're goin' to the Daulby Hall—there's a big Christmas Eve dance, wi' spot prizes an' a special non-alcoholic punch, an' mistletoe an' all sorts,' Rose said, following her cousin into the room and beginning to pile her belongings up on the bed. 'Then after that we'll go to Midnight Mass at St Francis Xavier's in Salisbury Street, so we'll probably be home even later than you, for once. Where're you goin', then? Is Tommy takin' you dancin', or something o' that nature?'

There was a pause whilst Mona carefully arranged her apricot jersey costume on two hangers and pushed them into the wardrobe. When she spoke it was lightly, however. 'I don't know, not for sure. I might—well, I might be goin' out wi' the girls from me first job, you know, the ones from the jam factory. It 'ud be a laugh, an' you know how hard it is when the fellers work shifts. Tommy may be on his perishin' tram.'

'Doesn't he know yet? Colm does. He's off today, tomorrow an' Boxing Day,' Rose said contentedly. She looked appraisingly round the room. 'Isn't it nice down here. I quite envy you, our Mona. You'll be able to use the bathroom, mornin's, instead of sharin' that old washstand wi' me. That means a hot wash an' all, because Mam always keeps the fire in, for the boarders.'

'That'll be a treat,' Mona said vaguely. She followed Rose's example and looked consideringly around the room. 'Yes, it is nice. In fact, I've been wonderin' ...' She turned and glanced almost measuringly at Rose. 'I've been wonderin', lately, whether I might not move out in the new year. I'm real comfortable wi' you an' Aunt Lily, you know that, but a friend's suggested we share a flat, quite near Exchange Station, an' once the snow starts an' the trams get later an' later, an' more an' more crowded . . . well, it might be an idea, even if only for the winter. Just because the journey would be shorter an' that.'

'No!' Rose said, looking, she imagined, as dumb-struck as she felt. 'But we thought you liked it here, Mam an' me. An' what about Tommy? I don't know whether you an' him's serious, but . . .'

'We aren't,' Mona said hurriedly. 'He's a lovely feller, but I don't think he wants to be serious about anyone just yet. He'll need to be in a better job than the one he's in now afore he starts thinkin' about gettin' hitched.'

'A better job than being a tram conductor?' Rose said incredulously. 'Why, Mona, me dad brung me up on a tram driver's wages an' you couldn't have had a nicer home than ours . . . an' look how his insurance helped Mam to manage when he were gone. Surely, if Tommy was serious . . .'

'He ain't,' Mona said hurriedly. 'How you do jump at a girl, Rosie! I said he's not thinkin' o' marriage an' I meant it. He's got real ambition, has Tommy. But I don't know if I'll take a share in the flat; it's a big decision, an'—an' I've not seen it yet.'

'Well, it's up to you, o' course, but I really did think you were happy here,' Rose said rather reproachfully. She could not help it, she had had to persuade her mother to take Mona as a lodger and now it looked as though her cousin was going to repay her by walking out—and in the new year, too, when the weather would mean that more money would go on fuel and good, hot food. They would not be able to replace Mona with anyone else, either, because Mam, Rosie knew, would not expect her to share her room with anyone other than her cousin. Just for a moment, Rose thought it would be nice to have her room to herself again, but then she remembered how good it was to have another girl to confide in from time to time, and sighed. Now that she thought about it, she rather enjoyed having a go at Mona's make-up or trying on her new blouse or skirt. But still, it was up to her cousin to decide whether she would stay or go.

'I am happy, I telled you I was,' Mona said. But she spoke absently, less as if she meant it than that she wanted to calm her cousin's fears. 'Honest to God, Rosie, I've been happier wi' you an' me aunt than I've been for years. I don't suppose I'll go, not really. But since the subject came up . . . oh, come on, let's go downstairs an' give Aunt Lily a hand with wharrever it is she's up to. Tell you what,' she continued as the two girls left the room and began to descend the stairs, 'I won't try to mek up me mind one way or the other until Mr O'Neill's back in his own room again an' we're sharin' once more. How's that?'

'Fair enough, I suppose,' Rose agreed. 'I can understand you wantin' a place of your own in a way, our Mona. You're older'n me, I expect it irks you more, sharin'. Only it won't be that long before one of us is thinkin' of marryin', then the other one will be left wi' our attic room all to herself.'

'Oh? Do you mean Colm is that serious already?' Mona said lightly. 'Because none o' the fellers I go around with have mentioned marriage. Not yet.'

'Nor has Colm . . . we're probably a bit young

yet,' Rose said, 'and we'd have to save for ages an' ages before we could even get engaged. But . . . but I do like him more than I've ever liked a feller before, even though he isn't a tram man.'

'You're quite, quite mad,' Mona said as the two of them entered the kitchen. 'You don't wed a feller for his *job*, Rosie, there's a lot more to it than that!'

Lily Ryder, making mince pies, looked up and smiled at them. 'Who's talkin' about gettin' wed?' she asked cheerfully. 'Don't say Tommy's popped the question, our Mona!'

'I don't know why everyone thinks that because Tommy an' me's good pals we're thinkin' o' marryin',' Mona said rather reproachfully. 'Tommy's got ambitions an' I reckon he knows he'll go further—and go further faster, what's more—if he isn't held back by a wife.'

'Well, queen, you'll find that when he meets the right woman he'll suddenly realise that money and ambitions come a long way behind marriage,' Lily said wisely. 'There, an' I bought a few sprigs o' mistletoe specially for you young folk . . . what'll I do with 'em? Give 'em to Gully?'

'Gully, Gully, give 'em to Gully!' the parrot squawked commandingly. 'Who's a clever boy, then? Gi's a kiss, gi's a kiss!'

'I'll give you a clout,' Rose said, wandering over to the pantry and taking a handful of sultanas from a large stone jar. 'Or would you settle for some sultanas, old boy?'

Gully, craning from his perch until his head was pressed against the bars, gave her to understand that he would settle for the sultanas, so she fed them to him one by one, then turned to her

358

mother. 'Can we help, Mam? We've changed the rooms round like you said. An' I told Mona she'd be able to use the bathroom, 'cos Mr O'Neill does. Was that all right?'

'Aye, that's fine,' Lily said. 'In fact over Christmas you'll both be able to use the bathroom, if you fit in with the fellers, that is. They need to shave, which takes a bit longer, but you won't mind that I dare say.'

'Hot water!' Rose said ecstatically. She remembered the early days in the house, before they had got their full complement of boarders and she had been able to use the bathroom each morning. 'When I marry it'll be a feller who can give me a proper, real bathroom, all to meself!'

Her mother clicked her tongue. 'There's not many wi' bathrooms in the city,' she said. 'I can charge an extra couple o' bob on the rent 'cos o' that bathroom. But you get your weekly baths, girls, you must admit that.'

'Oh aye, it's a heap better'n the tin bath in front o' the fire an' all,' Rose agreed. 'But it's so nice to get hot water straight from the tap, Mam, instead of having to break the ice on the jug.'

'You've not had to do that yet this year,' Lily said a trifle reproachfully. 'An' if you come downstairs you can always have a hot kettle. Only, what wi' gettin' the fellers their breakfasts . . .'

'It's all right, Mam, we were only kiddin',' Rose said, laughing. 'If it comes to breakin' the ice up there in the attic I'll come downstairs for hot water quick enough. Now how can Mona an' meself help you. You're off to Midnight Mass later, so we'll finish up for you so's you can get changed!'

'Well, alanna, it's been a fine day, so it has, and I wouldn't have missed one moment of it for the world! All the presents, an' the food, an' the singin' round the piano ... but d'you know what the best moment of all was?'

Colm and Rose were standing on the second floor landing, clasped in each other's arms. It had been, as Colm said, a wonderful day, with everyone exchanging presents at the breakfast table, then going off to church—those who had not attended Midnight Mass, that was—with the grand Christmas dinner served up on the best china and consisting of hot turkey, sausages, stuffing, bread sauce and every vegetable Lily had been able to lay her hands on.

Then in the afternoon they had played games and forfeits had been the silly, loving sort—to kiss someone beneath the mistletoe, to sit on a lap, to dance the tango whilst gripping, beneath one's chin, a large Jaffa orange. And at tea-time their own party—Lily and the two girls, Colm and Tommy—had been augmented by a variety of guests, for Lily had insisted that anyone in the Vale who would otherwise be alone should come to their house for a Christmas supper of cold meats, potatoes cooked in their jackets and a winter salad, followed by hot Christmas pudding and cream.

After supper the guests had departed and Colm and Rose had donned their coats and gone out into the frosty air. Despite their hopes it had not been a white Christmas, but above their heads the stars had appeared enormous in the black sky and a slender crescent moon had looked as though it were caught in the branches of the big old tree at the end of the road when they stared up.

The streets were deserted, though the lamps shone gamely, casting a primrose glow on the frost-rimed hedges, and the two had walked along, not talking, their arms round each other, breathing in the peace and beauty of the night. They had peered, as they walked, into the lighted windows, admiring Christmas trees, decorations and the girls in their prettiest dresses, the young men in best suits, for St Domingo Vale was a good area and most of their neighbours were in work and earning decent money.

But they hadn't stayed in their own neighbourhood; they had gone further afield, walking along Heyworth Street and seeing the little shops, which were always open, closed and the pavements, which were always crowded, clear of people.

'We'll go down to the docks, see what ships are in port,' Colm had said. 'I like to t'ink about the ferries goin' across to me home, so I do. I bet there's a party in the sailors' home an' all ... they're probably drunk as lords be now so we won't go too close, but we'll take a good look.'

But before they reached the docks they had to pass an area where the very poor lived, where the kids, even on a night like this, were out on the doorsteps, where from within doors they could hear the angry shouts of a father whose sleep had been disturbed or whose drinking had been deep, where the only fire had gone out hours since and where the women of the house came to the door to shout for their kids, hair unkempt, clothing ragged, quicker with a clout than a kiss even today.

Colm had put his arm protectively around Rose and tried to hurry her along, but Rose lingered. There were decent people here too, with neatly whitened doorsteps and tidy curtains, with clean, if shabby, children and a fire burning in the grate. And then they had seen, curled up in a darkened doorway, two children of no more than six or seven. They looked up listlessly as the two reached them and the elder, a skinny girl with lank hair and skin blotched with some sort of acne, held out a cupped hand in the gesture familiar the whole world over, the universal silent language of the beggar.

The two had stopped, appalled. On such a day, to see children like that! Colm had dug into his pocket and produced a handful of cash which he tipped into the small and filthy palm, speaking as he did so. 'Where's your mam an' dad, kids? Sure an' 'tis Christmas Day, you should be at home an' warmin' yourselves beside a good fire, not crouched on the step there. D'you live inside?'

The child took the money eagerly, cramming it into the ragged, cut-down man's jacket which she wore, but it was the small boy who answered. He looked healthier than his sister, if she was his sister, and had a pair of bright, intelligent eyes. 'No, we doesn't live 'ere,' he said, jerking a thumb at the door behind him. 'Me nanna used to live 'ere, but they took 'er away. We lives off of Netherfield Road, but Dad an' Mam are both in tearin' tempers, so we comes up 'ere, to be safer. Only . . . only we're awful 'ungry, me an' Suzie.'

'You've got some money now, chucks, so perhaps you can knock someone up,' Rose said. She dipped into her pocket and handed the small boy her own loose change. 'Here, take this.'

362

'Aye, an' Miz Cobbett on the corner will open if you knock,' Suzie put in. She stood up, then heaved the small boy to his feet. 'T'anks, both. We'll be fine an' dandy now, me an' Sammy.'

'An' if we takes some food 'ome, likely Mam'll keep Dad away from us,' Sammy said hopefully. 'Mam 'ardly ever wallops us, but Dad ...' He shivered. 'Dad can't 'alf swing 'is bleedin' belt.'

Rose and Colm watched until the small couple disappeared from sight, then Colm turned Rose towards him and gave her a hard hug. 'Scary, isn't it?' he said. 'That's what can happen, alanna, if you marries too young an' the kids keep comin'. Dear God, I'd not want to see any kid o'mine crouchin' on a doorstep on Christmas night, keepin' out of me way.'

'You never would be like that, any more'n your own father is,' Rose said. 'My dad—I wish you'd knowed him, Colm—never lifted a finger to me though we didn't have much money an' I think Mam and he was quite young when they wed. But I agree wi' you. They say it's better to marry than to burn, but ... well, I'd sooner burn a bit, like, than end up livin' in a place like this, wi' poor kids what I couldn't afford to feed, let alone dress decent.'

'It's a lesson, so it is,' Colm said as they turned by mutual consent and began to walk towards St Domingo Vale once more. 'We'll not marry till we've saved up a dacint sum, like, an' can afford a house wit' a nice bit o' garden, an' furniture, an' ...'

'I don't know why we're talking like this,' Rose said presently, as they turned into Heyworth Street once more. 'I'm not thinkin' o' marryin' for a good few years yet—I've not met the right feller, I dare

363

say. An' you've not met the right girl, eh, Colm?'

'I have so, and so have you,' Colm said, pulling her to a halt. 'I'd marry you tomorrow, Rosie Ryder, if I had the money. Don't say I've never axed you!'

'No, you haven't,' Rose said, dimpling up at him. 'We've only been goin' around together for a few weeks. Let's have some fun first, Colm!'

'Bein' wit' you is fun,' Colm said, squeezing her small waist. 'Shall us marry one day, though, Rosie? When we're older?'

'I'm not ruinin' me chances of marryin' a millionaire by tyin' meself to you, Colm O'Neill,' Rose said, laughing. 'But you never know, mebbe one day . . .'

So they had walked home, teasing one another, but with a vein of seriousness running beneath it all, And when they had reached the Vale, Colm had put his arms round her and given her a loving hug and a number of kisses, and had then stood back and regarded her, smiling. 'What say we start savin' up right away?' he said eagerly. 'An' you should come over to Ireland, so you should, to meet the mammy, an' Caitlin. Will you come, girleen? In the summer?'

'Oh, I don't know,' Rose said, confused. 'Isn't that sort o' . . . sort o' serious?'

And then Colm had given a kind of crow, and lifted her right up and twirled round and stood her down on the pavement again. 'Yes, it is alanna,' he said breathlessly. 'I'm serious about you.'

Rose stood there in the starlight, with a little breeze just stirring her hair, and looked up at him and thought that there was no one in the world that she would rather trust with her future than Colm.

So she stood on tiptoe and kissed him with deceptive lightness, then nodded her head vigorously. 'All right then; I'll be serious about you too,' she had said.

And now, with their arms about each other, they were saying good night and reliving their beautiful day.

'Go on then; what was the nicest part of the day?' Rose asked. 'Was it dinner? Or playin' forfeits wi' half the neighbourhood? Or Chinese whispers? Or . . . ?'

'It was you agreein' to be serious about me—and to comin' back to Ireland wit' me, next summer,' he said. 'Oh, Rose!'

'Oh, Colm!'

'Oh, gracious, you two, if you don't gerroff up to your beds you'll turn into pillars of salt, like that woman in the Bible!'

Lily had come quietly up behind them and her daughter and Colm sprang apart, guilt no doubt written all over our faces, Rose thought, turning towards the attic stairs. 'Sorry, Mam, we were just sayin' good-night and talkin' about what a great day it's been,' she said jerkily. 'Has Mona come in yet?'

'Just five minutes ago,' Lily assured her. 'An' Tommy come in wi' her, what's more, so mebbe this house'll settle down to sleep within the next hour or so.'

'Well I'm goin' up right now, an' since Mona's in Mr O'Neill's room she'll be able to lie in tomorrow or make a din, or keep the light on without wakin' me,' Rose said, walking up the attic stairs and talking over her shoulder. 'Oh . . . 'night, Colm. 'Night, Mam. See you in the morning.'

*   *   *

Mona, getting washed in the bathroom right next
door to Mr O'Neill's room, then drinking her cocoa
and cuddling down, wondered what her cousin
would have said had she known with whom Mona
had been considering sharing a flat. For, once
Garnett had got her on her own in the little private
room, he had sat beside her on the small,
comfortable couch, put his arm round her . . . and
suggested that it might be a good idea if he rented
a flat for her use—one in which he might visit her
whenever the opportunity arose.

Mona had been extremely shocked, to tell the
truth. The sort of young men she knew simply
didn't make proposals like that. They either
wanted to make love to you—which was only
human, she felt—or they wanted to marry you.
They did not, in her opinion, try to get the best of
both worlds by renting you a little love-nest in
which they would have, naturally, all the
advantages of marriage without any sort of legal
tie.

So she had told Garnett severely that he would
do no such thing. 'You want to have your cake an'
eat it, that's what rentin' a flat would be,' she said,
rather obscurely. 'If you want the goods, you
should marry 'em, Garnett. I never heard of such
goings-on! And anyway, there wouldn't be much
point in it for you, either. Why, you'd be payin' out
for a flat you weren't livin' in, but you'd go on bein'
bossed about by your mam an' your dad, just as if
you were still a single chap.'

'Well, I would be a single chap,' Garnett said
reasonably, having thought this over. 'And though
366

I'd have the rent of the flat to find, you'd still be working, wouldn't you?'

'I'd still be workin' if we was to wed,' Mona had said equably, reasonably she thought. 'Unless I fell for a kid, o'course. An' that's just as likely unwed as wed, they tell me.'

'Well ... but I don't think my parents would approve of me marrying so soon,' Garnett said after a few minutes, having examined the problem in his own mind, Mona supposed. 'Nor they wouldn't want me marrying a—I mean they wouldn't want me marrying someone whose parents they didn't know.'

'I've gorra mam ... an' a dad too, very like,' Mona said, indignation causing her to forget her posh accent totally for a moment. 'If you want me to dig 'em up an' bring 'em round to your house, I dare say it ain't impossible.'

'Dig 'em up? They aren't *dead*, are they?' said Garnett, sounding shocked. 'Only if they are ...'

'Course they aren't,' Mona snapped. 'I should ha' said find 'em up ... look for 'em, I meant. Me mam's in the Pool somewhere, that I do know, but me dad ran off years back. Still, if that's what you want ...'

'It isn't,' Garnett said, so hurriedly that he cut her proposed sentence off short. 'You don't understand. My parents aren't sn ... I ... I mean they're very nice people really, but they seem to have got the idea that I'll marry the daughter of one of Mother's friends. I won't, of course ... but on the other hand, I can't afford for them to cut me off without a shilling, just as I'm beginning to make my way in the world.'

'Oh, yeah? An' I suppose you're goin' to tell me

367

they'd be delighted to find you payin' rent for a flat wi' me in it,' Mona said shrewdly. 'I think if you put it to 'em . . .'

'No, no,' Garnett said, sounding harassed. Clearly, he had not expected such spirited opposition to his plans. 'The whole point of a flat, my dear Mona, is so that we can . . . we can enjoy a . . . a friendship, without . . . without interference from either my parents or . . . or your own.'

'Well, my parents wouldn't interfere with a wedding, but I'm not too sure about this flat,' Mona said. 'Tell you what . . . I'll ask me Aunt Lily when I get the chance, see what she thinks. Perhaps I'm wrong, an' it would be perfectly awright.'

'Your aunt?' Garnett said, his voice rising to a squeak. He cleared his throat. 'You . . . you don't mean Miss Ryder's mother? The aunt you live with? I really don't think it would be sensible to ask her. Remember, we've been quite careful to keep our . . . our friendship from both our families.'

'Yes, but that was before you suggested this flat,' Mona said in an injured tone. 'You can't expect me to move out from me aunt's place an' not tell her where I'm going—or who with! Besides, I told you, she's been like a mother to me and before takin' any big decision I should surely consult her.'

'I'd prefer it if you didn't mention the matter to Mrs Ryder,' Garnett said with some force, removing his arm from around her shoulders and turning so that he could look into her face. 'I have to work with Miss Ryder—suppose she were to let something drop before one of my brothers? Or my father? I tell you what, Mona, we'd best forget the flat, if that's the way you feel. I dare say it isn't quite . . . I mean I wouldn't want . . . that's to

368

say . . .'

He lost himself in the morass of half-sentences until Mona, taking pity on him, said: 'I'm sure you had your reasons, and it was kind of you in some ways, but perhaps you're right and we'll not mention the flat again.'

The rest of the evening had passed pleasantly, at least for her, though it did occur to Mona that Garnett's mind was not entirely easy. He kept giving her anxious looks and sometimes answered a remark quite at random. What was more, he took her straight home when she told him she was tired, and was rather vague as to when they might meet again. 'With Christmas so close, you'll want to be with your own people,' he had said as he helped her punctiliously out of the car. 'Have a good time . . . I'll see you after the holiday, no doubt.'

Mona had waved demurely and gone round to the back of the house, giggling to herself. The cheeky sod, she thought, wanting all the fun of marrying without the expense of a wife. Still, he made up me mind for me, so to speak. When I thought of bein' wi' Garnett and puttin' up wi' those great legs an' arms all over me, like a bleedin' daddy-long-legs, it was a lot easier to say 'no' to his little plans. He had no intention of marrying her. No, indeed! He was destined to marry 'Mother's friend's daughter', no matter how he might wrap it up, but intended to have some fun on the side first. And then, Mona thought, clicking her tongue at such innocence, he thought he could dump me and pick me up whenever he wanted to, because I'd be dependent on him for me weekly rent.

She had crossed the backyard and opened the door, still smiling. She realised that she felt free for

369

the first time since she had met Garnett. Now she would be able to tell Tommy that the affair was over and the two of them could spend time together openly.

Tommy hadn't been in the kitchen when she entered, but had come in as soon as the rest of the family had gone to bed. They had sat companionably in one chair, herself mostly in Tommy's lap, whilst she told him, with much amusement, the story of her evening. They had laughed together, but then he had astonished her by saying thoughtfully that she might do worse, at that.

'Worse? Wharrever meks you say that?' she had asked, round-eyed. 'Oh, it 'ud be awright for *him*, that I do see, but wharrabout *me?* I'd be cookin' me own meals an' doin' me own housework as well as havin' to purrup wi' that great leggy crittur pawin' all over me mornin', noon an' night.'

'Oh aye, but he couldn't be there all the time,' Tommy had said. 'An' when he wasn't, you an' me could have the love-nest all to ourselves. No doubt he'd be sure to tell you when he planned to come round, so's you could clear out any girlfriends you might have visitin', an' cook him a meal an' so on. You want to think hard before you turn down a free flat, queen.'

Mona had stared at him, speechless. He could not mean what he was saying; he must be joking. She took a deep breath and launched into speech. 'I don't believe me *ears*, Tommy Frost! The feller ain't suggestin' we live in tally, oh no, nothin' so wicked. He's suggestin' I move into this flat an' sit there like a dummy, waitin' for him. When I'm not workin', that is. Why, if I wanted that sort o' life I could ha' had it years since—fellers like me an' make suggestions. But I moved in wi' Aunt Lily because I could see that if I wanted a decent life wi' a proper marriage, kids, a nice house, then I'd not only gorra seem respectable, I'd gorra *be* respectable. Who'd marry me after I'd been at Garnett's beck an' call for a year or so, eh? An' where's the advantage to *me*? I'm losin' me good reputation just so's Garnett can have his way wi' me whenever he's got nowt better to do.'

'Who'd marry you? Me, for starters. Oh Mona, when your eyes sparkle like that I can't resist givin' you a kiss.'

He kissed the side of her neck but Mona pulled herself crossly away from him. 'Well, I dare say that's an advantage for me, seen from where you're lookin'. But from where I'm standin' it's all gain to Garnett an' nowt to me. Why, I'd have to buy me own food, do me own cookin' ... I'd be a sight worse off in every way.'

'Oh aye, I see what you mean, but he'd pay your way ... wouldn't he? I mean you'd run up bills, household ones, and you'd buy clothes an' that, or tek yourself off for a day at the seaside, perhaps. You'd tell him what the score was and he'd pay ... an' if he didn't you could persuade him to do so. After all, if he don't want his parents to hear what he's up to ...'

'That's blackmail,' Mona said. She was beginning to tremble and the heat was rising up her neck and flooding her face. She knew she looked like a bleeding beetroot and could have slapped her companion. 'How long would I last if I started in on that little game? Honest to God, Tommy, you're mekin' me feel quite ill. I didn't expect you,

371

of all people, to approve of what Garnett's tryin' on.'

'I don't, not really. I . . . I was just testin' you,' Tommy had said and had given her a squeeze. 'I want you all to meself, that's my trouble. An' if you didn't live wi' your aunt I thought it . . . it might be easier to see you alone.'

'Hmmm,' Mona had said, not entirely convinced. 'Well, I'm for bed. What wi' you argufyin' that there's nowt wrong wi' Garnett's cunnin' little plan, an' him a-pawin' at me I feel downright wore out. Goodnight, Mr Frost.'

'Oh, Mr Frost, is it? Very cool, very cool indeed,' Tommy had said, pulling a face at her. 'I reckon you're right an' I'm wrong, but I were only puttin' the other point of view. An' when I think o' the advantages of sharin' a roof, like we do, only a mad feller would want to change things.'

'I believe you; thousands wouldn't,' Mona said coolly, going over to the door. 'I'm in the bathroom first an' so you can mek a couple o' mugs o' cocoa whiles I'm washin'. You can knock on the bathroom door when you come up—if I'm not out, that is.'

Later, he had done so and she had taken her cocoa into Mr O'Neill's lovely room, hers for the duration of his time in Dublin, and sat up in bed for a little, to drink it and muse on what had been said that evening. And now she was comfortable and about to drop off to sleep, secure in the knowledge that she would be able to please herself about what time she got up in the morning.

When she heard footsteps in the hall outside, very soft footsteps indeed, she thought that someone was making their way to the WC, because

372

they had all had a pleasant time, which had probably included several drinks. Then she heard the sound of her door, opening very, very softly, and told herself it was Rose, coming to have a crack and to ask her what sort of an evening she had had. But when the footsteps came quietly on across the floor and stopped beside her bed she knew, really, what she had suspected all along. It was Tommy, here she hoped, to apologise for the things he had said earlier.

*　　　*　　　*

Colm and Rose had agreed that they would spend Boxing Day morning getting their thank you letters out of the way, because that was how they had spent Boxing Day morning ever since they had been able to write. It was not, however, an onerous task for either of them, since most of their presents had come from folk who could be thanked personally. Even so, Rose had received from an elderly neighbour a pair of blue woollen mittens and from one of her many aunts, now living away from the city, a calendar with a snow scene of robins on a holly log. Rose had half-expected that her Aunt Daisy would at least send Mona something, but not even a card had arrived from her.

Colm, of course, had more letters to do—one to Caitlin, thanking her for a shiny pair of bicycle clips, 'for to keep your trouser ends out o' the way o' the chain, when you've got a bicycle,' she had written on the label. Eileen O'Neill had sensibly dispatched a handsome shirt with two stiff collars, which she advised him to wear for best, and a pair of navy blue trousers which, she said, she had got 'very reasonable' last year in the Switzer's sale. And Sean had given his son two tickets to the pantomime at the Playhouse theatre and had very kindly added some money for other treats.

There was another good reason for writing their thank you letters this morning. Each had bought the other, without being aware of it, a handsome and expensive fountain pen. They had opened them in unison and had been both delighted and touched by the thought and tickled pink, as Lily put it, by the coincidence.

'Well, you're always writin' to your sister an' your mam,' Rose said self-consciously. 'D'you like the writin' paper an' envelopes Mam got you?'

'Everything's lovely, so it is,' Colm said. 'I know you use a pencil for your shorthand at work, but you did say, once, that you wished you had a fountain pen, an' didn't have to keep dip, dip, dipping when you was doin' exams.'

So now they settled down in the front room with the window table between them, and scratched away.

'What did you send your aunt? An' the neighbour?' Colm asked presently, blotting a page and putting it to one side. 'They're probably writin' to you at this very minute. I know Cait will be bendin' over her page, splutterin' away wit' her old school pen. An' likely me mammy too, because dinner's always cold on Boxin' Day.'

'I sent me aunt a box of dates an' some hairgrips,' Rose said. 'She loves dates and hair-grips are always useful. An' I sent Mrs Wilson Turkish Delight—one of them round boxes, it were hell to parcel up—an' the diary Eleanor at work give me—

because I got two, you know.'

'They'll be writin' too,' Colm said, nodding. 'I love to get letters, so I do, an' the day after we'll be gettin' a grosh o' the t'ings.'

'What did you get your mam in the end?' Rose asked curiously. She had helped Colm with a good bit of his shopping but his mother's gift was important and he had not actually chosen it whilst with her. 'You looked at gloves, an' stockin's, an' a vase wi' poppies on . . .'

'None of 'em,' Colm said, beginning to write once more. 'Vases are more for the house than for me mammy, an' the other t'ings seemed too . . . oh, too ordinary, somehow. So I paid all the money I could afford an' got her a warm knitted cardigan in blue and white wool. I just know she'll love it. It left me short for Caitlin, but you know what little girls are like—she doesn't care what a t'ing costs so long as it's pretty. So I chose some cheap pretties, an' put 'em in a box an' me daddy took 'em.'

'Oh, I wish I'd seen 'em,' Rose said wistfully. 'Why didn't you show me? You're lucky to have a little sister, but I've got Mona, who's like a big sister. It was real hard buyin' for her, though—she's got so much—but I chose careful an' I think she truly did like the stuff I bought.'

'They weren't that special, an' I got 'em at the last moment in the end,' Colm said casually. He looked carefully around him, then lowered his voice. 'Anyway, if you play your cards right, alanna, Cait'll be your little sister an' all soon's I've saved enough, so don't you forget it!'

'Good thing Gully's in the kitchen,' Rose said. 'Oh, Colm, it's been the best Christmas ever!'

'For me too,' Colm said fervently. He leaned

across the table and tried to pull her towards him but knocked over the vase of flowers—fortunately artificial at this time of year—which Lily kept in the middle of the window table and abandoned the idea, going round the table instead so that he could kiss Rose properly.

'Get off,' Rose said, rather breathlessly and a little late, when they parted. 'What'll we do this evenin'? Go to the pantomime? I do love the pantomime, though I've always been wi' me mam an' dad afore.'

'One t'ing at a time, alanna,' Colm said, returning to his own side of the table and starting another sheet. 'Let's get these done an' out o' the way before we start thinkin' about this evenin'.'

'I wonder if we ought to have asked Tommy an' Mona to come as well?' Rose said idly a moment later, finishing her second letter. 'I feel so sorry for Mona, Colm, because her mam never even sent a card. Oh, she's a nasty woman, real spiteful. Fancy, not sendin' a card to your own daughter!'

'Daddy only gave me the two tickets, an' I doubt it's too late to try to book more seats now,' Colm said, blotting another page and pulling the clean one towards him. 'I don't t'ink Mona minded too much, either. An' probably she an' Tommy 'ud rather do somethin' off their own bats. Likely they'd not t'ink much o' panto. They're both older than us an' Tommy likes a drink or two of an evenin'.'

'An' you don't, I suppose? Still, I expect you're right and they'd sooner go off together. It's odd, isn't it? They always liked each other but they didn't go out much, not together, I mean. We teased 'em, 'cos it were clear they got on well, but

376

they wouldn't admit to nothin'. Yet this mornin', at breakfast, they were talkin' about what they'd do today an' tomorrow an' the day after that . . .' Rose capped her pen carefully and shuffled her pages together. 'That's me lot. Are you nearly done?'

'Nearly. Only Caitlin loves a letter, so she does, an' this one's a bit on the brief side. She'll want to know all about the panto . . . tell you what, I'll leave it for now an' finish it off when we come home this evenin'.'

'Right,' Rose said. 'Mr Dawlish came in first thing this morning—did you hear him? He's asked Mam if she'd like to go to the show at the Empire—nice of him, weren't it?'

'Very nice,' Colm said cordially. 'Especially as it's the Empire an' not the Play'ouse! Well, me letters are just about done; let's go out for a walk, eh? Tomorrer we'll be back at work, so we might as well make the most of our time together.'

*　　　*　　　*

Lily had been surprised but very pleased when Mr Dawlish came into the kitchen, with his seabag slung over one shoulder, a gladstone bag in one hand and a big smile on his face, two whole days earlier than she had expected him. 'Mr Dawlish! What happened?' she said, crossing the room quickly and helping him to shed his burdens and to slip out of his heavy coat. 'You said you thought it 'ud be towards the end o' December before you was back in port again.'

'Oh, the skipper unloaded fast at the other end, 'cos his wife's expectin' an' he wanted to get home,' Mr Dawlish explained. 'Then we put on full steam—an' we've been lucky wi' the weather, so far. No really high winds to whip the sea into a frenzy an' make us late, see? So here I am!'

'And in good time for breakfast,' Lily said heartily. 'Would you like it now, afore the others get up? It's bacon, eggs, sausage . . .'

'I'd be glad of a round o' dry bread I'm that clemmed,' Mr Dawlish said. 'My, Mrs Ryder, but you're a cook in a thousand! All the way across the city I've been smellin' bacon from the houses I passed, an' hopin' you'd got one o' your big breakfasts on the go. Just let me wash me hands an' I'll lay the table for you.'

'I'll have mine wi' you,' Lily said comfortably. 'I'm pretty hungry meself. D'you fancy fried bread?'

Mr Dawlish fancied fried bread and it wasn't long before the two of them were sitting down to an enormous breakfast, with mugs of tea to hand and Gulliver, dancing on his perch, quieted by a handful of chopped-up bacon rind, which was very much to his taste and caused him to squeal with excitement when he saw the treat approaching.

They were half-way through their meal, having chatted inconsequentially of this and that—the run-up to Christmas, the voyage, the size of the turkey which the family were still eating—when Mr Dawlish dug in his pocket and produced a couple of tickets. 'Mrs Ryder, I suppose you wouldn't do me the honour of comin' to the theatre wi' me this afternoon? I met an old shipmate—he's ashore now, more's the pity—as I was walking up from the docks an' he told me he an' his missus were off to friends in Birkenhead for the day and would be missin' the show that they'd bought tickets for before the invite from their pals. He offered me the tickets for nowt, rather than see 'em wasted, so I gave him some money to buy his kids a few treats, an' now I've two tickets for the best seats at the Empire this afternoon. What d'you say?'

Lily looked hard at Mr Dawlish. He was probably about her own age, with bristly hair cut very short, steady light-blue eyes and a square, determined chin. He was not tall, barely a couple of inches above her own modest height, but he was broad-shouldered and capable-looking, with that air of reliability about him which Lily had spotted at their first meeting, and valued. Jack, too, had had just that look.

'I'm not bein' cheeky, Mrs Ryder,' Mr Dawlish said, plainly feeling rather uncomfortable beneath her scrutiny. 'If you feel it wouldn't be the thing . . .'

'No indeed, it's very generous of you,' Lily said quickly. 'But haven't you a friend you'd rather take? I know you've no relatives in the city, but . . .'

'I'd enjoy your company, Mrs Ryder,' Mr Dawlish said. 'But if you've scruples against bein' on too friendly terms wi' your lodgers . . . well, perhaps you'd like to take Mrs Kibble, instead? I'm quite willing—I just felt it a waste not to use the tickets.'

'I've no scruples of that nature,' Lily said at once. 'Truth to tell, I'd love to go to the theatre with you, Mr Dawlish. It'll gi' me a chance to wear me Christmas dress. What time do we leave?'

She had secretly expected to feel a little uncomfortable, walking along beside Mr Dawlish and then sitting next to him all afternoon, but she did not. He was good company, chatting to her

379

both walking down to the tram stop and on the tram itself, buying her chocolates before the theatre and an ice-cream in the interval, and generally making her feel ... well, valued, she supposed.

Making their way home again, she told him how much she had enjoyed the afternoon. 'It made me feel young again,' she said frankly, noticing how he shortened his natural long stride to suit her smaller steps. 'When I go out wi' Rosie or Agueda I always feel the responsibility for havin' a good time rests on me. This afternoon, I just enjoyed meself thoroughly. Thank you, Mr Dawlish.'

'It's a pleasure, Mrs Ryder. I'm home for at least a week this time, incidentally, so I hope you'll allow me to take you out again. What would you like to do next time? I'm sure Miss Ryder and Miss Mullins could manage to serve up an evenin' meal if you'd agree to come out for the day wi' me, an' to have dinner out an' all. Why, we could go to Southport if you'd like that.'

'Ooh, I used to love to go shoppin' in Southport,' Lily said, her eyes growing misty at the remembered outings. Herself with her hand warm in Jack's grasp, the child in Jack's arms, agog at the bright lights, the well-dressed crowds and the general air of holiday. 'That would be a treat, Mr Dawlish.'

'Then we'll do it,' Mr Dawlish said decidedly. He had tucked her hand into the crook of his elbow as they left the theatre and now he gave it a discreet squeeze. 'I'm really lookin' forward to this comin' week, Mrs Ryder!'

*　　　*　　　*

'It's been a better Christmas than I ever thought we'd have again,' Rose said on New Year's Eve afternoon as she and Ella were putting on their coats in the small ladies cloakroom at Patchett & Ross, preparatory to heading for the street. 'Mr Dawlish is ever so nice, he's been takin' me mam out an' about, an' that's meant that me an' Colm have been able to go out together most nights without me feelin' I'm neglectin' her. An' Mona's been goin' around wi' Tommy, they've been friendlier than they've ever been before, so it's been a good time. Of course me mam misses me dad, but at least it wasn't like the first year, when we felt guilty to smile, almost.'

It was a bitterly cold day, but so far, snow had not fallen, which meant that they had been arriving at work dry, at least. The two girls clattered out onto the pavement and turned right, lowering their heads protectively as the chill of evening met them. They were both on foot since Rose had obediently abandoned her beloved bicycle until the spring, after having a nasty fall as she coasted expertly— she thought—round black ice at the corner of Brow Side and Rupert Lane on her way home from work, so now she and Ella were heading for the nearest tram stop. They were warmly wrapped and very much looking forward to the evening ahead, for they were both going to New Year parties with the men of their choice.

'You shouldn't feel guilty because you're happier than you were last year or two years back; the pain of your dad's death was very new, then, but time's a great healer, so they say,' Ella remarked, pushing her hands into the pocket of her coat and shivering

381

as they turned the corner and met the wind off the river full on. 'And you're always sayin' as 'ow your dad liked you to have a good time, so don't you go feelin' guilty at havin' fun, Rosie. So your mam's off out tonight, eh? Wi' Mr Dawlish, I tek it?'

'Aye. They're goin' to a dinner dance at a big hotel on Hanover Street so Mam's wearin' a new dress an' her gold necklace an' so on,' Rose confided. 'We're all out, tonight, in fact, even Mrs Kibble. She's goin' to the club she belongs to an' takin' an old flame.' Rose giggled, turning her head sideways so that the wind did not whip her words from her mouth, and lowering her voice to a conspiratorial hiss she said, 'He's a Spaniard from where she lived when she were a girl, a retired seaman. So the house'll be empty till after midnight.'

'Aren't you all gettin' together to see the New Year in?' Ella said. 'I'm goin' to a dance, but I'll be home before midnight.'

'No point, because Mam's dance don't finish until the early hours, an' Mrs Kibble's goin' to welcome the New Year wi' her fellow countrymen. But I expect Colm an' meself'll be back soon after we've all sung "Auld Lang Syne" an' that, so's we can have a quiet cuddle by the fire afore we goes off to bed,' Rose admitted. 'I dunno about Mona an' Tommy, though. They're nearly always late.'

'Well, have a good time, then! See you next year,' Ella yelled as they parted, each to catch their own tram. Rose laughed and shouted her own good wishes, then glanced up the road and broke into a trot. Her tram, already well filled, was approaching; she had best get a move on.

She managed to get on despite having reached

the stop last, because everyone was in such a good mood. Two men hauled her aboard with great enthusiasm and she squeezed between them, hanging on to the nearest object, which happened to be the depository for used tickets, and craning her neck to see if there was anyone she knew on board.

She could see no one from her present perch, but when the tram reached her stop and she climbed down she saw Mona walking along the pavement, carrying something in a brown paper bag. She shouted and Mona stopped and waited for her to catch up. 'Wotcher, Rosie,' she said exuberantly. 'Guess what's in here!' She flourished the bag under her cousin's nose. 'One for each of us!'

'Not chocolates, I hope,' Rose said devoutly. 'I'm gettin' fat—no, don't you laugh, just think of all the eatin' we've been doin' lately! Go on then, what is it?'

'Sprays of orchids,' Mona said triumphantly, opening the bag in her right hand so that Rose could peep inside. 'Old sourpuss said I could have 'em half-price 'cos if they didn't sell today they wouldn't sell later. So I paid up for two an' took four, an' she never even noticed. She just bunched the others up in her bag, all crotchety and nasty because they were her idea, see? An' she's goin' to give them to her old mam an' pretend it's a special New Year gift, like. There's one person—no, two— what won't be goin' to a New Year party,' she added rather unkindly.

'Are you? Goin' to a party, I mean,' Rose asked. 'I know you're goin' out wi' Tommy, but you didn't say whether it was to a party or what,' she added.

'Colm an' me's off to the Daulby Hall. It'll be good fun tonight, there's bound to be balloons an' spot prizes an' all sorts.'

'We're goin' round to some friends of his,' Mona said. 'I've not met them before, though, so I'll wear me cream brocade an' a green chiffon scarf, an' the cream orchids wi' the dark orange middles will look just right.'

'What colours are mine?' Rose asked, peering towards the bags. 'I'm wearin' me blue, as if you didn't know,' she added rather gloomily. 'Sometimes I think I'm the only person in the world what has just the one dance dress.'

'Well, you ain't,' Mona reminded her. 'The gals at the Daulby mostly have one dance dress. Besides, you could have had another, only you went an' saved the money for your bottom drawer.'

'Yes ... well, Colm an' me's gettin' serious,' Rose reminded her. 'But we want to get a decent lot of stuff together before we name the day, an' you can't do that by spendin' your hard-earned cash on dance dresses.'

'No, I know,' Mona said as they turned into St Domingo Vale. 'Tell you what, why don't you borrow me peach taffeta? It'll suit you better'n it does me, because you're dark an' I'm fair, an' fair hair needs a contrast. I've bought a midnight blue silk wi' silver stars embroidered round the neckline, which I'd ha' worn tonight if we'd been goin' dancin', because if I marry, it'll be to someone who can afford to buy me all the sheets an' towels I want,' she finished on a note of defiance, Rose thought.

'Could I really borrow your dress?' Rose asked, adding: 'And as for marrying, you look all set to get serious wi' Tommy to me.'

'Tommy an' me's good friends,' Mona said evasively. 'But we both want more out o' life than the bare necessities. As for the dress, 'course you can borrow it. I'd lend you me satin slippers an' all, only me feet are bigger'n yours, they'd fall off you the first time you lifted a foot clear o' the dance floor.'

Giggling, the two of them made their way round the jigger, through the back gate, across the yard and into the kitchen, but they had barely shed their winter coats and hung them on the back of the door when the door flew open and Lily Ryder appeared. She was wearing a pretty pink dressing-gown and matching slippers, but her face was so pale that Rose said at once: 'What's the matter, Mam? What's happened?'

'Rosie, love, have you seen me gold necklace? The one made up of thick, twisted rings all set together, with a gold lily hanging from it? You know it, love—the family necklace.'

'Oh, Mam, don't say you've lost it,' Rose said, horrified. She knew how her mother valued the heavy gold necklace, for it had been Jack's grandmother's and had been passed down the family, Lily sometimes said, for the best part of a hundred years and would, in the nature of things, one day belong to Rose herself—and in time to Rose's daughter, if she had one.

'It isn't in me little jewellery case,' Lily said, her voice breaking. 'Oh, Rosie, when I went to look an' it weren't there, I couldn't believe me eyes! Your dad was so proud of that chain, it had been in his family for as long as he could remember ... I promised him I'd always take the greatest care of it

385

and now look what's happened. It's been stole an' I only knew this evenin', when I went to see if it could do wi' a polish before I wore it to the dinner dance.'

'Stolen? Mam, who'd steal your lovely things?' Rose said, feeling as if someone had tipped iced water down her back. 'Not . . . you don't mean . . .'

'I don't know who I mean, or who might steal it, I just know it's gone and this time it couldn't possibly be anything I've done, because I only wear it once in a blue moon, an' I scarcely ever look in the little jewellery case, as you know. It's tucked away safe in the back of me undies drawer and there it stays, and there it was when I got it out this evening, only it were empty. Oh Rose, Rose, what'll I do?'

'Ring the scuffers,' Rose said quickly. 'Mam, the necklace is valuable. If someone's pinched it then they deserve to be caught . . . and if someone's sold it, perhaps it can be traced. Honest, Mam, you must go for the police.'

'You must, Aunt Lily,' Mona said. 'Look, you're in a state—an' you're not dressed either. Rosie, you go an' telephone. I'll go up wi' your mam an' take a look round the room, just in case . . .'

'There's no in case about it,' Lily snapped. 'D'you think we've not searched high an' low, Mona? Me an' Agueda first, then we went an' called Mr Dawlish, so he helped us, then when Tommy came in for an early tea he looked an' all— an' went up to the police station an' telled them it had gone. Ever such a nice feller came down, but though he took details he was hopin' it would turn up and then I wasn't certain-sure it had gone. But I am now. It's been stole.'

386

It ruined the evening, of course. First, everyone searched the house, from attic to cellar, then they sat over a cup of tea and a sandwich, discussing who could have got into the house and how they could have known . . .

'There's no way,' Mr Dawlish said at length, voicing what they were all secretly thinking. 'This was an inside job—had to be. Yet I can't believe that any one of us could have done it—you've been so good to us all, Mrs Ryder! I suppose . . . parrots don't behave like jackdaws?'

'I looked in his cage,' Rose admitted, half ashamed. 'But it weren't there—well, I don't think I really thought it would be. It was just that we were lookin' everywhere, an' though Gully's a grand feller, he does pick things up sometimes . . . not that I've ever known him go for a necklace before. And anyway, how could he 'ave opened Mam's drawer and the box an' all.'

'I don't reckon he'd think much to it unless it were made of bacon rind,' Mona said. 'Oh, I'm sorry, Aunt, I know I shouldn't joke, but we're gettin' desperate when we try to blame the bleedin' bird. Someone's took it, that's plain. If it had been in the house we'd ha' found it by now. We're just goin' to have to leave it to the scuffers.'

'A fat lot they care,' Lily said tearfully. 'They looked at me as if I were tellin' fairy stories. Oh, they won't even try to find it.'

'We'll keep on at 'em,' Mr Dawlish promised. 'Well, the evenin' isn't over yet, Mrs Ryder. How about us goin' to the Daulby Hall wi' the young

387

'uns? It's too late for the dinner dance, but no need to let the night go entirely to waste.'

'Yes, Mam, do come,' Rose said. 'I'm sure the scuffers will do their best to get it back and I'm certain we've not left a pin unturned in the house. Why, tomorrow mornin' they may come to the door askin' you to identify it. And in the meantime, why not enjoy the rest of this old year?'

'Rosie's right, Mrs Ryder,' Colm said. 'Sure an' 'tis a terrible t'ing to have happened, but even a gold necklace isn't worth ruinin' your life for. Come on, show us how you can out-dance every man jack of us!'

'I don't know as I'm in the mood to dance,' Lily said heavily, but when everyone joined in the plea and Rose added that they could not possibly go off without her she consented to join them. So the women went to their rooms and presently, suitably gowned and made-up, the three of them joined Colm, Tommy and Mr Dawlish who went and flagged down a taxi so that they could travel in style.

But as she whirled in the dance and sipped a soft drink, Rose's heart was heavy. No matter how one might try to pretend that a cat-burglar had been at work, they must all know that this could not possibly be true. Whoever had stolen the necklace had been an opportunist—and this time, they could not hope to put the blame on the window-cleaner's lad. Someone had to have been in the house alone for long enough to rifle through her mother's dressing-table. It was an inside job, which meant that she could no longer look at any of their lodgers without wondering . . .

Except for Colm, of course. She knew him far

388

too well to suspect that he would ever take anything which did not belong to him. He was honest through and through and in any case would never have taken advantage of her mother in such a way. Lily Ryder had been good to all her lodgers though—and one of them . . .

It occurred to Rose, as she and Colm were dancing the last waltz together, slowly and dreamily circling the floor, that her mother might well not have looked into her little jewel case since they had moved in, and at first they had had lodgers who had only stayed for a matter of weeks. It was far likelier that one of them had walked off with her mother's necklace, and she had only just missed it.

Rose told Colm how her thoughts were going and he cheered up. 'Sure an' that's a likelier t'ing, so it is,' he said with obvious relief. 'I can't bear to t'ink any of us would take such a wicked advantage of your mammy's kindness. Yes, tell your mammy your thoughts; it'll cheer her.'

Accordingly, Rose asked her mother if such might have been the case and Lily, after some thought, admitted that it might. 'Because I've not so much as looked at it since we moved in,' she admitted. 'Well, if I never get it back, chuck, at least I can have the satisfaction of believing that we're all innocent of the theft.'

So it was a happier party who made their way home again in the starlight of the first day of the new year. And it was not until she was in bed and cuddling down that Rose had another, less pleasant, thought. Money, both small sums and large, had been going missing now for three or four months. They had blamed her mother's absent-mindedness at first, but it had not been the case

389

when what she now thought of as 'the window-cleaning money' disappeared. Was this just a weird coincidence? Uneasily, she admitted to herself that she did not think so. Someone in the house, she concluded unhappily, was a thief and unless they worked at it they might never find out who it was.

CHAPTER ELEVEN

January 1932 Liverpool

Sean came up Dale Street, looking round him at the great blocks of offices as though he had never seen them before. Ahead of him loomed the technical school and beyond it the free library, huge, impersonal places when compared with the homely Dublin streets, always crowded with people and warmer, to his mind, than the streets of this great, imposing city.

He had been away for two weeks, but it seemed a great deal longer, and he could not help reflecting that he was coming back to hard work and a lonely bed. Yet he knew, really, that he would soon settle down again, get into the habit of writing to Eileen and the child, slip back into his responsible job and his way of life without too much pain. But right now, at this very minute, with the wind following him up Dale Street and nipping spitefully at the back of his neck, he felt completely alien and simply wanted to be back in Dublin, walking the Quays, crossing Halfpenny Bridge, admiring the Custom House and the Law Courts, and believing them to be the biggest and best buildings in the world—until he saw the Liver Building for the first time, that was.

It was late afternoon and the streets were empty because the shops and offices had not yet spilled their staff onto the pavements and in the bitter cold and with Christmas behind them, few had ventured out. A solitary tram rattled along and its golden windows looked comforting; Sean's bag was heavy and he thought about catching it, then changed his mind. He would walk briskly and warm himself up and hopefully, by the time he reached St Domingo Vale, he would be feeling more cheerful and would be able to give a good account of his Christmas.

For he had had a marvellous time, there was no doubt about it. The Christmas presents from both himself and Colm had been received with rapture, all the little extras which he had saved so hard for had made every day special and he had sunk back into his home as into a soft featherbed, loving every moment, not allowing himself to remember that he would be leaving them, returning to the city where his work was.

Work, he reminded himself robustly now, was good. He crossed Byrom Street and went on into William Brown Street. He might as well get a tram, now he thought about it. He could pick up a number 13 and be home a good deal quicker, and once home, he could be sure that Mrs Ryder would put the kettle on and get him a good cup of tea, and probably some bread and jam, or toast. He hadn't eaten since early morning and then it had only been a boiled egg; he had felt too unhappy to eat, though Eileen had done her best to jolly him along with reminders that summer would soon be here and she was saving hard for that dream home, as was he.

When he came level with the next tram stop he joined the few cold, dark-clad people clustered there, glad now it came to the point to put his bags down for a moment. He hadn't taken all his things home because most of them wouldn't be needed— none of his working clothes, for instance—but one bag was heavy with more Christmas gifts for Colm and he had brought back a couple of loaves of Eileen's soda bread, because no one made it better, and a heavy pat of salted butter from the dairy round the corner, to say nothing of two jars of Eileen's gooseberry jam and another of the clover honey she particularly valued. 'Take two spoonfuls in hot water, wit' a good squeeze o' lemon, before you go to bed,' she had instructed him. 'It'll keep colds an' the flu away from ye. Caitlin's been fit as a flea this winter wit' lemon an' honey before bed.'

Sean, accepting the honey, had not admitted that he intended to eat it on hot buttered toast— and to share it with the Ryders and his fellow guests. He seldom ailed and saw no reason to waste good honey by watering it down, but he was by far too fond a father and husband to say so. It pleased Eileen to think, when his work was done in damp and darkness, that no Englishwomen could possibly know any good remedies for his health, so why should he tell her that Mrs Ryder, too, used honey and lemon for colds, as well as various other cures. It would only make his wife resent his landlady more.

For Eileen, he had realised quite quickly, whilst paying lip-service to his good luck in finding such a decent home for himself and Colm, had preferred it when he had lived in Lavrock Bank, with Mrs

Caldicott's rough-and-ready housekeeping. Sean, not fully understanding the workings of the female mind, had told Eileen enthusiastically all about Lily Ryder and her pretty daughter, and had afterwards regretted it. He was cross-questioned as to Rose's suitability to walk out with her beloved son and, at his first mention of Gulliver, Eileen had said, with a satisfied nod, that parrots were dirty critturs, so they were, and she'd thank him to keep well clear of it and not to bring any traces of it back home to Ireland with him. 'I'd never entertain keepin' a cage-bird,' she said. 'A cat now, that's different. Cats is clean—ask anybody. But parrots . . . aren't they always usin' foul language now and bitin' at folks if they get near to the cage? And they do their doings t'rough the bars as like as not. Oh aye, a decent, God-fearing woman would send that parrot to the rightabout, I'm tellin' ye.'

After that, Sean had not talked about the Ryders or about St Domingo Vale, and they had got on very much better. And the fun they had! Visits to the theatre, strolls round the markets looking for bargains and meeting old friends, evenings before the fire, telling stories of the tunnel, of his workmates. Then there had been a day trip, with a picnic, out to Finglas, to examine the cottage where the very old couple lived and to tell themselves what they would do with it when they moved in, how they would plant the garden, fish the river, harvest the hedgerows.

The weather had not been as bitterly cold as it was in Liverpool, either, or so Sean convinced himself now, standing shivering at the tram stop with his collar turned up and his muffler wrapped twice around his face. But presently the tram pulled up and the waiting people climbed aboard, and Sean jammed his bags into the space beneath the stairs and sat where he could watch them. He glanced around him as he did so, but there was no one he knew aboard; it was too early for the home-going rush and most shoppers had gone earlier, driven indoors by the icy wind. The conductor took his fare and Sean shrugged his muffler down—he would not feel the benefit if he remained wrapped up in the comparative warmth of the tram—and watched dismally as the city streets fled by. He wondered what Colm was doing now and also what Mrs Ryder was going to cook for their supper; then he remembered that Mona had been using his room and hoped that she had already vacated it. By the time he had got round to reminding himself that Eileen had packed, in addition to the soda bread, some of his favourite oat cakes, the tram was coming to a halt at the junction of Breck Road and Oakfield Road and he was heaving his bags out from under the stair, wrapping his muffler round his mouth once more and jumping down.

It was only a short walk now up Oakfield Road to the bottom of St Domingo Vale, where he turned left and began, for the first time since leaving Dublin, to think that life wasn't so bad after all. The house was grand and so were the Ryders. He got on well with Pete Dawlish and thought Tommy good company. So he opened the small wooden gate and walked up the path feeling a good deal happier than he had felt on arriving in the city. He was a lucky feller, now he came to think about it. He had good digs, a good son and some real friends at work. He enjoyed going along to the Sandon Hotel on the corner of Oakfield Road and

Houlding Street, and usually managed to make a pint last most of the evening. Yes, compared with a good few of their neighbours—and friends—in Dublin, he was doing all right.

Arriving at the front door, he rat-tatted. Usually, like everyone else, he went round the back, but it would be easier by far, burdened with bags as he was, to go straight across the hall, up the stairs and to his room. There, he could unpack the things he wanted to take straight down to the kitchen, tidy himself, maybe wash, since he had spent more hours than he cared to remember hanging onto the rail of a ship which tossed and laboured across the restless foam-flecked waves of the Irish sea, and eventually settle in once more.

His knock was answered by Mrs Ryder, who welcomed him with a hearty handshake and told him she would put the kettle on at once, if he'd like to leave his luggage in his room and come straight down.

'Miss Mullins has moved out?' he said. 'I was sure she would, but then it occurred to me she might t'ink I was catchin' the last ferry . . .'

'She moved her things out yesterday,' Mrs Ryder said briefly. She tried to carry one of his bags but he wrested it away from her, it was heavy, as he well knew. 'There's . . . there's been some changes, Mr O'Neill, but we'll talk when you come down to the kitchen.'

Agreeing that would be best, it occurred to Sean, as he climbed the stairs, that Mrs Ryder was not looking her usual self. In fact, she looked downright pale and peaky, not at all like a person who had enjoyed a happy and relaxing holiday. Of course, she would have been cooking and cleaning

395

just the same, since only himself and Dawlish, so far as he knew, had been away for Christmas, but even so . . .

He reached his room and found it immaculately clean and very welcoming. Mrs Ryder had put a vase with some rust-red chrysanthemums in it on the washstand and there was a new bedspread, blue with a scattering of flowers. It was the work of a moment to take off his outer garments and go along to the bathroom for a hot wash, then he returned to his room, took off his boots and put on his slippers, hung his coat on the hook behind the door and began methodically to unpack his bags.

Presently, with the food and some other oddments in a paper carrier, he left his room, shutting the door carefully behind him, and set off down the stairs. The clock in the hall showed that it was still not five o'clock, so no one else would be home yet. He decided he must ask, tactfully, whether his landlady was quite well, for he did not think he had ever seen her looking less like herself, and when he went into the kitchen and began to pile his things on the table, he saw at once that her attention, which would have been riveted on his doings once, kept wandering. She looked at the fire, at the stove, at the sink, moving restlessly and answering him more or less at random when he asked about her Christmas. So, being Sean, he asked the question direct: 'Lor' love ye, Mrs Ryder, what's been happenin' here whiles I was at home in Dublin? You look pale as a wraith, so you do, an' you've not been listening to a word I've said, which is not like you. I hope there's been no trouble?'

Mrs Ryder poured tea into two mugs and took them over to the table. Then she opened the biscuit barrel, sat herself down and gestured to the chair opposite. 'Yes, something has happened,' she said heavily. 'Sit down, Mr O'Neill, an' I'll tell you as much as I know meself.'

She began, quite simply, with the New Year festivities which had taken place just over a week earlier, and went on to explain the missing necklace. 'Tommy fetched the police,' she said tiredly. 'They was nice enough, but they said it were an inside job an' they searched all the rooms ... everyone was very good, but the necklace didn't turn up. Oh, Mr O'Neill, it just about ruined me Christmas and we'd had a real good time up till then. I went to the Daulby Hall wi' the kids, but me heart wasn't in it, and once midnight had struck and we'd sung 'Auld Lang Syne' I couldn't wait to get home here. You see, the necklace was real old, it had been in me husband's family a long time, an' ... an' I felt I'd let him down, because there's no denyin' that I'm careless wi' things. I'd not even looked into me jewel case since we left our old house an' arrived here ... an' I can't, I just *can't*, believe that one of me lodgers is ... is a thief.'

'Dear God,' Sean breathed. 'Well, I'd tek me oath Colm knows what's his and what isn't. The Brothers at school an' the Father at church knocked it into him, same's they did wit' me. And you've no reason to suspect anyone in particular?'

'No, not really,' Mrs Ryder said. 'But I've offered a reward, in the *Echo*, like the constable who came in the other day suggested. You see a gold chain's worth a good bit, but I'd give more'n it's worth to have it back. It would have gone to Rosie after me, an' to her child after her, the same as it did in the

397

Ryder family before. So by losing it, it's like as if I'd let Jack down, see?'

'I'm sure no one could t'ink such a t'ing,' Sean said comfortingly. 'But I can see you're very distressed an' wit' reason. But there's no manner o' use you breakin' your heart over it. It may yet come to light, or someone may answer your advertisement in the *Echo*.'

'I keep tellin' meself that,' Mrs Ryder admitted. 'But it's made everyone so *uncomfortable*, Mr O'Neill. We sit there at meals, carefully not lookin' at one another, and Rose and Mona go off to work so glum ... Tommy's cheerful enough, and your Colm has been good an' done his best to cheer us up, but it's been an unhappy week.'

'Well, I'll put some money towards this reward, so I will, an' mebbe you'll get a reply from the paper quite soon,' Mr O'Neill said. 'Now is there anythin' I can be doin' to help you towards supper, for 'tis hungry as a hunter I am after me journey!'

*   *   *

Rose was touched when her mother told her of Mr O'Neill's offer, particularly as it led to everyone else saying that they would put money into the reward as well, but as it happened none of them was called upon to do anything, because the advertisement did not bring forth a single reply.

Time passed. Sean O'Neill and Colm set off together most mornings, bound for the tunnel and their work there, and Mona and Rose went off too, one to the flower shop in the arcade, the other to Patchett & Ross.

Tommy was still on his tram, but he talked often

about starting up in some line of business of his own, as soon as he could save up enough money. He was, he told them, a dab hand with all sorts of engines, and rather fancied buying a lorry and doing deliveries. 'Then I'll buy another lorry, an' gerra feller workin' for me,' he told the family as they all sat round the kitchen table eating their supper. 'I could do the maintenance on the engines, you see, an' I reckon I could get plenty of work. First, I'd charge less than anyone else an' get the stuff delivered quicker, then me prices would rise an' folk would still come to me 'cos I was fast, see. Oh aye, you can get ahead in this world if you ain't afraid of hard work.'

Rose thought of Colm and his father, working on the tunnel, but said nothing. It would not be polite, especially for a tram driver's daughter, to say that collecting fares on a tram all day was scarcely liable to be regarded as hard work by a manual labourer. And anyway, so far as she could see Tommy was only dreaming and wasn't it natural to dream? She was getting on well at Patchett & Ross and sometimes considered applying for other, better-paid jobs when they came up, even though they mostly stipulated that they wanted young women with several years' experience But in fact she was extremely happy at work, enjoying having her own desk and typewriter in the small typing pool and beginning to be able to tackle quite complex tasks without having to consult either of the other girls. Ella, still working dispatch, envied her the nice desk job but it was only a matter of time, Rose thought, before Ella, too, would come up to the typing pool. Miss Rogers was getting married in April and would leave the firm then since she would be moving up to Scotland with her young man. When that happened, Ella was sure to be given the junior job and Rose hoped she would move up to work for Mr Lionel, and Miss Dupont would become senior secretary, working for Mr Edward mostly, and occasionally taking dictation from Mr Evans himself, on his rare appearances in the offices.

With Mona sharing her room once more, the two girls naturally talked about the disappearance of the necklace until they grew thoroughly bored with the whole thing and for some time had not even thought about the unfortunate loss. But lately, Rose thought, Mona had not been her usual cheerful, slapdash self. As February advanced, the weather began to seem almost springlike, and Rose and Colm had started to discuss what they should do in the evenings when the warmer weather came. But Mona had to be dug out of bed in the mornings and almost pushed off to work. She stopped going out in the evenings, especially since Tommy now seemed very taken up with his part-time job in a garage on Smithdown Road, where he was getting paid extra, and went to bed early, though Rose suspected that her cousin did not usually go to sleep. She simply lay there, gazing up at the ceiling, and when Rose asked what was wrong she said, waspishly, that nothing was the matter and would Rose kindly get herself into bed and to sleep, so that Mona could have some peace.

As the year advanced the missing necklace was forgotten by all of them, although Lily still mourned its loss. No more money disappeared, however. Lily's gold earrings remained in their little box, the money in the teapot on the kitchen mantelpiece waxed and waned, according to the day and time, and happiness gradually returned to the house in the Vale.

The friendship between Lily Ryder and Mr Peter Dawlish strengthened; they used each other's Christian names and it was more or less accepted that when Pete was home from sea, he and Rose's mother would go about together. It never occurred to Rose that her mother was growing fond of Pete—why should it? She could not imagine any woman who had known Jack being satisfied with the companionship of a mere seaman and accepted without question that the two spent much of their spare time together. She and Colm, however, were a different kettle of fish; they were now saving up as hard as they could so that they could both go over to Ireland when summer came. Marriage might still be a long way off, but a proper engagement was perfectly possible. A decent little ring could be bought and they had decided to get it in Dublin, after Rose had met Eileen O'Neill and Caitlin. Life seemed eminently satisfactory to Rose, though she feared that Mona was not as happy as she should be. Tommy, though still apparently fond of her cousin, was not the sort to spend all his time with her and besides, he was doing a good deal of overtime. Rose thought that Mona was seeing another feller, but she also felt her cousin was still hankering for Tommy. Still, Mona wasn't one to let a feller's change of heart get her down, so Rose guessed that she would soon return to her former happy self.

And then, most unexpectedly, Rose came home from the office one Friday night with what she thought was a cold. Only by Saturday morning she was feverish, aching in every limb, and tearful.

'It's flu, an' you'll give it to the lorrof us,' Mona said. 'Not that I'd mind a dose of flu—at least it would be a change to be tucked up in bed drinking hot lemon an' honey, whiles that old cat Ellis did her own bouquets.'

But flu doesn't come to them as wants it, Rose soon realised. Mona remained apparently immune but Mrs Kibble caught it, then Lily Ryder. Rose was the first to recover, but she was still very weak and listless after five days in bed, and, unable to return to work, found herself in the uncomfortable position of nursing her mother and Mrs Kibble, seeing to the house and cooking all the meals. Mona, working all day, could scarcely be expected to do much and Rose, though she let her wait on the invalids, did not want another patient and was extremely keen for Mona to stay fit.

So when the day dawned that Mrs Kibble got out of bed and came wearily up the basement stairs to 'give a hand with breakfasts', and actually stayed the course until elevenses time, Rose became a lot more optimistic. Colm and his father had been towers of strength, making their own carry-out and insisting that a breakfast of toast and tea would suit them just fine, but Tommy liked a cooked breakfast and Mona, too, had a healthy appetite.

Since her own recovery, Rose had begun to fall into the way of running the house and, though she was not yet able to go back to work, she almost enjoyed being in and out of the kitchen, finding housework a pleasant change from shorthand and typing, and other office tasks.

The flu epidemic had hit them in late February and within a week Rose had things well in hand.

She bustled about, cleaning, polishing, cooking and seeing that her mother drank a lot, took the medicine the doctor had left for her and began, as soon as she was well enough, to sit in the front room before the fire for a few hours before being helped back to bed.

'I don't know why Mam took the flu so much worse than you and I,' Rose said to Mrs Kibble as the two of them sat in the kitchen, companionably preparing a large pan of sprouts. 'We were up and about in no time, Mrs Kibble, but me mam is still a bit tottery.'

'She's suffering from working too hard to make Christmas a good one for us all,' Mrs Kibble observed, throwing a cleaned sprout into the pan and reaching for the next one. 'And she was upset about losing the necklace, too. I don't think she feels guilty, not now, because she's saving up to replace it, but it brought her rather low earlier in the year.'

'Well, she's better now. I think she'll get up tomorrow mornin' and probably stay up for the midday meal, then rest in the afternoon and get up again when we all sit down for our dinners,' Rose said. 'That was how you and I behaved when we felt strong enough. I've told Miss Rogers that with luck I'll be back in again next week—they'll be glad of me, since Miss Dupont went down with the flu two days ago and Ella's not feelin' too brave.'

'Well, before you go, let us have a bit of a spring clean of the bedrooms,' Mrs Kibble said practically. 'Your mam isn't going to feel much like heavy cleaning for a bit, but it should be done now the weather's improving a little. Why, we might even get the bedroom curtains and the bedspreads

403

washed and dried out on the line, if tomorrow is as warm as today has been.'

Rose agreed that this was a good idea and next day got up early, took her mother a cup of tea and a marmalade sandwich in bed, and told her that she should lie in until ten or eleven and keep well out of the way, since Mrs Kibble and herself intended to clean through the bedrooms.

'We'll leave your room for another day,' she said. 'But it's bright and windy today so I reckon if we get the curtains and bedspreads washed then they'll dry all right. And as Mrs Kibble says, if the weather turns nasty again we could be waitin' weeks to start a spring clean.'

Lily sighed, but said she was not yet up to spring cleaning and thanked Rose sincerely for her help. 'I dunno what I'd ha' done without you, queen,' she said. 'You've been wonderful, you've coped wi' everything, even when you had Mrs Kibble poorly in the basement an' me downright rotten up here. But I'm ever so much better now; in a few days I'll be able to cope wi' the house an' the cooking again, and you'll be able to get back to Patchett & Ross.'

'Yes, I've told them I hope to be back next Monday,' Rose said cheerily. 'But right now, Mam, you conserve your strength. Mrs Kibble an' meself will manage nicely if we know you're not overtaking your strength.'

Accordingly, Rose made breakfast and served it, and helped Colm with his carry-out. 'You don't want cheese butties *again*,' she told him, when he said accommodatingly that cheese would be fine, so it would. 'I've got a nice piece of boiled bacon— you can have that wi' some of our own pickled onions, an' a chunk of the fruit cake I made a couple o' days ago for afterwards.'

Colm beamed at her and blew her a kiss across the kitchen table. 'You're a real little treasure, alanna,' he said. 'You cook like a dream an' you pickle onions as good as me mammy.'

'You're not so bad yourself,' Rose said, twinkling back at him. 'I feel real wifely an' nice, packin' your carry-out an' seein' you off to work each mornin', Colm. I cut your dad's butties too, but I left him to choose his own pickles. He said the other day onions gave him the belly-ache.'

'Only when he eats too many of 'em,' Colm observed. He picked up his tin and the bottle of cold tea, and headed for the back door. 'Tell Daddy I'll save him a place in the tram queue.'

Rose nodded and smiled, enjoying the feeling of taking care of her man and all too aware that on Monday, when she started work again, she would be far too busy getting herself ready to see him off. It was all go in the mornings, though! Scarcely had Colm disappeared than his father came heavily down the stairs. He had breakfasted and then gone up again to clean his teeth, he said, and now grabbed his buttie tin and bottle and followed his son, shouting 'Cheerio, alanna' as he went.

Then it was Mona, slouching across the kitchen and saying she was sure she was in for the flu because she'd been sick when she first woke and wasn't that one of the signs? Rose agreed that she herself had been sick and looked anxiously at her cousin. Mona was pale and heavy-eyed, but when Rose suggested she might like to stay at home and they would fetch the doctor in, her cousin sighed heavily and shook her head. 'No, I'll be awright,' she said. 'Perhaps, if I still feel poorly tomorrer . . .'

Tommy was on early shift, so he had gone off even before Rose got up, though she had left him two hard-boiled eggs, a quantity of bread and butter, and of course his carry-out. Mr Dawlish was at sea and would not be home for another week, so Rose, greeting Mrs Kibble cheerfully as the two of them sat down to their own breakfast, thought gleefully that now they would be able to settle down to spring cleaning. Outside in the garden crocuses poked purple and gold noses up out of the rich black soil, and the birds were singing loudly and pursuing one another across the blue arch of the sky. It was a good drying day.

'Well, chuck, we might as well start. I'll get the copper on the go and you can go up and start stripping the curtains,' Mrs Kibble said. 'Bring down Mr Dawlish's stuff first, then the O'Neill's, then young Tommy's. Once they're on the line we can get the rest.

Rose, singing cheerfully, obeyed. Sean O'Neill had blue curtains and a blue flowered bedspread, his son had cheerful orange-coloured curtains and a bedspread in autumn browns and golds. Rose took them downstairs and helped Mrs Kibble to push them into the tub, and whilst Mrs Kibble pounded them with a dolly peg, she returned to the bedrooms to clean out.

'Rugs over the line and beat 'em till there's no more dust,' Mrs Kibble said breathlessly. 'Then we'll clean down the paintwork and scrub the linoleum. Oh, with a fine day like this to aid us it'll be done before you know it.'

Rose fetched the rugs from Mr O'Neill's room and rather enjoyed walloping them with the cane carpet beater. Then she laid them over a chair in the kitchen and went up for the ones in Colm's room. Being in a smaller room he only had two—one decent-sized brown one by his bed and a smaller rag rug in front of the washstand. She lifted them in her arms and saw a sheet of paper beneath the larger of the two rugs. It looked like a letter, but it was none of her business, so she carried the rugs downstairs and hung them over the line, beat hell out of them—and all the dust—and returned them to the kitchen. 'I'll scrub the lino now,' she told Mrs Kibble cheerfully. 'Then the floors can be drying whilst I tackle the rest of the rugs.'

Up in Colm's room again, she got down on her hands and knees, with a bucket of hot water and a bar of strong red soap, and began to scrub. She wafted the page of the letter under the bed and had to crawl to fetch it out again, then she glanced at it and smiled. She guessed that the round, childish scrawl belonged to Caitlin—Colm must have lost one page of his letter beneath the rug. She looked at the date, which was 26 December, and thought nostalgically back to Boxing Day, when she and Colm had sat in the front room writing their thank you letters, and Colm had told her that back home in Dublin, Caitlin would probably be doing the same thing.

Well, he had been right. She glanced at the letter, knowing she should put it on his bedside table, with his book to hold it down, but unable to resist a peep.

Dear Colm,

Oh it's been such a good Christmas! I got some lovely presents, so I did, but easily the best was my gold necklace! Oh you are kind, the

407

bestest brother in the world, Mammy says so too, she says me necklace must have cost a pretty penny and I was a lucky girl to have a brother who'd save up his money and then spend a grosh of it on his little sister!

Dear Colm, thank you, thank you! I weared it to Mass yesterday and everyone telled me how beautiful it was and how lucky I was as well, to have such a thing. I said Mammy might borrow it to go out with Daddy, but she said no, it was a precious thing and I was to put it away in its box in me room, and only wear it for very best.

Oh, I liked the chocolates too and the dear little bracelet but the necklace is me best thing and

The page ended there; clearly it had been a longer letter but the rest of it was either saved in a drawer somewhere or thrown away. Rose sat back on her heels and frowned. A necklace? A *gold* necklace? But of course Caitlin must have been mistaken, Colm could not possibly have afforded to send his little sister a gold necklace. Probably it was an ordinary gold-coloured one, which he had bought at one of the shops on Scotland Road and put in a nice little box. He was a good brother, he would get her the nicest thing he could afford . . . but a *gold* necklace?

Rose had put the letter on the bedside table; now she picked it up again and reread it with care, her heart beginning to thump. She could not believe that Colm had stolen the necklace, it was too absurd, particularly not to give it to his baby sister . . . but it was odd. Really very odd.

Still, it was useless to wonder, she had better get

408

on with her work. She began to scrub once more.

*   *   *

An hour later she went up to the room again, this time to replace the rugs. She took a deep breath and began to go through the chest of drawers. It was an awful, sneaky thing to do, she told herself, but she could not rest until she found the rest of that letter. Of course she knew, in her heart, that Colm would not take what did not belong to him, but . . . well, she would feel easier if she could read what else Caitlin had written.

She found letters, quite a bundle of them. Colm, it seemed, never threw one away. Caitlin's had a piece of thin red ribbon around them, his mother's a piece of blue silk. Feeling miserably guilty, she flicked through the pages until she came to one which did not appear to have a first page. She took it out, spread it on the bed, and began to read.

I'll value it always, so I will [the letter went on]. Mammy says the flower in the centre is a rose, but I think it's one of those blue things . . . an iris. Or maybe a lily. But it don't matter what it is, Colm, I love it and love it and you're the bestest brother in the whole world. Cracky says he'll buy me a ring one day, gold, like me necklace. Ha ha I told him, you've got to earn a grosh of money to buy gold!

Now I'll tell you all the other things I had, Colm. I had a box of coloured pencils from . . .

Rose stopped reading, feeling sick and frightened. A rose or a lily in the centre of the necklace? Ah,

409

dear God, her mam's necklace had a gold lily depending from the centre. Her father had given it to his wife on their tenth wedding anniversary, it was the only modern part.

'Rosie? Is the floor dry in Mr O'Neill's room? If so, I'll bring the rugs back up and we can lay 'em.'

Rose put the second page of the letter back into the bundle and, after a moment's hesitation, picked up the first page too and inserted it in its rightful place. It had been sneaky of her to read it, sneakier to search out the second page and all it had done was thoroughly upset her. She could not believe that Colm had taken her mother's necklace, she just could not! But suppose ... suppose someone else had taken it and dropped it in the garden, or the road, or along the jigger? Now if that had happened and Colm had picked it up—he wouldn't perhaps have realised its value. He would have sent it to his sister without a qualm. Wouldn't he? Wasn't that possible, and the most likely explanation? The only snag was that he had not realised, had not come clean when Mam had got so upset about her loss.

'Rosie!'

'Oh, right. Sorry, Mrs Kibble,' Rose said, crossing the room and going onto the landing. 'I'll come down for the rugs—the floors are dry. I'll just put them in place, then I'll fetch Tommy's curtains and bedspread down and begin turning out his room.'

For the rest of the day she worked steadily, but her mind was elsewhere. She could not make up her mind whether to ignore the letter or mention it to Colm. Surely, knowing as she did that he could never have taken what was not his, it would be all right just to *ask* him about Caitlin's present? But then he would have to be told how she knew that the present had been a necklace and about the flower hanging from the chain as well. And he would realise she had snooped through his things, had actually taken out the page of a letter from the bundle . . . oh, she could not tell him what she had done, she would just have to live with what she had found out.

'You're looking tired out, love,' Mrs Kibble said that evening, as Rose began to iron the curtains which had dried so beautifully out in the sunny yard. 'We shouldn't have done so much, with you only just over the flu yourself. I'll finish these, you sit down and take a rest.'

'I am rather tired,' Rose admitted. She left the ironing board and flopped into a chair, stretching her feet out towards the fire. 'What a blessing it's Lancashire hot-pot for supper, Mrs Kibble, at least all the work was done this mornin', more or less all we've got to do is serve up. Oh, what time should the apple pie go in?'

'It's cooked already, it only wants warming; there's a rice pudding in the back of the oven, though, which should come out; it's been simmering away for hours,' Mrs Kibble said, putting the cooled iron down in front of the fire and taking up the newly heated one. 'If you'd like to do that, Rosie dear . . .'

Rose got a stout cloth and brought the rice pudding out swathed in its folds; it was done, the skin crackly brown, the rice, she guessed, a lovely, thick primrose colour. She put it to one side and pulled the kettle over the fire. 'I'll make a cup of tea,' she said. 'Mam might like one, wi' a scone or a

411

Welshcake. It's another hour afore the fellers come in.'

'That's a good idea,' Mrs Kibble said, ironing away with great swoops of the flat. 'Is Lily coming down for the evening meal or will she have it in bed?'

'I'll ask when I take the tea up,' Rose said. 'I popped in during the afternoon, though, and she was sleeping like a baby. She looked really well, pink-cheeked and warm with the bedding pulled up round her ears. I wouldn't be surprised if she got up properly tomorrow.'

'Good, good. Let's hope no one else goes down with this wretched flu,' Mrs Kibble said. She finished the curtain she was working on and hung it tenderly over a chair-back. 'Presently we'll re-hang these and have that tea—I'm parched!'

*   *   *

'Ready, Rosie love? Then pass me over them hot plates an' I'll serve up.'

Rose, sitting at the table with Colm on one side of her and Mrs Kibble on the other, went on staring into space. Colm nudged her. 'Rosie, your mammy said . . .'

'Oh, sorry!' Rose got to her feet, then glanced back at her mother. 'Did you ask me to fetch you the mashed potatoes, Mam?'

Everyone laughed. 'Oh queen, you're in a dream again,' Lily said reproachfully. 'I dunno what's the matter with you lately an' that's the truth. I've got the spuds right in front of me, an' the sprouts an' carrots are in front of you. No, I want the plates off the back of the stove so's I can dish up.'

412

'Right,' Rose said. 'Sorry, Mam. I ... I can't seem to concentrate, somehow.'

'That's clear enough,' her mother said. 'How did work go today, queen? Your first day back's always tiring, I reckon.'

'It was fine, thanks,' Rose said. 'But I were the only one in, in the typing pool, that is. So Mr Lionel sent Ella up to give a hand, an' there's a new girl, Miss McMaster, who was doin' her best. I'll be glad when the others are back, though.'

Mona, picking up the serving spoon as Rose put the plates down in front of her mother, said: 'The others? Who's away now, then?'

Rose heaved a sigh. 'Mr Garnett's poorly,' she said. 'An' that's a blessin', since there's fewer folk to dictate letters. But since Miss Rogers an' Miss Dupont are still off sick, an' Miss McMaster don't do shorthand yet, there's too much work anyway.'

'Mr Garnett poorly? How long's he been off, then?' Mona said casually. 'I'll dish up the mash, Aunt Lily, if you'll pass me the plates as you put the salt beef out.' She turned to Sean, sitting beside her. 'Mash an' sprouts, Mr O'Neill?'

'Please, Mona,' Sean O'Neill said. 'I'm mortal fond o' mashed spuds—well, you know what they say about the Irish.

There was more laughter; Rose, joining in late, heard her own pathetic attempt at a giggle and felt ashamed. She took the plate from Mona and doled some carrots onto it, then handed it to Colm's father. Get a hold on yourself, girl, she thought desperately. Remember that no one here knows what you read in that letter and try to forget it. There's no point in dwelling on what's over and done with.

413

'Yes please, Rosie,' Colm said. Rose stared at him. Had she spoken aloud? She glanced around the table and everyone was laughing, looking at her. She felt the heat rise in her cheeks and said, stiffly: 'Does that mean you'd like some carrots?'

'Yes please, Rosie,' Colm repeated. 'You're in a dream an' a half this evenin', alanna. I t'ink you've gone back to work too early an' now you're too tired to t'ink straight. I was goin' to ask you to come to the flicks wit' me, but now I wonder if you'd be better goin' straight to bed an' havin' a good sleep so you're fresh tomorrow mornin'.'

Rose turned to look at him. His firm mouth smiled at her, his eyes were gently concerned for her. She realised, from his expression, that he knew something was badly wrong and wanted her to tell him, so that he could reassure and comfort her. Abruptly, the indecision which had haunted her ever since the discovery of the letter disappeared. She loved him, he was a good man, but whilst the niggle of doubt remained she could never be entirely at her ease with him. 'Well, I don't know if I'm up to the cinema, but I'd like a bit of an outin',' she said. 'Just a quiet walk an' a bit of a chat. Or a tram ride . . . we could go down to the Pier Head an' watch the shippin' on the Mersey. I like doin' that at night, when the shippin's all lit up an' excitin', makin' you think of foreign parts an' adventures, far-away places.'

'Right, that'll suit me, I'm after enjoyin' a walk meself, an' a look at the shippin',' he said easily. 'When the meal's cleared away, then.'

'I wouldn't mind a breath o' fresh air,' Mona said. 'Shall we tek a walk too, Tommy? Or are you workin' in that garage again?'

414

Rose thought that Mona rather missed his company. She knew her cousin was definitely seeing another man—or men—but she still felt that Mona would sooner have had Tommy. Only it seemed that Tommy wasn't into a steady relationship; he liked several girls rather than just one. How lucky I am, Rose thought, that Colm isn't like that. For the first time for several days she began to eat her food with appetite. Soon, very soon now, she would confide in Colm and have her doubts put at rest. 'We'll go as soon as I've helped Mam wit' the washing up,' she confirmed now. 'It'll be great to have a walk in the fresh air, Colm—I'm glad we're not goin' to the flickers, a walk will really do me good.'

*   *   *

Rose let Colm jump off the tram ahead of her and settled cosily against his side as they walked across the cobbles towards where the water glimmered darkly in the starlight. She felt safe and comfortable . . . happy, too. She would tell Colm, making a clean breast of how she had read his letter, and he would explain, forgive her, and she could go back to loving and trusting him totally once more. Not that I ever stopped, exactly, she reminded herself now, trying to keep up with his longer strides, but it's been worrying me, there's no doubt about it, and that's made me stiff with him a bit.

'Now isn't that a beautiful sight?' Colm said, indicating the dark expanse ahead of them. The tide was right in and the water reflected the lights of the shipping and also those on the Pier Head, so that the wind-ruffled surface was flecked with a thousand diamonds of light, some white, some yellow, some green and red. 'Do you fancy a sit-down or would you rather walk, alanna?'

'I'd rather walk,' Rose said peacefully. 'I feel so comfortable and happy, wi' your arm round me and the water sounds in me ears. I wonder if we could see Ireland, if we were further out? It's such a clear night I'd think the lights might show all that way.'

'Maybe,' Colm said. 'Now are ye goin' to tell me what's been after upsettin' you, alanna, or are you goin' on keepin' it to yourself? Sure and a trouble shared is a trouble halved, they say. Why not give it a try?'

'I'm goin' to tell you,' Rose said. Suddenly, it no longer seemed simple. 'Colm, you know you gave Caitlin a necklace for Christmas?'

'I did. She liked it. Mammy says she wears it every Sunday to Mass.' He chuckled. 'A week or so back she told the mammy that when she's a full-grown woman an' marries Cracky Fry, she's goin' to make him buy her earrings which match the necklace. Marry that varmint, mind, not just any ould feller.'

'Yes, well . . . the flower on it . . . what was the flower?'

She looked up at Colm. A frown creased his brow. 'A flower? I don't recall a flower on it, not as I remember. Why, alanna?'

'Colm, you must remember—you bought it for her, after all. Or didn't you actually buy it? Was . . . was it give to you? Or did you . . . did you find it?'

Even in the lamplight she could see the puzzled look on his face. 'Who'd give me a necklace, alanna—I'm a feller, not a gorl! As for findin' it—

what on earth are you talkin' about? An' why, in God's sweet name, should it matter?'

Rose hung her head. She could back out, pretend she was just messing about, say nothing further. Because if he had found it she was sure he would have said so, told her immediately. And if he hadn't found it . . . well, she didn't want to pursue that thought.

'Rosie? Does the flower matter? If it does I'll rack me brain . . . but I can't really remember, I didn't look that close. It might have been a daisy . . . or was it a rose? Sweet Jesus, I can drop Caitlin a line, ask her to let me know, only I can't see why it matters, alanna.'

'Well . . . it crossed me mind that you might have found it in the jigger, or . . . or in the yard, even. An' . . . an' it sounded like, well a *bit* like the necklace me mam lost, an' I just wondered . . .'

He gaped down at her for a long second, then caught hold of her shoulders and twisted her roughly round so that she faced him. He hurt her and she gasped, then tried to avoid meeting his eyes. He looked—oh, unlike himself. Darkly, bitterly angry.

'It crossed your mind that it might be your mam's necklace . . . it did that *now*? Your mam lost that t'ing at the beginnin' of January and now it's March, so it is. No, come to t'ink of it she didn't lose it, did she? It was stolen. And you . . . you've been t'inkin', all this time, that it were me . . .'

'No! Not all this time, Colm, I swear it on me . . . on me life! It weren't until I were cleanin' your room last week an' picked up the rug, an . . . an' found a letter from your Caitlin, thankin' you for a necklace . . .'

'You read me letter!'

'Well, yes. It were under the rug in your room . . . I scrubbed the floor, you see, an' the rugs had to be took up . . .'

'An' you jumped to the conclusion that I'd *stole* a necklace to give to me little sister for Christmas! You t'ought that of me!'

'No, no! It weren't anything like that, it were . . . not that you'd stole it, of course it wasn't! I thought you'd . . . you'd . . .'

Her voice trailed off. Rose put a hand on each of her flaming cheeks and took a deep breath. She was doing her best to explain and he wasn't helping by standing there glaring down at her as though . . . as though it were *she* who was in the wrong, *she* who had taken the necklace. She had felt ashamed of what she had suspected but now she was angry, too. 'Look, Colm, I *told* you I knew it wasn't you, it was just that the letter . . .'

He interrupted her again, without apology. 'You read my letter an' leaped to conclusions. An' just where did you put it? I save all me sister's letters, I read 'em over and over 'cos she's a clever kid and . . . But I did know I'd lost a page somehow, somewhere. It's not turned up again . . . where did you put it?'

Rose looked up at him in an agony of doubt. If she told, she would be putting herself so far in the wrong . . . but it had seemed all right at the time. She could not understand how an act which had seemed so natural then should seem so wrong, so horrible, now. But there was nothing for it but to come out with the whole truth or she could see the situation deteriorating even further. 'I put it back in the bundle of letters in your chest of drawers,

418

the bundle with red ribbon round it,' she said. She tried to sound calm, casual even, but her voice shook. 'I shouldn't have, I see that now, but at the time it seemed the best thing to do.'

'And that was three days ago,' Colm said. 'For three days you've looked at me and thought me a thief. Just because I gave me little sister a necklace an' your mammy had lost one. As if I would do such a t'ing! And as for readin' me letter, rootin' through me chest of drawers . . . I never would have believed it of you, Rose, if you'd not telled me your own self. Just shows I don't really know you at all.'

'And I don't bleedin' well know you, either,' Rose shouted, suddenly furious. She had done what she thought best, she'd not wanted to tell him how she had behaved but thought it the honourable thing to do and here she was, being accused of being an abominable snooper. When it was he, *he* who had possibly taken her mother's precious necklace. 'For all I know you're a known thief in Ireland . . . for all I know you come across one step ahead of the scuffers! So just you take all them nasty things back, Colm O'Neill, or . . . or I'll never speak to you again.'

'Don't bother,' Colm said. 'If you never speak to me again at least I won't have to hear you callin' me a thief. I'm off.'

He turned from her and strode away into the windy darkness. Rose stood where she was for a moment, gazing out across the black water and, even as she gazed, the diamond lights doubled and danced as the tears formed in her eyes and spilled down her cheeks.

*　　　*　　　*

'Rosie! Where in God's name have you been, queen? An' what the devil happened between you and Colm?' Mrs Ryder said some three hours later, as Rose came drooping in at the kitchen door. 'Colm came back hours ago, went upstairs, packed all his things, an' gave me a week's rent an' his notice. Mr O'Neill was out but he came in half an hour or so back an' he's got no more idea than I have what's been happenin' between you. We talked it out an' had a cocoa an' then he went up to his room an' came down again two minutes later wi' a note what Colm had left on his mantelpiece. It just said he'd go to one of the lodging-houses down by the docks for the night an' would arrange new digs tomorrow. He's ever so upset, queen—and to be frank, so am I. I can't afford to miss out on good tenants like Colm and it ain't as if he's a feller to lose his rag over somethin' you said, because he's not. So come on, what's goin' on?'

'We . . . we argued,' Rose mumbled, coming fully into the room and shutting the door behind her. 'He walked off. I said I'd never speak to him again unless he said he were sorry, an' . . . an' he said that would suit him very well an' went.'

'Now come on, queen,' Lily said robustly, helping her daughter off with her coat and hanging it on the back of the door. 'You must have said somethin' uncommon nasty to make Colm turn on you like that. What was it?'

'Oh, Mam, I wish . . . but it's no use, I said it an' now he's gone an' he'll never speak to me again very like,' Rose said tearfully. 'What's more, I don't *care* if he never speaks to me again, not right now, I don't.'

420

'Rosie, *what* did you say?' her mother shouted, pushing her down in the chair nearest the fire. 'Dear God, you're shiverin' an' cold as ice. I'll make you a cocoa whilst you tell me just what you said and no more messin'.'

So Rose, with both hands clamped around a mug of cocoa, told her mother just what had occurred and, when she finished, burst into tears. Lily stared at her without speaking for a moment, then got up from her chair and went over to her daughter, putting an arm round her shoulders and cooing lovingly. 'There, there, queen, don't take on so! But no wonder Colm took off when you more or less called him a thief to his face. Whatever made you say it, chuck? For I'll be bound you didn't mean it, didn't believe it. Just because the poor feller sent his little sister a necklace, that don't mean it was *my* necklace. Think straight, Rosie Ryder. That there chain o' mine was heavy enough for an adult, it would have pulled a kid of ten or eleven flat on her face at table, just the weight of it. And it wouldn't be suitable, either ... to say nothin' about havin' the lily hangin' from it. Oh, Rosie, what have you done?'

'I've ruined me life, except that so far as I'm concerned Colm bloody O'Neill can go back to Ireland an' welcome,' Rose said crossly. 'The thing is, Mam, I never *said* he was a thief, nor meant it. I only asked him whether he'd found the necklace an' ... an' thought it were a cheap bit of stuff an' sent it to his sister ...'

'What a horrible thing to say, as though he'd not bother to buy a proper present for the gal,' Lily said roundly. 'Look, Rosie, you've been an' gone an' put your bleedin' foot in it proper, and the only

421

thing you can do is find Colm and apologise real nicely. If he accepts your apology then you're a lucky young woman, for I'd as soon accuse me own flesh an' blood of theft as Colm. The O'Neills is decent people an' you'd no right to read the lad's letter, let alone . . .'

'I tried to take it back, tried to say I was sorry,' Rose wailed. 'But he wouldn't listen. He just walked away an' left me to get home under me own steam. And now I think it's all for the best. He said he wanted to marry me—well, he couldn't have wanted it very much if one little quarrel sends him off in a rage, so I'm glad it happened, that me eyes are open at last. And he can go to the devil as fast or as slow as he wants, but he'll go there without me!'

CHAPTER TWELVE

Rose got out of bed and walked across to the window. Mona, in bed still, groaned and sat up on one elbow. 'Whassa time?' she enquired thickly. 'Izzit time to gerrup?'

Rose, without turning, shrugged. 'Dunno. I forgot to wind the alarm last night. But it's light and any minute the sun'll come up.'

Mona heaved a huge sigh. 'Well, you wash first, then. That'll give me another five minutes under the covers.'

Rose, still examining the morning, did not reply. Over the distant rooftops she could see a line of deep orange-gold. What was that saying? Red sky at night, sailors' delight. Red sky at morning, sailors' warning. Well, if that was going to be true, today should be a real stinker. Which fitted in well with her mood, which was about as low as it could get.

Two weeks had passed since Colm had walked out of the house and out of her life. She had thought at first that his father would leave too, but he and Mrs Ryder had talked it over and he had decided to stay. Not that he held any brief for what Rose had done. But her mother had explained that it had all been a dreadful mistake, that her daughter was genuinely horrified at what had happened and was willing—nay, eager—to tell Colm so to his face, if only he would come around to visit them some time.

But Colm would not. So Rose had written a truly abject letter, to which she had had no reply. 'He's still very hurt, so he is,' Mr O'Neill had told her. 'I'm hopin' he'll come round, but there's no sign of it so far. He's in digs wit' a couple of fellers who work wit' us on the tunnel an' seems happy enough.'

After that the iron had entered Rose's soul and she became determined to be as indifferent to Colm as he seemed to her. She did not know where he was lodging and refused to try to find out. She steered clear of the tunnel when she went across the city and if she thought she saw the back of his head in a crowd—and she had done so a dozen times since the quarrel—she resolutely turned her steps the other way.

But she was beginning to feel awful lonely and to dream of him almost every night. Sometimes he was sweet and returned, apologising to her for his cruelty in not understanding her unhappy position when she had first seen the letter. At others he was cruel and came back with a young woman on his arm, introducing her as his affianced bride; then Rose woke up to find her pillow damp with tears. But she was still determined not to make the first move. 'He walked away, so he's got to walk back,' she told Mona defiantly. 'I went an' wrote him a real lovely letter, sayin' as how it were all my fault an' how sorry I was, and I know he got it, because his father told me so, but not a word would he write in reply, not a word!'

'He'll never come round,' Mona said. 'Damn it, Rosie, you called the feller a thief! You should go round and find him and tell him you love him and are very sorry for what you said.'

'I did not call him a thief,' Rose said wearily, for what felt like the millionth time. She still maintained that asking someone if they had found a necklace was not at all the same as accusing them of pinching it, but everyone else looked at her sideways when she said that, and clearly felt sorry for Colm and could not understand her refusal to seek him out.

So it seemed they had reached stalemate. Lily, who had read the tear-stained letter, said she thought Colm might at least have written some sort of reply, but Rose understood why he had not. He was not in love with her, he was glad to have the connection between them broken so easily and having escaped from her clutches he did not intend to do anything which might start the relationship up again.

'Rosie! Are you goin' to have first go at the washstand or must I gerrout of me bed an' drag you to the water?'

424

Rose grinned, but it was a pretty poor effort. She took one more look at the beautiful sunrise, then went over to the basin, poured cold water and dragged her nightgown over her head. Although it looked like being a nice day—the sunrise was more gold than red, she decided—it was still cold enough to make washing in icy water a penance, but she soaped herself all over, rinsed off and towelled herself briskly. Then she took her toothbrush and cleaned her teeth, using a bakelite mug of clean water to do all her rinsing in, though she spat into the slop bucket. Finally, she began to dress, informing Mona briskly that she had better get a move on or they would both be late.

'Why? You can't say that when the clock's stopped and you don't know the time,' Mona said, rolling heavily out of bed.

It occurred to Rose that her cousin was putting on weight; certainly when she tugged her nightgown over her head and began to dab unenthusiastically at her bare skin with the wet flannel she suseemed to have lost her waist—from the back at least. 'Mona, you're gettin' fat,' she said. 'You ought to bike to work, like I do. It keeps you in shape.'

'Oh aye? And how do I bike to work when I haven't gorra bicycle?' Mona said, heavily sarcastic. 'Anyway, I am not fat. And if I am, it's all the lovely grub your mam makes for us to eat. Oh, the apple puddin' I put away yesterday! I bet it's settled on me hips as though they were its home from home, though.'

'Well I don't suppose a bit of fat matters,' Rose said. She was buttoning her blouse facing the window. 'Oh, crumbs, that was the clock strikin' an' it's seven o'clock, so you'd better scamper,' Rose said. 'I thought we might as well use the bathroom now Colm's gone, but Mam said we'd only get into the habit an' she'd scalp us if we tried it.'

'Probably as well, if she's startin' a new feller soon,' Mona said, abandoning the washstand and struggling into a pair of fancy silk knickers which weren't going to keep her warm by the looks, Rose reflected. 'An' Tommy's talkin' about movin' on because he needs a better-paid job. We shan't know ourselves at this rate, Rosie.'

'Well, now I'm headin' upwards in the typin' pool I'm not that fussy about fellers,' Rose said untruthfully. 'They only hold you back. Still, I'm goin' to the Daulby Saturday night. Ella's comin' too. You never know who you might meet there.'

'It won't be Colm,' Mona said, shooting a sideways look at Rose. 'He won't go where he knows you an' I hang out. Why not try somewhere different? Somewhere nearer to the tunnel?'

'Because I'm no keener to meet Colm than he is to meet me,' Rose said firmly. 'What's gone wrong between you an' Tommy, incidentally? The whole household talks about me an' Colm, an' lays blame, but you an' Tommy split up and no one even asks why.'

'We had a ... a misunderstandin',' Mona said after a moment's thought. 'He thought I oughter do somethin' an' I thought I oughtn't. That was ages ago, mind, before Christmas.'

'You were still goin' out together at Christmas,' Rose objected. 'It's only lately you don't seem to see much of each other.'

'We were friends,' acknowledged Mona. She was making up her face before their small mirror with
426

quick, practised movements. Rose, who aimed a powder puff at hers and dabbed lipstick on her mouth when the fancy took her, realised that she had never seen Mona leave the house unmade-up. 'We still are. Only it's got kind o' cooler, you could say.'

'Like Colm an' me,' Rose said, trying to smile. 'Only we went straight from red-hot to ice-cold, you might say. Still, there's as many fish in the sea as ever come out of it.'

'Oh aye. Only ... well, I miss Tommy. I miss bein' with him, I mean. Still, there you are; if he's too keen on gettin' rich quick to bother wi' me, I'm best off without him.'

'Is he? Keen on gettin' rich quick, I mean?'

Mona, who was pulling her mouth into an odd shape in order to smooth on her lipstick, finished it off by blotting it with a piece of paper and turned to stare at her cousin. 'Keen? Honest to God, chuck, it's the only thing he really cares about. In fact it probably put him off meself. I mean, workin' in a flower shop you aren't ever goin' to make a fortune, are you?'

'As likely as workin' the trams,' Rose said, picking up her grey cardigan and her worn black handbag and heading across the room. 'He surely don't expect to become a millionaire tram driver, does he?'

'Nah ... trams are just useful on his way up, I think. You know he's workin' in that garage, evenings? He's savin' up for a lorry of his own, remember, and because he's good wi' engines he reckons he'll know a right 'un when he sees it. They come into the garage now an' then, an' when he's saved enough he'll buy one an' start his own

427

transport business. Oh aye, Tommy thinks big.'

'Well, when he's a millionaire he can jolly well give me a job doin' his typin',' Rose said, going out of the room and holding the door open for her cousin to follow. 'Because it don't seem likely that I'll ever marry, so I might as well have a decent job wi' good money comin' in.'

She set off down the stairs with Mona close on her heels. 'Huh! Haven't you noticed, queen, that rich folk stay richer by under-payin' everyone else? But you'll marry. Colm were just . . . just a hiccup.'

'I've been tellin' meself that ever since he walked away from me,' Rose said gloomily. She opened the kitchen door and walked across the room to the table, laid for breakfast. 'Only toast an' tea for me, Mam, I want to be in early today.'

*　　　*　　　*

Mona, walking briskly up St Domingo Vale and heading for the tram stop on Breckfield Road, thought back to Christmas and Tommy. She had been furious with him when he had told her to accept Garnett's offer of a flat, because she could see very well which way his devious little mind had been working. And when, the first night she had a room to herself, he had tried to get into her bed, she had been more furious still.

'You're not goin' to come in here, makin' use of me,' she had hissed, kicking out vengefully as he tried to scramble beneath the covers. 'I made up me mind when I asked Aunt Lily to take me in that I'd live a proper, respectable life. And that includes not whorin' for your profit, what's more, an' certainly not sleepin' wi' a feller who thinks so little of me that he wants me to set up house wi' another bloke.'

'Aw, Mona, don't be like that,' Tommy had said. Well, it had been more like a whine, really. 'You know I like you better'n I've ever liked a gal before. Why shouldn't we mek use of your havin' a bedroom—and a bed—to yourself?'

'Because I want to keep it to meself,' Mona pointed out. She knelt up and heaved him bodily onto the floor, where he made quite a clatter as he struck something on the lino by the bed. Mona feared he might have fallen into the chamber-pot and thanked her stars she had not used it tonight, but she said nothing of that sort. She just hissed: 'Gerrout of here or I'll scream the bleedin' house down!' and had watched him go before turning on the torch she always kept by the bed to check on the damage.

It hadn't been the chamber-pot, but the mug in which she had her cocoa; it was broken and she hoped, vengefully, that it had stuck into his horrible bum when he landed and made a nice deep slash. She looked forward to the morning, to seeing him limping down for breakfast pretending it was a touch of cramp, but having giggled over it for a few minutes she hopped out of bed, picked up the pieces of china and put them in a neat pile on her bedside table, then checked that the door was properly latched. There was a key in the lock so she turned it, got back into bed and was speedily asleep.

Truth to tell, she thought now, stopping at the tram stop, where a good many people had already gathered, he had been quite sporting about the whole business. He had apologised, said he was glad Garnett hadn't succeeded in persuading her to take on the flat, and came home from work that night with a large box of chocolates, which he suggested they should share whilst indulging in two penn'orth of dark at the Gaumont Palace on Oakfield Road. She had taken the chocolates but had not committed herself to the cinema. Who knew what he might get up to in the back row of the stalls? But then she had thought again; despite all she now knew about Tommy, there was no doubt that he attracted her. She really liked him; *two of a kind, two of a kind*, went through and through her mind when she thought about him, even though she now considered him to be selfish and immoral.

So she had gone to the Gaumont with him, graciously accepted a strawberry ice in the interval and held his hand throughout. Whether she had done so with a view to stopping it from roaming around or because she liked him she was still not absolutely sure, but it had cemented their new relationship; friends, not lovers.

She had not been at the stop for more than two minutes, however, before she saw the 43A approaching and began to move slowly forward, for other members of the queue might not be wanting this particular tram and she told herself she did not wish to be left behind. She eased her way so successfully, in fact, that she was first aboard and settled into a seat with a sigh of satisfaction. Nice to have time to think and to be sitting down whilst she did so. Once the tram got crowded, the bottom pinchers and gropers would try to get near a young girl in the crush and Mona, whilst not above handing out a hack on the ankle or a twist of any piece of groper she could grab, still preferred to sit down like a lady.

Relaxing now, with no need to move until Dale Street hove into view, Mona let her mind go back to her friendship with Tommy. She had been so successful in keeping him at arm's length whilst enjoying all the fruits of friendship that she supposed she must have got a bit cocky, over-confident. She had actually let Tommy walk her up the stairs after one particularly pleasant evening, dancing at the Daulby, though usually they parted, most correctly, in the kitchen or even at the foot of the stairs. But on this particular night—they were last in, having lingered on the walk home for a few pleasant kisses in various gateways—she had allowed him to put his arm round her and accompany her to her bedroom door. She now realised, of course, that it had been a stupid, crazy thing to have done. Because he had kissed her good night, not lightly or casually but properly, for the first time since the big quarrel. And as he kissed, the cunning devil had gently opened her bedroom door and somehow managed to manoeuvre both her and himself inside. And then he had gone on kissing, making a fuss of her, helping her ever so gently out of her coat, scarf, cardigan, blouse ... in fact, before she knew it he was cuddling and caressing her so delightfully that she had not wanted him to stop—had not been able to make him stop—and then they were sitting on the bed and she didn't seem to have any clothes on at all and he was rolling her so gently into the warm blankets, and following her, whilst murmuring that although he really must go to his own room, he would just warm up, having got real chilled on the

431

walk home from the dance-hall . . .

But it had only been once, Mona reminded herself sadly now. Just one night of wickedness, instead of the fourteen she might have enjoyed if she had known she was going to get into the family way anyhow. It seemed so bloody unfair, when you remembered how living with her mam, she'd behaved with the feller she'd thought would marry her and never a scare, even.

At first, she couldn't believe it. I'm poorly, that's the trouble, and me monthlies are late, she told herself. After all, no one could fall after one little kicking-over-the-traces like what she'd done with Tommy, she was sure it took more than that. Or did it? As time passed, it became clear that it could happen as easily after one loving as a dozen or more. She was going to have a baby unless she acted pretty quick and having a baby out of wedlock, she just knew, was one thing Aunt Lily would not stand.

She thought wistfully of Garnett, his money, his good position in the firm. What a fool she had been never to allow him any real intimacy! If she had she could have told him it was his child and he would probably have believed her, being a bit on the naive side. She had realised, right from the first, that Tommy would not want to be bothered with a baby. Nor with her, once she was a mother. Tommy liked to take her to dances and watch the other fellers envying him; she just knew he'd think that saddling yourself with a kid was for mugs who didn't know their way around. Men who intended to get on, who meant to be millionaires before they were thirty, didn't push prams.

So at first she hadn't told Tommy. But then she

432

had got desperate, because a girl she had once been friendly with told her that if you didn't 'take measures' in the early days it was too late and you had to have the baby, willing or no.

'What measures?' Mona had asked uneasily, though she knew, of course.

'Mrs Hancock,' the girl had muttered. 'Lives just off Netherfield Road. She's not cheap, but she's supposed to be all right. Some of 'em . . . well, the gals die, queen. You don't want to go to someone like that.'

'I dunno as I want to go to anyone,' Mona had said uneasily. 'Does it hurt much?'

'Well, not for long, anyway,' the girl had answered. 'But the earlier you goes the easier it is. I'll come wi' you, if you like. She helped me eight months back, so she'll know you're all right an' not a judy-scuffer or somethin' like that, tryin' to catch her out.'

'Thanks,' Mona had said. 'How much d'you say she charges?'

The girl had named a sum which made Mona blink. It would take several weeks' wages and if she had to spend all that time saving up then she'd probably be too far gone for the old witch to do the deed.

She had said as much to her friend, who stared. 'Wharrabout the feller?' she demanded. 'I made the feller pay up.'

'Oh. Yes, I suppose I could ask him,' Mona had said. 'He might lend me the money.'

'*Lend* it?' The girl was incredulous. 'He must be tight-fisted as a bleedin' Jew! Tell him it's give you the money or marry you, that'll mek him change his tune.'

The tram drew to a halt in William Brown Street and Mona gripped her hands into fists until she drove the nails into her palms. People began to get off, shoving against her knees as they passed. She had been forced to tackle Tommy, just as the girl had suggested, and his answer had been as nasty as she had feared. 'Havin' a *baby*?' he had said disbelievingly, as though he had never heard of such a thing. 'Look, Mona, you're a knowin' one, I trusted you. If you slipped up then you slipped up, but it weren't no fault o' mine, so you'll have to face up to it yourself.'

The old Mona would have given him a piece of her mind and probably blacked his eye into the bargain, Mona thought now, as the tram jerked into motion once more. But she was a newer, softer version now. She found she wanted someone to comfort and cherish her, to tell her to go ahead and have the baby and he would look after her. The child hadn't moved within her yet, but she felt tender towards it all the same. She didn't really want to go to old mother Hancock and let the old witch drag half her insides out, along wi' what there was of the baby.

But she could not say any of that to Tommy. Instead, she had pleaded feebly, 'I'll lose me job, Tom, if I don't do somethin' pretty fast. Couldn't you lend me the cash?'

'*Lend* it?' Tommy had said, in the very way the girl had done when Mona had first suggested a loan. 'And how would you pay it back?'

'Out of me wages. A few bob a week,' Mona had said. And then, suddenly sick, had turned away from him and headed for the back gate, for they had been talking in the jigger, Mona having hung around waiting for him to come off shift. 'It don't matter,' she had muttered dully. 'I'll think o' somethin'.'

But she hadn't been able to think of anything—her mind was a horrible, empty blank. She moped around at work, making mistakes in the bouquets, so that a dozen roses were carnations and a mixed bouquet for an important customer had included a pair of scissors for which the staff had searched fruitlessly all day. Only at home, with Rosie and her aunt, was she able to keep some semblance of naturalness and that was because she had somehow managed to tell herself that inside the house she was not pregnant at all, it was just outside.

She had only been sick a couple of times, thank the Lord, so that was all right. But sharing a room with her cousin had meant that she knew that sooner or later Rose would notice her burgeoning figure, and she had remarked upon it this very morning, though Mona had been able to turn it off without too much trouble.

'Dale Street!' called the conductor. 'Come on, gals, let's be havin' you!' Mona jerked out of her seat and made for the exit, telling herself that she would see if she could borrow the money off Rose when she got home this evening. She knew that her cousin had been saving up to marry Colm and to go over to Ireland this summer. Rosie was generous, always had been. She would lend the money, if Mona thought up a good story, and would be happy enough to get it back bit by bit. And I'll be back to bein' meself again, Mona thought pathetically, jumping heavily down off the tram and setting out towards the arcade. After all, it isn't so bad really, gettin' rid of it, because it isn't a real baby, not yet.

And I'll have proper ones of my own one day, when I'm older and married to a decent, respectable fellow. Not a fly-by-night no-good like Tommy Frost.

*   *   *

'Have a good day, Mona?'

Mona had been half-way down the Vale when Rose had come pedalling along on her bicycle and slowed beside her. Mona felt weary and dejected, but the sight of her cousin's smiling face made her grin too, especially when Rose got off her machine and slowed her pace to suit Mona's.

'You look worn out,' Rose said. 'Want a seater?'

Mona giggled and indicated her straight skirt. 'Can't, norrin this skirt, queen. As for a good day, how can anyone have a good day when they're workin' wi' that old cat Ellis? A lovely feller came in for flowers for his mam an' she wouldn't let me serve him, though she kept me servin' every other awkward cuss who come through the door all day, and grumblin' that I hadn't done anythin' right for weeks, what's more.'

'Oh, well,' Rose said tolerantly. 'She's jealous of you, I expect. But if you want to meet lovely fellers you ought to start comin' to the Daulby again. With me.'

'I might,' Mona said. 'Does Tommy still go?'

'Sometimes,' Rose admitted. 'But he hardly ever asks me for a dance. Well, he doesn't have much chance,' she added honestly. 'I'm steerin' clear of complications, like fellers who live in the same house.'

'I don't blame you,' Mona said. 'Oh Rosie, could

436

you lend me some money, d'you think? I'd pay it back, week by week.'

'Course I could,' Rose said promptly. 'What d'you want it for? Seen a nice spring costume, or a coat?'

'No. I want to get rid of a baby,' Mona said and stopped short, a hand flying to her mouth. What on earth had made her say a thing like that? Oh, God, let her not have heard, she prayed. Let her think I was joking.

Rose stopped too, and stood with her legs astride the bike and her mouth open. She glanced all round her—the street was bustling with people returning from work or going out for the evening—and lowered her voice to a whisper. '*What* did you say?'

'I'm . . . I'm in trouble,' Mona muttered. 'There's this woman who can help me, she lives off Netherfield Road. Only . . . only she charges a deal o' money, and . . .'

'And you've not got it,' Rose interposed. She moved nearer her cousin and dropped her voice. 'Whose baby is it, chuck? Won't the feller . . .'

'It don't matter who it is, it's me what's in trouble,' Mona said sharply. 'If you can lend me the money I'll tell the old cat I've got flu an' I'll go along to Mrs Hancock. It don't take long, I believe. Then everything'll be awright again.'

'Oh, but Mona, it's a sin,' Rose said earnestly. 'It . . . it's killin' someone, isn't it? I don't think Father O'Rahan would want you to do a thing like that.'

'He won't know,' Mona said defiantly. 'Who's goin' to tell him, pray?'

'Well, you; at confession,' Rose said. 'In fact I

suppose you should tell him before you do it, then he could tell you not to.'

'Oh aye? Well, he can whistle for me until it's over an' I'm meself again,' Mona stated. 'Gi' me the money, Rosie—lend it, I mean—and you won't have to think about it again. You aren't involved, norrin any way.'

'I am so,' Rose said. 'If I lend you the money, an' I suppose I will, then I'm comin' wi' you to old Ma Hancock's place. Women like that . . . well, I'm goin' with you or you don't get the money. Is that clear?'

'But if you go you'll split on me in confession,' Mona wailed. 'You dunno what it's been like, Rosie, facin' this for weeks an' weeks, an' then findin' out that To—I mean that the feller won't help. I don't think I can bear Father O'Rahan rantin' on at me and tellin' me I'm damned for sure. If you split I'll run away, honest to God I will.'

'I won't say a word, because I can't confess your sins, can I?' Rose pointed out equably. 'It's no sin to lend a pal a few quid. And since you've more or less said it, I'm ashamed o' Tommy. He's got plenty of money, he's always savin' up for this or that. Does he know what you're goin' to do?'

'No,' Mona muttered. 'But he knows I'm in the family way an' he just said I was a knowin' one and he'd relied on me to tek care of things like that.'

'He didn't!' Rose said, much shocked. 'Just wait till I get him alone, I'll give him a piece of me mind!'

'It don't matter, norrif you're goin' to lend me the money,' Mona said rather drearily. 'Tommy's got his way to make, I know that. He's set on havin' a good future, that's his trouble, so he hasn't got

438

time to worry about me, or . . . or babies.'

'Well, I'll lend you the money,' Rose said soothingly. 'Now come along, let's get home or Mam will wonder what's up.'

*   *   *

Despite her resolve to give Tommy a piece of her mind, Rose was unable to do so that evening, for he did not come in until both she and Mona were in bed. He was working at the garage, Mrs Ryder explained, and had taken sandwiches to work with him sufficient for an evening meal as well as for his midday break. He must have left at the crack of dawn next morning, too, because Rose made sure to be in the kitchen bright and early, only to find her mother clearing away his breakfast things. So later that day Rose withdrew the necessary amount from her savings account in the Post Office and tipped Mona the wink that all was well so far as the money was concerned. She had racked her brains to think of a better solution, but so far had failed to come up with one. For Mona, so bright and fun-loving, to be saddled with a fatherless child would, Rose thought, be disastrous. And if her mother knew . . . well, Mrs Ryder would not countenance her niece staying in her house, babe and all, Rose feared.

'I'm to go round, wi' the money, tomorrer after dark,' Mona muttered, as the two of them were getting ready for bed that night. 'Tommy's keepin' well out o' the way, you notice. I'm glad you're comin' too, Rosie—you won't let her kill me, will you?'

'Norrif I can help it,' Rose said grimly. She was

439

horrified both by what had happened to her cousin and the action she was about to take, but she saw that there was no alternative. She could get up at five o'clock and catch Tommy when he sneaked downstairs, shoes in hand, but doubted her ability to get through his self-satisfaction to force him to do his duty by her cousin.

The thought of getting up at five o'clock put her forcibly in mind of the story of the three little pigs and the apple orchard, and this made her smile for the first time since she had heard Mona's unhappy story. She did think, however, that she would keep an ear open and if she heard Tommy either sneaking up the stairs this evening or down them tomorrow morning, she would go out and tell him what was about to take place, hoping to make him see that he was forcing her cousin into a most sinful and dangerous action.

So, lying there in the dark, Rose listened and hoped. She had wound the alarm clock and saw by its luminous hands that it was after midnight; surely he would be in soon? He could not possibly still be working, he was clearly keeping out of the way.

She fell asleep soon after this, however, and because she was so tired, did not wake until the alarm sounded shrilly in her ear. By then, it was too late to catch Tommy, unless he had overslept. He did not usually leave the house until around seven fifteen, however, so Rose woke Mona, then picked up the tall enamel jug and scuttled downstairs, hoping to find him still at breakfast.

Lily Ryder looked up as her daughter entered the room. 'You're early,' she said brightly. 'Somethin' special on at work today?'

'No, but I fancied a hot wash; is the kettle
440

ready?' Rose asked, vaguely waving her jug. 'Tommy gone?'

'Not as I've noticed. Unless he went without his breakfast,' Lily said. 'Help yourself to hot water and then refill the kettle, chuck. You might give Tommy a shout; he'll be late for work, else.'

Glad of the excuse, Rose headed for Tommy's room, meaning to check the bathroom as she went, only Mr O'Neill was just going in as she passed it, so Tommy was clearly not in there. When she reached the room she tapped on Tommy's door and, when she heard no sound from within, cautiously turned the handle and pushed it ajar. The room was bright with daylight, the bed clearly unslept in. Slowly, Rose went right inside. It looked . . . odd, somehow. She crossed to the chest of drawers with the mirror propped up against the wall on top of it. She registered no hair brushes, no bits and pieces of change laid out on the top, no clothing scattered around. She pulled open the top drawer. Empty. She turned to the door; there was no dressing-gown hanging on the back of it, no pyjamas on the bed, no tin for Tommy's carry-out, no bottle for his tea. She noticed bitterly that the wastepaper basket was also empty save for an elderly copy of the *Echo*; it looked as though he had even taken his rubbish with him. It was a waste of time crossing to the wardrobe, but she did so anyway and swung the doors apart. Emptiness met her gaze, not a shirt nor a pair of old shoes were left, though a few pathetic coat hangers swung from the central bar.

Rose closed the cupboard again and went up the next flight of stairs to her own room. She gave Mona another shake and her cousin sat up

441

groggily, groaned and lay down again. 'It can't be mornin',' she muttered, trying to tug the bedclothes over her head once more. 'I don't want mornin' just yet, I can't bleedin' face it.'

'Well, you'd better make up your mind to it,' Rose said briskly. 'Because there's somethin' more we've got to face, chuck. Tommy's done a moonlight.'

Mona sat up, her eyes rounding. *'Wha-at?'* she squeaked. 'Tommy's done a what?'

'A moonlight flit, which means he's gone,' Rose said impatiently. 'Without tellin' me mam or anyone else so far as I know, without leavin' a note or his rent or nothin'. He's cleared out all his things, even the stuff in the wastepaper basket except for an *Echo* about a week old, an' the bed's not been slept in. Mam asked me to go up an' give him a call because he was late, so I went up and saw he'd gone.'

Mona swung her legs out of the bed and stood up. 'The bleedin', cowardly little rat,' she said fiercely. 'Still, he wouldn't of stood by me no matter what. I think I knew that all along.'

Rose remembered her mother, calmly cooking breakfast. 'Oh damn, I'd better nip down an' tell me mam not to bother with Tommy's breakfast, nor his carry-out. Oh Lor', I wonder how much he owed?'

She hurried down the stairs and into the kitchen where Mrs Kibble was now making toast under the gas grill. Her mother swivelled round on her entrance, then turned back to the bacon she was minding in the frying pan. 'Oh, it's you, queen. I thought it were Tommy. Is he on a late turn today?'

'He's skedaddled,' Rose said briefly. 'His bed's

not been slept in an' there are no clothes or anything in his room. I checked the wardrobe an' it was empty. How much rent did he owe, Mam?'

'Rent? Well, a week I suppose, since today's Friday,' Lily said, worried. 'But why on earth should he flit? Are you certain, Rosie love?'

'As certain as I can be,' Rose assured her. 'I can't understand . . .' she broke off. Could Tommy have actually run away from Mona because he knew of her condition? But surely he would have left her mother's rent money and some kind of note? She glance around the warm comfortable kitchen, but then remembered that presumably Tommy had made up his mind the previous morning since he had not been in the house, to her knowledge, since then. 'Mam, didn't he say anything yesterday, when he left for work so early? Didn't he leave his door key with you or . . . or mention that he might be going? You would have noticed if he'd gone with his suitcase an' his ukelele, and all his bits an' bobs?'

'He didn't, I'm sure of it,' her mother said firmly.

'What he must of been doin', Rosie, was takin' a few things every day, so's we wouldn't notice. Well, of all the mean, low-down tricks . . .'

'Perhaps he'll send the key through the post— an' his rent,' Rose said, but without much hope. She felt hot hatred for Tommy rise in her throat, almost choking her. It was bad enough to behave as he had towards her cousin, but to bilk her mother of the rent money and to leave with the key, which he could well have simply put down on his chest of drawers, seemed a petty meanness of the lowest kind.

'He might do that,' her mother allowed. 'Fancy

443

him flitting, though—an' him a tram man!'

'Aye, but there's bad as well as good in all jobs, I suppose,' Rose said. 'I must get dressed now, Mam, or I'll be terribly late for work. Tell you what, I'll pop round to the tram garage after work an' see whether I can learn anything about him. If he's still workin' the trams he must know we'd catch up with him, though. But surely he doesn't have enough savings yet to buy a lorry?'

'Buy a lorry?' her mother echoed. 'What on earth . . . why should he buy a lorry? He had a good job, didn't he?'

'Ye-es, but he had big ideas, Mona said he was always talking about getting rich, being a millionaire by the time he was thirty. Anyway, I'll see what I can find out,' Rose said, heading for the kitchen door. 'Mona an' me will eat his breakfast this mornin', Mam. Mona's bound to be upset; they were quite friendly and went out together now and again.'

'Aye, I thought they'd mek a match of it at one time,' her mother said as Rose slipped out of the door. 'Tell Mona grub's ready when she is, then.'

*   *   *

Mona thought that if she lived to be a hundred she would never forget the sheer awfulness of this day. From the moment Rose had told her of Tommy's defection she had felt as though the whole world was against her. He had been her lover and he had simply gone, leaving everyone in the lurch, not just herself. He owed Aunt Lily money, she presumed he had not given them the week's notice at work and no doubt other peccadilloes would surface in

444

the fullness of time. But worst of all, she must have been hoping, without even realising it, that he would stand by her after all, when she told him that she was going to Mrs Hancock's that evening to have an abortion: Yes, that was the word she had intended to use; abortion. Not 'getting rid of the baby', or anything of that nature. She had meant to tell him the naked truth, which was why, yesterday, she had gone to work with two handkerchiefs, one an ordinary one and the other liberally sprinkled with pepper.

She had waited until lunch-time to bring out the second handkerchief and had then, not surprisingly, been seized by a paroxysm of sneezing. Pressing her handkerchief to her red and running eyes she had sneezed and sneezed and sneezed. And Miss Ellis, the old cat, had bidden her, tartly, to take her germs and herself out of the shop and to stay away until she wasn't 'oozin' 'orrible gairms from every pore', as she had put it.

So Mona had intended to spend this morning making Tommy listen to her. Because she still thought that when it came to the last dreadful push he would probably stand by her. It was absurd, but she knew that whatever he had done she still felt as if he and she were meant to be together, so she was sure that the same feeling must nestle in his breast.

The trouble was, he had told so many lies, though not to her, admittedly. He had informed her quite airily that he had been brought up in a boys' home in London, but had run away from there when he was 'around thirteen'. So having been brought up in Liverpool was not true, nor was the fiction that his parents had moved down to London in order to get a job and had stayed there,

445

though he himself had preferred to return to the Pool. His name had been chosen for him because he had been 'found' in winter, during a spell of extremely frosty weather. He might stick to it, he had inferred, but then again he might not. He seemed content with his rootlessness, appeared to prefer it to the more normal sort of background— but then he didn't have much choice, Mona supposed drearily. And, of course, people who don't have roots and don't seem to want them don't want continuity, either. Or wives and babies, homes of their own, responsibilities.

However, she had not, until this morning, admitted any of those things. She had simply told herself that he would not willingly let her suffer the pain of an abortion, knowing that she might lose not only the baby but also her life and, whilst accepting with most of her mind that she might have to go through with it, at the very back of it she had trustfully expected Tommy to turn up trumps, to find a loophole for her, or to take her on rather than see her suffer.

But now . . . well, he had gone, but that did not mean she would meekly go back to work, her 'influenza' magically cleared; not she! She would go along to the offices of the tram company and see whether anyone could tell her where Tommy had gone—and why. And if they had an address— and surely he would leave a forwarding address— she would pursue him and make him listen to her.

Accordingly, Mona went downstairs, ate a hearty breakfast—the one that Tommy would have had, had he not absconded—and told Aunt Lily that she was taking a day off from the flower shop since, the previous day, it had looked as though she were

446

going down with flu herself. She waved Rose off on her bicycle then, with a glance at the sunny spring morning, for March was well advanced, she went upstairs again, changed her old wool dress for a blue linen jacket and matching skirt, perched a white straw hat trimmed with blue violets on her shining gold hair and set off to discover what she could.

*   *   *

As it turned out, she did not have to go out to the tram depot, since the first tram she caught had Perky Perkins as conductor. He was an old friend from school and had known Tommy as well as Tommy allowed anyone to know him, and the minute he set eyes on Mona he came over to her, his lips forming a whistle. 'Well, who'd ha' thought it?' he said, leaning against the arm of her seat and pushing his navy peaked cap to the back of his head. 'Tommy gorra-way just in time, so they tell me. Don't suppose he paid his rent, eh? Cor, wharra feller!'

'Just in time?' Mona echoed innocently. 'What d'you mean, Perky?'

'He's been runnin' some sort of a scam for weeks, so they say,' Perky said. 'He's been conductin', as you know, handlin' money, an' he'd got friendly wi' one of the gals in the offices an' he used to help her cash up. 'Course, he wasn't supposed to, but no one said nothin'. In fact, if he'd not got greedy no one would likely have noticed the discrepancies. But he did an' they did, an' the very day they'd decided to pounce, he goes off early an' don't come back.' He chuckled. 'Oh aye, he's a
447

fly one, Tommy Frost.'

'Oh. So he didn't leave no forwarding address?' Mona asked rather wistfully. She should have known it would not be that easy!' 'He owes a week's rent, no more, but he may have took more'n he owned. I don't know, me aunt hasn't checked yet.'

'A forwardin' address!' Perky chuckled. 'No, but he did leave a fair-sized clue. A newspaper, one o' the national dailies, in his locker. It were marked in the "Situations Vacant" column, so they reckon he's gone down there. The scuffers here are goin' to get the fellers in the Met to check the jobs out, though I don't suppose they'll find him. No, our Tommy's too fly for them soft southerners.'

'You sound as though it were a good thing to cheat on the tram company,' Mona said, folding her hands in her lap and lowering her eyes to gaze at her blue linen skirt.

Perky looked shocked. 'No, we all know it were wrong, but he were a laugh, were Tommy. I'd not like to think of him bein' chucked in a cell, like.'

'Nor me. But me aunt . . . well, that were a mean thing to do, Perky. She's widdered, makin' her livin' through her lodgers . . .'

'Mebbe he'll send the rent money on,' Perky said hopefully. 'Hey up, there's an inspector waiting at the next stop. I'd best look busy.'

'Right,' Mona said. 'I'm off at the next stop, anyway, Let me know if you hear any more, Perky.'

Mona got down off the tram and stood quite still on the pavement, thinking hard. Tommy had left nothing in his locker but a newspaper, and the paper had an advertisement marked in pen, which seemed to indicate that he had gone back to

London. Newspaper, newspaper, she mused. Now why did that sound so familiar? Odd, when you thought about it, that Tommy should clear everything out and leave just about the only thing which might give folk a clue as to his whereabouts.

She had got off the tram on William Brown Street and glanced around her. The free library was handy, and the museum, the Walker art gallery . . . but it was a glorious day and she wanted to think; surely nowhere would be better for that than St John's Gardens? She walked along the pavement and in through the wide stone pillars. Sunshine fell through the trees, softly dappling the paths and grass, and illuminating a green painted seat set amidst a glorious display of spring flowers—crocuses in full, brave blossom, daffodil spears, greeny yellow still, and several bushes of the brilliant yellow forsythia made her feel suddenly hopeful. There was an answer to the puzzle of where Tommy had gone and she was suddenly convinced that she was the only one who could possibly find that answer. She walked across to the wooden seat and sat down on it, staring down at the gold and purple of the crocuses at her feet. Concentrate, Mona, she told herself grimly. He talked to you in a way he talked to no one else, so just sit here quietly and think with everything you've got. Where would Tommy go, with his supply of illicit money? He would have left the newspaper on purpose, of course—it was just like him to lay a false trail. But there was something else . . . something important, if only she could think of it . . .

She concentrated and saw her cousin Rose's face, heard her voice: He's cleared out all of his things, even the stuff in the wastepaper basket, except for an *Echo* about a week old, and his bed's not been slept in.

That was it! The clue! Why should he take such care, clear everything out, except for an old copy of the *Echo*? The only sensible answer was that he didn't think the newspaper important, but had wanted to look again at something in it, just before he left the house for the last time. Of course he might have ringed an advertisement in that paper too, hoping to put them off the trail ... but somehow she did not think it likely. He must have known full well that his landlady would not pursue him down south—or up north, for that matter—just to get a week's rent.

Right. So the newspaper might tell her more than he meant it to. She would go home presently and read it from cover to cover. But now, whilst it was quiet and peaceful, she must go over and over in her mind everything that Tommy had ever said to her about his future. The lorry, for instance. The garage. The fact that he wanted to be a millionaire by the time he was thirty. But those were all lovely day-dreams really, not the sort of thing which happened to people like them.

She thought for a very long time and came to several different conclusions. There were things that Tommy wanted ... but she would go home now and read that newspaper.

*　　　*　　　*

Back at the house, Lily and Agueda went about their housework, and naturally they talked a great deal about the wickedness of such a handsome and

450

charming young man, and speculated as to where he was now. When they had cleaned through downstairs and done the bedrooms they marched purposefully into Tommy's room. Rose said he had taken the key, which seemed a strange sort of thing to do, but if he had left it somewhere they intended to find it.

They did. Under the paper lining the drawers in which until recently Tommy's underwear and shirts had lain. Agueda gave a cry of delight. 'There's the key, thank goodness, you won't have to have the lock changed, my dear. Now when this room has been turned out you must write out an advertisement and put it in the newsagent's window, that nice man in Heyworth Street has a good one. The advertisement will do for both Colm's room and Tommy's, for my dear Lily, it is just foolishness to continue to keep Colm's room empty. His father does not think he will return and, quite frankly, it would be a far from comfortable situation if he did. He and dear Rosie were so close once, to live under the same roof with neither speaking to the other would be dreadful indeed. So let the rooms and tell yourself that we are starting afresh.'

'I know you're right, really,' Lily said as they stripped the bed with practised ease and threw the bedding out onto the landing. 'But I feel so guilty over poor Rosie. She's pining for him you know, Agueda, though she don't say much. Pass me them clean sheets, love.'

They began to make up the bed and were just pulling the fresh bedspread over it when they heard someone come into the kitchen. A voice shouted: 'Aunt Lily it's me. Mona. Where are you?'

'Upstairs, doin' the bedrooms,' Lily called back, adding quietly to her friend: 'Eh, dear, these young things! Here we are, doin' Tommy's room out for someone else, and a couple of months ago I would have sworn that he and Mona . . .'

'Excuse me, Aunt, but I wondered . . . have you thrown away the newspaper you found in Tommy's wastepaper basket?' Mona said, appearing in the doorway. 'I thought it might be worth taking a look at it, to see why he didn't chuck it out wi' the rest of his rubbish.'

'It's in the kitchen, along wi' the lining paper from the chest of drawers,' Lily said. 'But it weren't the latest edition, chuck. I don't know as you'll find out much from that.'

'No, probably not. But I mean to look,' Mona said, turning to go down the stairs again. 'You never know—we might get your rent money back yet.'

'We've got the key,' Agueda said. 'It was under the lining paper in the chest of drawers. I half hoped for a note, or the rent money, but it was just the key. I wonder why he hid it there?'

'I don't know,' Mona said, sounding genuinely puzzled. 'But then he was an odd mixture. Shall I make you some elevenses whilst I'm down there? Say tea an' some buttered toast?'

'That would be very nice,' Lily said gratefully. 'You're a good gal, Mona, especially as it's your day off. You'll find a tin with some of my jam tarts on the second shelf in the pantry if you'd like to set them out as well.'

'Right,' Mona called; she was at the bottom of the stairs now. 'Ready in ten minutes, ladies.'

452

*   *   *

The newspaper had not been marked, or at least Mona did not think so at first. But when she began to look hard, she noticed that one or more advertisements had been carefully cut from the paper. They were not all advertisements for jobs, either. One was, but another was in the 'for sale' section. You blighter, Tommy Frost, you aren't goin' to make this easy for me, she told herself, carefully tearing out the appropriate sheet and folding it into her jacket pocket. But I'm not beat yet! This paper is dated 5 March, that's a fortnight back. I wonder if I can find up a whole copy somewhere in the Vale? But that means going from house to house, asking, and that will make people start to wonder. No, the best thing to do is to go down to Victoria Street and ask in the offices there. They're sure to have back copies of all their editions.

But for some reason she still did not want her aunt or Mrs Kibble to know that she was chasing after Tommy, so she made the tea, got out the tin of jam tarts, made some toast and buttered it, and sat and shared it with the two older women, not even allowing herself to think about the paper in her pocket until the tea was drunk and the food eaten. 'Well, I'm off again now,' she said then, getting to her feet. 'It's such a lovely day, I'd rather be outdoors than in. I might go out to Seaforth, or over to Woodside on the ferry.'

'That's right, love, you enjoy yourself,' her aunt said placidly. 'Will you be in for your supper, later?'

'I'm not sure,' Mona said. 'I might go to the cinema, or on to a dance. Anyway, I've got me key,

453

so don't worry about me.'

She got up and left the kitchen, walking briskly down the jigger and out into the road. She did not intend to walk to Victoria Street but would take another tram; you never knew, the conductor of the next one might know even more about Tommy. So it was with a bright face and burgeoning hope that Mona set out on the next stage of her search.

*   *   *

'She's hoping to find Tommy, of course, that's why she wanted the newspaper, to see if there was any clue in it,' Agueda said placidly as soon as the door had closed behind Mona. 'What a shame that two lovely girls should have been treated so badly by two nice young men.'

'We-ell, I don't think Colm treated our Rosie badly, I think the boot was on the other foot,' Lily said fairmindedly. 'And I don't think Tommy was a nice young man, though I grant you he was handsome and charming. Still, I get your meaning, Agueda. I don't think Tommy wants to be found, do you?'

'No, I don't,' Agueda said, chuckling. 'But Mona's a determined young woman. You never know, she may catch up with him yet.'

'If so, I hope she gets me rent money back,' Lily said rather gloomily. 'I'm beginnin' to suspect, Agueda, that the bits and pieces of money we lost might have gone out walkin' in that young man's pocket. But perhaps I'm wrongin' him. Maybe he'll send the rent money on when he's in work again. If he really has left the tram company, that is.'

*   *   *

There was no difficulty in acquiring the correct back copy of the *Liverpool Echo* and it was the work of a moment for Mona to spread her partial page over the whole one, thus enabling her to see the pieces of paper which Tommy had cut out—and taken with him, naturally. The first one read: *Thirty Foot Day Boat for sale. Diesel engine recently overhauled. Licensed for twenty passengers. Lying Fleetwood Harbour. Can be seen by prior appointment. Apply Box No. 2102.*

Mona frowned over this for a moment, then turned to the second advertisement which, to her relief, was self-explanatory. *Blackpool. Pleasant rooms in Lansdown Street area available for twelve-month let,* it said. *Suit single gentleman or young couple. Terms reasonable. Apply Box No. 2326.*

That's odd, Mona said to herself. Why is he interested in a boat for sale in Fleetwood and rooms in Blackpool? And whilst she was puzzling over it, the truth suddenly dawned on her. Her knowledge of geography was poor indeed, but she did remember from her one and only trip to Blackpool that Fleetwood had not been very much further on. She also remembered Tommy coming back from a weekend trip to Blackpool with several other tram workers, full of enthusiasm for the town.

'There's fellers there takes you for sea trips,' he had enthused to Mona on his return. 'Why, one will take you over to the Lake District—that's a good way, Mo. Tell you what, I reckon that's a good life. Takin' trippers all through the summer an' settlin' down to summat like waitin' on in a cafe—why, if you made the sort o' money I guess they do make, you could *own* the cafe! More fun than a lorry, because you'd meet people, probably they'd tip you the odd copper if you mugged up the chat a bit—the feller I went out with were glum—but I'd enjoy that. I'd tell 'em stories about the sea, about the town . . . oh aye, I'd do well at that.'

But being Tommy of course, within a week or so he was back on the importance of saving up for a lorry so he could start his own transport business, and his temporary interest in Blackpool and boats had gone right out of Mona's head. It occurred to her now, though, that despite his seeming openness, Tommy was a secretive fellow at heart. He'd muck around and tell you things, but the things that mattered would be kept close. He had trusted her to an extent, but clearly not enough to tell her he was flying the coop, nor to hint at his revived interest in boats and boating.

Having written down both advertisements on the margin of her cut-about sheet of newsprint, Mona returned the file copy of the *Echo* to the young lady behind the reception desk and left the office in a very thoughtful mood. He had not left the newspaper behind, she was now sure, with any intention of misleading anyone. It had never occurred to Tommy that anyone would be sufficiently interested in an old copy of the *Echo* to leaf through it, far less to notice that bits were missing and set out to discover what he had thought worth cutting out. Therefore, it stood to reason that he had taken the two advertisements with him because he intended answering them. What other reason would he have for cutting them out so neatly and carrying them away with him?

456

Mona walked along Victoria Street, thinking deeply. She scarcely noticed the shops and offices she passed, but came to herself at North John Street and began to think really hard. Just what had he done, the cunning devil? She must put herself in his shoes if she were to work out the puzzle. She could imagine him going in to work, pleased with himself because he was about to get right away from all this, and deliberately marking the old copy of the newspaper in his locker to make his colleagues believe he had returned to London. But it would never occur to him in a million years that someone might go to the trouble of tracing the advertisements he had cut out from the *Echo*. And of course, as he had never mentioned the boat idea to anyone but her, even if they traced the advertisements they would not make sense.

Satisfied on that score, she began to walk casually along the road, paying very little heed either to the huge office blocks towering above her or the shops, where her attention would normally have been riveted. She knew where he was! She would get a train to Blackpool and make him see that running away would do him no good—or not if he ran without her, at any rate. She was tempted to head straight for Lime Street station, but reminded herself sharply that she must not do—or appear to do—what Tommy had done before her. She would, instead, return to the Vale, pack a bag, tell her aunt she would be away for a day or two . . . Yes, that would be sensible.

Having made up her mind, she hurried. The day was still young, but she had no time to waste, Tommy had been in Blackpool—and, presumably, in Fleetwood—for two whole days. She needed to

457

catch up with him quickly.

* * *

It was a good journey by rail up to Blackpool and Mona arrived there before it was dark. She headed straight for the nearest newsagent's shop, where she bought a daily paper and asked the elderly man behind the counter if he could direct her to Lansdown Street.

He did better, he sold her a small street map and armed with this Mona set off. It was late afternoon and she was beginning to feel a great sense of urgency. Rose had given her the money to go and see Mrs Hancock, so if necessary she could book herself into a guest house for the night, but she wanted to find Tommy as soon as possible. As she walked, she planned her campaign as carefully as though it were a military exercise. She could not afford to muff this one chance, it had to go as she wished.

* * *

The woman who came to the door was fat, neatly dressed, hard-faced. Her greying hair was tugged back into a small bun on the nape of her neck and she eyed Mona warily before she spoke. 'Yes?'

It was not encouraging, but Mona bestowed upon the other her most charming and ingratiating smile. 'I'm so sorry to disturb you, Mrs Robbyns, but I believe you have a Mr Thomas Frost staying here?'

'That's right,' the woman said, and Mona's heart gave a great leap. She had tried several other

458

houses already and had been directed to this one because, the lady said, 'Her up the road—Mrs Robbyns—had an advert in the papers after her son John left 'ome.'

'Ah, I thought I had the right house,' Mona said cheerfully, employing the genteel accent which she used at work. 'May I speak to him, please?'

'We-ell, I dunno as . . .'

'We're hoping to be married when we can afford it,' Mona said gently. 'We had intended to leave Liverpool together, but I had to work out my notice, so thought I'd not be able to come up north. However, my employer has managed to replace me, so I collected the wages owing to me and here I am.'

'Mr Frost's took me last room,' the woman said quickly. Mona did not believe a word of it. 'We don't allow no funny business, not in a nice area like this. And any road, Mr Frost's out.'

'Up in Fleetwood?' Mona asked. 'With the boat?'

'Oh, he told you he'd bought it, did he?' the woman said, her face relaxing a little. 'No, he's not up in Fleetwood, he's at work.'

'Oh, I see. When will he be home? Can I wait for him in his room?'

The landlady looked shocked. 'Why, he may not be home for hours, Miss . . . er . . . and I don't allow ladies in me gentlemen's rooms. He's workin' at Macauley's garage on Dixon Road, though, if you'd like to go along there.'

'Oh, Macauley's,' Mona said airily, glad once more that she possessed the street plan of the town. 'I'll go along there, then. But I'll leave me bag with you, if you don't mind. It's a lot to lug.'

'Well, I don't know ...' the woman said doubtfully, but Mona stepped forward saying 'thank you so much' in a bright voice and dumping her bag at the foot of the flight of linoleumed stairs leading to an upper floor.

'Thanks, Mrs Robbyns,' Mona said, rubbing her aching arm. 'I shan't be long, I don't suppose. I'll just go along and have a word with my fiancé.'

'He never said nothin' about no fiancée ...' Mrs Robbyns began, but Mona pretended not to hear. She hurried along the road until a bend hid the older woman from view and stopped to consult her street map. Having discovered that she was going in the right direction she speeded up a little and presently found herself standing in front of a sizeable building before which were two petrol pumps and a large concrete apron. Walking across this, she came to the entrance of what must be the Macauley garage, since the name was written in large red letters across the façade. Before her was a pit, above which a car stood, and in the pit was a man who seemed to be screwing some object into the mysterious region of the car which she believed was called the exhaust.

There was very little of the man actually showing; she could see dark hair, a checked shirt and a brawny, black-smudged arm, but it was enough. Whoever he might be, he wasn't Tommy.

Accordingly, Mona walked around the pit, treading cautiously, and came upon another car, from beneath which protruded a pair of feet clad in shabby black plimsolls and legs in positively filthy blue denim overalls. She leaned forward and peered. 'Hello you down there,' she said affably. 'Can you come out for a minute?'

460

The legs jerked convulsively and there was a nasty thud. Head incautiously raised meeting bottom of car, Mona judged.

'Oozat?' a muffled voice asked. 'I'm tryin' to get this bugger fitted up before the owner comes back, an' I think I've cracked me skull.'

'Never mind, Tommy. I'll wait,' Mona said equably. 'How long do you think you'll be?'

There was a silence whilst, Mona imagined, Tommy tried to get a look at her without actually emerging from beneath the vehicle. Then he said rather sullenly: 'I dunno. Half an hour; mebbe twenty minutes. I'd near cracked it when you spoke.'

'Oh dear, and then you cracked your skull instead,' Mona said brightly, in her most 'society' voice. 'Look, there's a tea-rooms opposite. I'll go an' have a cuppa while I wait. In fact, why don't you join me there?'

'Too much black bloody oil all over me, that's why not,' Tommy said grumpily. 'I allus clean up afore I gets me tea.'

'All right then. I'll watch, and when you're ready, we can walk back to Lansdown Street together.'

'Oh,' the voice under the car said uncertainly. 'And just 'oo d'you think I am?'

'Don't be silly, Tommy,' Mona said severely. 'I don't usually invite total strangers to join me in a cup of tea.'

There was a brief but violent struggle beneath the car and the legs disappeared, crabbing slowly out of sight. In their place a familiar face, crowned with extremely dirty fair curls, looked up at her. 'Mona! How the devil ... What the 'ell are you doin' in Blackpool?'

461

'Looking up an old friend. Or rather, looking down on one,' Mona said, chuckling. 'Gerra move on Tommy, it's gettin' dark already, you know. Mrs Robbyns will wonder if we're late back.'

*   *   *

Mona did not ask herself what would have happened had she taken her eyes off the garage frontage for one moment, because she was very much afraid she knew. He would have scarpered, oily features an' all. But he wouldn't have got far, not with her knowing his digs and so on. And anyway, she didn't take her eyes off the garage, and presently, when she had drunk two cups of tea and devoured—she had had no lunch—two toasted teacakes and a slice of Victoria sponge, he came across the road and made an impatient sort of sign to her through the window.

Mona paid her bill and left, smiling affectionately at Tommy as she joined him. 'What did you think I'd do, when I found you'd gone missin'?' she enquired, as they strolled along the prom. 'I set meself to findin' out where you'd gone. I used me head and thought back, because I know you pretty well, Tommy. I remember how you'd talked about Blackpool, an' havin' a pleasure boat, an' of course I knew you've always been crazy about cars. You had to have a job for the winter, so I set meself to find your lodgings first, then where you'd be workin'.'

'I can't believe it,' Tommy said, staring at her. 'I were dead careful—there were others would want to know where I'd gone after all—an' covered me tracks. How in God's name did you catch up wi' me?'

'I told you. I know you inside out, Tommy Frost, that's how. And by the same token, what made you think you could walk out on me, an' leave me with a baby on the way. A baby, Tommy, that's a real person, not just a job you don't like or a landlady you don't respect. It's your baby as much as mine, you know.'

'It's your fault that you're in the fam'ly way,' Tommy grumbled, but he didn't sound annoyed. He was still puzzled, she could tell. 'Anyway, I've bought me boat.' He turned to her, his face flushing with enthusiasm. 'She's a real beauty, Mona, just what I've been dreamin' about. She holds twenty trippers, she's gorra first-class engine an' I'm the feller to keep it in good repair. She's called *The Lively Lass*, but I did think I might rename her ...' he glanced sideways at her, then quickly away ' ... only it's bad luck, they say, so she'll stay as she is for now.'

'That's good,' Mona said. 'You don't need bad luck, do you, Tommy? So when'll we get wed, eh? I don't mind a Register Office, seein' as I'm gettin' a bit heavy round me middle for floatin' up the aisle in white.'

'But I can't burden meself wi' a wife, not when I've just bought me boat an' got meself lodgin's,' Tommy almost wailed. 'You shouldn't of come, Mona, an' that's God's truth. You don't want to marry me. There's things you don't know ...'

'Norra lot, sunshine,' Mona said grimly. 'I know you've been stealin' money from the corporation, Tommy, an' they know an' all. They'd be very interested to hear where you are right now. An' you owe me aunt a week's rent, to say nothin' o' that

463

bleedin' necklace. Don't bother to deny it, you took it. So if you're really not interested in mekin' an honest woman of me as the sayin' goes, I just might go round to the local police station an' tell 'em they've a wanted man livin' in Lansdown Street.'

'You wouldn't!'

'I would, then. Tommy, I don't *want* to get rid o' this baby, I want to have it, an' be a proper mam to it. An' I want to be wi' you, you know I do.'

Tommy stopped looking hunted and for a moment smiled down at her with real affection. 'Oh aye, there's no one as suits me like you do, Mona. But I'm not cut out for marriage, responsibility, all that. You'd be better off wi'out me an' that's God's truth.'

'I don't think so. I've known a lorra fellers, Tommy, but you're the only one I've ever felt like this about. As if me life wouldn't be worth livin' without you in it somewhere. So what d'you say to that?'

'I dunno as I can take it,' Tommy said honestly. 'Suppose we wed, Mona, an' then it's too much an' I light out on you?'

'Well, I'll light out after you,' Mona said. 'We're on the same wavelength, an' that's God's truth, as you're so fond of sayin'. I found you this time, I'll find you next time. It's as though you're the magnet an' I'm the pin. Wherever you go, I'll find you, Tommy Frost.'

Tommy stood quite still for a moment, then swung her round to face him, his oily hands gripping the shoulders of her best blue linen jacket. He was smiling suddenly, lit up with an inner glow of happiness which she had not seen in him before. 'You're on then, Mo. I'll stand by you, an' I reckon

464

we'll do okay, betwixt us. Can you still work? Only I suppose you're goin' to mek me send the rent back to Mrs Ryder?'

'I can work,' Mona said. 'You can write a nice letter to me aunt, along wi' the money, an' you can tell her we'll pay back the necklace money somehow.'

'I'll do better'n that; I'll send her the pawn ticket,' Tommy said triumphantly. 'I meant to sell it, but I only pawned it. Mind, it's been in an' out a few times ... but the six months ain't up, she can reclaim it. As for a letter, I'll send one, but I won't send it from here. I'll persuade someone goin' down to London on the train to post it there ... that'll muddy the waters. Did you get a room in me digs? Old Ma Robbyns still hasn't let the small room over the porch.'

'She told me they were all gone,' Mona said. 'But why don't we move into different digs, Tommy, where we can be together? I know we oughter wait till we're wed, but that cake's been cut. No reason why we shouldn't get married in a week or so, but tell 'em we're married already. And tomorrer I'll get a job, so's I can help.'

'Right,' Tommy said exultantly. He turned to her, his oily face wreathed in smiles. 'Oh, I could hug you, Mo Mullins!'

'Wait till you've had a wash,' Mona advised. 'I say, Mona Frost sounds rather good, don't you think?'

'It sounds very good,' Tommy said. He took her hand firmly in his. 'I just hope the baby's a boy, so's he can help me wi' me boat. D'you know what, Mo? I'm rare glad you ran me to earth.'

465

CHAPTER THIRTEEN

'Rosie, there's a letter for your mam—it looks like Mona's handwriting to me.'

Rose had just run down the stairs and was about to set off for work, with a hand on the kitchen door, when Mrs Kibble hailed her. She stopped short and beamed at the older woman, who was crossing the hall with a number of envelopes in her hand. 'From Mona? Oh, thank God,' she said devoutly. 'I'll give me mam a shout.'

'It's all right, she's in the kitchen, we can go through,' Mrs Kibble said. 'I just hope it isn't bad news.'

'Well, nothing could be worse than silence,' Rose pointed out, opening the kitchen door and going through it. 'Mam, there's a letter!'

'From Mona? Oh, thank God,' Mrs Ryder said, echoing her daughter's words.

'That's right. Do hurry and open it, Mam, so's I can get off to work wi' a clear conscience. I've been that worried even my work's suffered, so Patchett & Ross will be just as glad to hear Mona's got in touch as we are.'

Lily Ryder took the envelope that Mrs Kibble was holding out and opened it with shaking fingers. She unfolded the sheet of paper, ran her eye quickly over it and gestured to the others to come right into the kitchen and sit down. 'We might as well be comfortable,' she said. 'There's a couple o' pages.'

She made as if to chuck the envelope in the fire but Rose reached over and tweaked it out of her hand. 'What's the postmark? Oh, it's London, posted the day before yesterday. Better hold on to it, though.'

Mrs Ryder gave her a bemused look but smoothed out the envelope, which she had crumpled in her hand preparatory to throwing it onto the kitchen fire, and took her own seat at the table. 'It's from Mona all right and tight,' she said, turning to the last page. 'Yes, it's signed Mona Mullins. Right, here goes, then.

Dear All

I do hope you've not been worrying about me, because I'm doing fine. I followed Tommy down to London and we're going to get married and make a home for ourselves down here, though he took some persuading at first! I'm sorry about borrowing money from you, Rosie, but I'll pay it back just as soon as I can, I promise. And I'm sorry for leaving you in the lurch, Aunt Lily, but I think you knew all along that it were Tommy for me, and I was sure, really, that he felt the same about me, so I followed him and found him, and all's well that ends well.

There's a lot more to say and to tell you, but I won't do it until I can clear everything up, which will take me a week or two. In the meantime, we're living in the same lodgings and very nice they are, too. We'll stay here for a bit, because you earn good money in London, then we'd like to move further south, because rents are awful high here.

I expect you wonder why I didn't write sooner. Well Aunt, it's taken me this long to find

Tommy, plus a couple of days to make him see marriage my way, but now we've settled everything and I wanted to put your minds at rest. I am very happy, far happier than I ever thought I'd be, and Tommy seems to have a big smile on his face whenever he looks at me, which is good.

I won't give you my address because we shan't be here long, but as I said, I'll be writing with a fuller story quite soon and in the meantime all my love to everyone.

Your loving niece,
Mona Mullins

'Well, I'm blessed,' Mrs Kibble said as her friend stopped reading. 'She might have thought how you'd worry though, Lily. She could have dropped you a line earlier, even if she could only have said that she was in London hunting for Tommy and quite all right.'

'I'm ever so relieved,' Rose said in heartfelt tones. 'I was so worried ... but I should have known Mona wouldn't do anything silly.'

'Anything silly? What sort of thing? And why should she?' Lily said at once. 'I did wonder, when she disappeared like that without even a note to tell us she wouldn't be home for tea.'

'Well, I knew she were very fond of Tommy,' Rose said, confused. 'I mean ... it seemed so odd him disappearing one day and her the next. As you said, Mam, he were one step ahead of trouble over money with the Corporation and when Mona wanted to borrow some money ... perhaps I should have guessed she wanted it for a train fare.'

'You never mentioned the money afore,' Lily

468

said suspiciously. 'Why not, chuck?'

'Mona made me promise not to tell anyone,' Rose said glibly. 'But she will pay it back, I'm sure. Mona's all right, really. I wonder what the next letter will say, though.'

'Wait and see,' Lily said rather grimly. 'I just hope it don't say that Tommy's lit out in the night and left her high and dry, the same as he did us. But this isn't the time to go speculating, queen, or you'll be late for work, and that would never do.'

Rose got her light coat off the back of the door and tied a headscarf over her hair. She said goodbye to Mrs Kibble and her mother, then went out into the yard. Her bicycle was in the shed and she wheeled it across the yard and into the jigger, then hopped along beside it, gathering speed, and jumped neatly into the saddle. She would not be late, she reflected, because she always gave herself ample time for the journey, but she would not be particularly early, either. But since she was always the first to arrive, and in fact now had the office keys in her charge for opening up, no one would know that she hadn't reached the office before eight thirty, her usual time.

As she cycled along, Rose pondered on her cousin Mona. She had been terribly frightened when Mona had failed to turn up that evening, but had been unable to confide in anyone. She had walked up and down the jigger, then up and down the road, and in fact, had it not been for Mr Dawlish, she would probably have gone up to the police station and admitted that she thought it was possible her cousin had done away with herself.

But Mr Dawlish had put the lid on such unfounded fears. He came up the road with his seabag over his shoulder and hailed her from afar. 'Miss Rose! Nice to see you, though I can't kid meself you're waitin' for me with such impatience. I suppose you're waitin' for Miss Mona—she's off for a trip, I gather. I saw her in Lime Street a while back, wi' a suitcase, waitin' for a train. Where was she off to, then?'

'I don't know. A suitcase, you say?'

'Well, a sizeable bag,' amended Mr Dawlish, falling amicably into step beside her. 'She looked excited, I thought. I did call out, but she didn't hear me. She was just about to step into a carriage, so her mind was on her journey, I guess.'

At her urgent request, Mr Dawlish had repeated his story to her mother and Mrs Kibble, and it seemed to Rose that all of them slept sounder that night because of it.

But as the days passed and no word came, as the manageress of the flower shop came round indignantly to find out what had happened to Mona, Rose's own particular worry began to resurface. Suppose Mona, in the grip of despair, really had decided to end it all? She might have chased after Tommy unsuccessfully and jumped into a river, or walked into the sea, or dived under a tram. Rose began to have nightmares and to spend time when she should have been working staring into space.

But that was all over now. Now they knew that Mona was safe, was with Tommy, and in due course no doubt they would be told officially that Mona was expecting a baby and—hopefully—that the two of them were about to marry. It'll be odd, Rose mused, turning into Dale Street and slowing with a foot on the kerb, if Mona marries before me—and her so determined only to marry someone rich. Still, Tommy might well be rich, the way he carried on. And Rose herself, alas, was undoubtedly destined to be an old maid.

She reached the office and turned into the short passageway which the staff used to take their bicycles into the building. She unlocked the heavy door, wheeled her bicycle inside and padlocked it to the banisters, then she ran lightly up the stairs to the main office and unlocked that door also, feeling the familiar little buzz of pleasure in the responsibility of 'opening up'.

Rose brushed her hair with great vigour to do away with the flatness caused by the headscarf, got out teapot, tea and cups, and went into the small reception area. She would remain on duty here, seeing to anyone who came up, until Miss Eastman, whose job it was to man the small telephone exchange and deal with customers, arrived.

Mr Garnett had recently purchased a large and rather fine parlour palm and an aspidistra for the reception area and it was Rose's pleasure to water the plants once or twice a week, and to feed them occasionally with stuff from a bottle with a picture of evergreens on the front. She liked the plants and did not agree with Mr Lionel, who said he was running an import-export business and not a hmm-hmmed house of pleasure, so she took great care of the plants, even dusting their leaves each morning and polishing the aspidistra, and only when she had done that and opened the big sash window opposite the reception desk did she sit down on Miss Eastman's swivel chair and pull a magazine out of the top drawer. It was a copy of *Woman* and she was following the serial story with great interest, so was speedily absorbed.

'Morning, Miss Ryder,' someone said presently and Mr Lionel came past her, arms full of the post since he did not trust Albert, the office boy, not to lose half of it on the stairs or half-landing. 'Nice morning.'

'Good morning, sir,' Rose said politely. 'Spring's on its way, I think.'

There was a short wait, then a group of employees all came heavily up the stairs together. Rose greeted everyone cheerily and presently was relieved by Miss Eastman, who came and sat behind the desk with her hair all anyhow and her cheeks scarlet from running—she was a plump, pretty girl who found the stairs a trial—and told Rose that she would be grateful for a glass of water when Rose had finished taking round the tea.

Odd that this morning feels different, yet it's just like every other morning, really, Rose mused as she made the tea and carried it round on the big black japanned tray with the exotic birds round the edge. But perhaps it's just because spring looks like arriving at last—and perhaps it's a bit because I know Mona's all right now, for I guess she'll have the baby and be happy, and probably marry Tommy.

But the thought of Mona marrying Tommy whilst she herself was not even seeing Colm was not exactly a happy one. She did not want to feel jealous of her cousin, but it was inevitable, she supposed, that the thought of Mona's happiness should make her think how very different her own lot seemed to be. A future of working for Patchett & Ross until she was old and grey, looking after her mother and the tall old house in St Domingo Vale, going to church every Sunday, watching other people marrying, having babies, fulfilling their role in life . . .

'Did you forget me drink o' water, Miss Ryder?' Miss Eastman said plaintively. 'Only I aren't half thirsty—I ran all the way from the tram stop on William Brown so's not to be late an' I'm fair parched.'

Rose's hand flew to her mouth. 'Oh, Miss Eastman, I must be going batty! I made you a cuppa and it's not even on the perishin' tray. Wait a mo and I'll fetch it through.'

With Miss Eastman discreetly sipping the cup of tea that Rose slid into the top drawer of her desk— the partners did not approve of a receptionist who drank tea whilst on duty—she was free to go to her own desk and start on her work. The other girls were already ensconced when Rose sat down, took the cover off her typewriter, arranged her notebook, pencils and rubber neatly on the desk, and picked up the first piece of work to read it through before beginning to type.

An ordinary day . . . so why did she feel so keyed up, so excited, as though something of immense importance was going to happen later on?

*   *   *

At six o'clock precisely Rose put the cover on her typewriter, slid her notebook, pencils and rubber into the top drawer of her desk, and went over to the central table to pick up the letters lying there. The office boy had stamped them and licked down the envelopes, and would be coming in a few minutes to pick up the whole lot and take it down to the postbox. Rose and Ella usually stayed until the boy had finished since Rose, the first one in, had to be the last one out, but as Ella still had not acquired a bicycle they only went a very short way together. Then Ella waited at her tram stop and Rose mounted her machine and pedalled away towards Everton, which, because it was uphill most of the way, took her twice the time it took to coast down every morning. 'Ready, Ella?' she said as her friend came back into the typists' room, carrying both their coats. 'Where's that wretched Bertie, then?'

'Mr Lionel's got some personal letters he wants puttin' into the box,' Ella said. 'Here he comes—I'd know them great thumpin' boots o' his anywhere.'

Bertie, hair on end, tie askew, entered the room at a canter and stuffed the letters into his canvas holdall. 'Sorry I's late, gals,' he said breathlessly. 'Mr Lionel wanted to mek some changes. Come on, 'en, we's ready now.'

'Your grammar is *vile*, young Bertie,' Rose said severely, helping him to shovel the letters into the holdall. 'Let's get a move on, because I'm on me bicycle, don't forget. Every morning I whiz into work like a bird, and every evening I puff and pant and work me knees to the bone to get up the hills to the Vale. Still, it's cheap and handy to have me own transport—and it's healthy an' all.' They trooped out of the room and Rose locked the door behind them, then turned to Ella. 'Has everyone gone, d'you suppose, I don't want to lock someone important in and find their skeletons still sittin' at their desk after the weekend!'

'Oh, you,' Ella said. 'Have you checked, Bertie?'

Bertie assured them that he had and reminded

474

Rose that the partners had their own keys anyway and would let themselves out and lock up behind them if necessary.

'An' 'oo cares if a typist gets skellingtoned?' he said cruelly, grinning at them. 'I wouldn't shed no tears, 'specially if it were that Miss Fazackerly; not that she'd mek skellington in a weekend. It 'ud tek a month.'

Rose smothered a giggle; Miss Fazackerly was plump as well as being sharp with the juniors. However, it would not do to let Bertie get away with remarks like that. 'Less o' your cheek, young Bertie,' she said, running lightly down the stairs and rounding the bannister at the end at top speed. 'You won't get to be managin' director by cheek, you know.'

She undid her padlock, slid it into her pocket and wheeled her bicycle out into the backyard, closely followed by Ella.

Bertie mounted his bicycle whilst still in the hall and whizzed past them, making a rude noise as he did so. 'Sucks to you, Ryder,' he shouted. 'See you Monday!'

Rose, locking the back door, sighed. 'Bertie's unsquashable,' she told Ella as they crossed the yard and entered the jigger. 'Mr Edward's really pleased with him, though. Says he's fast an' doesn't make mistakes. Oh, my knees are trembling at the thought of the hills ahead.'

'Go on, you love it,' Ella said as they emerged onto Dale Street. 'Come on, you can walk to the tram stop wi' me and I bet you'll beat me home.'

'All right,' Rose said, pushing her bicycle along beside the kerb. She glanced ahead of her as they reached William Brown Street, 'Isn't it light in the

475

evenings now? I can see the Liver birds clear as clear.'

Even as she spoke there was a sort of rumbling roar and the two girls clutched each other. 'What the 'ell was *that*?' Ella squeaked. 'Ooh, the ground shook beneath me feet, I swear it did!'

'Dunno . . . thunder?' Rose said hopefully. 'Oh, I know, it were an explosion. They have to blast their way through rock in the tunnel, Mr O'Neill's told us so many a time. Yes, that'll be what it was. Dynamite goin' off.'

'Well, I dunno . . .' Ella was beginning doubtfully, when another, more subdued roar reached their ears. Fainter perhaps, but somehow even more threatening.

People turned to stare down William Brown Street to where the tunnel workings started and a man near the two girls said anxiously: 'Were that comin' from the bleedin' tunnel? You often 'ears one 'splosion, but that were two. Mebbe there's been a roof fall.'

A roof fall! Rose looked around her. People were going about their business in an orderly fashion, now that the noise had ceased no one was even glancing towards the tunnel any more, but . . . a roof fall? Abruptly, hideous visions raised themselves in Rose's brain, memories of mining disasters, of books she had read, of the terrible toll of deaths when there was an explosion underground—and Colm was there! Other men she knew, too, but it was only Colm of whom she thought. In the brief split second before she began to move she had seen it all in her mind's eye—the darkness of the tunnel where lamps would have been extinguished by the fall, the great mounds of

476

rock . . . and Colm, white-faced and bleeding, lying on the ground, pinned to it by a great rock fall.

Almost without thinking Rose mounted her bicycle and fairly flew down the cobbled street, losing her headscarf almost at once because she had only looped it round her neck and not pulled it up over her head. A rock fall, the one thing all the men dreaded. It did happen, of course, when explosives were being used, but they had been lucky, so far. Of course there were always accidents and injuries, but because of the careful preparation there had been no disasters in the building of the tunnel. Or not, Rose thought wildly, until now.

By the time she reached the end of William Brown Street she was going so fast that everything was a blur; people, pavements, buildings. She could not even see the tunnel entrance, nor the piles of material and machinery which surrounded it. She was sure, now, that there had been a fall and that Colm, the only man she would ever love, was badly, perhaps mortally hurt. She must reach him, must tell him that she had never suspected him of anything at all, that she loved him, that she was sorry, with all her heart, for the thoughtless, stupid things she had said . . .

She was unaware of people dodging out of her way, she never even saw a horse and cart past which she flew, yet something warned her when she was approaching the end of William Brown Street and the beginning of the tunnel approach. She swerved violently to her left, hit a great pile of rock and rubble and flew like a bird off her bicycle and up. She saw the world turning crazily but did not realise that she was actually somersaulting through the air. Then she plunged to earth. Hard objects battered into her soft, yielding flesh and darkness, blacker than any tunnel, descended. Rose lost consciousness.

*   *   *

Colm O'Neill was finishing his shift when the double explosion sounded. He looked back, and his friend Davy Porter came after him at a run. He was cursing and holding a handkerchief to his eye. 'What's up, Davy?' Colm asked. 'You been fightin' again, feller?' Davy was an Irishman from Connemara, slow of speech but quick when it came to a fight and always determined to hold his own. Now he shook his head, his uncovered eye gleaming with amusement as he caught up with his friend.

'Fightin'? Not likely, me friend, I give rocks best when they t'umps me round the head, so I do. No, I was walkin' along, mindin' me own business, when a charge went off behind me, soundin' like all hell were let loose. So I thinks something's gone real wrong wit' the charges—someone said one charge went a bit crazy and 'stead o' startin' on the left o' the tunnel roof an' goin' round to the right in a circle, like, it shot out o' the hole an' lit across to the opposite charge an' acourse that went off too. But anyway, I were a runnin' like a hare in spring, wit'out lookin' where I were goin', an' I ran into the side o' the tunnel at full speed like, an' cracked me eyebrow open. See? An' the blood ran down an' made me t'ink I were killed.'

'Oh, well, if that's all,' Colm said mildly. 'Comin' for a beer? I'm off shift but me daddy's workin' an extra hour today. They'll serve us at the Trojan's
478

Head no matter that we're a bit early, like.'

'All right, old pardner,' Davy said. He was a great cinema-goer and loved Westerns. 'Let's mosey down dere an' have us a beer.'

The two men emerged from the tunnel, blinking in the daylight, though it was growing dusk, and began to climb the bank which would take them out of the works. Colm heard a sort of squeak and a shout and looked to his right—and saw, to his complete astonishment, a figure suddenly come flying over a large pile of earth and rocks, and somersault to a horrid stillness at the foot of the mound.

It was not light enough to see whether it was male or female, but Colm ran towards it. The dull thump of the impact made him fear that more damage had been done than a few bruises and he was first on the scene. It was, he saw, a girl and quite a young one, too, with thickly curling dark hair and . . . and it was Rose! His Rose!

*   *   *

Colm was still bending over her, trying to make her speak to him, when another man came round the mound of earth. He knelt opposite Colm, looking anxiously down into Rose's milk-white face. 'What 'appened, mate?' he said hoarsely. 'Poor little bugger—did 'er bleedin' brakes fail? She were comin' down the 'ill like a runaway 'orse when the bike 'it that mound of earth an' she simply shot into the air, turnin' over an' over. My, but that's a nasty wound on her forehead. Is she dead? Is she breathin'? We better send for a doctor, I reckons.'

Colm pulled himself together. He tried to gather

479

Rose into his arms—his Rose, his Rose!—only someone else came over and bade him leave well alone. 'If she's broke bones you could do damage, movin' the gal,' the newcomer said. 'There's a first aider comin' in a mo, 'ang on till 'e gives you the say-so.'

Colm reluctantly laid Rose's slender body back upon the ground. She was breathing and her heart was beating, he had felt it for a second as he held her. But the gash on her forehead was both long and deep, and the blood that ran from it looked dark and sinister to him. Apart from the forehead, he could tell nothing, but he knew she could have broken her neck, her back, anything. He looked up and saw that they were now surrounded by a circle of wide-eyed faces, one of them Davy. He fixed Davy with his steeliest glance. 'Go an' get someone, we've got to get her to hospital,' he shouted. 'It's me girl, Davy, the one I'm going to marry! Get a move on, or I'll . . . I'll break every bone in your miserable body.'

Davy didn't answer but he disappeared, and Colm sat back on his haunches and began to pray and to curse by turns. He cursed his pride and pigheadedness which had not allowed him to accept Rose's apologies nor to let him at least go up to the Vale and speak to her. And he prayed, harder than he had ever prayed in his life before, that the good God would let his little love live. She might be a lifelong invalid, she might never walk again, but he found that was secondary indeed to his desperate need and longing for her. She must live, so that he could tell her what a blind, obstinate fool he was, so he could tell her the real truth—that he loved her, knew she had never meant to hurt him, was sorry for the pain he had caused her.

Presently he saw Davy come pounding back and push his way through the crowd. 'There's a doc on the way and an ambulance,' he said breathlessly. 'Tell 'er it's goin' to be awright, Colm. Go, talk to 'er. I 'member in me first aid classes when I were in school that they said folk could often 'ear before they could move a muscle. Tell 'er it's goin' to be awright.'

*   *   *

They took her away from him once they arrived at the hospital. Colm would have followed as his love was put on a stretcher and rushed off down a long corridor, but a nurse stopped him. 'They've taken her for a thorough examination,' the young woman said gently, taking his arm. 'It will be a while before they can tell you anything definite.' She looked at him, at his stained and dirty overalls, at his calloused hands and the big, earth-clodded workman's boots. 'Do you know her next of kin? The doctor'll mebbe want a signature before they can operate. Why don't you go and tell her family what's happened, then you could go home and get cleaned up. You can be back before they take any serious action, I'm sure.'

Colm thought of getting all the way to Everton from the Royal Infirmary but got to his feet anyway. There were taxis . . . and he was filthy, too. He could get a message to Mrs Ryder, clean himself up and get back here in no time at all, if he just put his mind to it. 'All right, nurse,' he said, turning towards the hospital's swing doors. 'But I won't be long. If . . . if they need to operate, they'd not delay 'cos there was no one here to sign t'ings or tell 'em to go ahead?'

She smiled at him. She was stocky and plain, with protruding teeth and a poor complexion, but her smile transformed her into a beauty so far as Colm was concerned. 'No indeed, if they need to do anything they'll do it, never fear. Is she your young lady?'

'Yes,' Colm said baldly. 'She's me sweetheart. We're gettin' married when we can afford it. Nurse, is she . . . will she . . . ?'

'We'll all do our very best,' the nurse assured him. 'When you come back go to the reception desk and ask where you can find Miss Ryder, tell them Sister Bostock knows all about you. They'll see you get to the right place.'

'T'anks,' Colm breathed. 'Me name's Colm O'Neill. I won't be long Nur . . . Sister, I mean.'

He dived out of the hospital and was running along the pavement towards his lodgings, completely ignoring other passers-by, when someone grabbed his arm. 'Colm, me boy—how is she? Your pal Davy told me which hospital they'd took her to an' I come along as fast as I could. Where are you goin', son?' It was Sean, looking grim and worried but—oh, so dependable and sensible.

'Daddy, it's you! She's hurt bad, they want her mammy to know, they sent me out 'cos they'll be examinin' her for a while, they said to get cleaned up. Can you go back to the Vale, tell Mrs Ryder, get her here somehow?'

'I can,' Sean said, not bothering his son with a lot of useless questions, Colm thought gratefully. 'Don't go back to your lodgings, though. Nip into

482

the public lavatory an' clean up there, then go straight back. Don't worry, I'll be in the Vale before you can say "St Domingo".'

He hurried off without looking back and, blessing his father for his good sense, Colm shot into the nearest block of public lavatories, stripped off his overalls and scrubbed himself down, put the overalls back on inside out—they were cleaner that way—took a hasty drink from the little fountain by the doorway and left to hurry back to the hospital as fast as his weary legs would carry him.

*   *   *

She lay in bed, the covers pinning her arms to her sides, the huge wound on her forehead covered, now, with clean white lint and bandages. Her face was as white as the pillowcase and her eyes were dark-shadowed, but because she was clean and had been put into a hospital nightdress she looked better somehow, more normal. Just like any other patient who had fallen asleep at the end of a long day.

The curtains were drawn round her bed, creating an illusion of quietness, though it was only an illusion; beyond them the big ward buzzed with low voices and clicking feet, as visitors came to see their loved ones, and quiet, quick treads as nurses went about their business. Colm found a long stool underneath her bed and pulled it out, sat on it. Then he leaned his chin in his hand and just let his eyes feast on her small, chalk-white face.

Sister Bostock had been as good as her word. The moment he got back to the hospital he had been directed along quiet corridors, turning first

483

right, then left, then mounting stairs, threading his way towards the Sister's own ward. She had recognised him at once and smiled. 'That was quick, Mr O'Neill! Well, Miss Ryder has suffered a broken arm, a couple of broken ribs, some damage to the patella—but we now think it is only heavy bruising—and of course the wound to the forehead. That has been cleaned, disinfected and stitched. One of the theatre sisters told me that the patient seemed about to come round just before she was put under for her arm to be set and the patella—that's the kneecap, Mr O'Neill—to be gently bound into position, so that's a good sign. Now, of course, she's still sleepy from the anaesthetic, but you may sit with her on condition that you call me as soon as there is any sign of her coming round. Do you agree?'

Colm agreed. He would have agreed to anything which allowed him to stay near his Rose, watch that small, obstinate, much-loved face. 'But . . . will she get better, Sister?' he asked, as the nurse propelled him gently towards Rose's bed. 'Is her mind . . . all right? Did the blow on the head injure anything inside her head?'

Sister Bostock chuckled. 'She's fallen off a bicycle with some violence, Mr O'Neill. That's the sum total of it. She had a soft landing, too, from what I'm told—on a mound of earth, not on a tarmacadamed surface, nor on cobbles or concrete. She'll do very well, I'm sure. Now off with you, or I'll have to send a member of my staff to sit with her until she comes round, and we're mortal busy, as you can see. Visitors make a deal of work but occasionally'—she smiled at him—'occasionally one can come in useful.'

He said nothing more but left and took up his position beside Rose's bed. And began what he hoped might not be too long a wait.

*   *   *

Rose was floating in a blue sky, speckled with small white clouds. Now and then she saw one of the clouds approaching and could not prevent herself from entering it, and it was cold and wet inside, and made her feel weak and unsafe. But the clouds were small and the blue sky large, and most of the time she floated in golden sunshine, warm and comfortable and secure.

Presently she saw a cloud approaching and decided to try to float around it. She moved her arms and legs gently, but found it difficult, and as soon as she exerted real effort, it seemed that the cloud approached faster and enveloped her. She remembered reading *Alice in Wonderland* in school—or was it *Through the Looking Glass*? Whichever it was, there had been a path down which Alice had trod which, if she kept her eyes on her destination, seemed to give a wiggle and a twist which sent Alice off in the opposite direction. The clouds were like that, Rose decided. If you tried to miss them you immediately entered one. Perhaps if you headed for one as hard as you could, you would circumvent it.

Accordingly, she stared and stared at the nearest cloud and tried very hard to float right inside it . . . and suddenly, horribly, she became aware that the blue sky had disappeared, along with the gold sunshine. She was lying on something hard, which hurt her aching limbs, and staring at a huge, huge

485

cloud, all white and cold, which seemed as big as the blue sky had been and as limitless.

Hastily, she tried to look away from the cloud, to find again the gentle blue sky, but she could not. Her eyes were wide open and fixed on . . . on a ceiling. Where was she? What on earth had happened to her? When she tried to move arms or legs it was as though she were enveloped in warm but viscose treacle, which would not allow her to move so much as a finger.

She would have liked to look around, too, or to call out, but when she tried to move her eyes the lids simply got so heavy that she could not keep them up and she found herself verging on a dazed sort of sleep. And her voice would not, could not, function. Her lips moved a little, her tongue trembled against them, but no sound would emerge. She gave a violent heave at her lids and for a moment they actually lifted, allowing her to see it was not just a white ceiling above her, she was entirely surrounded by white. Her arms and legs were held captive not by treacle but by some sort of white ice, which gripped her whole body and would not let her move.

Fear came them, a fear which made her heart pound violently, her breath begin to come in little, painful gasps. And every time she took a breath a terrible sharp pain stabbed at her chest, making her give a tiny kitten's cry of protest. She was a captive, in pain, cold as ice itself and unable to see about her . . . she was so terrified that she almost stopped breathing, nearly ceased trying to understand what was happening to her.

Then she heard the voice. It was soft, deep—a voice she loved. It was saying, over and over,

486

'You're all right, alanna. You've broke a bone or two but you're all right. You're goin' to get well again, so you are, so's you an' me can get married, an' live happily ever after.'

It was a lovely voice and the things it said, though they did not make very much sense, were lovely things. And then the best thing of all happened. A weight lifted off one of her arms and a hand, warm, strong, infinitely comfortable and solid, took hold of her frightened, cold fingers. The hand smoothed and gentled her fingers until they, too, began to feel the first little thread of warmth, and the voice went on repeating that she was all right, that she had broken a bone or two but would be all right . . .

She tugged desperately at her eyelids; she would open her eyes, she would! She could see light now, bright light, and the soft mound of white that lay before her . . . it was a bedsheet, taut and tightly tucked, holding her into a perfectly ordinary bed. There was no ice, no clouds, no loneliness, not whilst the voice spoke and the hand held her own.

Rose gave a little sigh. 'Colm?' she whispered. She had meant to speak out boldly but it seemed a whisper was the only thing available right now. 'Colm? Are you cross?'

The voice began to say that of course it was not cross—and broke. She heard a sort of sob and then there was a face next to her own, a warm, familiar face, pressed against her cold cheek. She felt warm tears, whether her own or another's she could not tell, trickle across her skin, then lips kissed along her jawbone, up the side of her face and down across her small nose. She tugged even harder at her eyelids, which she had allowed to close as soon as she spoke, and saw a huge, dark eye, tear-filled, and a dark, arched eyebrow and a strong, familiar jaw-line, much in need of a shave.

'Rosie, me own darlin' girl. Oh Rosie, you're goin' to be all right, you are, you are!'

Colm's voice was wobbly with relief and love, but Rose, bathed in the warmth and security of his love, noticed nothing. She simply snuggled her cheek into the pillow and slept.

*   *   *

The next time she woke, Colm had gone, but a woman's figure sat on the stool beside her. Slowly and carefully, Rose moved her head. 'Mam! Oh, Mam, I can't seem to . . . I'm in the hospital, amn't I?'

'That's right, queen,' her mother said gently. 'Colm's been with you all night until I come over. He'll be back in a minute. He's gone out for a breath of air an' to stretch his legs because once you came round he weren't so worried, like.'

'Good. We're getting married soon,' Rose said vaguely. 'Mam, what happened? I remember talking to Ella and hearing a bang, an explosion, then . . . then I don't remember anything else until I found Colm bending over me and I were in this bed.'

'I don't rightly know meself, queen,' her mother admitted. 'Colm did say something about two charges going off and a pal of his being slightly injured, then he said you bicycled down the hill like a runaway horse, went front-wheel first into a great old mound of earth and rocks, and soared into the air like a swallow, landing on your poor head, which is why it's all bandaged, I suppose. Did you think something bad had happened?'

'I did,' Rose said slowly. She was beginning to remember her mad flight down William Brown Street, bouncing over the cobbles, pedalling like a mad creature, because she had feared for Colm's life, down there in the darkness and damp in the great Mersey tunnel. 'Oh Mam, I thought Colm might have been hurt bad and if he was, I wouldn't never have told him that I knew wi' all me heart that he'd never take nothing that weren't his. Why, he'd no more take a necklace he'd found in the street, let alone one that he knew were owned ... oh, Mam, I've been such a fool.'

'No bigger fool than me,' a voice said and Colm slid through the curtains. 'My poor little darlin' Rosie, I don't know what made me march out like a donkey, 'stead o' listenin' to you. But all that's behind us now, alanna. Right?'

'Right,' Rose agreed, smiling. 'Mind you, I've got a cut head—you may not want to marry me when you see me out of me bandages.'

'You've got two black eyes an' all,' Colm said, grinning. He sat down on the edge of the bed. 'But I'll put up wit' that, just to be back in me room at the Vale.'

Mrs Ryder clapped a hand to her head. 'To think I forgot! You'll never guess what come through the post this morning, you two.'

'Tell us,' Rose said sleepily. With her hand firmly held in Colm's warm clasp and his eyes lovingly fixed on her, nothing else seemed to matter. 'Is it nice or nasty?'

'Nice,' Lily said firmly. 'It were a pawn ticket. And a bank note.'

'What! Who sent it?' Colm said, instantly alert. 'Have you had a chance . . .'

'Yes. I went to the pawnshop an' handed over the ticket an' the banknote and I've got me gold necklace back, as good as ever. Can you guess where the pawn ticket come from, though?'

'Tommy Frost,' Colm said. Rose realised, with incredulity, that his voice sounded almost sad. 'I did wonder . . . but he was a nice feller, so he was, I didn't want to believe ill of him.'

'But you thought I believed ill of you,' Rose mumbled. She tried to sit up in bed but the movement made her head swim and she lay back on her pillows. 'Oh, Colm, will you ever forgive me?'

Colm moved up the bed and put his arms round her, then laid his cheek against hers. 'There's nothin' to forgive,' he murmured. 'As soon as you're out o' this we'll start makin' plans for our weddin', so we will. We've both got good jobs, we can afford a bit of a room . . .'

'You can have the attics; we'll convert the girls' big room into a nice bed-sitting room, and we'll clear the jumble out of the box-room an' make it into a kitchen,' Mrs Ryder said eagerly. 'You'll have to share the bathroom, of course, but you'll be better off than many another young couple. Poor Mona and that Tommy . . . but mebbe he'll turn out all right, wi' a good woman beside him.'

'Well, I don't know,' Rose said. She had told no one about the baby and thought, on the whole, that she had better continue to say nothing. 'We shouldn't do anything in a rush, should we? We always said we'd save up first, not do anything foolish.'

490

At these wise words, however, Colm looked mulish. 'Haven't I seen meself almost lose ye?' he enquired. 'Life's too short to waste, alanna. We'll go home to Ireland this summer so's you can meet me mammy an' Caitlin, an' we'll marry in September. Is that too soon for you?'

'No.' Rose sighed. 'I think you're right; we've wasted enough time.'

'Well, since you seem to have made your mind up, I think it's time I went home an' told Mr O'Neill what's brewing,' Rose's mother said, getting to her feet. 'I'll come an' see you again tomorrow, queen, unless they've sent you home by then, of course. The doctor seemed to think you'd mend fast, now you've come to yourself.' She slipped out between the curtains and Rose closed her eyes for a moment—or so she thought.

When she opened them again, however, the curtains had been pulled back from around her bed and the ward was in darkness save for one light over the door at the end. She sat up on one elbow, her heart bumping, and immediately a nurse in a starched white apron came rustling up the ward. She came over to Rose, smiling. 'Your young man left not five minutes ago,' she whispered. 'You were sleeping so soundly that I told him he'd just be a nuisance if he stayed. Now, could you fancy a nice cup of tea? I've just made a pot in the ward kitchen.'

'Oh, I'd love a cuppa,' Rose said longingly. 'I'm hungry, too, Sister.'

'I'll fetch in some biscuits,' the nurse said, smiling. 'You'll sleep all the better if you've taken food and drink. Why, very likely you'll be home in a couple of days, because you'll heal faster there, I

491

dare say.'

'I'm sure I'll get better quicker at home,' Rose said contentedly, when the tea arrived and was being deliciously sipped. 'My feller—the one who was here just now—is a lodger wi' me mam, so of course I'll get better quicker when I'm wi' Colm. We're getting married as soon as I'm well enough, but we nearly split up for good an' all . . .' and she began to tell the nurse all about the gold necklace and her terrifying ride which had nearly ended so tragically.

'It's like a story out of a book,' the nurse said, sipping her own tea and keeping her voice low so as not to wake the other patients. 'You're a very lucky girl all round, Rose Ryder.'

'I know it,' Rose said. 'Oh, don't I know it! I've been give a second chance, Nurse, an' I'm grabbing it wi' both hands.'

And presently, when the tea was finished and the biscuits crunched down, Rose snuggled under the covers, careful to keep her injured arm away from her body, and was soon fast asleep—and dreaming, in the happiest way, of Colm O'Neill.

EPILOGUE

It was a brilliant day, with the sun beaming down out of the blue sky and every bird for miles around, by the sound, singing its little head off. Caitlin walked along with a prance in her step despite her great age—she was going on fourteen—glancing around her constantly, because the streets were far emptier than she had previously seen them and it meant she could have a good look at everything. It was very early in the morning, but an early rising had been essential, for they had a special place reserved for them at the grand opening of the Mersey tunnel which her father and her brother had helped to build, and they had been advised to arrive in good time to avoid the crowds. It stood to reason that there would be crowds, because the King and Queen would be there, so everyone, naturally, would want to get a good place, so's they could boast, afterwards, how they'd seen the Royals.

But Caitlin would have an especially good place, because she was going to give the Queen the beautiful bouquet of sweetly scented flowers which she held in the crook of her arm. Her father had promised to put her well to the fore in the enclosure which held tunnel workers and their wives and families, and had bought her the white and gold lilies and dark red roses which she now held so carefully. Colm had laughed when he saw the flowers, because his wife was Rose and his

493

mammy-in-law Lily, but Caitlin had been far too excited to laugh. She had felt a little flutter in her stomach at the thought of her great moment, but now the moment was so near she wasn't nervous, not really—why should she be? She had on her best dress, pale blue with a white Peter Pan collar and turn-back cuffs, and her new, light-weight coat over it, which was a darker blue. 'It matches your eyes, queen,' the lady in Lewis's had said when she had tried it on yesterday. 'You look a real treat.' What was more, dear Rose had washed and set her curls so that they clustered round her face, shining like satin, and she had actually dabbed a little powder on Caitlin's nose, because: 'We're sisters, and sisters should share,' Rose had said, spraying some of her very own perfume behind Caitlin's ears and giving her the daintiest little lace hanky to tuck into her coat pocket.

Caitlin had met Rose before, of course, because she and Mammy had come over, almost two years previously, for the wedding, and Caitlin had given the happy couple a present which she had saved up for and bought her own self. She had liked Rose very much then, and liked her even more now, because Rose had told her a secret last night, the most important secret anyone had ever entrusted her with. 'We're having a baby, me and your brother, in early December,' she had whispered. 'Won't that be grand, now, Cait? You'll be an auntie. But we're not tellin' the rest of the family until the tunnel's been opened, so you're the first to know.'

Thinking about the secret made Caitlin glance behind her to where Rose and Colm walked, hand in hand, and as she turned her eyes front again, her

494

father, intercepting the look, winked at her. 'Nervous, alanna?' he asked, across her mammy. 'You needn't be—you're the prettiest girl I ever did see an' the whole city will be after envyin' you when you give the flowers to the Queen.'

'I'm a bit fluttery, just,' Caitlin admitted. 'But whyfor should I be nervous, Daddy? I'm too excited to be nervous.'

'I'm nervous,' her father protested. 'I keep t'inkin' suppose the lighting in me tunnel fails on us when the royal party drive through? Or suppose the mayor's late arrivin' an' can't get through the crowds?'

'Nothing's goin' to go wrong,' Eileen said firmly. 'And we're goin' to be so proud of you, alanna!' She squeezed her daughter's hand. 'A friend of your daddy's is goin' to tek a picture of you wit' his camera—imagine that! You'll be famous, so you will.'

Cracky, on her other side, gave a muffled snort and Caitlin immediately jabbed him hard in the ribs with an indignant elbow. He was only here because she'd begged and pleaded, he'd better remember that! When Daddy had written that he had been told he might bring his family to the opening he had also said he would pay for one of Caitlin's pals to come over ... and she had not hesitated. She had chosen Cracky and he'd been like an old alley moggy who'd stolen the cream with a grin from ear to ear. He had told her excitedly that he'd never crossed the sea, never thought to go to a foreign land, even if it were only England. What was more, he was clad from top to toe in borrowed raiment, mostly lent by friends of the mammy, he had better not forget that, either, or

495

the grand meals he'd eaten and the grand sights he'd seen.

But she was secretly rather proud of Cracky, who had somehow managed to behave himself so far for three whole days without once putting his foot in it. He had slept on a put-u-up in the front room of the Ryders' house, had scrubbed himself daily from top to toe and was taking great care of his borrowed plumage, besides eating everything offered to him at a seemly pace, with no cramming of the gob or talking with a mouthful—yes, Caitlin mused, she had been proud of him. She cast him a darkling glance, however, to remind him that despite being a little lady, she could still give him something to remember her by if he misbehaved.

But clearly, Cracky was mindful of his promise. He gave her the sweetest of gently forgiving smiles—Caitlin nearly malavoked him there and then, just to show him—and straightened his dark-blue tie. 'Sorry Cait,' he murmured. 'Sure an' the daddy's right; you look more like a queen than the Queen, so you do.'

Caitlin giggled; she couldn't help it. That was what she liked about Cracky, she decided; he could always make her laugh. And he looked downright handsome today, too, with his hair cut neatly—again, by Rose—and his white shirt collar so stiff it could have cut his own throat had he but bent his head too fast.

'Not far now,' her father said and Caitlin saw Eileen grip onto his arm with whitened fingers. Mammy's nervous, she thought wonderingly, and she isn't going to hand over flowers to the Queen, she hasn't been practising a little bob curtsy, or digging under her nails with an orange stick. The

496

bouquet, which was fresh and beautiful because Mrs Ryder had sprayed it with water just before they set out. Rose and Colm were chatting quietly and behind them Mrs Ryder and Mr Dawlish were walking very sedately, with Mrs Ryder's hand tucked into the crook of Mr Dawlish's elbow.

Rose's Mam and Mr Dawlish were getting married in September, Caitlin had been told when they first landed in Liverpool, and when that happened the house would be less crowded, because Mrs Ryder wouldn't need the lodging money so badly any more. Mr Dawlish was first officer on a transatlantic liner, and bringing home good money. And Colm had already got another job, since his work on the tunnel had ceased a few weeks previously. He had taken driving lessons, passed his test at the first attempt and now he drove a lorry from the docks to various destinations all over the north-west, carrying the goods which came from far-away countries. He enjoyed the work, which paid quite well, and best of all it meant he could sleep in his own bed each night.

But the best thing of all, to Caitlin's mind, was that her daddy would not be staying in Liverpool but would be coming home with her and Cracky and the mammy when they returned to Ireland the following day. He had worked hard for six years on the tunnel and had gradually climbed the ladder of success—that was how her mammy had put it when describing her husband's rise to her friends—until he was taking a great deal of responsibility and was very well thought-of by the senior staff.

He had saved and Mammy had saved, and then a cottage had come up for rent in Finglas and they had talked it over and taken Caitlin—and Cracky—

to have a look at it. It wasn't the one they had set their hearts on, things like that only happen in fairy stories, Caitlin supposed, but it was almost as nice—and it had more land.

'We'll take it, an' I'll grow 'taters an' cabbages an' leeks an' swedes,' her father had said. 'There's a bit of an orchard already an' we'll put in currant bushes, gooseberries, raspberries . . . I'll look after 'em when I've finished me work for the day, an' I'll get me a corrach so's I can go fishin' on the Tolka . . . sure an' we'll be happy as the day is long, Eileen me darlin'.'

Her father had known, Caitlin realised, that he would not get the sort of pay in Ireland that he had earned in England. Ireland was a poor country and did not pay its workers adequately for their toil. But he had applied for work with the Corporation, possibly as a road-mender, hoping he would be given a stretch of road near Finglas, and thought that with their savings, their garden produce and his earnings, such as they were, they would not starve.

'And I'll keep on earnin', so I will,' his wife had assured him. 'And Caitlin will be out of school in the summer and she'll no doubt earn too. Why, livin' in Finglas she could get a job in service in Dublin an' still get home o'nights, for I'll not have her sleepin' away from home. Oh, we'll be happy as pigs in muck, me dearest Sean.'

'Pigs! Aye, we'll have a couple o' fatteners, an' a sow or two down in the bit of orchard,' Sean had said happily. 'To say nothin' o' keepin' hens, an' maybe some geese.'

Caitlin was sure she would enjoy living in Finglas, but for the moment her thoughts were all

498

on the King and Queen, the tunnel opening and, naturally, the moment when she would reverently place her flowers in the Queen's arms. The Queen was rather old, but very grand, and so many people would be looking on! Not that they mattered; it was her own family who were important, this extended family of hers which now included Rose, Mrs Lily Ryder, Mr Dawlish—and of course Cracky.

'Not long now, alanna,' her father said, giving her an encouraging smile. 'There's plenty people about despite it being so early, but mebbe a good few of 'em's goin' to watch the King an' Queen openin' the East Lancs Road. Surely they aren't all here for the tunnel?'

'Don't worry, Daddy, we're still plenty early enough,' Colm called. 'But we'll be after havin' a long wait before anything happens, so let's find a good place and then we'll eat our carry-out.'

'Picnic. It's a picnic, so it is,' Caitlin corrected him. 'I've seen it! Sandwiches wit' cold ham an' lettuce, hard-boiled eggs, cold fried sausages in soft white rolls, little pink rosy apples . . .'

'Oh janey, you're makin' me hungry all over again,' Cracky groaned. 'Is it far, Mr O'Neill?'

'We're almost at Kingsway,' Sean told him. 'See over there? That's the tunnel entrance. Impressive, eh?'

'Great,' Cracky said almost absently. 'Where'll we have our carry-out?'

'Boys!' Caitlin said, disgusted. 'All they ever t'ink of is their bellies.'

'Down there,' Sean said, pointing. 'We'll get as close as we can to the barriers.' He turned round and grinned at his son and daughter-in-law, who were carrying, not without difficulty, two large covered baskets. 'Go careful wit' the grub, the pair of ye. Young Cracky's hungry already.'

'I wouldn't say no to a bite,' Colm admitted, putting an arm round Rose. 'Follow me, Daddy, alanna, an' we won't go far wrong.'

In an untidy group they hurried towards the place that Sean was pointing out to them.

*   *   *

It had been the grandest day in the world, Caitlin thought ecstatically as she climbed into bed that night. She was sharing Mrs Ryder's big double on the first floor this last night, so that Rose and Colm could be together, but the adults were still downstairs, talking over what had happened that day. Caitlin, however, had been glad enough to go to bed; almost fourteen she might be, but she was tired out and wanted to be alone to relive every lovely moment of this most momentous of days.

For Caitlin, as her father had promised, had a ringside view of the King and Queen, and had given her flowers, if not to the Queen herself, to a charming lady in a wonderful, flowing dress, who had promised to see that the Queen got them when she got down from her car in Birkenhead. 'There'll be no chance, now, of handing them to her,' she said consolingly to Caitlin. 'But you've got nearer to the King and Queen today than most people do even when they live in London and can visit Buckingham Palace every day.' And she had given Caitlin the sweetest smile as she followed the other members of the royal party who were taking to the cars once more.

After that they had met a lot of Sean's and

Colm's fellow workers and their wives and children, and then a large party of them, a great many Irish amongst them, had gone off to a spacious fish and chip cafe on the Scotland Road, where they had pretty well filled the place and had a supper which, Cracky had said blissfully, would number amongst his best and happiest memories of a very wonderful visit.

She had, throughout the day, been proud to be seen with Cracky. He had looked so smart, with his hair almost smooth, and if his face still reminded her of a bulldog burning to teach another dog a lesson, sure and he couldn't help that, could he? Her mammy said a person's looks didn't matter, and wasn't it the person underneath who counted, so though it was a pity that Cracky wasn't handsome, with regular feature and even white teeth ... well, he was Cracky, her best pal, which was all that mattered really. And presently, Caitlin slept.

*   *   *

Rose and Colm climbed into their bed in the attic room and put their arms about each other, and Colm smoothed the curls away from Rose's face and kissed along the line of her jaw and told her how much he loved her and how lucky they were. 'For when I came to England I'd been dotty over the silliest, most selfish girl in the whole of Dublin, an' I didn't care for me own daddy overmuch,' he whispered, though there was no need for quiet, since they were the only ones up here in the converted attics. 'Then I saw Mona, an' didn't I nearly do the same t'ing again, fallin' for yaller hair

501

an' a come-hither manner?'

'I knew it,' Rose said severely, snatching up his hand and pretending to bite his fingers. 'I could see right through you, Colm O'Neill!'

'Well, it didn't take me long to realise that me daddy was a grand feller, a daddy to be proud of. And sure an' I was even quicker to realise that little Rose Ryder was a pearl beyond price, so she was, an' poor Mona just . . . just a pretty face.'

'Oh?' Rose said, suspiciously sweet. 'And I've not got a pretty face, then?' As she spoke she picked up his hand again and fastened her teeth in his thumb. 'Rephrase that,' she said thickly, through thumb. 'Or I'll bite you so's you'll be scarred for life, you big jessy.'

'Oh, oh!' Colm shouted. 'She's disfigurin' me! Help!'

He got his thumb back and a punch in the chest at the same time. 'Shut up, you idiot, or someone'll be coming up to see if we're being robbed,' Rose whispered, giggling. 'I didn't know you weren't too friendly wi' your daddy, Colm. Why was that?'

'Well, I didn't know him too well,' Colm said after a moment's thought. 'It's hard on the women an' kids left behind when a feller comes across the water to work, an' I t'ink I got to believin' we could manage very well wit'out him. But he's a grand feller, me daddy. I'll miss him.'

'Me too,' Rose said soberly. 'He's got a good head on him, your daddy. If it hadn't been for his farsightedness, you'd not have gone for your driving licence, nor left the tunnel whilst the pay was still coming in regular. But now you're safe in a good job whilst all the other poor devils is just starting out to find work.'

502

'That's it. But though we'll miss Daddy, and the family, they're startin' on a new life which will be a deal better for all of them,' Colm said. 'And soon enough, alanna, we'll be startin' our own new life, because when your mammy becomes Mrs Dawlish she says they may move out an' leave us to pay them rent an' get ourselves some lodgers to make ends meet.'

'Ye-es, but they won't go *too* soon,' Rose said after a rather doubtful pause. 'I know I'll be stopping work in a few months, but I've always had Mam standing by, if you see what I mean. When it's just you and me running this place ... it'll be different.'

'It won't be just you an' me, don't forget this feller,' Colm said, laying his hand gently on Rose's rounding stomach. 'Believe me, alanna, he'll make it all worthwhile.'

'I know it,' Rose admitted. 'Mam's longing to be a gran, too. I just wish ... but it's no use wishin'. Wishin' butters no parsnips.'

'You were wishin' your daddy hadn't died on you,' Colm murmured. 'I wish I'd known him, Rosie. But at least you've never let your mammy believe that you grudged her marryin' again. You're kind, so you are.'

'I understand more how lonely she must have been, because when you stormed out that time I just wanted to die,' Rose mumbled. 'It did me good, that. If I hadn't remembered how I felt I don't think I could have been nice to poor Mr Dawlish when Mam told me they were engaged.'

'There you are, then—everythin' happens for the best, one way or t'other. Now are you goin' to let me get some sleep, Mrs O'Neill, or shall I be goin' to work tomorrer wit' great bags under me eyes an' me steps draggin'?'

'Me, stopping you? I like that! But hasn't it been a good day, Colm? One of the nicest days ever, I should think.'

'Aye, pretty good. Well, tomorrer I'll be drivin' through the tunnel—think o' that! Why, I'll be deliverin' in Birkenhead in a few minutes instead of havin' to drive right the way round. And though I'll be sayin' goodbye to Daddy tomorrer, in a few months I'll be a daddy meself. We've come a long way since first I come to St Domingo Vale, young Rosie, a rare long way.'

'We have,' Rose mumbled. 'Oh, and you shouldn't tek it for granted that we're having a boy; it could be a girl.'

'Oh aye? An' pigs might fly.'

Colm lay very still, ready to dodge, to catch her and kiss her, but there was no retribution for his daring and presently he realised why. Rose was asleep.

Colm rolled over and put his arms round her. It's a wonderful world, he thought contentedly. We'll never be rich or famous, but we'll be happy, me an' Rose, an' that's a lot more important. He began to think of the future, of the child which would be born in nice time for Christmas, of the work in store when his in-laws moved out. I should be like Daddy, an' plan an' save an' be farseeing an' sensible, he was thinking. I'll write a list tomorrer, I'll put down just what we'll be wantin' . . .

And Colm, curled round Rose, slept.

NMB

a.g.   PM

Mc

BN.
NG
BS.